HER
LAST
MISTAKE

T0204477

BOOKS BY CARLA KOVACH

The Next Girl
Her Final Hour
Her Pretty Bones
The Liar's House
Her Dark Heart

HER LAST MISTAKE

CARLA KOVACH

Bookouture

Published by Bookouture in 2020

An imprint of Storyfire Ltd.
Carmelite House
50 Victoria Embankment
London EC4Y 0DZ

www.bookouture.com

ISBN: 978-1-78681-885-0
eBook ISBN: 978-1-78681-884-3

Her Last Mistake is dedicated to parents, step-parents, guardians, aunties and uncles, siblings, grandparents, foster parents or even close friends – all those who are involved in any way or form with raising a child. It's so hard knowing if everything you did, or are doing, is right but just keep doing your very best. Xxx

PROLOGUE

Thursday, 9 April 2020

Holly ran into the hall, dropping the pregnancy test as the fire alarm sounded. Scurrying through the lounge, she skidded across the laminate flooring in her socks as she went to snatch the tea towel off the side. Heart thumping, she placed a protective hand over her stomach. There was no bump, not yet. It would be weeks before it showed, which gave her time to get used to how her life would change, if that was possible.

She opened the oven and spluttered as the smoke filled her lungs. Reaching in, she pulled the cannelloni out, almost dropping the brick of a baking tray onto the trivet. 'Damn it,' she yelled as the glass scorched the edge of her little finger. She was no domestic goddess and she knew it. She opened the window of her top floor apartment and coughed the smoke out of her lungs while the breeze circulated the fumes. The smell of herby garlic had been replaced by a nauseating acrid aroma. As the alarm hushed she placed her hand over her heart, willing the pounding to calm down. She'd only burnt dinner, no harm had been done – except to her finger. Without a doubt, there would be a blister there soon.

Finally she had the answer as to why she'd felt so yuck lately. At first she'd thought it was something she'd eaten. It started the night after she'd undercooked a chicken, around four weeks ago. Not realising it was still a little pink, she'd taken a bite. He'd spotted her failure much sooner, which is why he'd left her to clean up while he collected a pizza. Hours later they'd been laughing and rolling in her bed thinking nothing more of the chicken. She scrunched her nose as she recalled the next morning. That chicken had rendered her useless. She'd lain in bed, alone, clutching a bowl as the room swayed like a ship in a storm. *It's the chicken,* she had thought. *A day in bed will cure all.* She'd then dragged the covers over her head and thought nothing more of it.

'All this time it was you, little one.' She smiled as she picked the burnt cheesy topping from the soggy pasta. 'Saved. It's just cannelloni without the white sauce baked on top.' She emptied a bag of salad into a bowl. At least she couldn't mess up a bag of ready prepared salad.

The intercom buzzed. As she hurried back through the apartment, she glanced in the mirror. Her red hair was still clipped up except for a few strands that had cutely escaped, just the way he liked it. The steam from the oven hadn't smudged her mascara; she was good to go.

There was no way on earth the smell would go before he reached the top floor of the building. Her disastrous creation would be obvious.

She glanced at the floor and the pregnancy test stared back. She had to hide that for now, at least until he'd settled in for the evening. A smile beamed across her face. This baby was a chance for him to show her what he was prepared to do for love. She wanted a future with him and she wasn't going to hold back. He had made so many promises; it was now time for him to act on them. This was just the shove he needed. He was finally going to be pushed over the edge, straight into his new life.

'I see you burnt the dinner, Holly,' he said as he entered holding a bunch of red carnations while locking the door behind him. Holly – he used her name like a full stop. She didn't know whether his tone irritated her or turned her on. He sounded like a teacher who was about to go into detail about why she got a C instead of an A or a disgruntled boss who would follow with, *here's how you can improve your performance.*

Swiftly slotting the plastic test into her pocket as he jokingly waded through the smoke, she took the flowers and flung her arms around his shoulders, looking into his eyes before pressing her lips against his. His hand veered down, almost reaching the telltale wand that had poked out of her pocket. She threaded her fingers through his and drew his hand to her breast.

'This is a nice surprise. Who needs dinner?' She felt his other hand slot into the back of her tight jeans before turning her around and pushing her against the wall. She swiftly pushed the test back down. 'My God I've missed this.'

Laughing, she gently nudged him away. 'Later, you. I need to get these flowers into a vase. Shall we have a drink?'

He followed her through to the kitchen where he took a bottle of wine from the rack next to the little table. 'I think we'll go for a Merlot. It should complement the burnt whatever it is you've been cooking up.'

'Shut up.' She playfully slapped him as she popped the flowers into a vase. 'It's cannelloni and I've rescued it.' She smiled and bit her bottom lip, then gazed at him through her long eyelashes as she grabbed two plates and began dishing up. 'Sit at the table, I'll bring it over.'

'Wine? Or would you prefer a beer?'

He knew she wasn't keen on wine. 'Nothing. I have a drink.' She nodded towards the glass of lemonade she'd poured earlier. The blind fluttered as another gust of wind blasted through, bringing with it the smell of the chip shop on the high street. She pulled the window closed and swallowed. If anything would upset her stomach tonight, it would be the smell of battered cod mixed with burnt cannelloni.

'You're not joining me in a toast? One of my investments has,' he paused, 'well, I'll just say that it's been a good day in the hospitality sector. Can't go into details as yet as I don't want to jinx things.' He picked up his fork, ready to eat.

She placed the plates on the table and lit the candle, heart humming away. First the baby and now the news about his investment. Everything was going seamlessly. She couldn't have planned it any better. A lot of people would be hurt but as he'd often promised, they were going to move away and start a new life. Her whole existence over this past year had led to this. 'Does that mean what I think it means?'

His shoulders stiffened. 'You know I can't make any promises just yet. Can we drop it, Holly?'

'But—'

'I said drop it!' He slammed his fork onto the table knocking his wine over. 'Look what you made me do.'

What was meant to be a special moment had just been ruined. The stick in her pocket that had only recently told her that she was carrying the much-wanted little life inside her was threatening to snap under the pressure as she tried to remain rigid and still. He looked through her with clenched knuckles.

He stomped across the floor in his brown leather brogues and began wiping the wine from his crisp fitted shirt. It must have been a big day for him as she was used to him wearing more casual shirts over jeans. Something out of the ordinary had happened but that didn't excuse him talking to her the way he had.

With quivering fingers, she dropped the stick onto the table. This wasn't the way she planned to tell him but he had to know. 'Something has to change. I love you, but you can't shout at me like that again.'

A tear spilled into her salad; the little droplet on the butterhead lettuce leaf twinkled in the candlelight. She wouldn't look at him – she didn't want to see his face as the realisation dawned on him. She was going to have a baby and that was a fact. The news was meant to be good but here she was crying into her dinner while he huffed and puffed over spilled wine.

'I'm sorry, I shouldn't have shouted. What's this? Is this all a joke? Just tell me it's a joke.' He kneeled in front of her.

As she burst into loud sobs, she shook her head. Why couldn't he be as happy as she was? It wasn't as if they hadn't spoken about their future and the fact that she wanted children someday. The only difference in the plan was it was happening sooner than expected and she needed him. She couldn't do it all alone. One of his investments had obviously paid off. He could get rid of his business interests in Cleevesford and, that way, they'd never have to come back. All he had to do was take the plunge. All would be fine. He'd promised her that everything would work out.

She glanced up. There was no joy in his grimace and she knew she was going to have to go it alone. Why had she been such a fool? Everyone would laugh at her now.

'Stop it, come on.' He placed his arms across her shoulders and pulled her into him as she sobbed louder. 'I said stop it.'

'I'm having a baby, I can't just stop it. Look at you. I've given up everything to be here all the time, lapping up your empty promises. This is your moment to show me what I mean to you and I get it. I finally see you for what you are. You only love yourself. Get out.' She grabbed the salad bowl and flung the lettuce across his chest. She'd have her baby alone just like her mother had. It wasn't how she'd imagined her future to be. 'My only regret is wasting a year on someone like you.'

'You can't have this baby, you do know that.' He flicked the lettuce away and stood. Veins pulsed on his temples as his stare bored through her. He didn't scare her, he wasn't the first or last man in her life who thought it was his way or no way. She was a little older now, wiser, and she was going to stand her ground. He could stare all he liked. She was having the baby whether he was in her life or not. Bad decision? Maybe. What she wanted? Definitely –bad decision or not.

'I can and I will. My body, my choice.' She stood and walked towards the hall as he hurried behind her. 'Get out.' She pointed to the door. Seeing him react so unreasonably had been a first and it was going to be a last. He would never speak to her in that tone again.

'I'm going. Don't expect anything off me if you're not prepared to listen to what I want. I'll be in touch about everything we need to finalise.'

'Blah, blah, blah. It's always been about you. I don't know why I expected it would be any different. Just go.' She wiped her nose on the back of her hand and watched him through the reflection in the hall mirror. The same mirror that had reflected her red curls bouncing as she'd excitedly answered the door to him only half an hour earlier. Her blue eyes were now rimmed with angry swollen red lids. She flinched as he caught her looking. 'I said go or I'll call the police.' Her heart began to hammer against her ribs. Why wasn't he going?

'You think it's that easy.' He pinned her to the wall and gripped her throat, applying enough pressure to take her breath away. His fingernails drove into the back of her neck.

Gasping, she gripped his wrists but his strength had her locked in place. Every beat of her heart thumped through her head, louder and louder until her vision prickled. She could make out his grin, she could smell the wine on his breath and she shuddered as she felt his erection. She had been in a relationship with him for a year and it was at this point that she realised she knew nothing at all about him. He let go and she flopped to the ground, only having enough energy to protectively stroke her stomach.

He'd spared her.

She'd messed her life up the moment she'd waved at him across the bar in the Angel Arms all those months ago. She should have listened to her instincts telling her to stay away, that he'd be bad for her but he'd been her secret pleasure since. It's not like she'd only just met him, she knew him well. From that moment on, she'd got to know him a lot better, in ways she'd never imagined possible.

'You say a word and I'll kill you next time. Did you get that?'

She stroked her neck, hoping that he'd leave so she could cry her heart out. She was about to lose everything and he knew it. She hugged her body, not daring to catch his eye before he left. That moment had told her all she needed to know. *I'm a survivor. I'll get through this.*

His final words filled her head. *I'll kill you next time.* A few more seconds and he would have killed her. She understood the warning, loud and clear as she coughed and gasped. *Talk and you die.*

CHAPTER ONE

Saturday, 9 May 2020

'Here's to Kerry and Ed Powell, my beautiful daughter and my new son-in-law. This is for those of you who couldn't make Crete, enjoy the open bar and let's celebrate!' The father of the bride passed the microphone back to the DJ. 'Celebration' by Kool & The Gang blasted out and more partygoers joined the happy couple on the dance floor. Not Holly though. She'd spent all day ditching her drinks in plant pots, down the toilet, even on a carpet in the corridor outside Brendan and Lilly's room – that would be Lilly, the slimmer bridesmaid. The one who hadn't cost her oldest friend Kerry a further sixty pounds in clothing alteration fees because she'd got pregnant.

She touched her stomach; stroking it would be too obvious. Was that a flutter? She smiled as it happened again. Kerry giggled in her huge multi-layered wedding dress as she and Ed danced, then Kerry's gaze met hers. Only for a second, but maybe that had been long enough. Holly dropped her hands to her sides, leaving her stomach alone. Normally, an expectant mother would share this news and everyone would partake in the joy of hearing about her baby's first flutter, but she couldn't say a word. Her joy was also her burning shame.

Her baby was a secret. Her relationship was a secret. She was sick of secrets. No one had suspected a thing to date but her baby wouldn't remain a secret for long.

The music blasted out. She didn't feel like celebrating at all despite the happy dancers and drinkers surrounding her. The room had filled even more since the evening guests had arrived. She flinched as a group of men nudged her to get to the bar. As Samuel Avery, the landlord of the Angel Arms, pulled one of the guest ales at the secondary pop-up bar, he winked at her. She broke their eye contact. The other men at the bar began to shout and laugh, their rowdiness standing out from the crowd as they ordered a tray of free drinks. The father of the bride danced with his daughter as Ed pulled his new mother-in-law onto the dance floor. Francesca, one of the bridesmaids, re-entered the room and slowly turned in the middle of the dance floor, sporting a look that suggested she might be sick at any moment.

Hot and sick, that was how Holly was beginning to feel too. The venison followed by the lemon pie dessert was beginning to turn her stomach. She regretted following all that with the petits fours. A lot of things sickened her lately and the smell of fried onions coming from the hot buffet weren't helping. She lifted the hem of her sage green satin dress and made her way to the terrace of Cleevesford Manor where she hoped that fresh air and the expanse of woodland beyond the stunning gardens would ease her queasiness. Claustrophobia and pregnancy had got the better of her.

Gasping, she backed onto the cold wall, the music thudding as Kool & The Gang faded into ABBA's, 'Dancing Queen'. Her life as she knew it would soon be over. Today had been a façade as she watched her friend commit to the love of her life. All this happiness would soon end. There were lies, lots of them and those lies were coming out soon and people were going to get hurt. She wondered if her friends would ever forgive her betrayal. She, Lilly, Kerry and Fran had named themselves the Awesome Foursome when they were at school. Was the end of an era on the horizon?

His words swirled through her mind. *Say a word and I'll kill you.*

He wouldn't kill her. He wouldn't kill her baby. Words can be said in temper, they can be empty, and can be shouted on impulse. That's all it was. He wasn't going to kill her. Pinning her up against the wall was nothing more than an empty threat. Yes, he'd scared her, yes he was rough in bed, but kill her? People use that term all the time, they don't mean it and that gave her comfort.

Holly turned her head as she heard a rustling in the distance. Two men emerged from the dark foliage at the back of the garden followed by someone she recognised all too well. So that's how the extra guests were getting in. The whole of the Angel Arms were sneaking in for free drinks.

She flinched as the DJ's microphone squealed. Tables started to crash and glasses smashed as the DJ switched to 'I Predict a Riot'. Several men spilled out of the function room fighting as she ducked just in time to miss a flying bread roll. Kerry screamed as her mother, Alison, tried to pull her back. One of the buttonhole flowers landed at her feet as the scuffle passed by her. A carnation, just like those he used to buy her. She kicked it out of the way.

'I need to speak to you, now.'

Where had he come from? She hadn't heard him creep up on her.

'Your room, half an hour.'

'I've got nothing to say to you.' Tonight wasn't a good time. The last thing she wanted was a repeat of their last proper face-to-face conversation. He'd done a good job of keeping out of her way ever since that night in her flat. There was no way he was getting another opportunity to pin her to a wall and bully her into getting rid of her baby. He'd also taken his obsession with gripping her neck a bit too far – no longer was it slightly playful during their lovemaking, he'd gripped her like he wanted to suck the life from her. She rubbed the back of her neck, her fingertips touching the scar that he'd left.

'You're being stupid. We need to talk. Please?'

A gentle breeze filled the air, providing her with the clarity she needed. She was being stupid? It was he who had refused to talk any more about the matter of their baby. She glanced up at him, taking in his pleading expression. He wasn't the man who'd been so angry at her apartment, he was the man she knew and loved. Maybe he'd finally seen sense. She brought her hands down from the scar. Maybe her baby would have the father he or she deserved. His hand brushed against hers as he checked over his shoulder.

Francesca stumbled out of the function room through the bi-fold doors, one arm outstretched and her other hand across her mouth. Looking at her, she'd already been sick once down her bridesmaid's dress and Holly wasn't going to stick around to watch what was coming. Seeing Francesca throw up would be the very thing that would tip her over the edge, no matter how soothing the breeze was.

The gatecrashers fought, the staff tried to break things up, the mother-in-law ran out and began yelling across the garden like a banshee, and Holly felt numb to it all. Could she trust him? That question was filling her mind as chaos broke out.

As Francesca turned, he shifted his position so that she would only catch sight of his back. 'I'll see you in a bit. I'm just going to sort out this mess and I'll be up.'

Holly turned away from him, tearing a handful of flower heads from one of the table decorations as she hurried to her room. As she slammed the door behind her, she noticed the squashed carnation petals spilling from her clenched fingers. She sat on the bed and began picking out the petals and dropping them to the floor. Confused is how she felt. She'd wait and she'd see exactly what he had to say.

Half an hour had passed, then an hour. If he turned up, he turned up. She brought her knees up to her chest and pulled the quilt up to her chin. He wasn't coming. She switched off the light and closed her eyes, ignoring the revellers on the terrace below her room. She applied a light amount of pressure to her stomach hoping her baby would move again, but he or she didn't. The gentle beat of the music was hypnotic and soon she lost the battle with her heavy lids as sleep took over.

Heart in mouth, Holly jolted up in bed as a knock broke her dream. She almost tripped over her dress while stumbling across the unfamiliar room in the dark. She can't have been asleep for more than a few minutes, at least it felt like that and the music was still playing. As she opened the door a white flash of pain filled her face. Through peppered vision, all she could see was the dark outline of a head, backlit by the fading light from the corridor. That soon disappeared as the intruder closed the door.

Her nose stung as blood sprayed out. Why had he hit her? He'd come to talk. She tried to focus but her eyes had teared up from the blow to her nose. Was it even him? She tried to focus but all she could see were blurred dark images. Another flash of pain hit as her attacker grabbed her wrist and thrust her onto the bed.

'Don't hurt the baby,' she whimpered. Maybe he'd come to act on his promise. 'Don't kill me. I didn't say anything.' She had been naïve to doubt him. Another blow to the head came from nowhere. She had to get away.

Fight. Hit out. Thrash and run away. If only she could get to the corridor and shout like mad. Someone would wake up.

She opened her mouth to scream and her attacker thrust a pillow over her face, pushing hard. Winded by her attacker, she tried to wriggle beneath. Dark – she couldn't open her eyes. Dry material that tasted freshly laundered filled her mouth, along with the blood that was slipping down the back of her throat, drowning her.

Trapped and voiceless, two feelings that she was more than familiar with.

Panic rose as she tried to gasp but her attempt was fruitless. The sound of her own heart booming filled her ears as she continued her interrupted dream. The one in which she was walking her newborn in the park and people stopped to say how beautiful she was. In her mind it was a girl. As she slipped away, she kept thinking. He wouldn't kill her. He'd bring her around. Like at the apartment when he'd gripped her throat, it was just a threat.

The pulsating heartbeat in her ears faded as she slipped into another world. She strolled over to the calm lake, baby in her arms looking out at the ducks. Then it stopped, everything stopped for a second. It was as if time had stood still. No breeze, no trickling of water, the people stood like statues. What was happening? The shining sun got brighter and brighter, dazzling her, filling the whole landscape until she could no longer see as she entered her new serene world of nothing.

CHAPTER TWO

The sound of the ten o'clock news finishing filled the room as Detective Gina Harte pressed stop on the film she and her daughter, Hannah, had been watching. *The NeverEnding Story* had been Hannah's favourite movie as a child and they'd both watched it a million times but it still brought a smile to their faces. Hannah was sprawled out on the settee, hand half hovering over the tub of popcorn.

'I still love that film. It's a shame Gracie didn't get to see the end.' Hannah pulled the settee throw over the little girl who had fallen asleep on the floor. Strands of her long light brown hair reached over the cushion and a trail of dribble slid down her cheek.

Gina smiled. 'How's she getting on at nursery?'

'Good. She loves playing with the other kids. Every day I come home with another work of art for the fridge, which is why I brought a few over for your fridge.' Hannah paused. 'It broke my heart the first day I left her there.'

It had been well over twenty years ago when Gina had taken Hannah to preschool but it was a memory she'd never forget. Her little girl had immediately wanted to play with all the other children and Gina had hidden the lump in her throat and the tears in her eyes until she'd driven off to attend police training.

'They grow up so quick.' Gina paused. Her relationship with Hannah hadn't always been this good but they'd been talking more over the past few months. 'I'm glad you both came to visit. I mean it. It's lovely to have you here.'

'I'm glad you took some time off to be with us. Gracie always jibbers on about you. You're her hero.'

A lump formed in Gina's throat as she kneeled on the floor and gave her granddaughter a kiss on the cheek. 'I don't say it enough but you really have done a brilliant job with her. She's perfect.'

Hannah uncomfortably looked away. Gina knew she struggled to take a compliment.

'How's Greg?'

Hannah bit the skin on the side of her finger. 'Fine. Work is good. He's got a job for a building company now. New builds. He's away for the next week.'

Her smile was forced. Gina knew the effort it took to pretend. A smile that is natural takes little effort but Hannah had a grimacing line on her forehead and a smile that didn't match it. The light twitch in her temples showed Gina that she was subtly clenching her teeth together.

'So all is good with you both?'

'Couldn't be better.' Hannah placed the lid on the popcorn and swung her legs off the settee before stepping over her sleeping daughter and stretching.

'You know you can talk to me about anything.'

Hannah shook the crumbs from the snuggle blanket. 'I don't need to talk. Gracie and me, we're happy. Greg is doing well. My job is good and now that Gracie is at nursery, I've upped my hours.'

Gina waited for the next clue.

'Stop staring at me like I'm one of your victims or suspects, Mum.'

'I'm sorry. Bad habit.' She'd almost pushed it too far – almost. 'What are we doing tomorrow?'

Hannah shrugged. 'I know Gracie would love to go to Cadbury World.'

'Sounds like a plan.'

Gina's phone began to buzz across the coffee table.

'That's if you're available.'

DCI Chris Briggs's name flashed up and he knew that she'd booked the week off. She tensed up as she took the call. 'Briggs?'

'Sorry to call you. I know you've booked holiday but DS Driscoll's plane has been delayed. He's still stuck in Portugal and Wyre is visiting a friend in Staffordshire. She'll be here soon, but I need someone to meet me at Cleevesford Manor, now. We have the body of a young woman, looks like murder and we can't afford to lose any time. Forensics are on their way now. Please tell me you can be there.'

Hannah slumped back onto the settee, her gaze fixed on Gina. The expression she was reading on Hannah's face now was one of disappointment.

'I'll be there in about half an hour.'

'See you soon.' Briggs ended the call.

A shiver ran through Gina's body. She wasn't sure if it was a result of Hannah's reddening face or having to work that closely to Briggs again. Once her lover, now he was the keeper of her deepest darkest secret. She'd avoided being too close to him for too long, but now she was going to be working the next case with him until the other detectives in the department were back on the scene soon.

'Come on, Gracie. Looks like we're on our own tomorrow. I don't know why I expected it to be any different.' Hannah lifted the sleepy girl up and wrapped her in a blanket.

'I'll make it up to you, I promise.' Gina went to give Gracie a peck on the forehead but Hannah turned away. 'Don't be like that. I can't help it that a case has come in. Everyone else is on holiday or away. There's only me.'

'This was meant to be our time; you, me, and Gracie. You promised. Aren't there any other detectives?'

Gina shook her head. 'None that can get there now. It's a big case.' She turned away and dropped her hands in frustration.

'Hannah, it looks like a woman has been murdered. I have to be there because at the moment there may be a killer on the loose. I'm doing my best. I love you and I love Gracie, more than anything.'

'No, you love your job more than anything!' With that, Hannah was already halfway up the stairs.

'Goodnight, chicken,' Gina called out to Gracie up the stairs.

The door to the spare room slammed. Gina flinched as Ebony, her little black cat, began rubbing its head against her leg. 'At least you're not angry with me.' She glanced at the clock – if she hurried, she'd make it by half past midnight.

As she grabbed her bag and keys, Cleevesford Manor ran through her mind. She'd been a couple of times, once following a burglary and another time she took Gracie for an afternoon tea. The grand building had been there for centuries, owned by the same family. Its land, spread over acres, was the place to book for any extravagant celebration. She shivered, wondering who the woman was and why anyone would want to harm her.

She knew Hannah was right, she did love her job more than anything. She didn't love the people she came across all the time but she loved the fact that she was taking bad people off the streets. She wanted this killer in a cell. Maybe then, she and Hannah would be able to carry on with the week they had planned.

CHAPTER THREE

Sunday, 10 May 2020

He crossed his thumbs over her jugular as he reached his end. Her moaning below him only moments earlier had been all he needed to finish off.

'You can let go now.' Removing his hands, she rubbed her neck, stood and pulled her dress back down.

They wouldn't talk about this. Not because he didn't want to, it wasn't part of the unwritten agreement. He did what he was meant to do and he'd enjoyed it, but was it enough? He had a taste for something more, an intensity he couldn't explain or expect anyone to ever understand.

Was it enough? He asked himself the same question over and over again as he lay there in the darkness, staring out of the window at the stars in the clear May sky. Was it enough? That question was going to haunt him. It had to be enough. He rolled off the bed and slipped his trousers back on.

Nothing was ever enough. He needed more now, there was no going back.

A star twinkled. Maybe it was a planet. It was bright enough. She'd already left the room and he funnily missed her presence.

He exhaled. It wasn't enough.

CHAPTER FOUR

Gina drove along the half-acre long tree-lined drive, a string of fairy lights leading the way, and pulled up behind Briggs's car. An ambulance surrounded by three police cars was parked near the entrance.

PC Kapoor stood next to a paramedic who was hunched over a woman sitting in the back of the ambulance.

The nineteenth-century manor house stood proudly on the vast landscape and its gardens were the envy of many similar properties. This one had survived agricultural depressions and increased taxation during the early twentieth century. It had not only survived, it had been owned all this time by the Harris's of Cleevesford. Since the renovations, it had been a hub for the local community, a place for the well off to get married and the best venue for an award-winning cream tea. Gina wondered if numbers of people coming for a cream tea would drop for a while when news of a murder got out.

'Bernard is just sealing off the scene and PC Smith is herding everyone into the function room,' Briggs said as he stood by her car door.

'Who's that?' Gina pointed to the woman in the ambulance.

'That's Francesca Carter. She's one of the bridesmaids.'

'So it's a wedding?'

'A wedding reception. The couple got married in Crete and were having a party at the manor for everyone that didn't go abroad. We're trying to find out more and PC Smith is collecting a list of names, while finding out how everyone is related to or acquainted with the bride and groom. The couple are Kerry and Edward Powell.'

'And the victim? Do we know who she is?'

'She's been identified as twenty-five-year-old Holly Long. She was one of the bridesmaids. We should be able to go up as soon as the scene is secure.' He rubbed his emerging five o'clock shadow. 'How are you doing? I haven't seen much of you lately.'

'Good.' That was all she had to say. Now wasn't the time to share her thoughts. She wasn't going to go into the fact that she felt like she was balancing on a tightrope now that he knew some of her most intimate secrets, she wasn't going to tell him that her daughter was probably going to give her the silent treatment for cutting short their time together and she wasn't going to tell him how much she hated weddings. The thought of them made her teeth itch. The commitment, the feeling of suffocation as the words 'I do' are uttered. She scratched away the nervous prickles that were forming under her scalp.

Gina glanced around. Blue lights flashed across the front of the manor house. 'Have you spoken to Francesca Carter yet?'

Briggs shook his head. 'The paramedics are still treating her. She passed out when she found the body. Although, I think the whole ordeal has sobered her up a little.'

Gina headed into the building and glanced through the open doors of the function room. Small pockets of people were being ushered around by officers. A familiar face caught her attention – Samuel Avery, landlord of the Angel Arms. His ashen, troubled face had creased around the mouth and his eyes made him look a little older than his late fifties now the house lights were on. Gina couldn't understand what women saw in him.

Samuel moved his hand away from a crying woman's backside, her long blonde hair stuck to her face. Gina shook her head. They didn't always see much in him at all, he just took advantage. There was no look of sympathy on his face as he comforted the young woman, just a leer that suggested he was hoping that she would extend her need for sympathy to the bedroom if he pressured her hard enough. That was his game. She knew him all too well. As he turned, she caught him tucking the back of his shirt into his trousers. Gina would come back to Samuel later, once she'd checked out what was happening in the victim's room.

In the corridor, the mother and father of the bride were hugging their daughter and offering the teary young woman some reassurance. Her fluffed up dress had been torn at the side and a chunk of bread roll was caught in her large braided bun.

As Gina turned the corner to the staircase, the scene was well mapped out by the forensics team coming and going, all suited up, carrying boxes upon boxes up the steps, ready to start extracting and cataloguing all potential evidence from the scene.

She swallowed as she followed the action. Only an hour ago, she had been lying on the settee watching the end of a film with her family. So much had happened already. She was accustomed to being called out to handle a case but Hannah had never got used to it. When Hannah was a child, Gina had often bundled her daughter into the car and dropped her off at friends' houses so that she could work. Gina knew exactly where Hannah's resentment had come from.

'Here you go,' Bernard said as he passed her a forensics suit, a pair of gloves, hair cover and shoe covers. 'Put these on before we go any further and avoid the middle of the corridor.'

'Thanks.' She slipped the suit over her trousers and light jumper. As she followed him, she snapped the gloves on. Several evidence markers had been placed around the room already. Gina glanced at the one on the chest of drawers, identifying the blood that was smeared along the top. A trail of stepping plates marked the route they could all tread. A flash lit up the room as a suited body snapped away at the corpse, taking photos that would be emailed to Gina later.

There was nothing unusual about the room. It looked like a regular country hotel room. A brochure on the table in front of the window, a shelf containing tea-making facilities and a bathroom off to the right. Gina poked her head in; it looked as if it hadn't been used at all. A crime scene assistant passed her with several sample envelopes, a vial of liquid and some swab packs.

Gina's head began to throb as her gaze rested on the pasty-bodied woman. The woman looked to be in her early twenties. Her satin dress was dotted with blood and the blood from her nose injury had smeared across the pillow and was tangled in her flame coloured hair. There was something about the way she lay, her neck slightly up, not resting naturally on the pillow. She'd been placed there with her hands resting on her torso. A few white specks had been sprinkled around the pillow. She stepped in a little closer and could see that the specks were flower petals. It was then that Gina spotted the torn flowers on the floor, a mix of red and white carnation heads.

'Was the window locked?' Gina asked, but no one replied. Talking through a face mask wasn't easy. She repeated herself in a louder voice.

Bernard looked away from the evidence log. 'Yes, I checked that as soon as we'd set up. The catch was firmly on the sash window. The door had been left open.'

Gina visualised a featureless body and face entering through the door. Was the door left open by a drunken Holly or had she got out of bed to open the door? They glanced at the blood spatter. The smear on the chest of drawers had led Gina's eye to the fine spray on the pale grey wall by the door. Gina was no expert in blood spatter analysis, but she knew that one of the woman's injuries had occurred at the door, unless the perpetrator was bleeding too. Maybe Holly had put up a fight.

Gina's gaze fixed on the victim's nose as she worked through a theory in her head. Maybe Holly had answered the door to a knock and had been instantly hit, causing the blood to spray the wall as the instrument used to hurt her was drawn back. Was there a weapon or had she been hit with a fist?

'Any sign of the weapon used to hit her?'

Bernard mumbled through his mask. 'I can't be sure at the moment.'

Just as she suspected. They were midway through working a crime scene and she wanted all the information they hadn't collated yet, and she wanted it now. More markers went down, one for a clump of hair on the carpet and another for a sock behind the door. Again, Gina was drawn to the young woman's corpse. Most of her hair had tangled around her neck except one long strand leading from her head to her mouth. Her skin was almost translucent. Eyes, stark and open. Bed sheets tangled around her legs and body, an indentation left on the other side of the bed in the linen suggesting that another person had been lying next to her at some point.

Bernard stepped back and surveyed the room. 'From what I've seen, this room hasn't been cleaned or vacuumed very well. We've already found several different hair samples, old bits of bitten nails and don't get me started on all the fingerprints in this room. It's a forensics nightmare.'

Gina caught sight of a shelf holding several books above the bed, mostly Reader's Digest collections. She had to agree with Bernard as she stared at the thin layer of dust that led from one end of the shelf to the other. 'Cause of death?'

Bernard nodded to usher Gina out. For the time being, she'd seen enough. What she needed now were Bernard's initial thoughts on what the evidence was telling him.

She clunked on the stepping plates and followed him back out to the carpeted floor on the landing, allowing the crime scene investigators time and room to get on with their huge list of tasks. An outer cordon was being wrapped around the staircase.

'I need to get through. My room is there,' a teary woman said. It was the blonde-haired woman whom Samuel Avery had been comforting.

The officer blocking the route continued to apply the cordon. 'Really sorry but could you please join the others back in the function room. We'll let you know as soon as you can pass through.'

The woman stood for a moment as if waiting for the officer to change her mind. When she realised she wouldn't be allowed to pass, she hitched up her dress and went back down the stairs.

Bernard caught up with Gina and they pulled down their face masks. He scratched his escaping grey beard as he stood hunched over, looking down at her as he spoke. 'I'll give you what I know now and, as always, I'll prepare my report and send it straight your way. If I come across anything that I can share immediately, I'll call you.'

Gina nodded. 'Okay, thanks. But what can you tell me now?'

'You see the blood to her nose and face, there's a little bit in her hair too. Two injuries. Her nose is obviously broken, that's where all the blood came from. There is a slight split to her head; the nature of the mark suggests she was hit with something hard. I did notice a tiny smear of blood on the lamp base and that matches my initial thought that she could have been hit with that. As always, anything I say now has not been confirmed. Only a post-mortem and our lab results will verify everything or offer further or different evidence. The pillow beside her was also covered in blood but this had been positioned blood side down so that it wouldn't be seen straight away. Initial theory we are working on is that she was either killed by one of the blows to her head or smothered with the pillow.'

Gina nodded. 'Smothered?'

'I've already said this and I stick by it for now, the blood smeared all over the back of the pillow suggests there was a struggle. I would go with smothered.'

'And whoever did this, placed the same pillow back on the other side of the bed, blood side down when they'd finished.' Gina paused. 'It looks like our victim had also been placed on her pillow. I noticed she was tilted up slightly.'

'That's right. Someone placed her like that with her hands on her middle. It looks like flower petals were then sprinkled over her. And the indentation on the bed next to her suggests that someone else lay on her bed at some point. The positioning of the bed cover shows that this couldn't have been our victim. We need to get the samples to the lab and the body to the morgue before I can give you anything more.'

'Time of death?'

'Her body temperature suggests within the past four hours.'

'One more thing. Did you find a phone?'

He shook his head. 'No, not as yet. If we come across one in the meantime, I'll have it bagged and let you know.'

She knew that was all she was getting for now. The thought of Holly being suffocated with a pillow, panicking and trying to fight off her attacker sent a wave of nausea through Gina. She shook that thought away as she pulled her phone out of her pocket. There was a text message from Briggs.

Interviews happening in the function room. Wyre has arrived too. We'll pool everything back at the station in a briefing later. I'll get breakfast in for the team when we leave. No one will be going home in a hurry. I need you back on duty for the foreseeable. Briggs.

The last thing she could think about was food. She walked towards the large leaded window. As she released her brown kinked hair from the hair cover, a flash of light coming from the corner of the garden caught her attention. No sooner had it appeared, it disappeared. She tensed up as it happened again. Pressing her nose on the window for a better look, she could clearly see the light of a phone being held out and the head of a distant person.

As she phoned Briggs, she heard her heart thrumming in her ears. 'Pick up, pick up,' she muttered under her breath.

'Harte.'

'Get someone in the garden. Bottom left when you leave the function room. There was someone out there on their own a moment ago. I saw the light from their phone leading away and now it's gone. Stop them.'

She hung up and ran back the way she had come, tangling up the cordon tape as she hurried to the stairwell. 'Sorry,' she shouted back to the police officer. Darting down the stairs, her heart was beating out of her chest. She couldn't risk losing sight of him. If he was Holly's killer, she was going to be the one to bring him in.

CHAPTER FIVE

Gina sprinted across the lawn until she reached Briggs and PC Smith. 'We've called out, we've searched, but they're not answering. Two officers are continuing to search the woodland.'

Gina pushed her way past Briggs, calling out as she caught her breath. 'Police, you are leaving the scene of a crime. Come back now. Stop.' It was no good. Whoever she'd seen escaping through the back of the garden had long gone. They had a good enough head start. 'Damn it! Have you called for backup?'

Briggs's shoulders dropped. 'Of course I have, Harte. We have officers heading to the main roads that surround the woodland. If someone has left here, they'd have to come out on one of two roads.'

She didn't know why she doubted him. Maybe it was her increasing need to be fully in control of everything. She wanted to interview all the guests and staff, be with Bernard and the forensics team, be the one to chase their suspect into the woods and fields and be the one waiting at the roadside for him or her to emerge.

A man pushed his way through the officers on the terrace. 'Who's in charge here? I demand to speak to someone in a position of authority. Is it you?' He instantly looked to Briggs for an answer. This time the man was right – but in Gina's experience, the majority of the people she met asked the suited man on the scene if he was the one in charge. This time she didn't get to say she was.

'I'm DCI Briggs and this is DI Harte. DI Harte is the Senior Investigating Officer.'

Gina went to speak, her gaze fixed on Briggs as she realised he was stepping back and allowing her to take the lead on the case, as she had been doing for a while now. As soon as DS Driscoll landed, Briggs would be back in his office working the investigation, being the interface between the team and the press. She cleared her throat. 'How can I help you?'

'The name's Harris. Nigel Harris. I live in the cottage over there and this is my family estate.' He shivered slightly and buttoned up his tweed jacket. 'My staff have just called me away from my late game of bridge, saying that there's all sorts going on. They tell me a woman has been murdered. I can't have this malarkey happening on my property. My business has a reputation to keep so I suggest you take the body and hurry up off my premises.'

The man stood over six feet tall with a large round middle, his bulbous red nose reflecting the little bit of light coming from the manor house. His grey curly hair fell around the bald patch at the back of his head.

'Mr Harris. We won't be hurrying and the body will be taken when we are ready to take it. A woman has been murdered and the crime scene team are working their hardest to collect all the evidence. Your business is very important to you, I understand that, but the woman in there, the one lying dead in one of your rooms, she is important to someone. Imagine if she was someone you cared about, your daughter, your niece. You wouldn't want us to hurry up and leave, would you? You'd want to make sure we collected enough evidence and statements to convict whoever committed this terrible crime.' Gina felt a flutter in her chest.

The man let out a slight snort. 'That person is not my daughter and she's not my niece so just hurry about your business. I want you gone as soon as possible.'

'Well I suggest you don't tie us all up in meaningless conversation any longer.'

He stared at Gina for a moment before muttering under his breath as he walked back.

'Don't you just hate some people?' Briggs asked.

'Thanks.'

'What for?'

'You're in charge.'

He shrugged. 'I may be your DCI but you're in charge of this investigation. I know you won't let me down. Right, everyone is interviewing at the moment and hopefully all statements will be uploaded onto the system immediately upon returning to the station. No one is going home until that is done. It's impossible to keep this many people in one place for long and I don't want anyone missed.'

The two officers who had chased their suspect emerged from the hedge. Gina took a torch from one and pointed at the ground. There had to be something left behind, anything. A few cigarette butts were scattered around the muddy cut through. 'We need those bagged up. It looks like the masses have trampled through here. Shoe imprints upon shoe imprints are ingrained in the mud.'

'Why would so many people be coming this way?'

'Gatecrashers, guv,' PC Smith said.

Gina flinched as he broke her thoughts. 'I didn't hear you coming.' It had been a while since he'd been injured at a crime scene and it made her happy to see him back where he belonged, in uniform, helping with their investigation.

'You were all so engrossed in what was happening. We've been interviewing, as you know, and one of the bridesmaids, Lilly Hill, mentioned the gatecrashers. She said she'd like to speak to a detective in charge about Holly. Just look for the woman in the long green dress with blonde hair. She said it's important.'

'Thanks. While I'm catching up with the witnesses, I want you to find out if there were any photographers or videographers. I want all footage and photos of the night before anything can be lost or tampered with.'

'On it, guv.'

Lilly Hill could wait. The person she most wanted to speak to was the one who had found Holly's body.

CHAPTER SIX

Gina headed back out to the ambulance. 'We're finished now,' the paramedic called as he spotted her trying to catch his attention. He turned his attention back to the vehicle. 'You sit there as long as you like, love, until you feel a little better.'

PC Kapoor smiled as she stepped out of the ambulance. 'Guv?' the police constable said in a pitch that sounded as though it could crack windows. 'This is Francesca Carter.'

The paramedic walked around the ambulance and began speaking to a colleague.

'Thank you.' Gina stepped up and sat on the gurney beside Francesca. 'Ms Carter. I know this is hard for you, but could I ask you a few questions?' Gina asked in a gentle voice.

The woman looked up, revealing her mascara-streaked face. Gina cleared her throat as she caught the faint smell of vomit coming from down the front of the young woman's sage green dress. Her long brown hair was matted around the sides where she'd wiped her nose with her arm from ear to ear. 'I found her.'

'May I call you Francesca?'

She nodded as she pulled a blanket tighter around her shoulders.

'In your own words, can you tell me what happened?'

She wiped her forehead with her arm. 'I'd had a lot to drink and wasn't feeling well. I'd been sick and all I wanted to do was go to bed. Holly's room was next to mine on the first floor. When I passed her door, it creaked slightly and I wondered why it wasn't locked. That's when…'

'It's okay. You're really helping us. I know this is hard.'

A tear slid down her cheek. 'I pushed the door open. There was blood smeared on the drawers next to the door and I thought she'd hurt herself. I saw she was in bed so I called her name. She didn't answer. Then I thought she was asleep but I had to check that she was okay. I went over and shook her but still she didn't answer.' Francesca paused and swallowed. 'I turned the lamp on and saw blood smeared all over her face, and her eyes, they were glassy and staring at me but she wasn't moving. I ran out to the corridor and screamed for help. No one was around. I somehow managed to reach reception and told them what had happened. I felt really sick again but I passed out. I can't remember much after that, until the ambulance got here.'

Francesca tried to stand but fell back onto her bottom. 'Someone killed Holly. I don't want to be here. I just want to go home.' The woman folded her arms and bowed her head.

'I know you don't and I'm so sorry you've been through this tonight. Did you see anyone else in the corridor or around by the stairs?'

'I don't think so. It was just me.'

'Did you touch anything else apart from the lamp?'

'I can't remember. I think I touched some of the furniture.'

Gina glanced at Francesca's hands. Not a speck of blood on them, but her hands were a little make-up smeared. 'Francesca? Would you mind if we took some swabs and fingerprints from you for elimination purposes? We also need your dress and shoes. I'm sorry to have to ask you for these but you went into Holly's room. We need to catch whoever did this to her.'

She turned to face Gina.

For a second Gina thought she might object. She had to consider that at the moment they had no suspects and Francesca

Carter was the first person to arrive at the scene. She hadn't seen anyone else on the way there or back.

''Course.'

'Do you know anyone who would want to hurt Holly?'

'No, she was our friend and she never said she had any problems with anyone. She would have said something. We were all close.'

'We?'

Francesca wiped her watery eyes. 'Me, Holly, Kerry and Lilly. We've been friends since school. The Awesome Foursome.' She let out a teary smile.

'Was she seeing anyone?'

'She never said but she hadn't been spending much time with us lately.'

'Did anything happen tonight that seemed out of the ordinary?'

She shrugged. 'No, only that a bit of trouble broke out. Some gatecrashers had got in and were helping themselves to the free bar. Holly wasn't a part of that. I think I saw her outside. I went outside as I felt nauseous. She was talking to someone but I didn't see who it was.' Her brow furrowed.

'Could you tell me anything at all about that person?'

'It was a man. He was wearing trousers and a shirt.'

'Did you catch his hair colour? Colour of his suit or shirt? Height or build?'

'No. I felt really sick. My mind was elsewhere. Charlie, my other half, was a bit fed up with me as I'd been doing shots so I had that on my mind. As I said, I ran out to throw up and the man Holly was talking to faded into the shadows. I only wish now I'd properly looked. Do you think he could have been Holly's murderer?'

'We don't know all that has happened as yet. Forensics are still in the room at the moment. You've been really helpful but we'll still need a formal statement off you. PC Kapoor will come back in and talk to you about that.'

She nodded. Gina waved at Keith from the crime scene crew. He hurried over. 'Would you be able to take swabs from our witness while I catch up with Bernard? She went into the victim's room. Take PC Kapoor with you too.'

'Will do.'

'I'll leave you in the capable hands of the paramedics and our forensics expert, Keith. If you remember anything else, please call me.' She handed Francesca a card as Keith and the ambulance crew took over.

Briggs plodded out of the main entrance and headed over to Gina. 'Anything?'

'From what her friend and fellow bridesmaid, Francesca, says, Holly was seen talking to a man outside on the terrace, the one that opens out from the function room. We need to secure all CCTV. What kind of monster would do this to her?'

'Hopefully, we'll find out soon.'

Gina's gaze met his for a moment more than was comfortable. She almost hated Detective Sergeant Jacob Driscoll for being stuck in an airport when she needed him on a case. 'I best head back in to speak to the other bridesmaid, Lilly Hill. See what she has to say that's so important.'

She glanced at Francesca one last time as Keith took swabs and the paramedics reassured the woman. Could Francesca be their murderer? Francesca caught her eye then looked away quickly. Gina stared in her direction a moment longer but the woman didn't turn around for another look.

CHAPTER SEVEN

Gina half jogged back into the manor house. Huddles of people were dotted all over the main ballroom. At the beginning of the night, Gina imagined the room would have looked like every bride's dream, but now a thick pale green ribbon lay tangled on the dance floor. Vases of carnations had been spilled over the cream tablecloths and food had squashed into most of the carpeted floor. Balloons bobbed along the high ceiling and the cake had been smashed against the window.

The hoppy smell from the pop-up bar filled the air, that and onions. Gina swallowed as she made her way towards the woman in green. The man sitting beside her clutched his arm around her shoulder and placed his other hand on her knee. Gina slowed down her pace through the chaos as she observed the bridesmaid's partner sharing a short sharp stare across the room with Samuel Avery. Causing trouble again, that's what Gina thought. Samuel Avery was always trying to insert himself into the middle of someone's marriage and Gina didn't believe the man was capable of change.

'I'm Detective Inspector Gina Harte, Senior Investigating Officer. You wanted to speak to me?'

The woman blew her nose into a napkin and nodded. Gina recognised her to be the woman who she'd seen with Samuel Avery earlier. She shuddered as she remembered his searching hand on the top of her bottom. The same woman had also come upstairs while Gina was speaking to Bernard. Had she come to speak then about whatever it was she knew?

'Can you give us a minute?' Gina spotted the wedding ring on Lilly Hill's hand. The man nodded, kissing her on the forehead as he left.

She nodded and shivered. Gina eased the cardigan out of the woman's clutches and draped it over her shoulders. 'Yes. I don't know if what I've got to say will help but I've been friends with Holly for years and I notice things, changes. When this happened, I couldn't help but wonder…' She dropped her hands and looked up. 'I've given a statement. Maybe I've got this all wrong. It's just—'

'It's okay.' Gina placed a hand on the weeping woman's shoulder. 'May I call you Lilly?'

'Yes,' she said with a squeak as she choked on a tear and took a deep breath.

'What you have to say may be something, it may be nothing, but we won't know that until you tell me? Would it be easier to start at the beginning?' Lilly looked to be of a similar age to Hannah, maybe slightly older.

She wiped her hand on her dress. 'I've been trying to get together for a drink with Holly for weeks but she keeps making excuses and it isn't like her… wasn't like her.' Lilly paused. 'I can't believe she's not here any more. We've been friends since junior school. Anyway, I'd been worried about her.'

'Why were you worried?'

'I normally call her before I visit but she hadn't been answering her phone so I thought I'd surprise her. This was weeks ago and I can't remember exactly when. Holly had been depressed in the past, shut herself off from the world and, knowing her the way I do, I know the only thing that's helped is her friends, that's me, Kerry and Francesca. We've always been there for her, checking on her during bad times, encouraging her to get help.'

'You thought she may have been depressed?'

Lilly placed her arm on the table, dropping the napkin onto a half-eaten burger. 'Yes, and normally she'd open the door when she was like that but this time, or should I say the past few times I've knocked, I sensed she was in her apartment but not opening up. One time, I'm sure I heard another voice coming from behind the door, just a murmur. I even looked through the letterbox. She has a mirror in the hallway and I caught a reflection in it, just a slither of a blue shirt with some sort of print on it. I knocked and knocked but she wouldn't open up. It was just bizarre as we've never kept secrets. When I finally managed to catch up with her at the dress fitting before we departed for the wedding in Greece, she denied everything, said I must have been imagining that she was in when I called over. I know what I saw.' She paused. 'She didn't seem depressed, not like before. In the past when she'd been going through a rough patch she hadn't eaten and her clothes would look too loose but this time she looked to be a healthy weight, her skin looked good and she looked happy. I think she was hiding someone from us. I told Brendan, my husband, and he said she wouldn't do that. I know her better than him though.'

Gina flipped to a clean page in her pad and began to take notes. 'You saw someone in her apartment, wearing a blue shirt?'

'Yes, she was definitely hiding someone from us. I mentioned it to Kerry and Francesca but they didn't know anything either. I know she was seeing someone and something wasn't right. All day, she'd seemed off. We came earlier and helped to decorate the room for the party and have our hair and make-up done. When I spoke to her, it was as if she hadn't heard me talking. Her mind was on something else, that's for sure.'

'Yesterday?'

Lilly nodded. 'Yes, we got here about two in the afternoon. The venue had already set the tables up. We just had to receive the flowers and add the final touches.'

'Can you talk me through everything that happened from before the wedding to now?' Gina knew it was a lot to ask given the environment they were in and the fact that Lilly had started to yawn but she needed as much as she could possibly garner to work with when she got back to the station.

'The Friday before last.'

'Friday the first of May?'

'Yes,' Lilly replied. 'That's when Brendan and I flew to Crete for the wedding. Kerry and Ed were already there as were some of the wedding party. I couldn't get much holiday and neither could Francesca and Charlie, so we all flew out together on the Friday, ready for the wedding on Saturday. Anyway, the wedding went without a hitch. It was a small gathering, just family and a few close friends. Holly was there too. She'd been there for the whole week. She seemed fine at the wedding, happy even. I tried to talk to her about when I visited her apartment. I said it didn't matter if she was seeing someone but she wouldn't say anything. I kept pushing and eventually, on the night of the wedding, she got fed up with me going on and she walked away from me, mid-conversation, and went to bed. She was in the room next to me and I heard her sobbing and telling someone to call her back. It was as clear as anything as we both had our balcony doors open. I don't think she realised I could hear and I stood there in the dark, hoping that the person she left the message for would call her back. They never did and I was turning into mosquito food so after waiting for the best part of an hour, I gave up and went to bed.'

'Were you on your own?'

'Yes, I was tired. I think Brendan and everyone else was still at the bar. I could hear them all from the balcony even though I couldn't see them.'

'This is all really helpful, Lilly.' A lover, that's who Gina needed to find. The person in the blue shirt.

'The wedding was on the Saturday and we all flew back on the Sunday, that's Sunday the third of May. Before we knew it, the reception was upon us. I tried to call Holly several times when we all got back but she wouldn't answer. She was definitely avoiding me. I should have done more. I should have gone over to her apartment again and got it out of her.'

Gina made a note in her book.

Who was Holly seeing?

'Is there anything else you'd like to tell me?'

Lilly shrugged her shoulders. 'I woke up later that night, back in Crete and I was hot so I opened my balcony door a little and I heard something. It was about four in the morning, I guess. I heard Holly down by the pool pleading with someone. She was saying something like, *I can't keep this to myself any longer.* She may have been talking to someone who was there or on the phone. I have no idea. In the background, I could still hear some of the party at the bar too, no one specific, just a hum of voices. Holly must have gone back down after I'd fallen asleep.'

'Did you hear or see who she was talking to?'

She shook her head and a tear slithered down her cheek, plopping onto the table. 'Not even a shadow. I wish I did. I should have gone down and checked to see if she was okay. I was so fed up with her for hiding things from me and not opening the door when I went over, I turned my back on her. I could have done more—'

Gina had seen it all before. People argued and fell out all the time in everyday life and if the worst happened, they were quick to absorb all the blame.

The young man hurried back over and took Lilly's hand, helping her up. 'I think my wife has had enough for tonight.'

'I could have saved her,' Lilly yelled.

'Come on. We need to get you home. I've called us a taxi, we can come back for our things tomorrow when we're allowed in our room.'

'Could I just take your name?'

'Brendan Hill. You have our full names, address, and phone numbers. We're both tired and it's been a long day. We need time to grieve now. Come on, babe.'

'Thanks, Lilly. Here's my card. If either of you remember anything else, please call me.'

They'd been interviewed and all their details logged, so she couldn't keep them any longer. In fact, the whole room had thinned out since she'd started talking to Lilly. The DJ had left, the staff had started sweeping the food off the dance floor and Samuel Avery was packing the bar away with the help of his staff.

'Mr Avery.'

'DI Harte. I hoped we'd never meet again but chance has brought us together. I'm packing up and going and you aren't going to hold me up. I saw nothing, I know nothing and I'm nothing to do with anything.' He poured himself half a beer and swigged it back. 'That was good.'

The slight tremor in his hand told her he knew more than he was letting on or he had been gasping for a drink. His shirt hung over his middle and his skinny dark jeans reached a pair of brown shoes that had been splattered with beer. His dyed mousy hair was stuck to his forehead, telling of a hot sticky night of hard work.

'Elvis, grab this will you?' He shoved a box into the younger man's hand and a woman came along and helped.

Gina had met Elvis before, known to punters of the Angel Arms as the king himself because of his almost identical voice to the rock and roll legend. He went down well on karaoke night, so Gina had heard. She wracked her brains for his real name, Robin something. She'd find out later from all the statements.

Elvis nudged a glass off the bar, its fragments spreading far and wide with a crash. 'Dammit. Cass, get me a dustpan and brush.' He neatened his brown quiff before picking up the larger pieces of glass.

A thickset freckly woman pushed her curly brown hair behind her ears and sighed as she went away to get what he'd asked for, her leggings so stretched Gina could see her light coloured pants underneath.

'DI Harte, are you just going to stand around and hold me up all night or have you got something to say?' Samuel's thin lips upturned, deepening the smile lines around his eyes. It wasn't a genuine smile. Samuel didn't know the meaning of genuine. He said and did what he needed to do in order to get sex.

'I saw you with Lilly Hill earlier tonight, when I first arrived.'

He let out a laugh that sounded like a huff. 'So, what can I say? She's a bit of top totty. Thought if I showed her a bit of sympathy, she might be up for a quickie in the bushes after the coast was clear.'

'You haven't changed a bit.'

He poured himself another half. 'And what of it? Being hopeful of a shag isn't a crime.'

She refrained from rolling her eyes. 'Tell me about the gatecrashers?'

'I don't know anything about any gatecrashers.'

'Did you recognise any of them?'

'I'll tell you something, Inspector. I recognised near enough everyone in here. I'm from Cleevesford. I run a pub in Cleevesford. Everyone in here has crossed my path at some point. I have given every bit of information I have to one of your officers, the screechy-voiced bird who almost deafened me as she spoke.'

'Please don't refer to our officers as birds, it's disrespectful.' Gina knew he meant PC Kapoor.

'Whatever. It was her, little miss screechy.' He pointed across the room to Kapoor.

'Have you been here all night? In this room?'

He pointed at Gina and grinned. 'Trying to pin things on me again? I'd say this is harassment.'

She clenched her hands together. He had become embroiled in a few of their cases in the past and she'd never really had anything on him. 'I just need to know if you left the room.'

'Maybe I did, maybe I didn't. Screechy has my statement and that's all you're getting. Are we off, Elvis?'

'All done, boss. I'm going to wait with Cass in the van. Need to get out of this place.'

'You heard what he said. We need to get out of this place.' He swigged the last of his beer, grabbed a box of glasses and followed Elvis out.

Gina slammed her fist onto the empty bar, then noticed the bride being comforted by her new husband and parents.

'Guv. I got here as fast as I could.' DC Paula Wyre said as she hurried over, red faced. 'I've just chatted with Briggs and caught up with what's happened. He also confirmed that an officer has visited the victim's mother to break the news.' Her usual straight black hair was slightly fluffed up. Her checked skirt hem met her opaque black tights showing legs rarely seen at work. That was what having to attend a crime scene did after being interrupted while enjoying a night out.

Gina's phone beeped. She opened the email. 'Just in time. Would you please tell PC Kapoor to make a list of people who attended the wedding in Greece and then we need to head out to speak to the victim's mother. I have the address here. Meet me out the front when you're done.'

As Gina turned to leave she saw Samuel Avery grinning at another woman before slipping his number into her hand and leaving. He was wearing a blue shirt. Gina shook her head and looked around. So were many of the other guests. Had Holly turned down his advances earlier that evening and was he the man Francesca thought she saw at Holly's flat?

CHAPTER EIGHT

He walked between the trees at the bottom of the manor house and entered the thick woodland. The bustle had died down a little only to be replaced by press hanging around the front of the building. As he reached the clearing, he scanned the area. He was now far enough away to let it all out. Exhilaration, excitement, everything he'd bottled up so that he could blend in with everyone else while the police were asking all the questions. He'd comforted the weepy, looked sad and done exactly what had been expected of him. Playing the part had turned him on even more.

It was over for now. A wide grin spread across his face. He'd need to hurry back soon before he was missed. More than ten minutes and he'd definitely be missed. There were things to do. He needed to get away from this building as soon as the police gave him the okay. It wouldn't be long now.

Glancing back, the shining beacon of a building he'd admired for years now felt like a threat but he had to return. Everything had to seem normal.

He ran through the events of the night, reliving when he had his hands around her throat.

A swell filled his pants.

Was it enough?

That question again. It was enough, for now. But it wouldn't be enough for long. Still riding high on what had happened, he rubbed himself over his trousers, feeling an intensity like no other building up. He unzipped his fly and placed his hands in his underpants and smiled a little until he was shocked back into reality by a cracking noise coming from behind a tree. He zipped back up, cleared his throat and lit a cigarette, hoping that the watcher hadn't seen what he was up to. 'Hello,' he called as he blew out a plume of smoke. He focused on the dense woodland. 'Who's there?' He was by no means scared but the thought of someone hidden amongst the shrubbery, spying on him as he'd rubbed himself in the woods shook him a little.

A scrawny man stood and walked towards him, emerging from a hiding place behind a tree.

'You were running from the police earlier.'

The scrawny man nodded. 'I didn't do anything. I was leaving and they started chasing me. I heard that some woman was killed.'

'So why are you hiding?'

He shrugged his shoulders in his oversized denim jacket.

'I know why you were hiding. You killed her didn't you?' He was going to have some fun with scrawny man, scare him a little. He knew exactly why the man was in the bushes, hiding away from the police. He'd seen him in the function room earlier that evening and he definitely wasn't a guest, given that he'd snuck in through the garden. He wondered if the man recognised him but he didn't think so, it was too dark for either of them to make much out. 'Boo!'

Scrawny man flinched, his bottom lip quivering. 'I didn't. I was just trying to get out, I swear.'

'So you come here and hide in the bushes from the police and you're trying to convince me you didn't kill that woman.' He paused and took another drag on the cigarette. 'I tell you what, I won't say a word. What have you got on you?'

Scrawny man ran his fingers through his scruffy beard before giving up and turning out one of the pockets of his jeans.

'It's a lovely night. Moon's out. Not too cold and we will keep this as our little secret.' He patted the man's shoulder a couple of times before grinning.

Scrawny man stared as if waiting to be excused.

'Go on. Hop it.' Before scrawny man scarpered off, he grabbed a little packet from his hand and watched as scrawny hurried deep into the woodland.

He pinched the cigarette and dropped it in his pocket, along with what he'd taken from scrawny man. Taking a lungful of fresh air, he headed back. The air had never tasted so good. Everything tasted good, felt good and smelled good. Life was amazing, and now he had a little something to make it even more amazing.

The swell in his pants returned. Power was everything. The game, the fun, his hands around her neck. He was ready to start planning his next move.

CHAPTER NINE

Cass wiped the last of her eyeliner away from her puffy eyes. The waterproof stuff was the best – it had lasted through her tears back home and the sweat that had dripped down her forehead all night as she'd served the crowd, all for a measly thirty-five pounds cash in hand. She'd been stupid to volunteer to help Samuel and Elvis, especially as it had been Kerry's wedding, the girl who hadn't given her a second glance at high school. Maybe now, Kerry would appreciate a real friend, not her plastic friends, Francesca and Lilly. Maybe now that Holly had gone, there would be room for a replacement number four. The Awesome Foursome – what a stupid name.

She pinched the excess skin underneath her chin and held it tight, observing her face shape without it. Why did some women only attract more beautiful women to be friends? Cass would be a great friend, not like the others. She'd heard Francesca drunkenly saying that Kerry's new husband Ed was far too hot for Kerry – that wasn't loyal friendship. She'd also heard one of them say that Kerry had made the hugest mistake in marrying Ed, that he was a player. And Lilly had been saying to Brendan that Kerry's wedding hadn't been as genuine as theirs and that Cleevesford Manor was a bit of a grubby hole. Cass knew she shouldn't have heard Brendan and Charlie rating Kerry's backside ten out of ten but that's when she'd spotted her Elvis and Samuel sniggering along. So much bitching amongst so called friends. She clenched her fists. Having it out with Elvis in the morning would be her priority.

Cass hadn't heard Holly saying anything but she had spotted her ditching a drink in the corner of the room when she thought no one was looking. She'd seen the glance passing back and forth between Elvis and Holly and then Samuel. Did they know something she didn't? Elvis had been missing a couple of times but he was always playing up, cheating. Well not quite cheating, he'd call them friends. Was it cheating if he had women friends she wasn't friends with? She'd have done everything to make sure Holly wouldn't take him from her. He wasn't much but he was all she had.

She peered around the bathroom door and spotted Elvis lying flat out on their bed, one leg hanging over the edge as he filled the room with his growling snores. Falling asleep so easily hadn't surprised her one bit, not since she'd slipped an extra-large measure of vodka into his drink when they'd arrived home. They'd been in less than half an hour and it looked like he'd been asleep all night. As they sat in the living room winding down, he declared that he needed to go to bed. She feared he wouldn't reach their bed as he staggered towards it and that's where he'd been since.

She plodded over the creaky floorboards of their old rented house and kissed him on the forehead, just missing his silly Elvis quiff. He was no Elvis; he may have had the voice but his arms were like strings of spaghetti and he didn't have the moves, not in the same way. Some people were mildly impressed by him but most people laughed at him. He just couldn't see it. For a couple of years now, he was convinced he'd be a star and one day would make it to Vegas. I'll check out *Britain's Got Talent*, he'd say, and he did. He didn't pass the audition stage to get on the television. He wasn't bad enough or good enough to provide the level of entertainment the public had become used to seeing. He was Mr Mediocre.

Reaching over, she gave him a nudge. He snorted again. There was no waking him, which was good. As she ground her teeth, she gave up fighting the itch to find out the truth. She reached into his pocket and began searching for his phone. Pulling it out, she noticed he had a new message. As she pressed to open it, the screen flashed a password box.

CASS.

CASSANDRA.

He'd never used a password before. She threw the phone back into his pocket along with the unused party popper, old receipts and the small pile of cash he thought made him look like a big shot. If he'd definitely been cheating on her with Holly, she was going to find out somehow. Now that she was dead, the truth would come out and she wouldn't have to do the digging.

Cass grabbed her own phone and clicked the Facebook app. Her feed was full of comments about Holly's death. Already Holly's wall had been filled with 'RIPs', and comments along the lines of, 'How could anyone do this to such a wonderful person?'

Elvis's snoring changed tune to a deep guttural sound, making Cass flinch. Was Holly as wonderful as people made out? Cass believed no one could be that perfect. She would make it her mission to find out, but to do that she needed to be in the fold. Holly didn't matter any more. What mattered is that she could start again with Kerry. And she had her chance to do exactly that now Holly was gone.

Clicking on messenger, her finger hovered over Kerry's name. *Just do it, Cass!*

And she did. As easy as that.

CHAPTER TEN

As they pulled into the modern estate in Worcester, Gina enjoyed the tune of the early morning birds filling the air with their wake-up call. The Lyppards was one of many small housing developments in Warndon Villages. As one road snaked into an island and straight onto another road, Gina's satnav told her that the close she was looking for was next on the right.

'Well. It's been a long night but Briggs has promised us breakfast when we get back to the station and I am starving,' Gina said as Wyre stared into the darkness as they pulled in.

'Me too. I think I'll drop my standards and tuck in for once.'

Gina rarely saw Paula Wyre eat anything that was brought into the office. If the offerings weren't compatible with her gym workouts, she abstained.

'I was out with friends last night and we were going to have a late dinner after the band, but I got the call and headed back before eating anything so I'm starving. I can always work it off at the gym later.'

'Sorry you were called back. With Jacob's delay at the airport, we were a bit short-staffed.'

Wyre shrugged as Gina slowed down. 'What happened to that woman is terrible and I'm glad I'm here. I'm dreading seeing her mother though.'

'And me. I don't know how I'd cope if it were Hannah.'

One light was on in the whole cul-de-sac. It was the house where life would never be the same again. One person in this road had received an earlier visit from an officer giving them the worst news ever and their nightmare wasn't about to end with that; in fact, it was only just beginning.

They hurried across the block-paved drive and knocked on the door of the semi-detached house. The hall light flicked on and a blotchy-faced woman, a little older looking than Gina, answered while dabbing her eyes with a tissue.

'Marianne Long? I'm Detective Inspector Harte and this is Detective Constable Wyre. May we come in?'

The woman opened the door wider. She went to speak but coughed into her tissue instead. Another woman sat at the kitchen table in her dressing gown. 'This is my neighbour, Beryl. She came to sit with me after I got the news.'

'I'll put the kettle on.' Beryl tightened her towelling robe around her ample hips and walked with a slight shuffle to the sink.

'I can't believe she's gone,' Marianne said as she tucked her grey streaked brown hair behind her ears and buttoned her cardigan up. 'I want you to catch the bastard who hurt her! Tell me you will.' Marianne stared directly at Gina.

The ticking of the kitchen clock filled the silence as Gina paused. She wanted to catch the perpetrator as much as Marianne needed her to. 'I will do everything I can to find this person and bring them to justice.'

'Here you go, love.' Beryl placed a full teapot, some cups and a small bottle of milk on the table. 'I'll go in the living room. Just call me in if you want me. I'm not going anywhere, I promise,' she said to her friend as she left.

'She was murdered. No one has told me how or where. No one has told me anything. Have you arrested anyone?'

Gina shook her head. They had nothing but a million statements and a mass of bagged and tagged evidence that would take time to process. 'At the moment we haven't but I promise you wholeheartedly, we are doing everything we can. I mean everything.'

Marianne looked away, her eyes glistening with spent tears. 'What happened?'

'Late yesterday evening, Holly's body was discovered by a friend in her hotel room. We're still unsure of the cause of death. I'm so sorry, Ms Long.'

Gina could only imagine the pain and heartache this fellow mother was going through; and she knew a mother never stopped thinking about what their grown-up children might be doing. She often thought of Hannah, even though she lived far away and they were always at loggerheads. Hannah was the only real flesh and blood that Gina had left and to suddenly hear the type of news that Marianne had received would feel like it was the end of the world.

Marianne grabbed her straggly hair with both of her hands and pulled it as she yelled out. 'You've made a mistake. Tell me, it might not be her. I need to see her.'

'I can arrange that for you.' Gina knew it was definitely Holly. Francesca Carter had identified her. Her luggage had contained identification. 'Can you tell me a bit about Holly? It would really help us if we got to know her a little better.'

Marianne walked out of the room and came back a moment later with a tablet. She scrolled through her photos and placed it on the table, showing a photo of Holly. 'This is her a week ago, all dressed up for her friend Kerry's wedding. I emailed this photo to the officer who came earlier.' Marianne paused. 'She was so happy and I thought she looked beautiful.' A little cry escaped Marianne's lips. 'I know she was excited that her friend was getting married; she was always excited for other people but never herself. She thought she'd never meet the right person, get the good job, be good enough but I always told her she was. To me, she was perfect. She'd had a few boyfriends but never once did she introduce me to any of them. I asked her why.' The woman smiled through the tears. 'She told me they weren't good enough to bring home and if she ever brought someone home, it would mean he was the one. That's the thing about Holly. She was so guarded. She always thought something would go wrong. I wouldn't have minded her bringing friends or boyfriends home to meet me, even if they didn't last. I joked with her that she was embarrassed of me. She wasn't though. We had a good relationship.'

Ms Long flicked through the photos. 'This is Holly, aged five. I love this photo of her in her little school uniform. She was bullied at school in the early years but she'd stood her ground a little more, made some friends who looked out for her and things seemed to improve after that. Her friend Kerry had always looked out for her after taking her under her wing at junior school.'

'Can you tell me a bit about Holly's friends?'

The woman placed the tablet on the table and DC Wyre flicked over the pages in her notebook before pouring them all a cup of tea.

'They were really close: Holly, Kerry, Lilly and Francesca. They did lots together as teens: days out, shopping, playing with make-up, as teens do. They had their little dramas and fallings out, but nothing serious. When they all started work and began to leave home, they spent a little less time with each other. I worried for Holly then.' Marianne leaned back and sipped her tea while deep in thought.

'Why did you worry?' Gina swigged the tea, enjoying the warm liquid as it slid down her drying throat.

'She isolated herself a little. I used to call her most nights to see if she was okay. I wasn't smothering her; I was just worried as she lived alone. She stopped answering my calls all the time. That's when I knew she was feeling depressed. Since her teens she'd had a few minor bouts of depression but she always bounced back. I tried not to worry too much but I did and I called a lot. One day she snapped and told me she just needed some time to herself. That was only about three weeks ago. I thought maybe Kerry's wedding would be just the tonic she needed and when she called me before flying out to Greece she sounded fine, almost ecstatic. I suppose I stopped worrying. She said we'd catch up after the wedding and that was it.' She wiped a hair from her mouth and placed it behind her ear. 'She didn't call after the wedding but she messaged me, telling me she was busy catching up at work. That was the last I heard from her.'

Gina's mind flashed back to what Lilly Hill had said. 'Do you know if Holly was seeing anyone?'

'She never said. Do you know something I don't?'

'One of her friends thought so but they didn't have any idea who it might be. Did she mention anyone at all?'

Marianne shook her head. 'She never told me anything. I can't believe how little I know. How could I not have known that she was seeing anyone?'

'We can't confirm that yet, it's just an avenue we're investigating at the moment.' Gina hated the fact that she had to see people in Marianne's position when she had nothing to ease the pain even a little. 'Do you know of anyone Holly may have had a disagreement with? Did she have any known enemies?'

'I can't think of any. My daughter wasn't disliked by anyone. She had lovely friends and she was a good friend back. She never mentioned any relationships that had gone wrong or any friends that were fed up with her. She loved her work too.'

Gina rubbed her heavy eyes. 'What did she do?'

Marianne flicked to another photo. 'This is a photo of us. I met her for lunch in her dinner break. She'd started a new job for a microbrewery in Stratford-upon-Avon. She does accounts admin. I was so pleased for her. It was more money, better hours and they were going to pay for her to take some qualifications next year. She left school at sixteen and got her first job as an admin junior. Since then, she gained lots of experience but had no qualifications. She was so happy when she got the job.'

'And can I ask where she worked?'

'Furnace and Blower Ales.'

Silence filled the room and Gina was back to noticing the ticking clock. 'Is there anything else you can tell us that you think might help us to catch whoever did this to Holly?'

The realisation of what had happened hit Marianne all over again. Talking about Holly had distracted her slightly. Tears welled in her eyes and her lips trembled. 'No, I wish I knew more.'

Wyre topped up Marianne's tea and gave a sympathetic smile.

'I'm going to leave you with my card. If you remember anything, please call me straight away. No matter how small it is, call me.'

Marianne's shaky fingers emerged from the cuff of her cardigan and she gripped the card, sniffing as she began to fill up again. 'I think she'd had a bit of an argument with someone at work a few weeks ago. She said it was nothing and the air had been cleared.'

Gina leaned forward over the kitchen table. 'Did she say who she'd had this argument with?'

'No. She said it was nothing but I know my daughter and I can tell when something is troubling her.' Marianne closed her eyes and swallowed her tears down.

'We really are so sorry for what you are going through. If you need to be put in touch with bereavement services, please call me and I can help you.'

A tear streamed down her red cheeks. 'Thank you.'

As Gina and Wyre scraped their chairs on the tiled floor, Beryl came back in and placed an arm around her friend. 'Come on, love,' she said as she hugged her friend. 'Let it all out.'

'We'll see ourselves out.' Gina nodded at Beryl as they left.

'That was horrible, guv.' Wyre closed her pad and popped it in her pocket.

'I hated every moment of it. I suppose we really need to visit her workplace. What was it called again?' As Gina opened the car door, a neighbour came out and got in his car. It was officially morning and neither she nor Wyre had been to bed all night.

'Furnace and Blower Ales, in Stratford.'

Gina's phone beeped. Briggs.

We've made an arrest. Remember the person you saw leaving the scene at the back of the garden? We have him. Uniform picked him up walking down one of the two roads.

'We need to get back to the station, now.' Gina started the car up and pulled away.

CHAPTER ELEVEN

'Can you confirm your name?' Gina's voice echoed through the interview room, a tone of annoyance cutting the silence as she waited for Phillip Brighton to answer. Wyre stared sternly at the man as Mr Ullah, the duty solicitor, whispered in his ear.

Shrugging, his shoulders almost got lost in the material of his denim jacket. His belt had been removed when he'd arrived at the station, causing his jeans to slip to his thighs, exposing the grubby cream waistband of his boxer shorts. Spending an hour in a cell should have given him time to think, but he was still refusing to tell them who he was. The man barely blinked and this made Gina uneasy. His stare fixed on her, then across to Wyre as he scratched a few flecks of dried skin from his beard.

'You have been charged with the supply of Class A and Class B drugs. What do we have?'

Wyre turned over the page in the file. 'Twenty-five wraps of cocaine and a bag of cannabis have been seized, along with four hundred pounds in cash.'

'Phillip Brighton. We have you on file and your fingerprints don't lie. This isn't your first offence. It isn't even your second offence. You're looking at a long custodial sentence so I suggest you start talking about last night.'

The suited solicitor whispered once again in his client's ear and Phillip Brighton didn't say a word.

'Mr Brighton. You were picked up by officers on Blossom Lane, which runs along the back of Cleevesford Manor. We found you in possession of a substantial amount of Class A and B drugs, along with a wad of cash.' Gina needed to prove to herself that he was the man running away from the building. 'I saw someone who fits your build from the window of the manor, using a phone as a torch before disappearing into the woods.' She couldn't have identified him in a line-up. 'You may or may not know that a serious attack took place last night resulting in the murder of a woman, so you need to start speaking. We are presently going through all the CCTV from the manor. If you were there, we will find out.'

She was bluffing. There was CCTV but she had no idea how good any of it was until they sat down and went through it. She knew that DC Harry O'Connor had arrived at the station a short while ago and she'd tasked him with that very job.

'Okay. I was at the manor but I didn't kill any woman!' He kicked the leg of the table.

'I'm not saying you did.' He paused and twitched slightly, then again. Just a little shake of his neck. 'I need you to tell me what you saw. Do you know Holly Long?'

'Never heard that name.'

Gina pushed a photo of Holly across the table. 'Do you recognise this woman?'

'I've never seen her before. Look, if I tell you what I do know, will you drop the drug charges?'

Gina slowly shook her head. 'I will make it known that you cooperated fully with our investigations.' Phillip Brighton had been caught with the drugs and the cash and he was a known drug dealer in the area. She knew he was small fry in the big scheme of things but still, she couldn't magic these charges away. 'Phillip. Can I call you Phillip?'

'Phil. I hate Phillip.'

'Phil. A woman was murdered last night and we are interviewing everyone. Can you tell me when you arrived at Cleevesford Manor, how you got there and what you did?'

Mr Ullah whispered a few more words and Phillip nodded.

'I wasn't dealing, I just had some stuff on me for personal use. I heard that there was going to be a free bar and I turned up, taking my chances on getting a few drinks.'

'Where did you hear about the free bar?'

'The Angel Arms. I was in there having a quiet drink and someone let on that they were heading down to Cleevesford Manor.'

'Who?'

'I don't know. I overheard some of the lads talking. They were joking about milking some geezer called Trevor for a few free drinks. He's the bride's dad, apparently. I headed over there about an hour later. That's how long it took me to walk. I think the others caught a taxi. They said to climb over the stile on Blossom Lane. It's a short walk through the woods and there's a cut through at the back of the garden. I couldn't exactly swan in through the front door, could I? I didn't have an invite. The aim of the game was to guzzle as many drinks as possible before we got chucked out.'

Gina knew he'd gone there to sell drugs but now wasn't the time to interrupt him.

'Carry on.'

'I got there about half nine or ten, I think. When I came out of the toilets, I saw that all hell was breaking loose when the father of the bride could see that we didn't belong. Food started flying, a few shirts were ruffled and most of us were thrown out onto the terrace. I waited outside and had a smoke until things died down and then the cops arrived and I heard people saying something about a dead woman. I knew I needed to get out. I shouldn't have been there and I knew this would happen if I stayed. I ran to the back of the garden and I got a bit lost in the woods.'

Didn't want to get caught with all the drugs in your possession more like, Gina thought. 'You didn't come when you were called.'

'I fell asleep. Like I said, those drugs are for personal use. I had a smoke and I fell asleep in the woods.'

Gina didn't believe any of it. 'You went from running away in a panic to falling asleep.'

'Yes.'

Gina cleared her throat and glanced across at Wyre who raised an eyebrow. 'Okay, what happened when you woke up?'

'I saw someone, but as I say, I was half stoned and it was dark but I know what I saw. He was feeling himself in the bushes.'

'Feeling himself?'

The man rolled his eyes. 'Wanking. He started to wank and I startled him.'

Something about what he was saying and the way he was saying it told Gina that amongst his lies, this was a truth. Even Phillip Brighton wouldn't have embellished his story with something so bizarre.

'You're saying you saw a man masturbating in the bushes?'

'Yeah, well starting to. It was way after things had died down. I'd been out of it for a while. I don't know what time it was but it was late or should I say early.'

'What did he look like?'

He shrugged again and leaned his chin on his chest as he slouched back, his beard draping over his stained yellow jumper. 'It was dark and I was a bit stoned. All I could see was his white shirt.'

'Height? Build?'

'Taller than me.'

Gina glanced at the file. Phillip Brighton was only five foot six. Most of the men there had been taller. 'Much taller or a bit taller?'

His stare was so intense, his eyes looked as though they might pop out of his head. 'How am I meant to know? The ground was uneven and as I said, I was stoned. Average, tall, not sure. Not fat. He had a suit jacket on.'

'Hair colour, features?'

'He had a nose, two eyes and a mouth. He could have had hair – I don't know. It was dark. I couldn't see. I. Don't. Know.'

Gina dropped her pen on the desk.

'I do have something.'

Gina and Wyre sat up a little.

'He was smoking.'

They were looking for a smoker.

'Can you tell us where you saw him?' There was a chance he may have left something behind. A cigarette butt, a footprint, anything.

'There's a small clearing. You follow the trodden path through the woods from the cut through in the garden. When you reach the oak trees, there is a small clearing. I fell asleep behind one of the oaks, in a bush. That's where he was. Are you going to put a good word in for me?'

'That's all for now. I will add in your file that you cooperated.'

'You'll tell them I wasn't dealing, that my stash is personal?'

Ignoring him, Gina continued. 'When you went to the toilet, was there anyone else in there who can corroborate your whereabouts?'

'I was taking a dump and I was on my own in the cubicle. No, I didn't take anyone in with me.'

'Did you go upstairs at all?'

'You're trying to fix this on me. I didn't go anywhere but the shitter. I didn't go up no stairs and I didn't do anything I weren't meant to be doing.'

'That's not entirely true. You shouldn't have been in the building.'

'You know what I mean. Tell them,' he shouted to Mr Ullah. The solicitor whispered once again and Phillip pointed his shabby boot at the table and kicked the leg again, almost losing his boot. 'Bloody hell! And I want my laces back.'

'You know the rules.' Gina knew he'd get his laces when he eventually left but not while he was in custody. She doubted Phillip Brighton was a suicide risk but the rules were there for a reason. 'Anything else you can tell us?'

'My client has been most helpful in your investigations. He's told you all he knows and has given his full cooperation. I insist on a break so that I can liaise further with Mr Brighton.'

The investigation had just notched up. She was considering Phillip Brighton as a suspect in the case. He was in the building at the time of the murder. He claimed to be in the toilet and no one saw him in there. They had his DNA and fingerprints on file. Question was, would they find evidence of him having been in Holly's room?

'Interview ended at ten thirty a.m. on Sunday the tenth of May—' Phillip leaned back and stretched in the plastic chair. 'What is that on your jumper?'

'What?'

Everyone in the room spotted the tiny fleck of red on his yellow jumper. 'That?' Gina pointed to the bloody fleck.

'How would I know?'

Gina leaned in a little closer. 'It looks like blood to me.'

His eyes widened.

'There's no evidence for that,' Mr Ullah said as he slammed his paperwork down on the table. 'My client is here to answer to a charge of supplying drugs—'

'And now I want him to tell me why he has what appears to be blood on his jumper when he was at the scene of a murder last night.'

Phillip Brighton stood and kicked the door. 'I didn't do anything. I want to go. Let me go. Let me out.' He hit the door several times.

'Sit down, Mr Brighton.'

The man stared as his shoulders dropped. He took two steps back and slumped into his chair.

'I need your clothes.' She was sure that Phillip Brighton was shaking in his denim jacket.

He trembled as he almost ripped the jacket from his own back before throwing it onto the table. 'Have it. Have everything. Have it all!'

He stood and manically shouted and grunted as he began peeling his clothes off. His solicitor tried to whisper something to him but Phillip pushed him away. He pulled the jumper over his head and threw it onto the floor before finally kicking his boots off his feet at the wall.

If the blood on his jumper was a match for any blood samples taken from Holly's hotel room, Phillip Brighton would have a lot of explaining to do. Gina pulled a pair of gloves from the draw next to the table and snapped them on. She picked up the jumper. 'We'll get these to the lab. Thank you for your cooperation. In the meantime, we'll get you something to wear.'

CHAPTER TWELVE

Cass's fingers trembled as she opened the message.

> *Thanks for your thoughts, Cass. I can't believe what hap-*
> *pened. Poor Holly, and our reception was ruined. I don't*
> *know what to do. My mum has barely said a word and my*
> *dad keeps telling me everything's going to be okay. It's not*
> *though, is it? Kerry.*

The open message showed Cass that Kerry had begun to type another reply. Cass had to keep the conversation going. Now was her big chance. Kerry stopped typing.

For years, Cass had tried to strike up conversation with Kerry but nothing had worked. Once primary school friends, Cass had found herself dumped in favour of Holly. Timid, little Holly – the girl who would do anything Kerry asked of her. Cass had been the opposite. She was loud and clumsy. Now was the right time to be a friend to Kerry once again. She'd missed her for years. She'd missed having the fancy cakes her mum used to make and the fun sleepovers, when it was just the two of them. Everything was perfect until Holly came on the scene. Lilly and Francesca soon followed and they made up the popular gang. Cass had become history. Not for long though.

Cass twirled a strip of coarse hair between her fingers. She hadn't fitted in with them all those years ago. Her freckly skin became a little spotty with the early onset of puberty. Her figure became more ample, setting her apart from her athletic peers. Now was her chance to make things right, to get her friend back. With Kerry on side, she could also probe her for information, find out if she knew anything about Elvis and Holly or, indeed, Elvis and anyone. Kerry knew everything, she always did.

Nothing changed with age, it just meant more candles on a cake at the turn of another year. Right now, she felt like that dumped nine-year-old once again, but this time, she was going to fight to win back her friend. With Holly out of the way, she had hope. Gaining Kerry's trust was a part of the new plan.

Cass hit reply and began typing her message in the little box.

Kerry, what happened was terrible and if there's anything I can do, just ask. You're one of my oldest friends and it hurt like hell to see you so upset yesterday. I know we haven't spoken in a while but a friendship like ours never dies. I'm totally here for you. Just ask. Anytime. Shall I pop over to your house?

No response.
Don't you dump me again! Not when I'd do anything for you.
She stared at the screen. Nothing. Kerry was now offline. 'Dammit.' She slammed her phone on the bedside table causing Elvis to stir. 'Morning, sleepyhead.'

'What time is it?' he murmured as she wiped a trail of drool from his cheek and squinted at the ray of sunlight that had seeped through the gap in the curtains.

'Nearly eleven.'

He fought with the sheets and tumbled onto the floor, dragging them off her. She knew he had to work and she'd let him sleep in.

'My head hurts, bloody hell.' He pressed his temples. 'I didn't even have a drink. I feel pissed.' He stumbled to his feet and almost hit his forehead on one of the low beams by the window.

Maybe she'd given him more to drink than she thought. His phone beeped. He grabbed it, taking it with him to the bathroom. It was obvious he was hiding something.

She followed him in and he placed the phone on the window-sill. 'Why don't you call in late?' She pulled her nightshirt over her head and wrapped her arms around his naked torso, while inserting one hand into his jeans and caressing him. He had to want her. Whoever was messaging wasn't important and she would show him just how unimportant they were. She began running her tongue over his shoulders, grimacing as her taste buds recoiled from the sweat and deodorant on his skin.

'Cass.'

She undid his jeans while catching his reflection in the shaving mirror.

'Cass? Stop it.'

She snatched her hand back and stepped away, grabbing a towel to wrap around her body. 'What?' She tried to swallow but a mass was forming in her throat, a familiar lump. Tears began to spill down her cheeks. 'I thought you loved me.'

'For heaven's sake. Let's not do this now. I have to go to work and I feel like utter shite. I don't know why you're acting so weird, but not now.'

'What's that?'

'What now?' He gelled his quiff and took a swig of mouthwash before spitting it into the sink.

'The love bite on your shoulder. Who is she? Was it Holly?'

'It's a bruise, you idiot. We moved barrels and boxes all day yesterday.'

'I know a love bite when I see one.'

'You clearly don't. And Holly was murdered last night. Your comment, it was in bad taste.'

He didn't want her, she knew it. She glanced at his shoulder again. Maybe it was a bruise. She stared at it. It could be a bruise.

As he stormed out of the bathroom gripping his phone, he almost pushed her over.

'Ouch. That hurt,' she yelled as she let out a sob. She was getting no sympathy from him. If Holly had been standing there naked with her hands in his pants, he'd have called in sick.

She gazed in the mirror tiles above the bath as the front door slammed. She was no looker – no wonder he was straying. Elvis was the karaoke king and had become a bit of a local celebrity. She saw how some of the women watched him perform. She slapped her face hard, once and then again. 'You're ugly, ugly—'

Crumpling to the bathroom floor tiles, she clung to the towel and wept. She hated herself and all she'd become. Maybe she wouldn't eat today, at least try to lose a few pounds. It was all her fault. But she could change, be more like them. Be more like Kerry, especially if she stood a chance of becoming best friends with her again. Gaining her trust was one thing but she had to show herself to be worthy.

She crawled along the floor and pulled herself onto the bed, which is where she would stay. Elvis didn't want her and Kerry hadn't messaged back. The repulsed look in her boyfriend's eyes would stay with her for the day. It wasn't just a rejection; he was sickened by her. She squeezed her flesh and poked it as she yelled, wanting nothing more than to slice it away. 'Revolting. You're ugly, you're disgusting. You can change things but you don't. You're ugly.' She wouldn't eat today. No food, not a morsel.

A message flashed up. Kerry was back. She wiped her face on the quilt and her heart rate sped up.

Cass. Thank you, but I'm fine. Take care, mate.

She threw the phone to the floor. You do not get to dump me again Kerry Reed, or should I say Kerry Powell now?

CHAPTER THIRTEEN

'Guv, I've arranged the viewing at the morgue for midday so we haven't got much time.' Wyre dried her face on a paper towel. 'I feel a bit more human after a quick wash.'

'Thank you for being there. I know it's been a long night. Have you called Marianne Long to let her know?' Gina asked.

'I have. She'll be there.'

As they entered the incident room, Gina grabbed a Danish pastry and bit into it, enjoying the buttery pastry that oozed apricot jam.

'I'm so sorry, guv. Mrs O and I had had a few to drink last night and I didn't hear the phone.' O'Connor grabbed the last pastry. 'I'm here now.'

'Good. Wyre, after the morgue, you can head back home and have a nap and O'Connor, you can take over. We've been up all night. I'll plough on as long as I can and I want to make a dent in this case today. That means I want you all on it. Go through the interviews. O'Connor?'

He rubbed his shiny head and adjusted his tie. 'Guv.'

'CCTV. How have you got on?'

'Not good. The only camera working is the one pointing over the front door. Oh, I tell a lie. Lord of the Manor himself, Nigel Harris, has one more working camera pointing at his safe in an office on the bottom floor. No one went in that room all night and nothing was stolen, so that camera tells us nothing.'

'Damn, I was hoping to see some of the gatecrashers but they all infiltrated the party through the back terrace after sneaking in through the garden. Did we get Holly on any of the footage?' She popped the last of the pastry in her mouth and rubbed her gritty eyes. All the coffee in the world wasn't going to cure the heaviness that had infected her body, spreading from limb to limb. She needed sleep and she needed it soon.

'She shows up on it twice. Once on arrival in the afternoon at thirteen thirty-six, then once again at twenty-one, zero five. I'll show you.' O'Connor clicked his mouse and his laptop screen came alive. He pressed play and the isolated slice of video began. 'It's a bit grainy but you can tell it's definitely Holly.'

Two people finished smoking and entered the building. One of the members of staff came out and took the ashtray from the bench out the front. They all watched, waiting for the moment. Holly appeared, lifting the hem of her long dress as she stepped carefully towards the steps, alone. She glanced back and fluffed her hair up while looking at her reflection in the door, then she stopped and turned, taking a moment before going in through the main door.

'That's all we have.' O'Connor pressed stop on the recording. 'After that, a few people come out to smoke, then they go back in. No one else comes from around the side of the building like she did.'

'Rewind that clip, back to the two smokers.'

O'Connor clicked his mouse again.

'That's Samuel Avery out there smoking just before Holly appears. Then he goes inside. Go through Avery's statement again and all the others. Was he back at his bar all night or did he leave for a while? Also, Francesca Carter, one of the bridesmaids, said that she saw Holly talking to a man on the terrace. They were tucked away in the corner. It could be that she left him there and walked around the building. I haven't had the chance to go through all the interviews yet. Did anyone see Holly after the terrace or walking through reception?' Gina gazed around as O'Connor flicked through his notes and Wyre checked the system.

'Smith, you were there too.'

PC Smith poured a sachet of sugar into his coffee. 'I took a fair few statements and I have read through Kapoor's too. There are absolutely loads of them. One hundred and twelve to be precise.'

'Anyone?' Gina needed the team working quicker on this but she knew that analysing the contents of over a hundred interviews wouldn't be an easy task.

O'Connor rubbed his head. 'From what I've read, no one saw Holly after she went back in through the front. It could be that she went straight up to her room. A lot of the guests couldn't be sure that she wasn't around, they just didn't see her. There were a lot of people there, then add the gatecrashers to that – possibly another ten of those – and add to the mix that a lot of them were off their faces, we have a lot of unreliable witnesses. There's a lot of "not sures" and "maybes" in the mix. No one can say for definite that they saw Holly after nine fifteen.'

'I just hope forensics come up with something.' Gina placed a finger over her lips as she thought. 'Anything back yet?'

Wyre leaned back in her chair. 'No. There was so much taken away, I'd be surprised if we hear soon. Bad news though, guv.'

Shoulders slumped, Gina sighed. 'Go on.'

'I read Alison Reed's interview notes. She's the mother of the bride. Holly's room was used for getting ready. The hairdresser came. They all did their make-up in there. The table props were stored there, looking after those had been Holly's job. People came and went all day.'

'That's all we need. Was there a photographer or videographer?'

Briggs entered with an empty cup. 'Yes, the photographer left about eight. Her details were taken last night from Alison Reed, the mother of the bride.'

'And the photos?'

'They've been emailed to me, all of them. Over eight hundred raw photos. I'm just downloading them now then I'll get them uploaded onto the system. The *Warwickshire Herald* has been onto me already. I'm just preparing a statement.' Briggs passed them and headed to the kitchen.

PC Smith, O'Connor and Wyre all waited for further instructions.

'We know what we have to do. So much work, so little time. I want all of those photos scrutinised. Anything that looks out of place, any of Holly, I want them flagged up for my attention. Another thing. Smith?'

'Yes, guv.'

'Take Kapoor back to the manor. Phillip Brighton, our man in custody who has been charged with supplying drugs, claims to have seen a man masturbating in the woods. He gave us the location of the clearing. I want this checked out and want forensics to go in first. I think we can all agree that this is unusual behaviour and I want this man found. His description of this man was poor. Brighton claims it was dark and he was stoned. Not much to go on but we may just have a shoe print, a cigarette butt, anything. We have to consider this person to be a person of interest. Also, Brighton's clothing has been taken and has gone to the lab after we spotted what looks like blood on his jumper. If this turns out to be Holly's blood then he'll be high up on our list of suspects.' Gina glanced at her watch. 'I've got to get to the morgue.'

Wyre stood up, ready to accompany her.

'Any word on Holly Long's phone? Bernard didn't find one at the scene.'

Everyone shook their heads.

'To me, that's strange. People are glued to their phones. She must have had one. I'll ask her mother when we see her.'

As Gina packed up her notebook and laptop while finishing her coffee, DS Jacob Driscoll walked through the door and dropped three packets of chewy sweets onto the central desks. 'Bloody airports. I've had my fill of lying on a floor while waiting for the dodgy plane to be replaced.' He yawned. Gina stepped back and held her breath. The sweaty smell coming from her colleague told her he hadn't even been home to freshen up. 'I came straight away. Emergency, you said.' His short hair shone on his head, the precise cut around his ears giving him a well-preened look.

'Have a wash and be ready to go to Furnace and Blower Ales this afternoon.'

'I gather you're not taking me for a pint?' He lifted up his armpits and grimaced as he inhaled.

She left him with a telling smile as she snatched her coffee cup from the desk. 'I'll meet you by the car,' Gina called across to Wyre as she hurried to the kitchenette.

Her phone beeped as she almost collided into Briggs. She pulled it from her pocket.

Gracie and I have left. At least we know where we stand at the Cleevesford Cleaver B&B. We're off to Cadbury World – alone. Not even a message or a phone call. Thanks again. ☹

Gina threw the cup into the sink, breaking it. Her daughter had checked into a bed and breakfast for the rest of her stay. Hands shaking, she steadied herself on the small strip of chipped worktop. 'Why the hell didn't I call my daughter?'

'Don't worry, I'm fine.' Briggs brushed his fingers over his crumpled shirt and a bit of his usually tidy hair flopped forward. It had been a long night for them all and there was no chance of popping home for a sleep.

'Sorry.'

'We haven't spoken for ages. In fact, we haven't spoken properly since—'

'I can't talk about that here. You know I can't.' A flash of pain shot through her head. Briggs knew her secret. He'd known it for a while but she couldn't think about that right now. Not yet. He said he'd understood but now it felt as though he was badgering her for more. Not satisfied with what she'd given already.

'We need to talk soon. Really, Gina, we do.'

A look passed between them. The kindness in his eyes that she'd been so familiar with wasn't quite there. He gave her nothing but a vacant expression to fathom.

'I'm sorry.' This is exactly how she didn't want to feel. That's why secrets were best being kept and she'd blown it.

He placed a hand over hers. 'Stop saying you're sorry.'

As he left, all she could feel was the warmth he'd left behind on her fingers and that would soon be gone. He'd read her well. She'd wanted him to touch her. She felt the frostiness within spreading through her body as she thought of Marianne Long and her next appointment of the day.

The morgue – she was going to be late.

CHAPTER FOURTEEN

Gina headed along the corridor and was met by a suited woman, her hair in a tight bun and her glasses dangling over her chest on a piece of cord. 'Come through.' She opened the door leading to a small, whitewashed waiting room where Marianne Long was sitting.

'I have to see her, I have to,' the woman repeated in a quivering voice.

Gina nodded to Wyre who took a seat.

'I can't believe someone hurt her like this. She's such a gentle girl.' Marianne paused. 'Was. Someone has taken her from me and if I find out who they are, I swear I will kill them.' The teary woman began to seethe, breathing rapidly as she slammed her fist into the wall. She stood back and shook her hand out.

'Ms Long. Are you ready?' Gina placed a hand on her shoulder and the suited woman used her pass card to open the door.

'Have you got children?'

Gina nodded. 'I have a grown-up daughter.'

'You understand then.'

Gina was glad she didn't. She couldn't begin to understand what it would be like to lose Hannah in this way; in fact, even though they weren't speaking again, she couldn't imagine losing Hannah at all. She swallowed the mass that was forming in her throat as the door closed, leaving Wyre behind in the waiting room. Her colleague was exhausted. Gina was shattered too and it was setting her emotions alight. Gina looked away, unable to observe Marianne's expressions as they took the long walk to where the bodies were stored. This was no place for her to crumble.

'Through here.' The suited woman opened another door. Holly had been laid out ready, a sheet brought neatly over her shoulders on a stainless steel table.

'Thank you.'

Gina guided Ms Long through, feeling her quivering beneath her coat. The woman almost crumpled. Gina hurried beside her and helped her remain standing. The woman nudged her away and leaned over, kissing her daughter once on the forehead before standing back.

The wound to her head had been cleaned and she looked almost angelic. Long red hair neatly framed her face and her pale skin made her look completely drained of blood.

'I don't want to leave her. It's cold in here. Holly hated the cold.' A tear streamed down her cheek and the woman turned to the wall. 'You have to get the animal who did this to her. You have to.'

Gina closed her eyes and tried to imagine different things. Gracie, her cat sleeping in her bed. Briggs – his warm hand over hers. Anything but the young woman in front of her, triggering something of her own past that she couldn't bear to think about. Her own wedding night, the gasping and pain. A shiver started in her legs as she tried to evict her horrible memories and think of Gracie. Her granddaughter, the little girl she loved so much, even though her daughter thought she had no time for either of them.

'Goodbye, my love. Sleep peacefully.' Ms Long pressed the exit buzzer and hurried back into the corridor.

Grateful of the distraction, Gina followed. 'Ms Long – Marianne – we haven't managed to locate Holly's phone.'

'I always make jokes about that. She was never without it. Either that or her trusty pink tablet.' Marianne smiled as a tear ran down her cheek. 'I moaned at her sometimes for ignoring me while she was texting or browsing Facebook. I'd do anything to be able to moan at her again.'

'Again, please accept our sincerest condolences. I can't begin to imagine what you're going through.' Gina swallowed the lump in her throat.

'Thank you.'

'We want to catch this person more than anything. To do that, we need to learn all we can about Holly. Would you have a key to her apartment?'

Marianne nodded. 'I was meaning to go there. I just wanted to feel close to her.'

'Could we please meet you there so that we can take a look too?'

She sniffed and pulled a tissue from her pocket, wiping her sodden eyes. 'Of course.'

Gina made a note to catch up with Marianne later that day. For now, she needed to find out who Holly was arguing with at her workplace.

As Gina and Wyre left the building, Gina took a couple of deep breaths.

'That bad?'

'Yes. I don't know how Marianne Long is going to get through this. I couldn't even tell her when her daughter's body would be released.'

Wyre yawned again.

'I need to find out who Holly was arguing with at work and why. I'll drop you back and take Jacob with me. You need to get some sleep.'

'How about you, guv? You look like a walking corpse.'

'Thanks.'

'I meant, you look tired.'

Gina smirked. 'I was just having you on but I agree, I do look like a walking corpse. When I've been to Furnace and Blower Ales, I'll head home for a shower and rest. I've checked. They are open today which is good for us.' She could send O'Connor and Jacob, or PC Smith and either detective, but she wouldn't. She had to be there. She had to interrogate this person with her eyes as well as her questions. Going home wasn't an option. Holly had some sort of disagreement or argument at her workplace and Gina needed to know what that was about and if it led to her murder.

CHAPTER FIFTEEN

Staring at her phone, Cass began spreading several slices of bread with peanut butter and chocolate spread. That would follow the multipack of crisps and half jar of jam, scooped straight out with a spoon. Nausea swept through her. They hadn't been shopping and she hadn't cared after promising herself she wasn't going to eat today. Elvis would get a meal of some sorts at work and he wouldn't ask if she'd eaten or not.

Her phone beeped.

Just having a break. Look, I'm sorry about this morning. I'll make it up to you later. Elv. X

Too late. She'd seen the disgust on his face at the sight of her naked. It had happened all too often, leaving her looking desperate when he'd rejected her advances. It wasn't like when they'd first met a year ago. He couldn't get enough of her. They'd done it in his car, in the work van, in the cellar at the pub. His hands were all over her, all of the time. She bit into the stodgy sandwich, forcing an uncomfortable amount into her mouth, crumbs puffing out as she let out a sob, the peanut butter sticking to the roof of her mouth.

She knew exactly what he thought of her now. And Kerry, she'd only just gained an inroad to her friendship and she'd lost that too. Everything she'd done was for nothing. No one wanted her. She swallowed the bread and washed it down with a swig of fizzy orange straight out of the bottle. Again, she filled her mouth and continued until four of the slices had gone. Acid rose at the back of her gullet, a reminder of how she'd failed again. One day without food, that's all she had to achieve to prove she could do it. *Ugly, disgusting, failure.* No wonder Elvis was looking elsewhere. No wonder he didn't want her like he once did.

She prodded her stomach and slapped it hard, then again until it reddened and the skin prickled. She parted her dressing gown and pinched her thighs. Grabbing the knife she'd used to cut the bread, she traced a line across her thigh. If only she could slice her disgusting layer of flesh away, just like that. A small prickle of blood emerged, contained in its skin until it was ready to pop. She placed the knife back on the table and shoved her stubby fingers into the chocolate spread jar before placing a blob of it into her mouth as she sobbed.

She reread his message and replied, getting chocolate all over the screen.

Am I losing you?

Who was messaging her man? He didn't answer her message. Maybe he was taken up with her, whoever she was. That had to be a sign.

She needed a friend. She needed someone. Kerry. *Keep it cool and polite. She'll need a friend soon and I'm here waiting. After all, one of Kerry's besties was murdered at her wedding reception. I will be a good friend. I'll be the best. Just like old times.*

She answered the earlier message from Kerry. K*erry. You take care too. I'm here if you need me. X*

Playing it cool was beyond her. Impatience was setting in already. *Answer me, answer me,* she kept repeating in her head. *One of you, say something. Elvis? Kerry?*

She swiped the chocolate spread off the table. Holly took Kerry from her all those years ago and she was going to get her back.

She didn't care how, but Kerry was her friend, her best and only friend and she'd forgiven her for being horrible back then. The glass from the jar shattered, covering the tiles and her bare feet. She didn't care. All she cared about was fixing her sad meaningless life. She wrapped the bread up and wiped the blood globule from her thigh. No more food today. She'd had enough. She could claw this back by not eating again – not failing.

CHAPTER SIXTEEN

'Someone forgot to put sunscreen on,' Gina said as she parked the car in the brewer's car park.

'Shut up, guv! I knew I'd never live this red nose down. I fell asleep on the sun lounger and Jennifer had gone to get a massage.'

'You two make a sweet couple. The crime scene investigator and the detective. Your parents will be as proud as punch on your wedding day,' she said, teasing him.

'Shut up. Enough. We're a long way from weddings.'

The brewery looked like a large barn and was adorned with their signage and logos.

'So this is where Furnace and Blower Ales are made?'

Gina nodded. 'Yes, and as we know this is where Holly Long worked. Her mother, Marianne told us that Holly had had an argument with someone here but she didn't know who or why.'

'What did she do?' Jacob rubbed his nose and flinched a little.

'Some sort of accounts admin but her mother didn't entirely know.'

Gina rang the buzzer, focused on the little camera above it and was buzzed into a tiny holding room with two doors leading off it. She tried one of the doors but it was locked. 'I suppose we just wait.'

A yeasty smell seemed to be coming from everywhere. 'I'd love a pint.' Jacob smiled.

'When we've solved this case, I'll buy you one.'

'I'll hold you to that, guv.'

A man with an identification card pinned to his jacket pushed open the door in front of them. Gina could see that his name was Rick. 'Hello. Who are you here to see?'

Gina held up her identification. 'We'd like to talk to Holly Long's manager.'

'Has something happened?'

'We would need to discuss that with Holly Long's manager first.' Gina needed to know who Holly had been arguing with before speaking to the other staff.

'That would be me. Rick Elder. Come through. We can talk in the lounge.'

They followed Rick along the corridor that led to a room with a floor to ceiling window. A large mural was painted on the wall depicting the brewing production cycle, from the hops being harvested to the final bottle of ale. Several cosy couches were positioned around small coffee tables and a single white carnation in a miniature vase adorned every table. Gina shuddered as Holly's body covered with the little petals scattered all over her torso flashed through her mind.

'We try to make the staff as comfortable as possible when they take breaks. Fortunately, no breaks are due for another half an hour.'

Gina took a seat on the couch and pulled out her notes, as did Jacob.

'I love the smell of this place,' Jacob said, with a smile.

Rick ignored Jacob's comment. 'Now can you tell me why you're here?'

Gina crossed her ankles and placed her hands on her knees. 'Unfortunately we have some bad news. I'm sorry to tell you that Holly Long was murdered last night and we're conducting investigations.'

Rick removed his glasses and rubbed his eyes. 'Are you serious?'

'I'm afraid so.' She paused, giving the news a moment to sink in. 'We need to ask you a few questions, about Holly.'

He walked over to the coffee machine and pressed a button. 'Want one? I could do with one.'

They both nodded. Gina needed a coffee more than anything. Her lips hadn't been wet since her morning coffee during the briefing and she was beginning to feel even more headachy. As soon as she was done, she'd be heading home to work before having a shower and catching up on some sleep.

'Here.' Rick placed three cups down and dropped a few sachets of sugar onto the coffee table.

'I was surprised but glad to see that you were open on Sundays.' Gina sipped the hot coffee.

'We're a twenty-four seven operation. We have orders coming out of our ears and are hoping to secure bigger premises soon. It's been tough stepping up production but while the going's good, we keep going.' He paused. 'I'm sorry. Things aren't good. I only saw Holly on Friday. She mentioned that her friend who got married in Greece was having a reception in Cleevesford. She said she was looking forward to it.'

Jacob flicked over to a clean page in his pad.

'How did she seem when you last saw her?'

He shrugged as he stirred some sugar into his drink. 'I didn't know how to take Holly. One day she could be all smiles, the next she looked like she'd just lost her dog or something.' He slapped himself on the head. 'I'm sorry. I have this way about me. I sometimes say things that aren't appropriate. I shouldn't have mentioned death. Idiot.' His leg jittered slightly as he took a sip of his drink.

'It's okay, Mr Elder. Please go on. How did Holly seem on Friday?'

He inhaled and put his glasses back on. Gina guessed he was in his mid-thirties. No wedding ring, quite handsome with his light stubble and designer suit. Gina wondered if the man in front of her could be the man Holly was hiding in her kitchen. Mr Blue Shirt.

'On Friday, she seemed distracted. I'm the office manager amongst other things, which means I'm responsible for everything in the office and when things go wrong, I normally have to deal with them. I had a few billing complaints. Holly had wrongly charged a few customers and had sent out a couple of letters containing confidential quotes to the wrong clients. She also sent a notice of court action to a debtor who had paid the week before. I guess what I'm saying is her mind wasn't on the job. She'd complained of having a headache, feeling sick, feeling tired, anything. I suggested she go to the doctors, she said she was fine.'

'Did this result in any conflict?' Maybe the person Marianne heard Holly arguing with was sitting right in front of her.

'I'm afraid it did. She'd go on about how much she loved this job and wanted to progress further, to behaving like she didn't care. She'd come in late, took longer breaks and was always checking her phone. I had to have a word with her.'

Jacob's pen scrawled across his pad as he caught up. Gina rearranged the cushion behind her so that she could lean back a little. 'What was said and how did she take it?'

A slight redness flushed across Rick's face. 'I didn't enjoy our chat. She was defensive, saying that she was being picked on but she loved the work. She wasn't happy with me.'

'With you personally?'

He nodded.

'Had something more than work gone on between you both?'

'Okay, I slept with her but it was three years ago. She thought she'd be okay working for me when I interviewed her but it seems she found us working together uncomfortable. I think that's what her funny moods were about.'

Gina wondered if that could be the case but she remembered how Lilly had mentioned Holly's depression. Could Holly have been going through a bad patch and brought it to work? Maybe

Rick had made his way to the party last night through the same route the gatecrashers took.

'You say three years ago?'

He nodded and finished his coffee. 'I met her in a nightclub in Redditch. We'd both had a few and went back to my flat. We woke up with a hangover in the morning. She got dressed, said she'd call me and that was it. I really hoped she would call for ages. One-night stands weren't something I really did but I was out with friends and I really liked Holly. When she came for the interview, I was thrilled. A part of me hoped she might want to go out on a date but being her manager, I could never ask. She would have had to be the one who'd asked me. Workplace dating isn't frowned upon here like some places but I didn't want to complicate things unnecessarily.'

'Did your relationship rekindle in any way?'

He shook his head and bit the inside of his mouth. 'No. When we shared that night together, we were both a little merry from the drink and music. I realised I had no idea who Holly really was, I just built an image of a person who didn't really exist. This Holly, the one working here, wasn't anything like the creation in my head. She looked angry all the time, then sad. I offered to listen if she needed to talk. No strings attached – obviously. I'm here for all my staff. Happy workplace is a productive workplace, and all that. I was prepared to let her mistakes last week go. I felt she had potential. We all have bad weeks, it's just that Holly had a few more than the rest.'

'Thank you for being so candid about your relationship. Can you tell me where you were last night between the hours of nine and ten?'

His stance stiffened as he sat on the edge of the opposite couch. 'Really? Am I a suspect? She just works here. I slept with her once three years ago and I've been nothing but totally honest about everything. Others in the office will back me up.'

'We just need to eliminate you, Mr Elder.'

'I was at home alone but I was FaceTiming my sister.'

'Can we see your message history, between you and your sister?'

His brows furrowed. 'I don't have my tablet with me and I don't use Messenger on my phone as I find it too distracting, so no. I'll write my sister's details down if you really want to check.'

Jacob passed the man a sheet of his notebook and a pen.

He snatched it off the table and scribbled a name, address and a phone number down. 'She lives in Australia. I was trying to catch her before she went to work.'

Gina would get his alibi checked as soon as she got back to the station. 'Did Holly socialise with anyone from work?'

'Nah. We, all the staff, often met at the pub after work but Holly never joined in. I know she lived alone and, before you ask, I didn't go stalking or anything. She told us she lived alone. It just surprised me that she didn't want to come out. There's a core of us ranging from early twenties to mid-forties and we do all sorts. Bowling, cinema nights. She wasn't interested. She seemed too preoccupied.'

'In what way?'

'Like I said, she was always staring at her phone like she was waiting for a call or a text. I'd catch her looking out of the window, biting her nails when there were piles of work to do.'

'Was she like this all the time at work?'

He shook his head. 'No, only the past few weeks, maybe a month. That's when she started messing up small things at work. I'd say she had something on her mind.'

'Thank you, we'll be in touch.'

'I should have been more understanding rather than reprimand her over her errors. Maybe I could have done more.'

Gina closed her pad and passed Rick Elder a card. 'If you think of anything else, call me.'

He placed it in the slit in his phone case. 'There is one more thing. Elissa is on holiday but a couple of weeks ago she came to speak to me in confidence. She heard Holly crying while in a toilet cubicle. She asked Holly what was wrong and Holly told her to go away.'

'When will she be back?' Jacob asked.

'Two weeks yesterday.'

'Thank you,' Gina said as they made their way back to the main door.

'What did you make of all that? He's a little weird.' Gina pressed the central locking button on the car key and the lights flashed once as the doors opened.

'I don't know. He answered everything we asked but he didn't seem at all upset by what had happened. If I had just been told that you'd been murdered—'

'Thanks, Jacob.' Gina let out a snort of laughter.

'You know what I mean. We're colleagues. If that happened to you, I'd be gutted and we haven't even had a one-night stand.'

Gina got into the car. 'It's nice to know someone would be upset.'

He laughed and looked away.

'What?'

'Nothing.'

'Just say it, Jacob.'

He burst into laughter. 'Briggs would be upset. Have you seen the way he looks at you?'

'No, no and no. Don't you dare go there, Driscoll.'

'I'm just pulling your leg, guv. Of course we'd all miss you and we'd all be sad if you were unfortunately murdered. I don't feel his reactions were genuine. There was just something about him.'

'I agree. He was a bit odd. Maybe it's just the way he is, as he explained, or maybe there's more to it. We'll check his alibi for starters. I need to work out what time it is in Australia.'

She got into the car feeling her face flushing. If Jacob could see through Briggs's feelings for her, could everyone else? She had to talk to him and it had to be soon.

As Gina pulled off a few drops of rain hit the windscreen. 'Best get on with it. We've got to get to Holly's flat in a short while. Marianne Long called earlier to say she'd meet us there. While I drive, give the team a call and update them with all that we know.' She glanced back at the brewery as she turned the car in the car park and spotted Rick Elder at the window. He ran his shaky fingers through his hair, turned and walked back towards the offices.

Jacob's phone beeped at the same time as Gina's.

'Email,' he said as he checked.

'What is it, Jacob?'

'The post-mortem is scheduled for first thing.' He paused to read. 'We have some results back. The blood smeared on the drawers in Holly's hotel room does belong to her, as does the blood on the wall. Her blood showed no alcohol or drugs at all in her system but get this.'

'What?'

'She was pregnant.'

Gina swallowed. The murderer had not only taken Holly's life, they'd taken that of her unborn child. 'I want the foetus's DNA sample taken without delay.'

CHAPTER SEVENTEEN

The beast has escaped and it was never going back in its cave now, he was more than just a player – he had an urge. Lives would be ruined but he didn't care as long as his life wasn't ruined. He wanted to feel the pulse of a woman throbbing through his thumbs as he throttled her. It was a feeling of power like never before and they loved it, he could tell.

She loved it and she was begging for more. He'd give her more when he saw her later. She'd asked where he'd been going. He had work to do. That was his excuse. After all that had happened, he didn't care if she believed him or not. He made her feel good, helping her to float in her sea of misery. *I am God and she knows it. I can attach that weight around her neck at any time but I'll never let her drown, not her. The world needed at least one person who understood his needs and desires.*

He watched as the young woman pulled her bags out of the car, no doubt filled with her sage green dress. She must be sporting one hell of a hangover following the previous night's drinks and the unfortunate event. He'd seen her wandering about in a stupor. What a let down. He'd always thought more of Francesca.

Francesca Carter, the most beautiful one in the room last night. A pang of guilt left his thoughts as fast as it came.

She flicked her long brown hair over her shoulder. He loved the look of tragedy sweeping across her face. There was something about a sad, grieving woman that turned him on, especially a young one. In his mind, he is lying on top of her getting turned on as she screams for more. Then he does it. He brings her hair around her neck, using it like a rope to cut off her air supply, tighter and tighter until she's blue. Her red lips will throb for him and he knows what he gives her will be the gift of pure pleasure.

Would he unravel the rope of hair and allow her to gasp in huge gulps of air? Maybe, maybe not. Until last night, he'd have said yes, but now it was all about him.

He walked up her drive wondering whether he should offer to help as she struggled with her luggage.

'Bastard bag,' she said as the stringy handle twisted around her wrist one too many times, threatening to cut the blood flow to her arm.

All I see is the indent on your flesh from the stringy handle and I want you, Francesca.

She untangled the string and threw the bag to the block paving before kicking it over and over again, then breaking down. Slamming the boot closed, she leaned over and sobbed onto the cold black metal.

'Frannie, I'm really sorry.' He hurried over and held her.

'Where did you come from?' She nudged him away.

He hadn't washed properly this morning, let alone taken the time to shower. Time had been against him. Maybe that's why she wanted him to get off her. She hadn't been that cold at the wedding reception. She'd been drunk and her arms had snaked around every man there at some point over the course of the evening, including him.

'Come here.' He pulled her closer and stroked her hair. Her rigid body crumpled in his embrace and he felt a slight shiver running through her. He took a few strands of her hair and wrapped them lightly around her neck, disguising his movement as comfort. Within seconds, she'd pushed him away again. Francesca is going to be harder work than he'd anticipated.

A stir filled his pants. Francesca couldn't be allowed to feel that, it seemed inappropriate. He didn't need her telling anyone about that. It could ruin him and blow his plans right out of the water. 'Where's Charlie?'

'He'll be home soon. He's just popped to get some shopping.'

Damn. He didn't have long to enjoy her company even though she looked reluctant to let him in.

Her hair.

Her neck.

The smell of lightly fragranced soap as she passed, subtle lemon.

Her soft cheeks and the feel of her bosoms crushing against his chest for that couple of seconds had taken his breath away. Thrum, thrum, thrum. Blood flushed around his body and his heartbeat quickened a little with excitement. The beats went from fast to deep, filling his body with a desperate need for her.

'Can we talk?'

'I don't know.' Francesca looked around as if someone might be watching. 'I'm not in the mood for talking. I really just want to be alone.'

Look hurt, look hurt, look hurt! Forcing the corners of his mouth to downturn, he cocked his head to the side. 'Please. It'll only take a minute.' He reached out and cupped one of her hands with both of his.

Her shoulders dropped as she pulled away. 'I was just going to make a drink. Do you want one?'

Of course he did. He needed a coffee to calm himself down. Brandy would be better. Would a drink be enough? Was she alone in there? He glanced up at the front of the house, lined with tall conifers either side. No one had seen him come and he had parked a fair way back. 'Yes, please. Thanks, Frannie.' *It's so easy when someone trusts you completely. I need to work on Frannie a little more. She isn't as desperate as Holly was. People like Holly always give trust away with ease and wonder why everything in their life has gone wrong.* Not him, he worked hard on being trusted but he trusted no one.

'You coming?' He could see the wary expression she was wearing but that didn't bother him one bit. He'd won her around.

He smiled. 'Let me get those bags for you.' Ever the gentleman.

CHAPTER EIGHTEEN

As Gina pulled up past the bus stop on Cleevesford High Street, she glanced up at the flats and spotted Marianne Long waiting in the communal corridor on the top floor. A soft breeze fluttered through the slightly open window and a grey cloud had formed overhead. O'Connor pulled up beside her. Jacob gave a little wave in his direction, out of the window. O'Connor stepped out of his car and got into the back of Gina's.

Gina turned a little in the confined space so that she could address Jacob and O'Connor. 'Right, we're looking for any sign of someone else in Holly's life. Remember, Ms Long has lost her daughter and I don't want to make this any more painful for her than it has to be. We are looking for clues as to who she may have been seeing. I spoke to one of the bridesmaids and she said that Holly was acting a little strangely, that when she visited Holly wouldn't open the door to her. This same friend said that she looked through the letterbox and saw the back of a man reflected in the hall mirror. He was wearing a blue shirt, that's all she saw. We have not as yet managed to locate Holly's phone or her pink tablet. For someone who is described as glued to it, by her mother, this is strange. There is a chance she left it at home. I want to find it.'

'Got it, guv,' Jacob replied.

'And thanks for getting here so quickly, O'Connor. When Ms Long called, I didn't want to put her off until later. We need to find out all we can, and fast. She doesn't yet know that her daughter was pregnant and this is something I will need to tell her. Ready?'

They nodded. All getting out of the car, they crossed the road. Ms Long spotted them coming and hurried down, letting them in through the locked front door. Gina's mouth watered as she inhaled the smell of frying fish in the shop underneath the flats. The High Street was built in the thirties and the building in which Holly had lived had once been a bank. Developers had used a side access door, converted the middle and top floors, leaving the bottom floor as the chip shop, which had been there for as long as Gina could remember.

'I couldn't go in,' Marianne said as she led them up the stairs, keys jangling between her jittery fingers.

Gina was grateful that she hadn't. She wanted to see exactly how Holly was living without anyone moving things. 'No neighbour,' Gina said, noticing that it was a tiny block with only one apartment on the top floor.

Marianne poked the key towards the hole and missed, scratching the wood on the door.

'Shall I?'

Marianne nodded and handed the keys to Gina.

'Ms Long, I'd like to search around your daughter's apartment in the hope that we find something that helps the investigation. I just need your consent to do that.'

'I want this person caught. Do whatever you need to.'

Snapping on a blue glove, Gina entered first, turning the hall light on. All the interior doors were closed. The scent of an air freshener tickled Gina's nose, a sneeze definitely on the horizon. She walked through, followed closely by Marianne, then Jacob and O'Connor. She opened the door to the lounge where the evening light shone through the window, casting shadows from the trees on the opposite side of the road. It looked as if spooky fingers were reaching out into the apartment. Gina shivered. A slight chill in the air gave the apartment a vacant feeling, but something else was adding to this sense of unease. Everything looked so clean and perfect, pretty much like a show home. The furniture looked designer in every way. Holly was basically an accounts clerk. This brand-new-looking apartment seemed a little out of reach for someone on her wage. Maybe Gina had it wrong but something wasn't adding up.

Every surface shone and not a fleck of dust or lint spoiled anything. Gina hurried through to the kitchen. Shiny from every angle. The smell of disinfectant and bleach was overwhelming.

'Holly hated mess and dirt. She'd always clean things up straight away. Knowing her, she would have made sure everything was lovely to come back to after her night away.' Marianne walked over to one of the cupboards and opened it. Every tin, plate and cup had its place. She picked up the only thing that cluttered the worktop, an opened bottle of red wine. She opened the top and winced. 'I think this has had it.'

Gina felt a sharp pain run through her head, the need to sleep almost overwhelming her. If it wasn't for the fact that they were in a murder victim's apartment, she'd love nothing more than to curl up on the sofa in the other room and have a nap. Another sneeze was building up. Gina's nose twitched before the sneeze escaped. 'Excuse me,' she said as she continued. As she blew her nose, she opened the bin – empty.

Gina glanced back at the wine. Would Holly have been drinking if she knew she was pregnant? They knew nothing about how Holly felt about her situation. Could the wine belong to a visitor? Possibly the man with the blue shirt? 'Can you call Holly's number? Maybe we'll be able to locate her phone.'

Marianne ran her fingers over a Little Miss Sunshine apron that was pinned to the back of the kitchen door. 'I bought this for her birthday last year.'

Jacob went to speak and Gina pressed her finger against her lips, hushing him.

Marianne left the kitchen and hurried to the one bedroom and sat on her daughter's bed, grabbing her pillow and inhaling it. 'She's never coming back.'

The bedroom was just like the other rooms, perfectly clean and tidy in every way, not a thing out of place.

'May I?'

'Yes,' Marianne replied.

Gina carefully opened the wardrobe a little, half hoping to find a blue shirt, or any man's shirt, but there was nothing but women's clothes – Gucci, Armani, labels galore. The bottom of the wardrobe was full of neat lines of women's shoes, including a couple of pairs of Prada. She slid open the drawers, one by one, and once again, only Holly's clothes filled them. The bathroom. If a man was staying, there would have to be some items of his.

'Let it all out, Ms Long,' Jacob said as he sat with the distraught woman.

Gina crept along the landing and opened the last door, the one she hoped would yield something helpful. Like the rest of the apartment, every surface gleamed. She opened the storage unit and the medicine cabinet. Prescription antidepressants, in Holly's name. That confirmed the depressive episodes that Holly's friend spoke of. The drawer under the sink – only Holly's things once again. There was no sign of another person ever being here and, worst of all, no sign of her phone or tablet.

The sobbing had stopped and Gina went back into the bedroom. 'Ms Long, we really need to find Holly's phone. Could you please try to call her? Maybe it's in the flat somewhere.'

'I don't have her mobile number. I call her on the home phone.' Marianne looked a little confused as she paused. 'She was meant to give it to me when she had a new phone but she never did. Time just passed and I didn't ask again. She was always on Facebook. We messaged and FaceTimed mostly. That seemed enough.'

'How long had she had her new phone for?'

'Three months, four maybe. She said she had a new contract. I can't be sure. As I say, she used her tablet mostly but only on Wi-Fi. I'm going to miss her FaceTiming me.'

The mystery of the missing phone and tablet was the thing that was worrying Gina the most, along with how clean her flat seemed.

Jacob and O'Connor joined Gina on the landing outside the apartment, giving Marianne a few moments to herself. 'O'Connor, will you go to the apartment below and ask if they've heard anyone in the flat above today or indeed any other day? Anyone who wasn't Holly. Also ask at the chip shop if they have any CCTV pointing in this direction. If anyone entered this block today, I want to know. I need to know that someone didn't come in and sanitise the place, just to satisfy my own curiosity. Oh, one last thing. Find out if the communal bins have been emptied.'

'I'll go now.' O'Connor began stomping down the stairs, his large feet almost seeming too big for each step.

Marianne left the apartment carrying a stuffed rabbit. 'This was her childhood friend, Flopsy Dopsy.' She smiled fondly as she held the rabbit closely.

'Ms Long. There's something else we need to tell you and I don't know whether you want to go back inside to sit down.'

'You know something? Have you arrested someone?'

Gina shook her head and gulped. 'Shall we go inside?'

'I don't want to go inside. Whatever you need to tell me, you can tell me here. I don't want to go in and be reminded that I'll never see Holly again. I can't.' She took a few deep breaths and steadied herself on the window ledge.

'Okay, I'm sorry. I need you to know that Holly was pregnant. We have just found out.'

The woman shrieked. 'It gets worse. How could anyone do this to her? How could they? Who's the father?'

'That's what we need to find out. None of her friends knew that she was seeing anyone. Can you think back? Did she mention anyone to you?'

'No! If she had, I'd tell you.' The woman broke down and gripped the rabbit. 'I need to get out of here. I'm suffocating.' She gasped as redness spread across her neck.

'Breath in and out. Count with me. One, two, three.' Gina continued breathing with Marianne until she regained control. 'Come on. Let's lock up. May we keep this key for now? We'd like to come back for a further look.'

Marianne nodded. 'I will need it back though. Someone is going to have to sort all her things out.'

'Of course.' Gina held her arm out for Marianne to hold onto. She took it and shakily went back down the stairs. 'Would you like a lift home?'

'No, I'll be okay. I have my car.'

'Do you have anyone at home who will stay with you?'

'Beryl, my neighbour.'

After helping Marianne into her car, Gina watched her drive away, holding her own tears back in. Her white knuckles gripped the key as she thought about her own daughter. In her mind she could see Hannah lying in Holly's place in that deathbed at Cleevesford Manor. She shook that thought away and grabbed her phone. Maybe she should call Hannah or pop to the bed and breakfast. Hannah wouldn't want to see her but Gina had to see Hannah. She had to know what was happening in Hannah's life, the bit Hannah was holding back on. Secrets led to parents like Marianne having no clue as to what was going on in their grown-up children's lives. Not Gina. She had to know. She had to at least try. She went to press Hannah's number on the phone and stopped. She couldn't. As she placed her phone back into her pocket, it vibrated.

I need to speak to you later. Yours or mine?

It was Briggs, her DCI and her past lover. She had put him off for far too long. Her stomach flipped and she almost wanted to heave as she sent her reply.

Mine. About 8.30.

O'Connor almost made her jump as he approached her car with Jacob. 'Nothing from the neighbour below and the chip shop's CCTV isn't working.' He scratched his bald head and began trying to decipher his notes. 'The neighbour below said she'd been out all day but she didn't hear anything early this morning. She did, however, say that she'd heard Holly arguing with someone a few weeks ago but she couldn't hear anything specific or remember when. She just heard raised voices. I took a statement but it really doesn't help. She doesn't remember ever seeing anyone coming or going. She didn't have much to do with Holly and she works long unsociable hours as a nurse. She can't remember when this happened and she can't even remember the time of day. I'll update the system as soon as I get back to the station.' That at least confirmed that someone else was visiting Holly's apartment.

'And the bins?'

'Emptied on Friday.'

Gina glanced at her watch. The Angel Arms would have to wait, for now.

'Call forensics. I want the contents sifted through, just in case anything was thrown away from her apartment after the bin lorry had been.' O'Connor placed his phone to his ear and walked away. If someone else had been to the apartment and left something in the bin since the last collection, she wanted it found. 'I want to know who Holly had been arguing with.'

CHAPTER NINETEEN

Gina snatched the paper file off her desk and hurried to the incident room. Several officers were processing all the statements they had taken. PCs Kapoor and Smith were just finishing up for the evening and closing down their computers. As ever, Gina was grateful that they were once again on her team.

'You still here?' Gina said to Jacob as he finished off a chocolate bar.

'Yes. Jennifer is working late on everything taken from the scene at Cleevesford Manor. Apparently there's absolutely loads so they're all working late. I'm probably going to head home in about half an hour. I just wanted to update the system with everything from today. Rick Elder has been added so I'm nearly done. We've tried to contact his sister in Australia to confirm his alibi but the phone was off. It's first thing in the morning there now. Maybe it's just a little too early. If I don't get any joy soon, I'll contact police over there to see if anyone can help us.'

Gina smiled as she zipped up her laptop bag. 'Great work. He's still a person of interest at this point. So far, we can't confirm his alibi. Even then, it's not watertight. We may need to look into getting his message and video call data from Facebook if he won't offer it up, but we don't have enough evidence to go there yet. Let's see what the investigations bring but keep him in the forefront of everything for now. O'Connor?'

He stopped mid walk, cup of coffee in hand. 'Guv.'

'Please update the board with Rick Elder's details. The system has been updated. You'll find everything you need there.'

'On it now, guv.'

'Oh, forensics and Holly's bin. Have they gone?'

'Yes, about half an hour ago.'

Gina glanced around the room as she fiddled with the buttons on her jacket. There was no sign of Briggs. He must have already left and be getting ready for their chat. A throb filled Gina's head. On top of the chat-to-come and lack of sleep, she knew she wasn't going to be good company. She checked her phone again. Nothing at all from Hannah. She tried to call but the phone went straight to voicemail. A lump formed in her throat. Marianne Long would never get through to her daughter again. Gina had to know Hannah was safe with all that had happened. There was something Gina needed to do before heading home, and it couldn't wait. She punched out a message to Briggs.

Make it nine. Gina.

Briggs would have to wait another half hour.

Gina turned the heating up to full in the car. The May evening was chillier than expected. Maybe it was the tiredness kicking in or the darkness that had fallen that gave her an unsettling feeling in the pit of her stomach. As the car warmed, Gina felt a wash of calm flushing through her body. But there was nothing calm about the evening, not a jot. Hannah hadn't answered her call. She turned into the dark street and pulled up alongside the Cleevesford Cleaver where Hannah was staying. Only one light was on in the front of the old building. The fact that it had once been a butcher's many years ago sent a shudder through Gina. She always thought the name was a bit sinister given its history. She remembered her father taking her to a traditional butcher to get their Sunday roasting joint as a child. The smell and sight of death always turned her stomach. Blood, a pig's head stuffed with apples. The cleaver placed on a bloody metal surface and the sound of the chop as it cracked through bone.

A figure walked across the lit room and leaned on the window-sill. Gina remained in the dark, parked alongside a hedge. There was no way Hannah would see her watching but the thought of being caught didn't put her at ease. The double-fronted building had some old-style charm with the large bay windows and the heavy burgundy front door. A solid building that would survive everything. Gina glanced up, hoping to catch sight of Gracie; just a quick glance, then she'd go home to face Briggs.

Her body stiffened as she caught sight of the man. A short, sharp dizzy spell made her jerk up in her seat. *No, no, no, this can't be happening.*

CHAPTER TWENTY

Slamming the car door closed, she ran to that huge burgundy door and knocked over and over again. The guests normally had a key. Someone had to let her in. She had to warn her daughter.

'Mum! What on earth are you doing?' Hannah leaned out of the top window, her face reddening.

'Let me in.' Gina pressed her palm against the door, desperate to hurry through.

'No. Just go home, Mum. I'll call you tomorrow.'

'Where's Gracie.' The thought of that man being around her granddaughter made her skin crawl. It was bad enough that he was in a room with her daughter. She knew something was wrong between Hannah and her partner, Greg. She had sensed that Hannah had been lying. Had she been with him when Gina had looked after Gracie a few days ago?

'She's with her Nanny Hetty. She's fine.'

Gina was flung back as the main door opened and a man hurried out. She darted in, running to the top of the stairs and banging on the door to Hannah's room with both hands.

'I said I'd call you tomorrow,' Hannah said as she opened the door. 'What are you doing, spying on me?'

Gina fought to gain her breath back. 'I wasn't spying. I tried to call you and I was worried when you didn't answer. A woman was murdered last night and I guess I panicked. Please let me in, love.'

Hannah let go of the door and ran her fingers through her stark blonde hair.

'Hello, Detective Inspector.' Samuel Avery gave her a sickening grin as he placed a hand on Hannah's back.

'How dare you. Leave my daughter alone. This man—'

'This man what, Mum? What? Seriously, I need you to go home and leave me alone. You're interfering.' Hannah brushed him away and as she sat on the double bed, the floorboards creaked, shaking the mirrored wardrobe slightly.

'Does Greg know?' She stared at her daughter's eyes, her dilated pupils giving her away. Her speech was very slightly slurred. Gina charged across the room towards Samuel. 'If you so much as even touch her, I will—'

'You'll what?'

What would Gina do? What could she do? Two consenting adults in a room together. He was too old for her, too sleazy. He was everything bad she could think of. Was he her daughter's and granddaughter's future? She hated him. All the times the police had been called to his pub because he'd inserted himself into some woman's marriage and been punched by a jealous husband. Then there was the story during the case of missing Deborah Jenkins. One of her friend's had said Deborah had been petrified when Avery had assaulted her, but Deborah never reported it. After the case had been closed, Deborah herself had said she just wanted to forget that moment with all that had gone on. The man in front of her was trouble and now he was in her daughter's life.

'He's dangerous, Hannah. You need to tell him to go.'

Her daughter stared hard at her. Gina glanced around the room. There weren't clothes everywhere, no underwear on the floor. The bed looked made, but what was he doing here? Her daughter had had a drink. She knew exactly what he was doing.

She inhaled the faint smell of rum, Hannah's favourite and spotted the empty miniature bottle on the bedside table.

'Mum, you're making a fool of yourself. Just go. Please.'

'You heard what she said.' Samuel stepped forward and went to grab Gina's wrist.

'Don't you dare touch me or I'll take you in for assault.'

He held both hands up. 'You look a little shaky. I was just going to steady you, that's all.'

'I'll be keeping an eye on you.'

His flowery blue shirt barely touched his non-existent skinny waist. Blue shirt. Her mind flashed an image before her. When Lilly Hill was looking through Holly's letterbox, she caught sight of a blue shirt in the hall mirror.

'That sounds like harassment to me. I suggest you go and leave us to it. Have I hurt you, Hannah?'

Hannah shook her head.

'Did you invite me in?'

Hannah nodded. 'Mum, please go. I'm fine, see. All is fine.'

'Fine, fine, it's all fine.' She had lost this one. Gina stepped backwards out of the room, her gaze alternating between Hannah's and Samuel's. She left, stamping her feet down every step.

'What's going on? If you don't keep it down, you'll have to leave.' At last, the man who ran the rat-infested dump of a bed and breakfast had surfaced. His half-asleep look and dirty vest told Gina all she needed to know. An owner that took little care of his business.

'I'm leaving and the pleasure's all mine.' She slammed the main door and hurried back to her car, glancing up one more time. Samuel grinned through the condensation on the glass as he slowly drew the curtains. He hadn't been stationed at his bar all night at the wedding reception. He had opportunity to kill Holly. He had now been bumped up to the top of her list. As soon as she'd attended Holly's post-mortem, she would be heading straight over to the Angel Arms. One thing was for sure. With Gina turning up like that, Hannah was safe. There was no way he'd hurt her now, not tonight. She pulled at her knotty hair and hit the steering wheel. Samuel Avery had crossed a line when it came to her daughter.

CHAPTER TWENTY-ONE

Snaking the car through the deserted country roads, Gina took each corner a little too quickly. She felt the car skid slightly as she took the last bend that led to her house, tyres screeching as she pulled onto her drive next to Briggs's car. She got out and slammed the door, stepping close enough to the house to activate the security light.

'I thought you had stood me up.' He grabbed a bag from his front seat. Gina could smell the Chinese food escaping.

'I'm not hungry.'

'It's been a long day—'

'I know, I know. It's been a long day for all of us.'

He followed her to the house as she opened the door and walked in, leaving him to close it. The cat meowed. 'Okay, Ebony, I'm getting your food now.' She hurried to the kitchen and began slopping a pouch of cat food into a bowl. Without any gesture of thanks, the cat greedily tucked into the meaty chunks.

'Has something happened?'

'You could say that.' Gina turned away and faced the back door, fighting a tear of anger. Was she upset? Was she angry? Both. She was everything all at the same time. Confused. Never in a million years would she have expected the biggest sleazebag in Cleevesford to be in her daughter's room.

'Gina, what's happened? You can tell me.' He placed one of his large shovel-like hands on her shoulder. He was hefty but so gentle. That was something she had loved about him and possibly still loved about him.

'You know I had a bit of a falling out with my daughter?' She turned around, hoping that he wouldn't see the remnants of the tear that she'd just wiped away. There was no tear but she knew her eyes would have that watery look about them and he'd know.

'You mentioned that earlier.'

'She's staying at the Cleevesford Cleaver. She wasn't answering her phone and I got worried so I drove over after work.' She grabbed the tea towel off the side and wiped the worktop with it. 'When I got there, my daughter was in her room with no other person than Samuel Avery and I lost my temper.'

He placed an arm around her and she crumpled into his chest. 'He's a despicable human being. I can see why you're so upset. You didn't do anything stupid, did you?'

'What do you take me for? Of course I didn't. Unless stomping down steps and slamming doors qualify as stupid. Can we not have our talk tonight? I'm not fit for anything. I need to work on keeping it all together for the case.'

Gina pulled away slightly. She could see the disappointment in his expression but she couldn't have the talk, not with everything that was going on. Her mind was all over the place and the last thing she wanted to go through were the finer details of how her ex-husband Terry died, or more so, how she watched the life leave him at the bottom of the stairs on that stormy night. Briggs had been patient with her for a long time. He sensed her trauma when it came to talking but as the holder of her secrets, he deserved to know everything, and soon she'd tell him, but not tonight.

'Okay for now, but you have to stop shutting me out. How do you think I feel when you ignore me or try to avoid me?'

'That's why I wanted us to end, because of this, and it would have been worse had we carried on. People can see that we share something. They don't know what. It's not obvious, but I can't deal with the fact that I know, okay?'

He pulled a couple of bottles of light beer from the carrier bag. 'I struggle when it comes to dealing with everything too. This isn't just about you, Gina.' He grabbed the magnetic bottle opener from the fridge, cracked open the beers and passed her one.

'I know. I'm sorry.' She took the bottle and sipped the cold beer. 'I don't know if I can face food, not after what's happened tonight.'

He began opening the foil containers on the kitchen table, then he grabbed a couple of plates and some cutlery. 'You need to try. We're both running on empty.'

He was right, as always. The part of her that was breathing a sigh of relief at having postponed their conversation had been replaced with a churning anxiety after seeing Hannah with Samuel Avery. She slumped at the kitchen table and slopped some of the sweet and sour onto her plate. Staring at it, she knew she'd struggle to get it down. She pushed the chunks of pork around with her fork and an image of the pig's head on the butcher's slab flashed through her mind. She dropped her fork in the food, wishing he would just go home and leave her to wallow.

A few minutes passed and the food had already started to form a skin across the top as it cooled. The silence was too much. 'I'm sorry. I'm not good company.'

'Gina, why won't you tell me all that happened? I know you keep your secrets pent-up. I see what you put yourself through, the nightmares and the crippling anxiety. You hide it so well from the others, but not from me. I've seen you wake up in the night, full of fear. I know I wasn't meant to hear your most personal words at your mother's graveside but I did and I can't un-hear them. We can't go back, only forwards. And we can't stay in limbo. That isn't an option.'

She felt her resolve crumbling. For so long her past had remained all hers but now he knew. 'It tears me up, Chris. I don't think I can talk about it all. I feel that if I do, I may not even be the same person ever again. I'm so scared of losing *me*.'

'Have you ever thought that you might gain *you* back?'

She pushed her plate away. 'He was so cruel to me – Terry. When we investigate these cases, such horrific cases, there are elements of each that often trigger flashbacks. I've tried hard to bury everything so that I can move on but they won't leave me alone. Each of my personal stories of abuse and cruelty are mine to tell. That's the only power I have over them. I had no choice when he was doing the things he did to me but it's like I'm in control and I don't want that control taken from me. Besides, he can't hurt anyone else, he's dead.'

'Are those thoughts controlling you, though?'

Her voice quivered with each word and her heart began to thump. 'Probably, but I'm a survivor. If nothing else, I've proven that over and over again. Believe me when I tell you this, if I hadn't accidentally pushed Terry down the stairs that night, he would have killed me. I know that much. I wouldn't be here now.'

Her throat began to close and her hands started shaking. Pushing him was one thing, but holding back until he'd passed away before calling an ambulance, that was on her. Coughing, she ran to the sink and poured a glass of water as she gasped in a few breaths of air. The kitchen seemed distorted, like it was swirling on an axis. The sound of the cat meowing for affection was as pleasurable as nails scraping a blackboard. The cat jumped through the cat flap into the garden, taking the noise with it.

'Come on. You've got this.' He held her close as she let it all out.

She had felt a release. Was she losing her grip or was she feeling unburdened? That was a question she couldn't yet answer. A moment, just the briefest of thoughts entered her mind. Like a picture in a film. Her on her wedding day, walking up the aisle towards Terry. Those moments of doubt had crossed her mind. She should have run out of that registry office and never looked back. Life could have been so different but if she hadn't met Terry, she wouldn't have Hannah. Every step up that carpeted aisle had felt like she was walking on glue. She would never forget the look in her own mother's eyes. The one she ignored that said, *you don't have to do this, my love.*

She felt the calm beating of Briggs's heart against her ear and she didn't want the moment to end. For once she felt safe, but he couldn't stay. They both knew that. Besides, safe was just a feeling. She wasn't safe. He wasn't safe. No one was safe when a potential charming predator was hell-bent on inserting themselves into your life. No one. And now, they had another predator to contend with, one that had taken Holly's life and that of her unborn child. Had this perpetrator charmingly wormed his way in before gaining her trust and subjecting her to the most horrific of deaths? Now was not the time to lose her focus.

CHAPTER TWENTY-TWO

Monday, 11 May 2020

Jacob shuffled into the room behind Gina, taking a seat. Being present at post-mortems was never a pleasure.

'Can I get either of you a drink?' the young man asked.

Gina caught a glimpse of the scalpel gliding through Holly's taught skin and she swallowed. 'No, thank you.'

The man closed the door, leaving them to it.

'I'm surprised he didn't offer us a bit of breakfast. Just the thing to help us through a post-mortem.'

Gina glanced across, taking her dark straggly hair into her hands and forcing it into a ponytail using the elastic band she always kept in her pocket. 'You've got to be joking.'

'Chill, guv. I'm definitely joking. I know I always say this, it doesn't matter how many times we've seen this happening, it never becomes easier. I'm just glad we're behind glass. I couldn't take the smell today.' He gave a little wave to one of the assistants.

'Jennifer?'

'I know, you can't tell with all the garb she's wearing.' His gaze locked onto hers for a couple of seconds.

The clean crime scene assistant snapped away, cataloguing every part of the process. One of Holly's organs was removed then dropped into the scales; Gina guessed at it being her liver. The assistant with the form and pen scrawled a few notes and nodded back at the pathologist. He began calling out measurements along with a commentary.

Gina twiddled her fingers in her lap and looked down for a second but the urge to watch was overwhelming. Holly's red hair had been tidily placed to one side, eyes closed, skin bluish and as pale as skin could get. Gina had seen the photos of the young redhead. She had been pale in life but death almost gave her skin a translucent look.

Gina glanced up as her stomach contents were being placed in a tin.

'You okay, guv?'

'This isn't my favourite part.'

'Mine neither. Such a tragic loss.'

Gina slowly nodded. 'What do you and Jennifer talk about at night?'

He let out a slight laugh. 'Not this, that's for sure. Films, music, art.'

'Art? Since when did you have an interest in art?'

Any conversation that acted as a diversion from what was happening was most welcome. She didn't normally get too squeamish but today the post-mortem just added to the uneasy feeling in her stomach. After an unsettled night with both Hannah and Holly running through her every spare thought, and her conversation with Briggs waking her every five minutes, a banal conversation was just what she needed.

'Jennifer has opened my eyes to so much. We now have a shared passion for Salvador Dali and René Magritte.'

'A bit of surrealism?' Gina could have laughed. Her whole life at the moment felt like it was a work of a surrealist creator pulling her strings. Between what was happening and the weird dreams, she pushed images of Dali's melting clocks to the back of her mind. 'I'm glad you're both happy.' A flash of Dali's 'Carnation and Cloth of Gold' entered her mind as Gina thought back to

Holly's body. The flower petals had to mean something even if they were just snatched from the table centrepieces. Had the killer chosen them with thought or was the carnation simply a coincidence? She felt the cogs of her mind kicking into action. 'Carnations – the Mother's day flower.'

'What?' Jacob glanced her way.

'Someone left carnation petals on her torso for a reason. Holly was going to be a mother. Let's keep that in our thoughts as we investigate.'

Jacob slowly nodded in agreement.

Swabs and samples were being catalogued and the body was being sewn up. Gina hoped they had all they needed and that Marianne Long would be able to start arranging her daughter's funeral.

The pathologist stepped to the side and headed towards the shiny stainless steel sink. After scrubbing himself, he left through the other door.

'I suppose we best get the low-down.'

The door opened. 'Ah, DI Harte and DS Driscoll,' the pathologist said as he straightened his Pink Panther tie. He held out his arm revealing a crisp white cuff as he gestured for them to leave the room. 'Lovely to meet you both again. It's a shame the circumstances are always so macabre.' His eyebrows arched. 'Follow me. There's a room down the corridor where we can talk. We have a lot of the forensics results back too and I'm happy to talk you through what we've got.'

The pathologist held the report in his hand, smiling as he led the way to a tiny room with three mismatched plastic chairs surrounding a small coffee table. 'Have a seat.' He slipped his glasses from his pocket and pushed them up his thin nose.

'So, what do you have for us?' Gina rested back onto the plastic chair, resisting leaning too far back when it creaked.

'Holly Long, aged twenty-five.' He scanned his eyes across the report. 'I'll obviously need time to prepare my official report but this is what I have for now. Her nose was fractured, just slightly on the right of the bridge. This would have caused some bleeding and looking at the blood spatter photos and reports, we can confirm that the blood on the wall by the door did come from her nose.'

'Taken by surprise?' Gina imagined someone knocking or calling through the door and Holly answering. Was it her lover? The baby's father? She opened the door to someone she knew, or could it have been a call from staff? Room service, maybe. She thought back to the reports she'd read. The staff all had alibis. Her mind flitted back to the drug dealer, Phillip Brighton.

'Could have been. The other main injury is that of the blow to her head. The actual size of the cut to the right side of her skull is two point three centimetres. I have matched this to the lamp measurements and the edge of the base fits this measurement. We also have a blood match to the lamp. Holly Long's blood is on that lamp.'

'There was some evidence at the scene showing that she may have been smothered with a pillow. Can you confirm this?' Gina thought back to the blood on the pillow that had been placed back on the other side before her body was left to look like she was sleeping.

'I was just coming to that one. Look at her eyes.' He passed a photo across the table. 'See the little bloodshot prickles? This is a sign of suffocation. Also, we pulled out fibres of the pillow from her bloodied nose. The fibres were found in her mouth and throat too. If you look at her skin,' he passed another photo to Gina, 'petechial haemorrhaging – during asphyxiation blood vessels break and can leak into the skin, causing this.'

Gina passed the photos back. 'Can you email these over to me?'

'Of course. I can get these sent this afternoon.'

'Are there any more signs of a struggle?'

'Yes, she has a broken rib. Given the bruising on her body, it looks like someone straddled her and held the pillow over her face.

There's no doubt that this would have been traumatic for the victim. Confusion and dizziness would have set in after a few seconds and that soon would have been followed by unconsciousness and death. There was also bruising to her wrist, colour consistent with it occurring that evening. She could have been grabbed or pulled. The fingerprint measurements will be in my report. Also, her body still contained a lot of its heat when the forensics team arrived. No rigor mortis, but you already know that there was only a small window of time when her murder could have happened.'

Gina glanced at Jacob's notes. He'd got it all down. 'And the foetus?'

'The foetus weighed in at 14.9 ounces and was measured at 4.1 inches long. Sex, female. Holly Long was about fifteen weeks pregnant.'

Gina scrolled through her diary on her phone. 'So, she would have conceived around the week of the twentieth of January?'

'That would be a good estimate. There was something else.'

Gina exited her calendar and looked back up.

'There were a couple of scars on the base of her neck, consistent with fingernails digging into her skin. The measurements have been logged. I will send these to you too. Two rows of half-moon scars. Someone must have gripped her like this – may I demonstrate on one of you?'

Gina nodded and the tall pathologist leaned over her, placing his two thumbs gently on her throat as he gently pressed his nails into the back of her neck. As the nails pinched her flesh she felt her stomach sink and her heart rate speed up. He let go and sat back in his chair. 'Do you see what I mean?'

Gina nodded. She saw what he meant and she knew how it felt. She knew what it was like to gasp until her oxygen supply had been cut off. She knew how it felt to look into the eyes of someone who was clearly enjoying every moment as her vision had prickled.

'Are you okay?' The pathologist pushed his fringe to the side. 'Guv?'

'Yes, I'm okay. It's just such a horrible way to die, suffocation. No, I'm fine. I suppose what Holly went through has just become more real. Thank you for demonstrating.'

'That's where the light scarring could have come from, anyway. Unfortunately, I can't say when this could have occurred. Going back to other things, we found no other blood on Holly apart from her own. No semen, no other bodily fluids and no skin from a struggle under her fingernails. As for DNA, I know from the reports I've read that the lab has a lot to process still.'

'I know, I think the whole party had been in the room at some point during the day, plus it hadn't been properly cleaned between customers. It's proving to be a nightmare. Anything else?'

The pathologist smiled. 'This is an unusual one. I noticed a slight shadow at the back of her throat.'

'And.' Gina's pulse began to race.

'The head of a carnation with all the petals removed had been pushed right back.'

Gina shivered. 'So we know where the petals had been torn from. That's made me feel a little queasy. Poor Holly. Any more surprises?'

'No, that really is it.'

'Thank you. I suppose we best go. We have a pub to get to.' Gina felt the urge to get out.

'Lucky for some.'

'If only. We have to get to the bottom of these gatecrashers, so not for pleasure unfortunately.'

'If there's anything else specific you need to ask, just pick up the phone. Otherwise, I'll get started on the report. Are you sure you're okay?'

She nodded. The pathologist had applied barely any pressure at all when he placed his hands on her neck. It was no more than a tickle and now with the news of the flower head in Holly's throat she almost wanted to gag. She felt her face reddening as they said their goodbyes and left the building.

'Any thoughts about all that, guv? That was a lot to take in.' Jacob placed his notebook in his pocket and checked his phone as they hurried across the car park.

'The person who did this was quick. They took her by surprise, startling her with a fractured nose as she opened the door. I'm just running a scenario here. Maybe her attacker then grabbed her by the wrist and thrust her onto the bed. She would have been kicking up a fuss by now or maybe she was stunned. I can imagine a blow to the nose would be instantly disabling and I'm guessing that the person who attacked her would know that. So the attacker has her on the bed and she's starting to fight back maybe, this is when the attacker grabs the lamp and hits her over the head, stunning her again. They then take the opportunity to weigh her down with their body weight and smother her with the pillow. This is a really violent attack.'

Jacob gripped the car door handle and got in.

Gina placed her keys in the ignition. 'Then Holly's attacker places the pillow used to smother her back in its place. Why even do that? There is blood on the drawers, blood on the wall, blood on Holly's head and face. Neatly placing the pillow back wouldn't disguise what happened. They went to the effort to place it facing down so that the blood was hidden from view, then they leave without even closing the door properly. Before that, they place her neatly, put a flower head in her throat and sprinkle petals on her torso. This person was deeply affected in one way or another by Holly's pregnancy – of that I'm sure.' She pondered for a moment. 'The initial attack had been thought through. Stun and go in for the kill. But the finish, it's shoddy. This is the finishing of a panicked person, an emotional person but no one saw anyone looking panicked at the party following the time of the attack. Whoever did this must have composed themselves almost immediately.'

'Complicated. I'll never understand what drives someone to do something like this to another person.' Jacob shivered as he put his seat belt on. 'Late breakfast or pub? Which first.'

'I'll treat us to a pasty from the garage after we've been to the Angel Arms.'

'Right you are!'

She drove out of the car park and felt a knot forming in her throat as she thought about facing Samuel Avery once again. The day was going from bad to worse.

CHAPTER TWENTY-THREE

The smell of beer-sodden carpet wafted through the doors of the Angel Arms as Gina and Jacob entered. A girl who couldn't have been much older than the legal age to work in a pub smiled, showing off her braced teeth. Gina opened the buttons of her jacket and smiled. 'Are Samuel Avery and Robin Dawkins here?'

The girl straightened out the stripy tank top over her crisp white balloon sleeved shirt and furrowed her brow. 'Robin? I don't know anyone called Robin.' She glanced at Jacob and smiled.

'Elvis, sorry. He's known as Elvis.'

'Ahh, I see. Elvis, I never did get it. He thinks he's the karaoke king but in my opinion, he's a bit off key. They're in the beer garden, smoking.' Two elderly men queued up behind Gina, waiting to be served. 'Do you want a drink or shall I serve him?'

Gina stepped aside.

'Your usual, Billy?'

The man nodded. 'And his usual too.' He pointed his walking stick at his drinking partner.

'I'll bring them over in a minute.'

Jacob leaned on the bar. The girl glanced over and smiled – his action man looks often made him a little bit of a hit but unlike Samuel Avery, Jacob would never take advantage of someone so young or cheat on Jennifer. 'Were you working here on Saturday night?'

'Yes.'

He stood up. 'Great. We'll be back to chat with you in a minute. Thank you.'

'You're welcome,' she called as she began measuring a couple of drinks from the top shelf. 'Who are you?'

'DS Driscoll and DI Harte,' he said as they walked off.

'I pity anyone that has to work here,' Gina said as they walked past the toilets toward the beer garden.

The slabbed patio was full of wooden tables and chairs. Moss grew through the gaps in the tiles and beer bottles and cigarette ends were scattered all over the garden.

'Samuel Avery, Robin Dawkins,' Gina said as she walked up to them, Jacob catching up with her.

'Not you again. Turn the porn off, Elvis?' Samuel Avery let out a pantomime laugh.

The younger man slammed the laptop he held closed and stood up from the table.

'Chill, Detective Inspector, or can I call you Gina now that we're practically family?'

'You will never be my family.'

He shrugged and grinned as he swapped his weight between his feet. 'What's this all about? Come to tell me to keep away from little Hannah again? I can't help it that I'm irresistible to women.'

He lit a cigarette, inhaled and blew out a plume of smoke. He was a smoker like the man their drug dealer spotted touching himself in the clearing on the night of Holly's murder. Had Samuel Avery gone back to the venue after taking the van full of kegs back to the pub? He wouldn't even need to drive. Had the location where his crime had taken place lured him back? Had being there given him a thrill? He could have taken the country walk at the back of the town that led to the woods, easily avoiding the police that were guarding the comings and goings on the road.

'Were you alone after leaving Cleevesford Manor?'

'What do you think? Oh, maybe I brought Elvis and Cass back for a three-way.'

She'd come to expect this type of comment from Avery.

'Seriously, I came back. I was knackered and I went to bed.'

She glanced at her notes trying not to imagine him with Hannah, feeling her knuckles clenching around her pen. 'Tell me about the gatecrashers. They were a group of locals that frequent the Angel.'

'Everyone who lives in this town and likes a drink frequents my pub. It's the main boozer in Cleevesford. What makes you think the gatecrashing issue is anything to do with us? Do you know anything about any gatecrashers coming from here, Elvis?'

The younger man shook his head, his quiff bobbing as he moved. 'Err no, Sam.'

'Are you sure? It was an open bar. It would be financially beneficial to you if more people were to come and drink all night, run the tab up even more, so to speak.' Gina watched as he paused to think of a retort.

'First you come and have a go at me for being in your daughter's room. She invited me in, believe it or not. Secondly, you think I invite a load of boozers over to a function to run up a bill. I do a good job at events and earn a pretty packet. I wouldn't do that. I pride myself on the ales I sell. I don't need a few gatecrashers to boost the coffers. You're barking up the wrong tree.'

Gina took a tiny step forward. 'Why do you look so worried then?'

'It's you lot. You're always on my case. Your daughter's lovely, you know. You should stop letting her down, Detective Inspector.'

Jacob caught her eye and gave a subtle shake of his head. Now wasn't the time to bite. 'You weren't behind the bar all night. In fact, neither of you were. Some of the witness statements say that it looked like you and Robin were shirking off, wandering about and mingling while the woman who was working with you did all the work.'

'My Cass is a good one,' Elvis said with a snigger.

Avery nudged him in the stomach with his elbow, reminding Gina of a couple of schoolboys playing the teacher up at the back of class.

'Okay, we did mingle, but we were around all the time. The most wandering off we did was to go outside for a smoke or the toilet. That's all.' A bead of sweat formed at Avery's hairline.

'How well did you know Holly Long?'

Samuel Avery rolled his eyes. 'I only knew her from the pub. She came in a few times with Fran, Kerry and Lilly. Only occasionally. They're all locals and they've virtually grown up in the town. How could I not know them?'

'Have you ever had any type of relationship or friendship with Holly Long?'

He stared at Gina, a grin spreading across his face. 'I have never been in a relationship with her, we've never shagged and we've never spent a meaningful moment together. I barely know any of them. I just know them to look at. I think that's all I've got to say to you unless you're arresting me?'

'Should I?' Gina felt her confrontation hackles rising.

He shrugged. 'Got anything on me?'

Gina paused, her stare meeting his. This was war and she had lost the second battle to him. First, her daughter, and now, her lack of evidence to place him in or near Holly's room at the time of her murder. She turned and headed back towards the bar.

'That was a bit intense, guv.'

'You're telling me. We need to speak to the bartender. Double check whether she knows anything about the gatecrashers.'

They approached the bar and waited for the two couples wearing business attire to get their drinks. Gina flashed her identification. 'We need to talk to you about Saturday night. Could I take your name?'

'Oh sure, it's Leslie Benton. What's this about?' The girl took a sip of her water and sat on a stool at the end of the bar so that they could talk a little more privately.

'Have you heard about the murder at Cleevesford Manor?' Gina sat while Jacob scribbled a few notes down.

'I saw it on Facebook and gossip is rife around here. It's all anyone is talking about. In fact, people are looking now.' She pulled up her balloon sleeves and placed her elbow on the bar.

Gina glanced back. The group in suits pointed towards Gina as they spoke. 'The wedding reception was invaded by a group of gatecrashers that we have been led to believe came from here. I need the names of everyone who was in on Saturday night and I need to know who left and when.'

'I can do that,' the girl replied. 'I haven't been working here too long but I do know most of the customers by name. A crowd of them did leave here together on the Saturday night.'

Gina nodded. 'That's good. Can you tell me what time that was?'

'Probably around eight or nine. I don't have an exact time.'

'Do you know what instigated them all to leave? Did something happen?'

The girl looked puzzled as she thought back. An orange glow from the bar lighting caught her hair. 'Yes. It was Phil, someone called Phil, always wears a denim jacket. He said the call had arrived. They whispered for a while. I jokingly asked them what was going on but they didn't answer. They finished their drinks and left.'

It all made sense. Just as Gina had suspected, a tip-off had come in from someone at the party, telling them all to head over to the manor for free drinks. 'Did this seem unusual?'

'Oh definitely. They were hardened drinkers. We normally have to prise them off their seats at the end of the night. Did one of them hurt Holly?'

'We're just trying to establish where everyone was at the time. Thank you for that. Is there anything else you can tell us?'

The girl leaned over and whispered in Gina's ear. 'I know Phil deals drugs. He offered to sell me some coke once. Please don't say I said anything as I don't want to lose my job. He's one of our bigger spenders. I overheard him mentioning that he was going to offload some gear that night.'

Gina noted what she had said on Jacob's pad and he gave her an understanding nod. He wrote 'CCTV' underneath her note. He was right. The Angel Arms's CCTV would show those who left the premises and at what time. She also knew of Phillip Brighton's arrest for drug possession and dealing. His property would have been searched by the arresting team and she would catch up with them soon.

'Could he have hurt Holly? I mean he gives me the creeps, the way he looks at me.' The girl checked over her shoulder, making sure no one would hear.

'We are looking into all possibilities at the moment. Has he said or done anything to you that you'd like to mention?'

She shook her head. 'No. I just feel like he's always watching. He has these beady eyes and he stares a lot. He just gives me the creeps, that's all.'

'If you're ever worried, please do call us. Here's my card. If you hear, see or remember anything that you think will help us with the case, please call me.'

A man cleared his throat loudly and tapped his fingers on the bar. 'Anyone serving?'

'I best go back to work.' As she left her stool and served the man, Samuel Avery headed towards Gina.

'You still here?'

'I'll need your CCTV for Saturday night.'

His shoulders dropped. 'How did I know you were going to ask that? Any sign of trouble in this town, you always want my CCTV. Of course, Detective Inspector. You can have whatever you like, but we best make it quick. My date has arrived.'

Hannah flicked her long blonde hair and took a seat at the bar. Her casual dress was nipped in at the waist by a chunky belt. 'Mum? It's you again. I wish you'd just leave me alone.'

'It's not all about you, Hannah,' she said as she stepped outside, Jacob following.

'What was that about?'

Gina took a deep breath and rubbed her tired eyes. 'There appears to be something going on between Avery and my daughter. That's my daughter, Hannah. You remember her, don't you?'

'Of course I do. Sorry, guv. Wish I hadn't asked. Tell you what, I'll go in, get the CCTV and meet you back at the car.'

Her phone rang. 'O'Connor. What have you got?' Gina asked as she gazed at her daughter through the pub's leaded bay window. Hannah sat on a bar stool and flicked her hair as she smiled.

'The blood results from Phillip Brighton's top have come back but that's nothing, the blood was his. But there's more.'

'Okay, give it to me.'

O'Connor paused for a second. 'During the search of his bedsit, the officers not only found all the usual stuff to convict him of dealing – scales, little bags, drugs, money. They found a password-protected pink tablet. It's the same make and size as the one Holly owned.'

'Holly's missing tablet? I want him ready and waiting for my return.' Gina took one last look at Hannah and hurried to the car to wait for Jacob. Hannah would have to wait.

CHAPTER TWENTY-FOUR

Cass stared at her phone, then back at the cake. *Don't eat it, don't you dare. If you want friends like Kerry, you have to look good. Be the part.* She snatched the cake from next to the filing pile and flung it in the tin bin by her feet. It wasn't just Kerry, it was Elvis. Whoever he was texting would soon be history. His hands would be all over her once again. She began pretending to sort the papers in alphabetical order by client name. Pretending was fine. It's all she had to do that day at work, that and answer a phone that rarely rang. Shut off in her own world, she could imagine what Elvis was up to and how Kerry was spending her day. Would Kerry be back at work considering what had happened to her best friend at her wedding reception?

Kerry worked for Daddy's company. There would be no back-to-work interrogation by an uncaring manager. Even Ed worked for the company – handsome Ed or Fox Mulder as Cass liked to call him in her thoughts. She'd watched reruns of all *The X-Files* episodes many times and, in her mind, Ed was Fox. That family had everything; health, wealth and happiness in abundance. Cass had enjoyed some of that as a child when she'd been Kerry's best friend, especially the wealth, before Holly took her place. But Holly was as dead as yesterday's reception flowers that stood upturned in her bin. The best friend place in Kerry's life was vacant and Cass had to take it back.

'There's a few spare slices of cake left. Want some more? I bet you do.' Melody tottered past in her heels, holding a box.

'No, thank you.' Why would she want more cake? They were all in it, trying to encourage her to eat more so they ate less. It wouldn't work. She knew them too well. They could keep their cake. She wasn't going to eat today. 'Hey, Melody?'

The woman turned back, just before the double doors.

'I'm going on lunch break in half an hour. I have to go somewhere. Could you man reception for me, please?'

'Of course. I'll take this cake around, grab a drink, then I'll head back. You going anywhere nice for lunch? Got a date with Elvis?'

Cass knew they all gossiped about her, made her the brunt of all their jokes. She'd caught a couple of nasties in marketing imitating her and Elvis, replacing the words to some of the real Elvis's most famous songs with jokes about how they saw her relationship. 'No.' The woman waited for more. Cass wasn't going to give her any more ammunition to pass on. No was all she was getting. 'Half an hour then?'

Melody nodded and hurried off. Pulling several old tissues from her bag, Cass covered the cake in the bin and dragged some of the dead flowers over it. If Melody saw that, it would be another thing to gossip about. She'd heard them talking about her hefty weight, citing it as funny as they never saw her actually eat. Soon things would change. She would get her friend back, tidy herself up, get her relationship back on track and they would all see her differently. For now, she had a truth to find and one way or another she was going to get it. She leaned over and slipped her shoes back on, not her low-heeled Mary-Jane's, but the flat pair she kept for frosty days that had long passed. It was time to take action. Sitting around sending poxy messages just wouldn't cut it.

She moved the flowers aside and lifted the tissues in the bin and stared at the cake. Just a few morsels. She poked her finger in the creamed centre, scooped it out and licked it. It was just a taste and the bin was clean. Her stomach grumbled hard. After her evening binge when Elvis hadn't come home straight after work, she promised herself no food today but every pore of her body screamed for sugar and salt. She poked her finger into the cake again and scooped out some more cream.

'Cassie? What are you doing? You should have just said if you wanted more cake. Why is yours in the bin?' Melody stared, red lips in a slight o shape as she awaited an answer.

Cass grabbed a piece of paper from her notepad and wiped her finger. 'It wasn't what it looked like.' Who was she trying to convince.

'Is everything okay?'

Cass nodded, keeping a calm exterior, the one she'd practised long and hard when what was inside felt like it was shooting in all directions. 'I best go.' She grabbed her zip-up jacket from the back of her chair and hurried out. 'See you later.'

Dammit! Melody saw everything. She hurried to her car, holding her fuzzy curls in place as a gust of wind caught them. Everything was going wrong. She kicked the bushes at the back of the car park, wanting to yell and scream. She had to make things right, make her own destiny. *I'm on my way.*

CHAPTER TWENTY-FIVE

'Phillip Brighton. Here we are again. Our murder victim, Holly Long was missing a pink tablet and we found one matching the same description during our search of your bedsit. What can you tell me about this?' Gina held up the exhibit photo of the pink tablet.

He shrugged his shoulders and said nothing on the advice of Mr Ullah, his solicitor, who was whispering away in his ear.

'Does this tablet belong to Holly Long?'

The suspect ignored every question, simply shuffling in his grey tracksuit bottoms.

Gina had to go through the motions for the tape, asking question after question she knew he wouldn't answer. As she came to an end, she sighed, asking the final two. 'Can you give us the password to the tablet?' Gina paused. 'How long have you had it?'

She exchanged a glance with Jacob.

'Interview ended at twelve fifty-four.'

Gina grabbed all her paperwork and left the interview room.

'Are we charging him, guv?'

She exhaled slowly. 'He had opportunity, no one can confirm that he was in the toilet where he claimed to be and he didn't see anyone. We have his DNA on file and looking at some of the reports that came back, I don't think Phillip Brighton's have been flagged up as being found in Holly's room but they are still working through everything. That's not to say it won't come up. It would make our case tighter when we put it to the CPS.' The

Crown Prosecution Service would decide if the evidence was good enough to charge him with. 'If we arrest him, we can keep him in again while we conduct further enquiries. Holly is missing a pink tablet and one of the same make just happened to be in his bedsit. That's too much of a coincidence and he's not talking. We can't let him walk out on bail today; that might risk him tampering with any potential evidence.' Gina turned away and marched back into the interview room.

'My client would like some lunch.' Mr Ullah stood.

'Your client will have to wait. Phillip Brighton, I'm arresting you on suspicion of the murder of Holly Long on the evening of Saturday the ninth of May. You do not have to say anything. But it may harm your defence if you do not mention when questioned something which you later rely on in court. Anything you do say may be given in evidence.'

She left the room, giving both Phillip Brighton and his solicitor time to talk.

'We need that tablet cracked now,' Jacob said. 'Why would he want to hurt Holly Long?'

'I wish I knew. Where is the tablet?'

Jacob followed her along the corridor. 'It's with the tech team. It shouldn't take too long to get into.'

'And we'll be either charging him or letting him go.'

Jacob nodded. As Gina turned towards her office, Wyre's hair shook from side to side as she jogged towards them both. 'Guv, Francesca Carter is in the waiting room. She's asking to speak with you about the night Holly was murdered.'

'Thanks, Paula. Let's hope this is the break we need. Have the forensics come back on Francesca Carter's clothing yet?'

'Let me just check.' Wyre pulled out her phone and checked through their emails. 'Yes, only this morning. O'Connor has marked this one done so it must have been added to the system. Nothing alarming found on her, only her own secretions. Her hair was found at the scene, this could have been when they all had their hair and make-up done or it could have been left there on the evening of the murder. There was also a smear of blood on her hand that was swabbed and it is Holly's.'

'She did go into the room and touch both the lamp and Holly. Thanks for the update. I've read the notes from her interview so I'll bear all that in mind when I speak with her.'

Gina hurried towards the waiting room and smiled at the desk sergeant, Nick, then turned to see the young woman sitting on a plastic seat, hugging her knees with her oversized bag filling her lap.

CHAPTER TWENTY-SIX

What are you doing in there, Frannie? The slow walk into town had led you to the police station. Why? I need to find out what you know, and I will.

He walked past the wall and headed to the public car park on the grounds just opposite the station and he leaned against the fence, checking his phone. Far enough away to avoid detection from either Francesca or the police but close enough to spot her burnt orange knee-length trench coat that covered her perfect figure.

Your coffee was terrible yesterday, Frannie. I'm not sure if you made it that badly on purpose to hurry me out, and you don't trust me – that much I know. I can see I have work to do when it comes to you. When I stood next to you in the kitchen, you moved and it wasn't subtle or polite. You didn't spare my feelings at all. Trust needs to be earned. I'm good at that. Whether I have the time to waste, that's another question entirely.

He closed his eyes and imagined stroking his fingers through her hair. It was up today, a loose bun, which reminded him of Holly. He'd prefer that Francesca leave her hair flowing down her back, ready for him to wrap it around her neck. He stretched his twitching fingers, already desperate to act out his thoughts, then he curled them into a fist.

'You alright, mate?' asked the man in the paint-splattered tracksuit as he got into his white Transit van.

He loosened his clenched fists, the moment ruined. He'd just been at the part when her lips would begin to turn blue. 'Yes, mind your own business.'

'Stuff you. Was only askin'.'

He walked away towards the other side of the car park, watching the man stick two fingers up at him as he pulled out onto the main road. Was that image in his mind enough? He inhaled and imagined breathing in the scent of lemon, the smell he'd forever associate with Frannie from now onwards.

Back to the moment.

He's wrapping her mane around her neck and watching her stark stare plead with him to unleash her but she's enjoying it too so he carries on.

Is the thought of it enough?

Her voice is nothing more than a croak and she gasps air as he releases her from her own hair.

No, it wasn't enough. He needed to feel it fully. He needed to feel the end.

He unbuttoned the top button of his shirt letting the light breeze cool his reddening face.

He turned his attention back to the station knowing that she could be ages. When she came out, he'd be waiting. A quiver ran through his body. Maybe Holly had said something to Fran and maybe she was telling the police. If that was the case, the police would come for him within the next couple of hours, he knew that much. He'd have a lot of explaining to do. Two hours, three hours, maybe four. When would he be in the clear? No more risks and no loose ends. If he were to get a second chance, he was going to tie them up, good and proper.

Come on, Frannie. Show me your hand. I'm waiting for you.

CHAPTER TWENTY-SEVEN

'Have a seat. Can we get you a drink?' Jacob asked as he indicated for her to sit.

Francesca Carter shook her head and removed her orange raincoat. 'I just want to get this over with.'

Gina sat next to Jacob in the little room and gave Francesca a slight smile. 'What can we do for you?'

Jacob began to scrawl the date and a few details at the top of the page.

'This is off the record so you can stop making notes.' She put her bag by her feet and leaned forward, her long pale pink talons resting on the desk between them.

'Okay, but bear in mind that someone murdered your friend on Saturday night and if you have information that could help us catch the killer, we would need to record it properly.'

She looked away and ran a hand across her eyes. 'What I am going to say may well have nothing to do with Holly but I had to say something. Do you know what I mean?'

Gina nodded.

'There's no denying I was drunk, so drunk at times I struggled to stand, but I soon sobered up when I saw Holly's lifeless body. I don't think I've ever come around so fast.' She paused and scraped her chair closer to the table.

Jacob closed his notepad and leaned back.

'Go on, in your own time,' Gina said.

'I spent all night awake, not knowing whether to say something, blaming myself, but you know what, he took advantage and I need to get this out of my system.' She took a couple of deep breaths. Her nails tapped on the table as she trembled. 'I left the function room just as the disco had started and went to the toilet. I came out feeling a little light-headed so I thought I'd hang out under the stairs to the first floor, just for five minutes until I felt a bit better. The light seemed so bright so I faced the wall with my head on my arms, blocking the light out, thinking, regaining my composure – whatever you want to call it. That's when I felt a pair of hands snaking around my waist. At first, I thought it was Charlie—' Francesca stared at the wall.

'Charlie?'

'My husband. I thought he'd come out to check on me. He was rubbing my back tenderly and I was enjoying it. When I turned it wasn't him and before I knew it that tosser had his lips pressed against mine and his hands up my dress. He pushed his fingers into my pants. I tried to get him away from me but he was strong and had all his weight on me, pinning me against the wall. I heard people coming and going but I didn't shout. I don't know why I didn't. For a moment, I thought if someone saw, they would think I was cheating on Charlie and I'd never do that. But I was drunk and I know what people think when you're drunk. I should have said something when you interviewed me in the ambulance but it hadn't sunk in. Eventually, I managed to push him away. He called me a prick tease and walked off. I feel so stupid. I didn't want Charlie to find out. I still don't, which is why I didn't want it to be official. I just thought you should know. What if he hurt Holly after I pushed him away and ran off? I should have said something. It's probably my fault Holly was killed.' Francesca wiped her eyes and pulled some of her hair around her face as if trying to hide behind a few strands.

'Francesca, what happened to you wasn't your fault. Whoever did this should not have touched you or kissed you. Thank you so much for coming forward. I know it can't have been easy to tell us what happened. You're right to bring this to our attention. If someone did this to you, who's to say he wasn't capable of doing much more. It would really help us if you went on record with this or at least told us who you are talking about.'

'I know what people are like. Some of them would say I was drunk, a bit flirtatious and dancing with anyone around, but Charlie, I just don't know what he'd say.'

Gina placed her hands on the table. 'What do you think he'd say?'

'I think he'd be livid. Not at me, at him. I just don't want any trouble. Cleevesford is a small town. I grew up here. My best friend's wedding reception has already been ruined and all I'm going to do by reporting this is to add to an already bad memory.'

'Any real friend would want you to feel safe enough to report an assault. I'm sure she will understand.'

Francesca stared at the mottled grey wall behind Gina and Jacob.

'I have to do this. It's the right thing to do.'

Gina slid the box of tissues across the table.

'You can get your notepad back out. It's okay. I'll deal with whatever comes my way. I'll have to. It was Samuel Avery, the landlord of the Angel Arms.'

A slight shiver travelled up Gina's spine, resting at the base of her neck. She almost snapped the biro she was gripping as she pressed the tip to the page. The man who was worming his way into her daughter's life as they spoke had committed an assault on a young woman only a couple of days earlier.

CHAPTER TWENTY-EIGHT

As Cass finished her filing, she noticed her phone lighting up. It was probably Elvis. He'd be seeing if she was okay, maybe trying to make up with her. She skidded across the tiled floor in her tights and grabbed the phone. Her heart rate picked up and she smiled.

Are you free to talk? I just need someone and it would be lovely to catch up after so many years. I'm so sorry I've been distant but with all that happened, it's been hard. Thank you for caring. Kerry. XXX

She went to reply. *Don't mess this up, Cass. Don't mess up like you always do.* She'd seen Kerry crying at the kitchen table at lunchtime and she'd reached out at the right moment. She didn't expect things to move this quickly.

I can come straight after work. I finish at five. XXX

Straight after work, she could pop into the supermarket, grab a bottle of wine and they could chat away, just like old times when they were best friends, but back then they shared sweets. This time, they will drink wine and talk as adults do. Best friends again. She wanted to run around and do a dance. Jump with glee. She had her best friend back and life would only get better. A moment of guilt washed through her as she thought of Holly. She swallowed, knowing she should feel something but she didn't. Holly's death was helping her to get her best friend back. It would be her and Kerry from now on. No, Francesca and Lilly would get in the way, or maybe they'd accept her being a part of the new fold.

Pulling a vanity mirror from her bag, she gazed at her reflection. She didn't belong in their world. Her round face and dark eyes made her look tired and bloated. She hadn't eaten much at all. A couple of finger scoops of cream from a piece of cake barely counted. Her mind flashed back to the piles and piles of bread, the chocolate spread and the jam. She snapped the mirror closed and dropped it back into her bag. Transformation wouldn't happen overnight. She'd take things slowly. For now, Kerry wanted her support and she was going to give as much as she could.

Melody came through the double doors with one of the other women from the marketing department. She glanced across then back at the woman. They both laughed as they went into a meeting. It never ended. Maybe if she and Kerry became best friends, there may be a role for her in her family's business. Kerry, her new number one priority. Elvis could wait. She'd get to the bottom of what was happening in his life sooner or later. One day he will slip up and leave his laptop on or she'll see part of a message flash up that actually means something. She didn't expect things to move this quickly.

Thank you. You're a real friend. Can we make it a little later, about eight? There are some things I have to do. See you later. K ☺

Even the sound of another one of her colleagues giggling and pointing as she passed couldn't ruin this moment for Cass.

CHAPTER TWENTY-NINE

Gina stormed into the Angel Arms with Jacob in tow, the place already packed out with people finishing work and coming in for a few drinks before going home. Her daughter swivelled around on a stool and rolled her eyes as she downed what looked like a gin and tonic.

'Samuel Avery, please could you follow us.'

He grinned and threw a towel over a beer pump as he followed her and Jacob out of the bar and into the car park. 'Come to harass me again? Didn't want anyone to hear so you brought me out here. Am I warm?'

'You couldn't be any colder. You need to come with us to the station. I'd like to interview you. You've been accused of a serious sexual assault.'

'I haven't done anything.'

'That's not what Francesca Carter is saying.'

'What the hell. She's making it up! I haven't assaulted anyone. This is because of your daughter, isn't it? It's because you can't bear to see lovely little Hannah hanging about with me. That's what this is all about.'

Gina waited a few seconds before continuing. 'This is about you, Mr Avery, and a very serious accusation against you.'

Avery's stare lingered on Gina, a moment longer than comfortable. 'Okay, I'll come. But I didn't do anything and I'm sticking to that. Do I get a lift?' He smirked as he walked ahead.

Hannah burst out of the door, leaving it crashing to a close behind her as she hurried over to Samuel's side. 'What's happening?'

Her daughter looked a little unsteady and the hair that had lain shimmering over her back earlier that day took on a tangled and slightly sweaty appearance now. 'Hannah. Please go back to mine or to the B&B. We'll talk later.'

She shook her head slowly. 'Why are you trying to interfere in my life?'

'This isn't about you, Hannah.'

Jacob opened the back door. As Avery bent over to get into the car, he made a phone gesture to his ear as he caught Hannah's attention. Gina inwardly smiled. Hannah would soon find out what Avery was like. He'd have to tell her why he was questioned at some point or he'd tell someone who would tell someone else. Cleevesford was a small town and word often got around quickly.

'Mum, why are you doing this?'

Gina tugged Hannah's sleeve and pulled her towards the wall. 'I've told you, this is nothing to do with you. I don't want to see you hurt so please go to mine or just get out of here. We'll talk later.'

'Why is he in the car? What are you doing to him?'

'Hannah, you're asking too much of me. I can't tell you, you know that.'

'Fine, if you want to be like that. I'm going back in there and I'm having another drink. Then I might have another and another. Just go and do whatever you've got to do. You can't keep him in that long anyway.'

Gina felt her stomach turn as she saw what reminded her of teenage defiance in her adult daughter's eyes. She also reminded herself that she hadn't won many of their battles back then and she wasn't about to win this one. She just hoped that in the morning, when Hannah had nursed her hangover, she'd speak to her and, maybe then, they could have a proper talk about what was going on.

'You coming, guv?' Jacob called out.

Gina turned away and hurried towards the car.

'She's a lovely girl, your Hannah. Nothing like you,' Avery said as he caught her gaze in the rear-view mirror. Gina placed the keys in the ignition and drove through the town. As they passed Holly's flat and the chip shop she caught sight of Samuel Avery looking out of the window in the direction of her apartment. Was he thinking back to another time, when he was there in her apartment wearing his blue shirt, or was he checking out the chip shop? Gina couldn't tell and that made her want to scream.

A message from Wyre flashed up on Gina's phone. She caught the words *pink tablet* and *cracked*. The tech team had managed to unlock the tablet that they'd found at Phillip Brighton's bedsit. She passed the phone to Jacob.

Jacob smiled from the passenger seat as he read the message.

She turned her attention from the rear-view mirror and focused on the road ahead even though she could still feel the weight of Avery's stare and she wondered if he'd cooperate during questioning. She already knew the answer to that thought.

CHAPTER THIRTY

'Samuel Avery's in interview room three, guv. There's no rush, he's refusing to speak until his solicitor arrives.' Wyre led the way to the incident room.

Gina gazed around, trying to take in all the changes to the board and surroundings since she'd left earlier that day. The crime scene photos were pinned next to Holly's photo. Whether the assault on Francesca Carter had anything to do with Holly's murder was something she was clutching at right now. She imagined a frustrated Samuel Avery taking himself up the stairs after being rejected. Had he then decided to harass Holly, knowing that she was alone in her room? Maybe she had then told him to go away after he knocked, sending him over the edge.

Gina knew they needed more than Francesca's word and she doubted Samuel would confess. They had to at least try to find out who had passed as Francesca was being assaulted under the stairway. 'Can you please go through every witness statement again, see if anyone mentions seeing anyone under the hotel stairs before the gatecrashers arrived. And if anyone even mentioned just being around there, I want them contacted. We have to find someone who will corroborate her story.'

'I'll take that one up, guv. I'll get onto it now.' Wyre flicked a spot of fluff from the lapel of her pristine black suit before heading to her desk.

'Oh, would you please set up a new board for the sexual assault but keep it within this room. Both are separate crimes but we can't rule out a link as yet and I want us to be working together on them. Smith?'

'Yes, guv.' The PC awaited further instruction.

'Wyre is going through all the statements again to see if we can place anyone else at the stairs in the hotel at the time of Francesca Carter's assault. As she passes you names, you and PC Kapoor can take them and speak to these witnesses again. I know it's time-consuming but I don't want that smug tosser walking if he assaulted Francesca. He's already walked too many times. Also. O'Connor?'

'Yes, guv.' He stopped scrolling through the interviews.

'As soon as Avery's solicitor arrives, let me know. I want to be the one to speak to him.'

'Sure thing. I have the pink tablet here.' He placed it on the central table and a few of the others quietened down so that they could hear what was going on.

'What have you found out?'

'The transcripts from all the emails and messages were sent from the techies and I have the unlocked tablet in front of me. I hate to say this, guv, but it doesn't look like this was Holly's tablet. It's registered to Millie Brighton and Phillip Brighton has since filled us in on who she is. It belongs to his sister. I called her to corroborate his story and she said he stole it from her a couple of days ago. Apparently, he's always stealing her things and was probably intent on pawning it.' O'Connor picked his pen back up and began tapping it on the edge of the desk. 'Also, there is a lot of dirt on the tablet and none of the fingerprints on the tablet match Holly's.'

'Dammit! How could there ever be two pink tablets out there that have become a part of our case? So we are still no wiser? We have Brighton on drug charges only but he still had opportunity as far as I'm aware. I know we have to let him go for now and he'll answer to the drug charges soon but I want you all to keep digging. He, like Samuel Avery and Holly's manager, Rick Elder, are still on the suspect list. Any contact with Mr Elder's sister in Australia? Can she confirm that she was FaceTiming with him at the time of the murder?'

'She can, guv. We're just waiting for the actual records to come back. We've put in a request but, as we know, it takes time.' O'Connor stopped tapping the pen and Gina's shoulders relaxed slightly.

'Keep him up there until we have more than his sister's word.'

'Oh, one other thing.'

'What's that?'

'There's a strawberry gateau in the kitchen. Mrs O made it. Thought we could do with something nice. There's not a lot left but if you get in quick, there may be a slice for you.'

'That's dinner sorted,' and she meant it. The last thing she'd be doing when she got home would be wasting time preparing food. She needed to soak in the bath and clear her muddled mind. This case was filling every spare brain cell she had. That and her issues with Hannah.

'Another thing. Anything back from forensics? Have they been keeping you updated?' She caught Wyre's gaze.

Wyre opened her emails. 'Yes. They said that the cigarette butts found at the clearing where Phillip Brighton claims to have seen a man touching himself are still being processed and there are an awful lot of them. No one on file has been flagged up, which means whoever they are, they aren't on our database. There were so many footprints, forensics don't know where to start. They are mostly made up of layered partials as the ground was soft and a lot of the gatecrashers had trampled it to get to the cut through. It's also used by dog walkers and ramblers. It's a popular route.'

'Do we have the full names of everyone who attended the actual wedding ceremony in Crete?'

Wyre nodded. 'Yes, and we've crossmatched them to the reception. Everyone at the ceremony attended the wedding reception
at Cleevesford Manor.'

'What we don't know is who Holly was talking to in the small
hours in Crete. Her words were something on the lines of, not
being able to keep things to herself any longer. Given that we now
know about the pregnancy, I think she may have been referring
to that, but who was she talking to? We also can't be sure if she
was talking to someone in front of her or speaking on the phone.
There is so much to this case. Right, stay with it. You're all doing
a brilliant job but we need to catch this murderer. Let us not
forget how violent a murder this was. One more thing; well, two.
Anything come of searching the communal bins behind Holly's
apartment and has someone been through the wedding photos?'

O'Connor smiled. 'Nothing from the bins and nothing from
the photos either.'

'Right, let's get back to it. I don't want this person wandering the
streets any longer than needs be. The press are going to be all over
this too. One more thing, not a mention of the flower head being
placed in Holly's throat to anyone. Only the killer would know this.'

The conversation amongst everyone picked up a little as the
detectives and officers turned back to their screens, getting on
with the mass of tasks that lay ahead.

She hurried out to the kitchen, knowing that Avery's solicitor
wouldn't be long. She had a few minutes to wrap up a piece of
cake to eat later.

'Briggs, you made me jump!' As she turned on the kitchen
light, he was standing there, sipping a coffee. 'Why are you
standing here in the dark?'

'I'm enjoying the peace. My head hurts and the press are
going berserk. I haven't been off the phone all day. One of the
papers has reported using the headline and tagline, "Wedding
Night Strangler – A murderer is terrifying the residents of a

small Warwickshire town." A tabloid, of course. It seems our favourite reporter Lyndsey Saunders finally got her promotion and is working for the gutter press. Also, Holly's case is really touching the public. There's a lot of fear out there and I get it. Young woman killed in that way. She was just ordinary in every sense. People worry that it will happen to them and I can't offer them any reassurance at the moment. I just hope there was a really personal motive behind this murder and it won't be repeated. In the meantime, I'm working on another press statement just to appease the reporters that are metaphorically knocking the door down. So far it's emails and calls, but I know before long they'll be camped outside the station. We're monitoring social media too.'

'Shall I make you a drink?'

'You got a double scotch?'

'If only. I think there would be a few takers out in the incident room.' She smiled and gazed into his eyes for a few moments before flicking the kettle switch.

'Thank you for opening up to me the other night. I know you're not comfortable talking about your past, but it helped me to understand. I hope it helped you.'

She swallowed and stared at the steam bellowing out of the kettle's spout. It had and it hadn't. The relinquishing of control gave her an uneasy feeling in the pit of her stomach, a light churning. 'I suppose time will tell.'

'I meant what I said at your mother's grave. This stays with me and I swear that to be true.'

'Swear what to be true?' Jacob stood in the doorway, serious expression plastered over his face. 'Am I missing a cosy chat?'

Briggs gave a smirk. 'Don't be daft. I was just talking about the reporters. They always think we're holding information back on them and it's true, they know it, we know it. I think I might explode one day if they don't stop tying up every line we have. I swear that to be true!'

Jacob burst into a fit of laughter. 'You should see your face, guv.'

Gina tucked a stray clump of hair behind her ear. 'It's been a long day and I can't see it ending any time soon. I just want Holly's murderer brought in, that's all.' A flutter caught her throat, making her voice a little croaky. She poured the water into the cups. 'Want one?'

'Do I ever? Thanks, guv.' She pulled an extra cup from the cupboard, made him a drink and passed it to him. As Jacob left, her tense body almost crumpled.

Briggs placed his warm hand over her shirtsleeve and gave her a little squeeze. 'Come on, Harte. Let's get our minds back on the case. There will be plenty of time to talk after.'

She knew that had been close. Jacob could already see a fondness in the way Briggs looked at her. She didn't need him to jump to conclusions that were no longer there. Or were they? They may not be ripping each other's clothes off every night but a thick air of sexual and emotional tension often threatened to expose them to others.

Wyre entered and hurried straight to the boiled kettle. 'I'm glad that's hot, I need a caffeine kick. Guv, Samuel Avery's solicitor has arrived. I showed him to the interview room. He's waiting for you.'

'Thanks, Paula. Get onto those witness statements and find me someone who can back up Francesca's version of events. I know he'll walk if we can't find anyone. Don't worry about the gatecrashers with this case, it was before they arrived. That should eliminate all the people we had leaving the Angel Arms on the CCTV that Avery gave us.'

Wyre made a drink and hurried back out of the kitchen. Briggs began rubbing his temples and half closed his eyes as he caught the glint of light that bounced off the silver kettle.

'Right, time to grill Avery.' She smiled at Briggs and turned the light off, leaving him alone in the darkness.

CHAPTER THIRTY-ONE

'It was consensual. I was in the corridor and she called me over and dragged me towards her. We kissed and things got a little heated. She rubbed me over my trousers and I reached up her dress. That was it. We were playing about and the constant interruptions put us both off. I don't know why she's saying this.'

Avery began fiddling with the hem of his shirt, the same blue shirt that was taunting Gina's thoughts. An image flashed through her mind. Avery in Holly's flat, telling her to be quiet as Holly's friend knocked and peered through the letterbox. Neither Holly nor her lover had banked on the mirror in the hallway giving away what they were doing. Had he gripped her around the neck, leaving the half-moon fingernail scars behind?

'She's fitting me up. They all do it after. They play away behind their husbands' backs and rather than face their old man's music, they lay the blame on a geezer like me.'

Avery glanced back with a grin at his solicitor.

'Once again, did you grab her from behind while she was trying to compose herself under the stairs?'

'She told me to meet her there. I stroked her and began kissing her neck and she responded. She knew it was me. What bit of "she told me to meet her there" don't you understand?' The solicitor whispered in Avery's ear. 'Sorry, I don't mean to sound loud. It's just an awful thing to be accused of when you've done nothing wrong.'

Gina knew of the solicitor – he had a reputation for getting the guilty off. There was no way Avery would be arrested if he stuck to his story. Without further evidence, she relied on him tripping himself up in an interview. She should've known better. Avery was a seasoned liar. 'She says you pinned her up against the wall before kissing her against her will.'

'I've told you what happened and that's it. You're just pig sick that your daughter likes me. That's what it is. You think this will keep me away from her. I tell you something, you don't know a thing, always thinking you know it all, DI Harte.'

A shiver ran along the nape of Gina's neck, like icy fingers teasing their way around. She inhaled sharply, trying not to conjure up her past. She held her hands to her neck as if trying to release the invisible fingers while reminding herself not to lose her grip. 'She then says you pinned her to the wall under the stairs and pushed your hands into her underwear.'

'She had her hands on my crotch. Shall I put in a counterclaim for assault? We were kissing and touching, doing all those things that turned-on people do. Have you never felt the thrill of foreplay, Detective Inspector?'

Gina met his stare and felt her knuckles tightening as a slight grin formed on his lips.

'My client has been over what happened more than once so if you have no evidence, I suggest you let him go. He won't be saying any more on the matter.' The solicitor stood and peered through his round glasses as he inserted all his paperwork into a folder.

'Interview terminated at seventeen thirty-three.'

Gina hurried out of the room, leaving Jacob to finish up. She ran into the toilets and gave the bin a swift kick. Once again she'd failed when it came to Avery. She'd failed her daughter too as he'd be back out there with her that same evening. She grabbed her neck and massaged her nape as she tried to forget her own wedding night that followed the marital vows she'd bitterly regretted. Almost choking, she grabbed the tap and turned it on, splashing cold water over her face as she gasped in lungfuls of air until she felt light-headed.

'Here you are, guv.' Wyre entered and smiled.

She splashed her face again. 'I failed with Avery. He's walking out as we speak. I can't face it.'

'We'll get him. The investigation won't stop just because he denies doing any wrong, you know that. It was obvious he'd deny everything. Someone has to have seen something. There were too many people around. We'll keep looking.'

She forced a smile. 'I know we will. I can't get all defeatist over this. I think it's because it's him. Anyone else, I could've dealt with but Avery, he really gets to me. Did you have something to share?'

'You're going to like this. Carrying on from the door to doors, one of the PCs has reported back that someone matching Phillip Brighton's description was seen trying to get into Holly's block of apartments about three weeks ago.'

'He claimed he didn't know Holly. If that was the case, what was he doing outside her apartment block? Can we pull the miniscule amount of CCTV we know of on the surrounding roads, going back as far as possible?'

'Definitely.'

'We now know that Phillip Brighton knew Holly Long even before the wedding. Could it be too much of a coincidence that he was there to see someone else?'

Wyre shrugged. 'It would be a huge coincidence.'

'We need to speak to him. Is he still here?'

'No, he's gone. Once we established that the pink tablet was nothing to do with Holly, we had to let him go.'

'What conditions was he bailed on?'

'He's meant to report to the station at ten every morning until his case is heard at the Magistrates Court.'

'This day just gets worse. We're going to see him at his bedsit. I want to get to the bottom of this without delay and this can't wait until ten in the morning. I want to know why he was visiting Holly's block of flats three weeks ago.'

As Wyre left, Gina pulled a paper towel from the dispenser and wiped her pale face dry. Her eyes had darkened and a few lines creased around the edges. She removed the band from her hair and allowed it to fall over her shoulders before fluffing it up. What on earth did Briggs see in her? Before leaving, she felt the back of her neck once again and her heart fluttered as she touched it in only the way Terry used to touch her. He'd lure her into a false sense of security by tickling her neck and the first time, on that night, she'd felt nothing but tenderness. After that, it was merely a trigger for what was to come. *Just leave me alone, Terry. Please, you've hurt me enough.*

She threw the paper towel in the bin and left. Finding Phillip Brighton was now at the top of her list. She had to let Avery go, for now.

CHAPTER THIRTY-TWO

Fran threw her phone and orange coat onto the corner settee after ending the call with the police. Just as she'd expected, that slimeball Samuel Avery had denied what he'd done to her and he was roaming free to assault some other woman. She was right to tell. If he did it again, her statement was on record and that's what counted.

'Charlie,' she called, but the only sound was the echoing of her own voice in the hall. 'Charlie?' The heating was on as were a couple of lights. She hurried to the kitchen. She had to tell him exactly what had happened before she lost her nerve. 'Charlie.' He was nowhere to be seen. She tried the handle of the back door. It was unlocked. She glanced across the lawn and over towards the shed. The padlock was still on. He wasn't in there.

A piece of paper lay on the kitchen floor. She bent over to pick up the note and began to read.

> *Be home about nine. Popped to Mum's to help her to put a curtain rail up and my sister's back from her travels. Come over if you want. We can all get a takeaway. Love you. Charlie. XXX*

She slammed the note on the table. Not only had he left the back door open at a time when there was a murderer walking the streets, he'd left half of the lights on too. She locked the back door. As she hurried through to the lounge, she grabbed her phone and tapped out her reply.

*I'll give it a miss if you don't mind. Think I'll have a bath
and see you when you get home. Love you too. XXX*

There was no way she could sit with his family all night,
gushing over his little sister's travel snaps while she had all this
going on at the back of her mind. She needed to stay focused
on telling him what had happened at the party and how she'd
been to the police station to report it. She headed up the stairs,
unbuttoning her blouse while she walked. The washing basket
on the landing had overflowed. They hadn't touched it since
going to Crete. She pulled her tight trousers off and opened
the bathroom door. A chill ran through her as the shower
curtain fluttered in the breeze. She hurried across the tiled
floor, pulling the window closed. A movement caught her
peripheral vision. Remaining still, she grabbed the liquid soap
dispenser and gripped it before turning around with it above
her head. Reaching for the plastic curtain with her other hand,
she swallowed before swiftly pulling it back to reveal nothing
but an empty bathtub. Placing the dispenser back on the sink,
she let out a little laugh and turned on the bath tap. Her mind
was running away with her. It had been a long and trying day.
She inhaled the lemon oil as she drizzled it into the bathwater,
then removed her bra and pants.

The door to the spare room creaked as she reached down to feel
the temperature of the water. Grabbing a towel, she wrapped it
around her tiny curves and gazed across the dark landing, listening
for anything. As the breeze let out a gentle howl, the door creaked
again. 'Charlie!' She hurried across the landing. They'd be having
words when he got home. It might be May but it wasn't summer
yet. It was still too chilly to leave all the windows open. Stomping
across the landing, she pushed the door and as suspected, the top
window was open. She slammed it closed. Maybe now, she could
have that bath in peace.

Stepping in, she felt the initial burn of the hot water hugging her ankles before she cautiously sank into the water and lay back, immersing her head under the water while holding her breath. As she opened her eyes, she spotted something grey or blue shimmering through the water. The bathroom was white. There was no grey or blue. Bursting through the water, she rubbed the oil and water from her bleary eyes, gasping for breath.

'What are you doing here?' She grabbed a flannel and held it over her breasts. 'Get out. Now.'

He grinned and took a step forward in his all-in-one boiler suit. 'Charlie is on his way home.'

After dropping the note into the bath with his gloved hands, he kneeled beside the bath. They both knew Charlie wouldn't be home for ages.

She went to grab the shampoo bottle to hit him but her trembling hands betrayed her, taking all the strength from her aim. As she tried to stand, the oil she'd poured into her bath made her slide back down. Knocking her head on the side of the bath, she slipped beneath the water. He grabbed her by the hair, dragging her to the surface as she coughed out flecks of water.

'Isn't it good, being on the brink of death, then coming back?'

She went to grab him but he forced her head under once again, leaving her there for longer. *Don't inhale. Hold your breath.* It was too long. She inhaled a mouth full of water, then another. An intense spasm filled her throat. He pulled her to the surface again and she coughed and spewed the bath water out. 'No, please,' she gargled. A dark vignette formed around her vision, closing in as she almost lost consciousness. Breathing in short, sharp bursts, blood pumped around her body, each beat of her heart sounding in her ears, filling her head.

'Tell me you don't feel alive.'

She coughed and gasped as she went to grab him. She couldn't go under again. He'd kill her. He intercepted her grip, bending her fingers back until she whimpered and withdrew. 'Please don't kill me. Why are you doing this to me?' Tears ran down her face and dripped into the bathwater.

'It's simple. I saw the way you looked at me when you invited me in the other day. I can't let you bring me down. You know, don't you?'

'I won't. I don't know anything. Just go home and we can both pretend this never happened.' She burst into a coughing fit.

A grin spread across his face. 'Too late. Besides, I like it.' She felt him wrench a length of her hair and wrap it around her throat. As he throttled her with her own hair, all she could do was stare at him, hoping that he'd see the pain in her eyes and let her go. Her face dipped below the water's surface once again. One glance back at him through the rippling water told her that this was her end. He bit his bottom lip with closed eyes, which told her he wasn't letting her go. One last grab at the shower curtain brought the whole pole tumbling down. That move got her nowhere; it merely depleted what little bit of energy she had left. She flapped her arms, spraying the room as her vision started to fade. It was like being dragged backwards, the blackness of the vignette getting larger until her sight was almost gone. She let out one last croak as he brought her to the surface and all she could hear was his whisper.

'Was it enough?'

She thought of Charlie and Holly as her muscles tensed one last time.

*

He grinned as he took a step back. The feel of her squirming beneath him still tingled through the latex gloves. He scurried down the stairs after checking that no sign of him had been left behind, then he darted out through the back gate, aiming to run the three blocks to his car. He grabbed the holdall that he'd left in a hedge, tucked the boot covers and gloves into the side pocket, and ran. He'd rushed to get over and when he'd seen Charlie leaving, he'd seized the opportunity. It had been handed to him on a plate when he'd opened the unlocked back door and read the note.

Was it enough?

No.

It was only the start.

He felt a stir in his boxer shorts, the very pair that Holly had given him for his birthday. With one urge taken care of, he had another that was forming and he knew there was one person who'd be more than happy to attend to that one. She'd be waiting and he was ready.

He'd been careful. Would his crimes catch up with him if he didn't give up?

Was it enough?

Could it have been better? He nodded and grinned. It was also too easy.

There would be a next time…

CHAPTER THIRTY-THREE

Cass tried to call Elvis one more time to tell him she wouldn't be at home when he finished work but, once again, it had gone straight to voicemail. 'Message me when your phone's back on. Why aren't you answering my calls?' She placed the phone in her zip-up bag and hurried up the long winding drive. The cutesy street lamps that lit up the hedges led the way to the huge double-fronted house. Having a wealthy family ensured that Kerry would never be like Cass, living in an unkempt rental property with zero chance of ever owning her own home.

As she reached the front door, she took a moment to take in the mature gardens and perfect weed-free block paving, and the large silver feature balls that shone under the security light. She walked around the gleaming Mercedes, consciously making an effort not to allow her bag to brush against the silver paintwork. A scratched car wouldn't get her back into Kerry's inner circle. She rang the bell and waited. Glancing across she saw the little camera next to the bell and smiled. Was Kerry watching her? Making sure she wasn't a dangerous intruder. She gave a little wave just in case. Her once best friend neared the door. Cass could just make out her outline through the narrow strip of glass. *Smile*, she thought.

She gripped her bag, then held it more casually. *Don't look so tense, Cass.*

'Cass, hi. Thanks for coming over. Lovely to see you after all these years. Sorry but I don't think I'm much company at the moment.' Kerry's streaked blonde hair fell over her shoulders. The light shining through it showed the many shades that made up the overall honey tone. Her large green eyes and petite features seemed wasted on the pink track bottoms and the oversized T-shirt she was wearing.

This wasn't the Kerry she recognised from her Facebook photos sporting flawless skin and fitted clothing, always showing off her slender figure. At school, Kerry always owned and wore the newest of trends and had the most stylish of haircuts. She was everything the other girls at school aspired to be. Now, without her make-up, she looked so ordinary, if not slightly pockmarked. Maybe they had more in common than Cass thought.

'Cass, are you okay?'

She realised she'd been staring. 'Sorry, yes. It's just been such a long time.' She reached into her bag. 'I thought you might need this.' She held the bottle of bargain rosé wine up and smiled. Instantly, she wondered if she should have spent a little more on the wine, not getting the bottle from the fiver basket. Kerry was more of a vintage woman, she guessed.

'That's lovely of you. Well, don't stand on the doorstep all night. I best get the corkscrew out.'

Cass knew there was no need for a corkscrew. She followed Kerry through the large hallway with its reception sofa and wide central staircase. Underneath stood a large white plinth containing a vase full of dying carnations, the same ones from the wedding reception centrepiece.

At twenty-five, Kerry had everything. There was no way Cass could ever invite her to her scruffy flat. She would bet everything she had that the corner of the bathroom, or should she say bathrooms, wouldn't have a regularly recurring patch of mildew spores reaching for the lighting. She could also guarantee that Kerry wouldn't need to place a collection of buckets around the house during rain showers. She wanted to slap herself. Kerry was her friend and her soon-to-be best friend. She couldn't envy her. Envy was an ugly trait, one she wished hadn't plagued her so readily.

Kerry led her through the double-door entrance into a large open plan kitchen and dining room with a table that seated around twelve. She grabbed two wine glasses from a cabinet and sat on a chair. 'Well, sit down. Take your coat off. Get comfortable.'

Cass smiled as she undid her Primark coat. She would also bet that Kerry didn't own any clothing that had come from Primark.

'Hearing from you reminded me of back then. I won't lie, it's been a bad few days. None of us can believe what happened to Holly.' Kerry poured them both a glass of wine and stared at the pink liquid.

Cass was sure she could see a bubble of water building up in the corner of Kerry's eye. If there's one thing she'd learned over the years it was to listen to people and never look shocked. Always keep a straight but friendly face and people would spill out their secrets and thoughts. 'I'm so sorry about what happened and I know we haven't spoken for a long time but we're friends and I'm here for you.'

Wiping a tear away, Kerry half smiled. 'I treated you badly at school. I can't believe you're here now. For years I thought about you. I thought you might never want to speak to me again. I was just a stupid kid. That's no excuse, I know, but I want to make things right. Losing Holly like we all did has made me realise how precious life is. I didn't want you to go through life hating me.' Kerry sniffed as she wiped her eyes.

'As you said, we were just kids. It doesn't matter any more. How are you coping?'

Kerry shrugged.

'It's okay, we don't have to talk. We can just drink.' Cass took a long swig of the wine and almost pulled a face. It was as sour as anything. She wished she'd picked the Zinfandel instead of the house wine but money was an issue. She didn't have everything and she definitely didn't have parents that propped her up financially, like Kerry did. 'So, where's the new husband?'

Kerry shrugged and poured some more wine. 'Who cares?'

'Oh, I'm sorry. I really should mind my own business.'

'You weren't meant to know. I bet you think I'm such a loser now.'

'Of course I don't. I mean, I'm the loser. Look at you, you really have your life together. Me, I'm stuck in a damp flat with a job I hate.'

Kerry walked across to a wooden unit and opened the door. 'Here, let's properly drink to us both being a pair of losers.' She placed two tiny shot glasses down and poured a couple of Sambucas. 'We never got to drink together as teens. We missed out. Let's make up for all those missed times. Drink.'

Cass stared at the glass. She'd never really done shots. The drinking culture had missed her out during her teen years. The most she'd had was a bottle of wine and Elvis had to carry her home from a friend's house. She swore she'd never get into that state again as she'd spent the night on their bathroom floor with her head leaning over the toilet bowl. She sipped the liquid and coughed as she watched Kerry down the shot in one.

'What's your fella like with you?'

Cass shrugged. 'He's okay, I think. Sometimes I'm not so sure. I don't know where he is half of the time but when we're together, he can be lovely.'

'So you're not sure if he's the one?'

She shook her head. 'No. He'll do.' She giggled a little to lighten the mood. 'How about you? Is Ed the one?'

'I married him.'

'That's not what I asked.' Cass took another sip of the Sambuca. 'I'm sorry. Elvis always tells me I'm too nosy.'

Kerry flicked her hair over her shoulder. Cass noticed the clip in strands beneath her layers. Those beautiful lengths of silky hair weren't all hers.

The smile on Kerry's face dropped. 'I don't trust him. He's cheated on me before.'

Cass coughed as she almost choked on her drink. So much for keeping a neutral expression.

'I know, I know. I thought things would change when we committed. Do you know what I mean?'

'Yes.' Cass knew exactly what Kerry meant. Her relationship with Elvis had changed immensely over the past few months. He'd gone from all over her and completely turned on as soon as they were in a room together to *meh, I'll do it if I have to*. However much she craved his attention, she knew she could never marry him. Forever was a big commitment; one which Kerry and Ed were already failing at. 'If I'm honest, I know Elvis isn't the one. I just like being with him at the moment. I bet that sounds horrible. I think he might be seeing someone else though.' There, she'd said it. Now Kerry might say something if she'd heard any gossip.

Kerry let out a snort and poured another Sambuca. 'You're falling behind.'

It looked like Kerry wasn't going to say anything. Maybe Cass had got it wrong about Elvis seeing Holly. Cass knocked the rest back, taking her breath away as the liquid burned her gullet. 'Fill it up.' A rosy glow flushed up her neck and her face burned up a little, in a nice way.

'What can I say? Ed and me. I think Ed enjoys the lifestyle.'

Cass could understand that. She'd once enjoyed the lifestyle that came with being Kerry's best friend. When that went, she'd felt so ordinary and it had stung even more when the beautiful people – Holly, Fran and Lilly – had stepped into her shoes.

'We had an argument today.' She paused and stared out of the window into the darkness that spanned acres of fields. No doubt one of them would house the stables for all her horses. 'He thinks our life isn't exciting enough. I mean, we have everything we flipping well want. Holidays, cars. How can it not be exciting?

I was obsessed with him, couldn't bear to let him go at whatever cost, so we got married. My dad wasn't happy about it. I mean, we'd only been together a year and we rushed it. My dad wanted me to get a prenuptial agreement but I couldn't ask him. It just felt so… cold. I wish I'd listened because since the reception, I've barely seen him. Holly died a few days ago. I need him to be here and he—'

Tears began to spill from Kerry's eyes. Cass was almost relieved that the drinking had ended. Another Sambuca and she'd be hoping Elvis would call her back just so that he could come to rescue her. She scraped her chair on the heated floor tiles and placed an arm around Kerry. It was just like old times.

'I was thinking of staying with my parents while I cleared my head. What a failure! Twenty-five and going back home.'

Cass was never going to lose her best friend again, whatever it cost. She gripped Kerry a little closer, closing her eyes as she comforted her broken friend.

'Ouch,' Kerry said as she pushed her away and wrenched one of her hair extensions from the crease in Cass's coat. 'Do you mind if we call it a night? I could do with being alone with my old friend, Sambuca.'

A message flashed up on Kerry's phone and the name lit up. It was from Lilly. Kerry scooped it up and paused while she read it.

Something had changed. Kerry was withdrawing.

'But… I want to be here for you.'

'I know and I'm grateful. Maybe another time. I'll message you, promise.'

Kerry really was desperate for her to leave. Her phone rang. It was Ed's name flashing up this time.

'Do you need a taxi? I can get you one.'

Cass shook her head. She wasn't after Kerry's money or help. 'No, I'll be okay. The bus stop's just down the road.'

'Message me tomorrow?' Kerry smiled. 'I really am grateful that you came. Thank you. I may be better company another day; my head is everywhere at the moment.'

Kerry stood to see her out and before Cass knew it, her friend gave her a light hug before closing the door, leaving Cass wholly unsatisfied by the whole experience. She looked up and then it hit her. The friend that had it all didn't really need someone like Cass, but she did need a confidante and tonight had been a start. Perseverance was all she needed.

Her stomach rumbled and the alcohol on an empty tummy began to churn. She couldn't resist the urge of food any longer. She almost wished she'd eaten the cake at work. Cass checked her phone as she followed the windy drive all the way back to the main road. No reply had come through from Elvis. She checked her watch. He was scheduled to finish work a few hours ago. She tried to call him but his phone went straight to voicemail.

CHAPTER THIRTY-FOUR

Gina tapped the window again, the one left of the communal door that was firmly locked. After ringing his buzzer several times, they soon realised that Phillip Brighton wasn't in. 'I wonder where he went?'

A twig snapped beneath her foot as Jacob shone his torch in her direction then through the window. 'He's probably back out there selling drugs. I doubt people like him change overnight.'

She nodded as they peered through his window. A pile of washing filled almost one half of the room. This was mixed with several pizza boxes, odd shoes and a mangled umbrella. His bed was pushed against the wall in front of the tiny worktop that displayed the microwave. His soiled bed sheets had been pulled back to reveal a stained mattress.

'No wonder he doesn't want to stay in. Dammit. I really needed to speak to him. Maybe he's gone.' Gina pressed her face against the glass and peered through again. What Phillip owned wouldn't be much to leave behind. He had a past record of drug abuse and dealing, and not all of his crimes had taken place in Cleevesford or even Warwickshire. He was a drifter, travelling from town to town. 'What were you doing at Holly's apartment, Phil?' The sound of an argument coming from a house a few doors away filled the night air and was soon followed by the barking of several dogs.

Jacob stepped back. 'It's no use us staying here. Shall we go and get a bite to eat?'

Gina thought of the cake in the fridge at the station but a takeaway was sounding far more appealing in her head. 'Sounds like a plan. We can grab some food and head back to the station. Let's hope our bailed drug dealer turns up at the station for his ten in the morning appointment. Something is telling me he's scarpered.'

'You have little faith, guv, but then again, I was wondering that myself.'

Gina's phone buzzed. She snatched it from her pocket as she followed Jacob back to her car. 'O'Connor?'

'It's Francesca Carter, guv.' The line crackled slightly as her signal dipped. She took a step back and it cleared.

'What about her?'

'Her body's just been found at her house. Forensics have been called and are already there cordoning the place off.' He reeled off a summary of what he knew.

Gina checked her watch. 'Dinner will have to wait.'

Jacob glanced back.

'Francesca Carter is dead. She appears to have been drowned in her own home.' Gina grabbed the door handle and slammed the car door shut with full force. 'We spoke to her today and she was fine. She was alive. Phillip Brighton and Samuel Avery were released and this happens.'

'We best get over there.'

She clipped her seat belt in and started up the engine. Another violent murder in less than a week. The pressure to get results had just been turned up to full. 'How many bridesmaids were there?'

Jacob flicked through his notes. 'Three.'

'So only Lilly Hill is still alive. Give O'Connor a call back. Get someone to check on her.'

Two out of three bridesmaids was a bit too much of a coincidence. There had to be a connection.

CHAPTER THIRTY-FIVE

He walked over, wearing only his boxer shorts, to the bed where she eagerly awaited him. Enthusiastic as ever, she bent her leg up and teased a few curls over her shoulders. She knew what was coming and she wanted it. Frannie hadn't realised what a gift he'd given her and if she hadn't have known things about him, it could have been so different. Frannie could have enjoyed this as much as the woman in front of him did.

He kneeled on the bed, right between her legs and pulled the tie from her hands. They both knew what was coming next. Goosebumps prickled her skin, each bump defined by the subtle lamp on the bedside. He crawled up further, running his large hand firmly up her legs, brushing her hips until he straddled her. She gulped and fixed her gaze on his.

Looping the tie around her neck, he smiled. They were both electrified by what they were about to do. She wriggled beneath him, taking the weight of his body with a slight expulsion of air as he rubbed against her, teasing her senses.

He felt her movements matching his and they knew it was time. She went to grab the tie, to loosen it but he wrenched her hand back, bending it at the wrist until she let it go over the side of the bed. He'd driven all the way back for this and now he was getting his reward.

'Shush,' he said as he placed his index finger across her lips and kissed her nose. All she had to do was lie back and let him get on with it, enjoy it, take it all in.

Was this enough?

It was definitely enough for now. It would have to be, but there was someone else. Her time would come soon. He wrenched the tie and watched as her face reddened but she knew better than to resist.

CHAPTER THIRTY-SIX

Jacob held the inner cordon tape up as Gina hurried underneath, nodding to the PC who guarded the scene. A couple of teenage girls hung around at the end of the drive and they were quickly joined by a woman wearing jeans and a jumper.

'What's going on,' she called out. 'I live just over the road. Is Francesca okay?'

Gina took a few steps towards her. Now would be a good time to check out what at least one of the neighbours had seen. 'Have you been in all evening?'

The woman nodded. The two girls stepped closer. Gina could see the resemblance now. They were her daughters. Both of them had the same dark skin tone and slight build. 'I've been in since about five. Is Fran okay?'

Glancing at the girls, Gina called her to one side. 'May I have a word with you?'

'Sally, take your sister in. I'll be back in a minute.'

The slightly taller girl nodded and took her sister back to their house.

'What's this about?' Her short curly hair bounced as she settled on a spot and stood, arms crossed in front of her.

'That's what we're here to find out.' Gina didn't want to say too much. She had no idea if Francesca's parents had even been told. The last thing she needed was for them to find out that their daughter had been murdered on social media. 'Have you seen anyone around here acting suspiciously this afternoon or evening?'

She shook her head. 'No. I came back from work and made dinner. That's what I do every night. The girls have just got back from swimming so they wouldn't have seen anything either. They came in and told me that the police were outside.'

Gina had hoped for more.

'Has someone broken into the place? I keep telling my husband we need to invest in better security.'

'No, it's not a burglary. There's been an incident and we're investigating at the moment.'

'Is it something to do with her husband? They're a funny couple.'

That piqued Gina's interest. From what O'Connor had reeled off to her, her husband, Charlie Carter, had been at his mother's fitting a curtain pole earlier that evening but knowing more about them could be of some help. 'What makes you say that?'

'I don't know. When they first moved in a few months ago, I thought they seemed lovely but they shout all the time. She's always yelling at him about something, often trivial things like how he positions the bins back when they've been emptied. Then he will yell at her when they're coming home from shopping. I think they had money worries. They seemed to be shouting about her spending habits. I don't think it was just me who heard it all, the other neighbours probably did too – they have been rather loud. My husband keeps saying that Charlie loves himself. Charlie is rather well preened so I think he's just a bit jealous.' The woman laughed a little. 'That was it really.'

'Well, thank you for your help, err…'

'Annie.'

'Thanks, Annie. I best get back to my work.' Gina left the woman behind the cordon and headed towards the door. She now had something to discuss with Charlie Carter. Their arguments would be a start. Could Charlie Carter have arranged for someone to hurt Francesca on his behalf? He may not have been present at the scene but that did not warrant crossing him off the suspect list, not yet.

She hurried along the drive, past the forensics van and the police cars. Several crime scene investigators huddled around discussing what they would be doing and Bernard towered over them all. Slipping his beard into a beard cover, he nodded her way. Jacob was standing near a well-trimmed hedge, talking to Jennifer. He placed a loving hand on her arm and she smiled as she did up her forensics suit.

'You got here fast.' Bernard passed Gina a coverall, gloves, hair and boot covers and she began speaking as she slipped them on.

'We were only around the corner following up on another lead. No luck with that tonight. Have you assessed the scene as yet?'

He nodded. 'I'll take you up in a moment. Two of my team are in the bathroom taking the crime scene photos. The husband is with an officer in the kitchen. He found his wife's body so I'm sure he'll have a lot to say to you.'

'What are your initial thoughts?'

Annie, the neighbour she'd spoken to only minutes earlier, had returned with her husband and several other neighbours and they were beginning to flock around the cordon.

'I think we should go inside.' Bernard glanced at the forming crowd.

Gina agreed. A little privacy would make things easier. She followed Bernard through the front door, straight onto the stepping plates in the hallway and up the stairs.

'We'll go in the spare room to talk.' They took a left through the first door.

As Gina followed him, she glanced to the side and saw a woman in a white suit snapping away in the bathroom.

'Finally, a place with no eavesdroppers. Right, we got here forty minutes ago and sealed the scene off immediately. What we have is the body of a young woman identified by her husband as Francesca Carter. She is lying dead in the bathtub. My initial thought is that she died by drowning.'

'Intentional or accidental?'

A serious expression washed over his face. 'Definitely intentional. There are signs of a struggle. The bathroom is soaking wet and there is a lot of red bruising to her chest and neck. A clump of her hair has been pulled out and discarded onto the bathroom floor. Her ankles and feet have bled quite a lot and there is blood on the taps. It looks like she'd been kicking them during the struggle. Everything is leading us to conclude that her death was intentional. The shower curtain and pole are on the floor too.'

'She or the perp may have grabbed it.'

'We will need to carry out the post-mortem to confirm exact cause of death.'

Gina felt her head beginning to thump. She wanted to stand in a dark room, just like Briggs had been doing. She wanted the noise of everything to quieten just for a moment so that she could order her chaotic thoughts. 'Only a few days ago, Holly Long was suffocated to death. Today, Francesca Carter has died in what looks to be a drowning. Both starved of oxygen but both being killed in different ways. Both had been bridesmaids at the same wedding. Can you give me the time of death?'

'Given all that we've tested and found so far, the water temperature in the bath and that of the body suggest that Francesca Carter was killed approximately two hours ago, give or take half an hour each way.'

'So around seven this evening?'

'Give or take half an hour to an hour each way. Do you want to see the scene before her body is taken away?'

She nodded. She didn't want to see any such scene. She wished there wasn't one to see, but she owed it to her victim to see exactly what her attacker had done to her. A sinking feeling washed through her. Only a few hours ago, Francesca had been

in the station telling them of the assault against her and Gina
had failed in her duties. Samuel Avery had walked. If he'd done
this, she knew she'd struggle to forgive herself. She felt a lump
forming in her throat as her gaze fixed on the bathroom.

Bernard covered his mouth and beard again, then beckoned
her to follow him.

Lights on, the starkness of the bathroom almost made her
wince. The crime scene assistant sidestepped around her and out
of the door, giving Gina and Bernard some room to step inside.

The young woman lay crumpled in the murky bath, the sole
of her bent over foot wrinkled. Her large brown eyes had a glassy
death stare where she'd finally rested on the curve of the bath.
She looked more petite than Gina remembered. When Gina lay
in the bath, she often had to throw a leg over the side as it never
felt long enough. Francesca was almost cocooned by the tub. Her
brown hair splayed all around her.

'Any sign of flowers anywhere?'

'No, none. We found her phone though. It has been catalogued
and placed with the evidence.' Bernard awkwardly waited by her
side. 'There was also a note found in the bath but the ink had ran
all over the page. I couldn't tell what was written on it.'

'Thank you.'

The shower curtain had been pulled from the rings, some
of which had pinged across the room, lying broken on the
floor. Gina took a step back. Before she went, she needed to
speak to Francesca's husband. She needed to be able to read
his expressions herself and she needed to get to the bottom of
their relationship.

'Keep me updated as you get results.' What she really wanted
to know was if something had been lodged in Francesca's throat.

Bernard nodded and gave a muffled reply under his mask.
'Will do. We're going to be collecting evidence for most of the
evening and through the night. I'll keep you posted.'

Gina let out a sigh as she left the room and pulled her mask away from her face. A bead of sweat had trickled down the side of her temple and onto her ear. The panic that must have been coursing through Francesca's body during her murder was already starting to haunt Gina. She swallowed and took a deep breath before heading downstairs to see what Charlie Carter had to say.

CHAPTER THIRTY-SEVEN

Charlie Carter sat at the kitchen table with his head in his hands and a glass in front of him. The bottle of Irish whiskey stood open. He swigged the contents of the glass and refilled it.

'I wish I'd stayed at home and waited for her. She should have come over to my mother's and spent the evening with us. Something was wrong. I know it. She hadn't seemed herself since Holly's murder.'

Gina gently stepped into the room and sat at the table opposite him. 'I think the murder of a close friend would do that to anyone.'

He shook his head and looked up with glassy blue eyes. 'It wasn't that. She wasn't telling me something. I should have been there more but I just wanted to go back to work. I couldn't be around all this grief and misery. It's just not me and not many people understand that. I'm not a tea and sympathy kind of guy.'

His defined jaw and stubble made him look quite ruggedly handsome but his hair really smartened him up. The classic cut gave his dark hair a precise side-parted line. He was older than Francesca by about ten years, Gina could tell that much. She also knew what secret Francesca was holding onto, that of the sexual assault she'd reported, but now wasn't the right time to upset her bereaved husband even more.

He slammed his fist onto the glass table, making all the fixings underneath shake. 'I should have been here. I shouldn't have gone to work. What kind of husband leaves his wife and goes off to work after something so horrible has happened? She must have died hating me.' He swigged his drink down in one.

'Would you like us to contact her parents?'

'I've already called her father. Her mother died a few years ago. He should be here in a couple of hours. He's absolutely devastated, as am I.'

Gina pulled out her pocket notebook. 'I'm so sorry this has happened but we need to catch the person who did this to Francesca and we need your help. Would you be able to answer a few questions?'

A recurring twitch on his cheek caught her eye. She knew he was grinding his teeth behind his closed mouth.

'Yes, of course I will. If you find out who did this, I'll kill him myself.' He snatched the bottle and poured another drink.

'Can you please tell me where you were today?'

'Am I a suspect?' He tilted his head to the side and scratched his stubble.

'These questions are just routine.'

He exhaled slowly and leaned back in his chair. 'I was at the office from nine in the morning. Then I was at court between ten and twelve. Back at the office about twelve thirty as that's how long it takes me to get from the courts to my office. I left the office about five and came home. Fran wasn't in. I left her a note in the kitchen.' Gina remembered what Bernard had said about a note being found in the bath.

'What did you write?'

His brow furrowed. 'I can't remember the exact wording. I just said I was at my mother's fixing a curtain pole and I told her to come over so that we could all get a takeaway but she didn't want to come.'

'What is it you do for a living?'

'I'm a solicitor. I practise family law, that's why I was at court this morning and it's also why I didn't want any time off. My client was going through a difficult time with not having any contact with her child.'

'Can you think of anyone who would want to harm Francesca? Any known enemies?'

He leaned forward and placed his head in his hands. 'I don't know why anyone would want to hurt her. She was such a sweet person. I can't imagine my life without her even though we have our petty squabbles. I don't know what I'm going to do.'

Gina made a few notes. He'd admitted to squabbling with his wife. She needed to know a little more. 'What did you argue about?'

His hands dropped back to the table with a thud. 'I didn't hurt her. I was at my mother's. I came back and found my wife in the bath, dead. Why is this relevant?'

For a moment, their gazes met, neither wanting to say the next word. Gina gave him a moment. Sometimes silence acted as a prompt.

'If you must know, we argued about money, that's all. I earn a substantial sum but Fran, I love her to bits—' A moment of realisation hit him as he closed his eyes, trying to force away a potential tear. 'I will always love her, you understand.'

Gina nodded. She had a dead ex-husband and if the hatred she still felt towards him was as strong as Charlie's love, then yes, she understood.

'She liked to spend. I could see our bank balance going down all the time. She had no idea how to budget. The clothes, the holidays, it was as if she was constantly trying to keep up with her friends who all seem to be more well off. I'm from working-class stock. My mother had to budget for everything so I suppose the reckless spending worried me. Anyway, I didn't mind for the first couple of years. When she agreed to go out with me, I felt like the luckiest person in the world. She was funny, beautiful and she made me feel like I was her everything. I'd just come out of a bad relationship myself and I'd hit an all-time low. Drinking, being late for work; I'd lost weight. She saved me. I don't know what I'm going to do without her. If she was here now, I'd tell her to spend everything. It wouldn't matter. It's just money.' He leaned back and stared up at the ceiling. 'I can't do this now. I need time to let this sink in.' He got up and moved over to the worktop.

'Thank you, Mr Carter. I promise you we'll be doing everything to catch whoever did this to your wife. Just to warn you, we will be putting out an appeal on the news. We need witnesses to come forward.'

'Do it. Do whatever you can. Just catch who did this.' He began to breathe through his teeth and stood against the worktop as he seethed. He crouched over the sink and let out a roar.

All Gina could see in Charlie Carter was a broken man. Footsteps echoed through the hallway and Jacob peered through the door. 'Guv, can I have a word?'

She nodded as she removed a card from the small pile she kept in her pocket. 'Mr Carter, we will need you to make a formal statement as soon as you can. If, in the meantime, you remember anything, however trivial you think it might be, please call me straight away.'

He took the card and stared out of the kitchen window at the garden. Gina glanced out at the back gate. A crime scene assistant was swabbing the catch. 'Do you keep your gate locked?'

'We tried to remember to lock it but we never did. This is a safe neighbourhood. We've never worried about these things.' He held his hand out and looked away as if to say that was all she was getting out of him that night. Gina sensed she needed to leave him alone.

She left him to his grief in the kitchen and followed Jacob out. 'What is it?'

'Footprint in a patch of earth just outside the garden. Size nine and a popular brand of work boot.'

Carla Kovach

It was more than she expected but less than she'd hoped for. 'Average and popular. Narrows it down a little but not much, but I'll take that for now.'

She saw a pair of Charlie Carter's shoes under the stairs. Bending down for a quick look at the underside, she shook her head. 'Elevens. Call the bride. We need to speak to her. Two bridesmaids is too much of a coincidence and this can't wait until tomorrow. Find out where Samuel Avery is. Also, put a look out on Phillip Brighton. If he wasn't in his bedsit at the time of Francesca's murder, where was he?'

CHAPTER THIRTY-EIGHT

Fat tears plopped onto the empty chip wrapper. Cass wiped the slithering damp from her glistening face as she checked her phone. There had been no reply from Elvis and despite Kerry telling her to message tomorrow, she'd gone ahead and messaged her during the bus journey home. Kerry hadn't replied either, but she'd read the message. She hated herself for being so impatient and chips, pie, a sausage and three scallops had filled a temporary gap.

A cramp seared across her upper stomach. She was in for a night of stomach hell and the lingering smell of grease was making her guts turn, that and the thought of the Sambuca she'd sipped with Kerry. She hadn't wanted them. Deceptively, her stomach had screamed for the food but now all it did was rebel at the contents she'd guzzled at super speed.

The key turned in the lock. Elvis was home. He kicked the stiff door and it bounced back from the jamb on the wall as he muttered obscenities against their landlord. 'Cass. You in?'

She grabbed the chip papers and wedged them into the plastic bin, swiftly dropping the lid on it. Snatching the tea towel, she began wafting the smell, trying to get rid of it.

'Are we having chips? I'm starving.'

She sat at the table, her back to him as she wiped a tear away. 'I had no idea when you'd be home so I didn't get you any chips. I tried to call but you didn't answer.'

He kicked the table leg. 'I'm not allowed to do anything without you nagging me. My phone battery ran out.' No sooner

had he said the last word of his sentence than his phone beeped.
'But I managed to charge it at the Angel.'

'So, is that where you were?'

He paused and walked over to the cupboard, opening the
doors. 'Here we go with the questions again. Do I ask where you
are every minute of the day?'

Now she thought of it, he never asked her a thing about her
day. It was as if he didn't care. He always expected her to be with
him when he wanted her around. She helped him and his slimy
boss, Samuel, with their functions and got paid a pittance. She
did these things to help him and he never appreciated a thing.

'It's all about you, isn't it?'

'And what the hell does that mean. I work all the hours I can
get so that we can get out of this dump and just because I want
a couple of hours with my mates, you're on my case.'

She wanted to ask who these mates were but the more she
spoke, the worse things would get and that could result in him
walking out again. Besides, when she got closer to Kerry, she
knew she'd change, and that would show him. She'd rip the rug
from under his feet and watch him tumble.

'Why have we got no food?'

She shrugged.

'You see to yourself. How selfish. That's you all over, isn't it,
Cass? Selfish with a big fat capital S. Look at this.'

She turned to see what he was pointing at.

'Beans, a tin of tuna, parsnip soup – I mean, who eats parsnip
soup?' He opened the fridge. 'Cauliflower rice and not much
else. You buy this crap and neither of us eat it. Do you think it
just looks good in the fridge? We both know that it'll end up in
the bin and you'll stuff your face with the shittiest food going.'
She glanced away, shame burning on her face. His phone beeped
again. He pulled it from his pocket and preened his quiff as he
read the message. 'Stuff it. I'll get my own food.' He picked up

the wine receipt she'd thrown on the worktop. 'What's this? Are you sitting here drinking when I'm not here? Is that why you're like this?'

'No. Let me explain.'

His phone beeped again.

'Wait,' she called as he stomped out of the room. 'Don't go.' Even with him yelling at her, she still wanted him to stay and not to run to whoever was texting. Her bottom lip began to quiver. She had been selfish. She'd thought about herself and her need to fill a gaping emotional hole when she'd passed the chip shop. She hadn't known when he'd be home otherwise she'd have got him something too and now he'd gone.

Her mind wandered over all the possibilities that could make up Elvis's secret. Was she someone he worked with? A pretty girl had started at the pub, maybe it was her. Or, maybe it was someone he met at the wedding reception a few days ago. He hadn't seemed himself since. They had their moments but something had changed and she wondered if this was the end of their relationship. She mulled over her conversation with Kerry. She'd confessed to not being totally in love with Elvis. Maybe he could sense that, which is why he was spending his time with someone else. There wasn't much binding them together apart from a shared tenancy on a crummy flat, one she could just about manage to pay on her own if she really had to. She had to get to the bottom of what was happening.

She checked her watch and her phone. No reply from Kerry. Her friend had seen the message an hour ago and nothing, not the simplest of replies. She grabbed her coat and left. Now that she and Kerry's friendship had been rekindled, she wasn't about to let it slide.

CHAPTER THIRTY-NINE

'Mrs Powell, we're so sorry to disturb you. May we come in?' Gina glanced at Jacob as Kerry Powell stared at their identification. The young woman's face was smeared with mascara and several of her clipped in hair extensions were tangled in her own hair. Her enlarged pupils, red cheeks and the pungent smell of stale alcohol gave her away.

'Why are you here?' Kerry filled the doorway, swaying from side to side as she waited for an explanation.

'It might be best if we come in.'

Kerry stared and grinned before allowing the door to swing back. She led the way without telling them to follow.

'I think that means enter,' Jacob whispered.

The large hallway screamed wealth. Gina now understood who Charlie Carter was referring to when he mentioned Francesca's rich friends. She spotted the dying flowers under the stairs.

The large double doors led to the hugest kitchen and dining room ever. A shot of Sambuca and an empty bottle of wine sat at one end of the table. Gina's shoes clipped on the porcelain tiles, the sound echoing through the room as she took a few more steps closer to the table.

'Sambuca? There's plenty for all of us.' Kerry smiled at them and gestured for them to sit.

'Not while on duty,' Jacob replied.

'No, thank you.' Gina had come to ask her questions but she wondered if Kerry was in any fit state to answer.

'I'd offer you a coffee but,' she shrugged, 'I haven't got any.'

Her speech was a little drawn out but Gina understood her perfectly. 'Are you okay?'

'As okay as anyone is when their best friend was murdered at her wedding reception. I don't know the meaning of okay. I have a husband now. Fat lot of good he is. Where is he? Who knows? My whole life is falling apart.' Kerry leaned forward over the table and began to sob.

Gina nodded to Jacob and he flicked to a new page in his notebook to write down that Edward Powell wasn't at home, with the time next to it. 'Have you been on your own all day?'

She shook her head, rubbing a mixture of snot and tears into her straw-like hair. 'My friend, Cass, came to see how I was a while ago. We had a drink.'

'How about your husband?'

'I don't know. I never know. He said he was busy working then he was meeting with friends. He just left me here, like this, like he does all too often. If I go AWOL, he moans like mad. How could he leave me like this?'

Gina passed her a packet of pocket tissues and the young woman removed one and blew her nose. 'Do you have anyone who will come here and be with you?'

Kerry passed her mobile phone to Gina. 'My mum. Her number is under Mum. Can you tell her I need her? Her name's Alison.'

Gina could tell Kerry was the type of person who mostly got people to do things for her. Given what she was about to tell her, she'd let it slide and call her mum for her. She pressed the number and a woman answered. 'Hello. This is DI Harte and I'm with your daughter, at her house. She's asked me to call. Could you please come and be with her?'

The woman agreed and ended the call after a few concerned words.

'You look like you've got something to say, DI Harte.'

Gina swallowed and cleared her throat. She knew O'Connor had since called Francesca's family but given what had happened to Holly, Kerry needed to know about Francesca too. 'Shall we wait until your mother arrives?'

'No. I want to know what you have to say.' Her brow scrunched, like that of a child about to have a tantrum.

'I'm afraid I have some bad news.'

Kerry shrugged. 'I've had the worst so spill. There's nothing up there,' she held her hand above her head, 'that could be worse than what happened to Holly. Nothing.'

Gina doubted that. 'I'm so sorry, Kerry. Francesca Carter, your friend, has been murdered this evening. I really am sorry.'

Kerry's bottom lip shook before she burst into tears. 'No, she can't—'

'I know this is hard and you must be shocked, but someone out there did this to your friend and we need you to answer a few questions so that we can find who did it. Would you be able to do that?'

Screaming out, she wrapped her arms around her front and bent over the table. 'No! Who's doing this to me?'

'To you?'

'They are my friends. It was my wedding.'

Gina went to speak but then stopped, allowing Kerry to cry until her sobs subsided.

'Can you please tell me more about you, Francesca and Holly? How you all met and how you know each other.'

Kerry went to sip the shot of Sambuca but changed her mind and placed it back down. 'I think I've had enough to drink. Fran and Holly, we met at primary school. We have been best friends through our childhood and our teens. We've always been close, meeting up for lunch regularly, speaking on the phone. We've helped each other get over bad boyfriends. We've held each other's hair back in nightclub toilets when we had too much to drink. I love them both like they're my sisters. There's also Lilly, she's the fourth one in our group – the Awesome Foursome – and the other bridesmaid at my wedding. We've always been friends. I thought we'd all be besties until the end and now two of them are gone. Who would do this?'

'That's what we're trying to find out. Can you think back to your wedding in Crete?'

Kerry scraped the chair on the tiles and hurried to the sink and poured a glass of water. 'I can't stand the stale taste of that stuff any more.' She pointed to the bottle on the table as she dragged her feet on the floor and sat back in her chair. 'What would any of this have to do with our wedding? Please don't taint that memory too. It's bad enough that Holly was murdered at my reception.'

'We have to ask. When we interviewed Lilly at the reception, she told us that in Crete on the night of your wedding she went to bed early, leaving everyone at the bar celebrating. She heard Holly arguing with someone outside, by the pool. We don't know who she was talking to. I know this is a long shot, but can you remember anyone being missing during that evening or during the early hours of the next day?'

'I was pretty wasted.'

'Or do you remember anyone seeming a little off or did Holly say anything to you?'

'This has got something to do with her secret man, hasn't it?'

Gina crossed her ankles under the table. 'Do you know who that was?'

She shook her head. 'She kept denying there was a man, but Lilly saw him through Holly's letterbox. She wouldn't let her in when she went over, even though she was in. I really don't know who he was though.'

Sighing, Gina pulled a photo from her notebook. 'Do you know this man?'

'Everyone knows him. That's Phil the Pill.'

'Phil the Pill?'

'He's got a pill for everything. I shouldn't say any more.'

Gina took the photo back. 'We found drugs and money on him on the night of your reception. He was at the venue and he didn't have an invite. We know why he was there.'

'Okay. Everyone knows he dabbles and passes on a few light drugs, mostly pills and weed. Someone must have called him for some stuff or maybe he was chancing it by turning up.'

'How about Holly? Did she know him?' Gina already had reports of him being at her apartment block. If she could prove that Phillip Brighton knew her, then she'd have reasonable grounds for further questioning.

'Definitely. We bought some weed off him once. He lives in Cleevesford. He drinks in the Angel Arms. Everyone knows him.'

'He was seen outside her block of flats a few weeks ago. Do you know why he'd be there?'

Kerry leaned back and wiped her nose once again. 'Maybe this man in her life fancied a smoke. Holly didn't smoke or do drugs. I don't think it would be her putting in an order or maybe she was buying it for him.'

Gina popped the photo back in her notebook.

Kerry placed her palm on her forehead and began pressing. 'My head isn't good.'

'You're doing really well. Just one more thing—'

The main door burst open bringing with it a light breeze through the large building. 'Kerry, love. What's happening? Oh my goodness, look at you.' Alison Reed, the mother of the bride walked in. From the statements, Gina knew she was a little older than herself at forty-nine, but she looked much younger. Her sun-streaked straight hair flowed over her shoulders and down her back as she moved with elegance in her skinny jeans and calf length boots. Her svelte figure could have had her mistaken for a teenager from behind. Her light swing coat fell over her shoulders. On another day, Gina could have been convinced the two women were sisters. 'What are you doing here?' The woman stepped back, staring at Gina and Jacob.

'I'm afraid we've had more bad news. Francesca Carter has been murdered this evening and we needed to speak to Kerry.'

'What for? Kerry wouldn't have had anything to do with that.'

'I'm not suggesting that she did but both Holly Long and Francesca Carter were bridesmaids at your daughter's wedding.' Witness statements had clearly placed Kerry in the main reception room at the time of Holly's murder.

A pale Kerry nestled into her mother's arms and began to weep quietly.

'I think she's had enough of a shock tonight. Is my daughter safe when there's some crazed murderer on the loose?'

Gina didn't know. She hoped that Kerry was safe. 'As she's alone, it might be best if someone stays with her.'

'Where's Ed?'

Gina wanted the answer to that question too but Kerry simply shrugged.

'Come on, baby girl. I'm taking you home with me tonight. I think she's had enough for now.' With that, Alison Reed helped her daughter up. Taking her coat off, she placed it around Kerry's shoulders. 'It might be best if you call her tomorrow.' The woman picked up the Sambuca bottle. 'Looks like she's had a few too many. Yes, tomorrow would be best. Come on. Follow me out, I'm locking up.'

'Can you set the alarm, Mummy?'

'Of course. Come on. Dad's making you some food. Looks like you need something to soak up the alcohol.'

Gina rolled her eyes at Jacob as the woman led her exhausted drunken daughter towards the door. Within minutes, they were standing on the winding drive, listening to Alison's performance car whizzing off down the road.

As the breeze picked up, the trees in the garden rustled.

'Did you hear that?'

'What?' Jacob looked across the lamplit lawn.

'I thought I heard a twig cracking.' She walked over to the dense clump of trees and listened carefully. Not a sound came from them. She pulled her torch out of her bag and shone it through the gap. 'I think I'm cracking up. Lack of food probably.'

Jacob smirked as he walked towards the car. 'I know how you feel. I'm hallucinating pizza.'

Jacob's phone beeped at the same time as Gina's. She read the message from O'Connor.

We found a receipt in Francesca Carter's bag, dated the 11th April. One for the cash purchase of a meal at Piccolo's, an Italian restaurant on the edge of town. Her husband has no idea who she had this meal with. He didn't even know she'd had a meal there without him. It is apparently their special place. It's where he proposed to her.

'Not another spanner in this investigation. Who on earth was Francesca out having dinner with? This gets more confusing by the minute.' Gina opened the car door and slumped in the seat. 'Right, back to the station.'

'I've just read the email that has followed. No one has managed to locate Samuel Avery or Phillip Brighton. Both of them weren't where we'd expect them to be when Francesca was murdered.' Jacob scrolled down to the end of the email, his phone lighting up the car's dark interior.

Gina pressed send on a quick message to Hannah. She needed to know if Avery was with her.

'We can add our groom to that list, Edward Powell. I want to know where he's been.'

CHAPTER FORTY

Tuesday, 12 May 2020

Gina threw her keys on the kitchen table and glanced at the kitchen clock. Two in the morning. After the initial briefing and updating the boards, uniform had been tasked with door to doors and the team were on the lookout for Samuel Avery and Phillip Brighton. There had been no word from Edward Powell, their missing groom.

She glanced at her phone. There was still no word from Hannah either. After driving by the bed and breakfast on the way home she had made a mental note that Hannah's car hadn't been parked around the front. Gina felt her stomach sink and her body weaken a little as she imagined her daughter being away somewhere with one of the very men in the town she despised. Avery couldn't be her future too. In her mind, they'd already had the wedding and Gracie was calling him Daddy Sam. No, that couldn't happen. Her heart thumped as she tried Hannah's number again and it rang. Within seconds the call was cut off. *Not good enough.* She called again, then again.

'Mum, do you know what time it is?'

'Why didn't you answer my message earlier, Hannah?'

There was a pause. Gina heard a crashing of objects hitting the ground.

'Bloody hell! I've knocked a glass of water over now.'

'Where are you? You weren't at the Cleaver when I passed it an hour ago.'

'Last time I looked, I'm a grown adult who can do as she pleases. If you really must know, I'm not staying there tonight.'

Gina took a deep breath and furrowed her brow. 'Is he with you?'

'Who?'

'Samuel Avery. Is he with you now?'

'Of course he isn't.'

Steadying herself against the worktop, Gina gazed down at her feet. He wasn't with her; that meant he was out there somewhere but not at his pub, where he also lived. The images of Hannah and Avery's wedding were vanishing. Maybe she'd jumped to the worst possible conclusion. Hannah was having a little bad patch in her relationship and maybe she had been seeking a little comfort in Avery, the expert manipulator, but he wasn't with her now.

'Where are you?'

'At Nanny Hetty's. Gracie wasn't feeling too well so I came over a couple of hours ago and said I'd stay for a bit. I fell asleep on the couch.'

'Is she okay?'

'It's nothing, just a bit of a sniffle. Apart from that, she's having a lovely time catching up with family and they love her being here.'

Gina's shoulders dropped. 'Hannah, it's really important that you answer my next question as honestly as possible. Were you with Samuel Avery this evening?'

There was a long pause. 'He came over to the bed and breakfast about ten. He said he was checking that I was okay. It was a bit random.'

'Why would he be checking that you were okay? Is something the matter?'

There was a tap at the front door. She crept across the dark lounge and peered out of her front window. Briggs's car was parked next to hers. She unlocked the door and pointed to her phone. He smiled, came in and sat on the sofa in front of the log burner. Gina hurried back into the kitchen, closing the door behind her. Whatever Hannah had to say, she didn't want Briggs to hear for the time being.

'Hannah. What's going on with you and Greg?'

'I don't want to talk about it but I will tell you something, Sam hasn't done anything wrong.'

Gina wondered why he'd turned up to see Hannah at ten in the evening. What had he been doing before? 'How did Sam seem when he turned up?'

'A little distant, if I'm honest. Don't freak out, Mum. He seemed a bit lost so I walked outside with him for a while. Then he went on with this stupid little spiel about how beautiful I was as he stroked my hair.'

Stomach tightening, Gina waited patiently for Hannah to continue. One wrong word could lead to Hannah dropping the call and turning her phone off.

'It's not that I can't handle that type of thing. It's just—'

Gina felt her teeth clenching together. After the accusation from Francesca about the assault, her mind flashed to an image of Hannah fighting him off, getting in her car and hurrying over to Gina's dead ex-husband's mother's house to be with Gracie.

'His hands were getting a bit spaghetti man. That's all. I told him to go home and said we'd talk in the morning.'

'And?' Had that one word ended Hannah's flow?

'And what? That was it. He held his hands up, smiled and said sorry. He said he'd call in the morning and went on about how he shouldn't have come to see me. He seemed a bit, I don't know, depressed, then he said he had to get back to the pub. You know, Mum, he's not that bad, I think he's just a little lost.'

A little lost – Gina hoped that her daughter wasn't falling for that act. Samuel Avery had just changed his strategy. Gina knew he hadn't been at the Angel all night and he hadn't gone back to the Angel later either, so where had he been and who had he been with? Or had he been stalking Francesca, waiting for her to come home before seizing his opportunity to kill her. So far, her theory didn't contain enough evidence to arrest him, not after already questioning him. She needed to dig deeper or, she knew for sure, he'd kick up a huge stink.

'Mum, I can hear stirring in the other rooms. I think I've woken the others up. I could do without Gracie waking up too. Can we speak tomorrow?'

'Did he assault you?'

'No! For heaven's sake, he fancies me, Mum, that's all. Look, it was nothing. It's not like some guy hasn't got all spaghetti hands on me before. He stopped. He left me alone when I asked him to. It was nothing so let's leave it at that. Goodnight, Mum.'

Hannah ended the call. Gina opened the fridge door and slammed it hard, rattling the two old bottles of tonic in the fridge. Thoughts of Avery turning up to see Hannah, his hands snaking around her daughter's body while she pushed him off, filled her mind. What also angered her was that Hannah's acceptance of his behaviour had normalised it to the point she'd even talk to him the next day as if nothing had happened. Her mind whirled with thoughts of Hannah and Greg and the many possibilities of what might be going wrong between them.

The kitchen door creaked open and Briggs peered through. 'Everything alright?'

'I'll fill you in over a drink. Gin and tonic?'

'I won't be able to drive home if I say yes.' His gaze met hers.

She leaned closer to him and smiled. 'I have a very comfortable couch and my cat would love a slumber party.'

Ebony meowed as she ran over to her dinner bowl and crunched on a chunk of dried food.

'I just love sleeping on a couch.'

Gina poured the tonic over the gin and passed him a glass. He took a sip and cocked his head to one side while shutting one eye. 'There's a lot of gin in there, Gina.'

'There certainly is.' She took a swig. 'It's been a long day and I need to sleep – the gin will help. Why are you here?'

'Can we sit?'

She nodded and followed him into the lounge. He'd lit a small fire and the log had just taken hold of the flames. They both sat in the dark room, staring at the flames that danced away.

'You don't trust me, I know you don't. I understand why you wouldn't trust anyone. I needed to come here and remind you of what you have on me and the power that secret holds.'

She scrunched her brows and gave a small laugh. 'You haven't killed anyone.'

'I threatened to set a suspect up with a crime he hadn't committed and I did it to keep him off your back.'

'Is this about Stephen?' Terry's brother, the man who was so similar to her abusive ex-husband.

'It still plays on my mind. You know me, I'd had a clean career up to that point. Only you know that I threatened to pin an unsolved historical murder on him by creating evidence.'

'But there was no real evidence. You couldn't have followed it through.'

'He didn't know that and he still doesn't. What I'm trying to say is that this bit of information could absolutely ruin me; pension, reputation, the lot. You could arrest me at any point and I'm sure Stephen would happily shout about the injustice of it to all who would listen. I will keep your secret forever and I know you'll keep mine. I just wanted you to trust me, that's all. I want you to know, I'm on your side.'

She shook her head and placed her gin glass on the coffee table. 'Those two things aren't in the same league, are they?'

'No, my crime was well calculated, yours was a result of years of abuse. I know who'd be demonised more. I know who would have a harder time in prison. The abused wife against the corrupt DCI.'

He was right. She'd never thought of things that way. He slipped off his shoes and put his feet up on the sofa, lying on the cushion as he watched the logs crackle. The glow of the flames flickered in his irises. She slipped her own shoes off and curled into his body, allowing him to spoon her. He placed his large hand over her shoulders and placed his chin on her head as he kept her warm. Soon the fire would burn out and a chill would bring them back to reality.

She shivered as she thought back to Avery and her daughter. With her alarm set for five thirty, she'd be back at the station soon, sifting through all the new leads, if indeed there were any. A gentle snore filled the room. It had been a long day. Gina wouldn't be sleeping through that but, equally, she didn't want to leave him to go to her cold bed upstairs. Her phone flashed. It was a message from Bernard. Carefully, she slid her arm out of Briggs's embrace and selected the message. Finally, they had their forensics link between the two murder scenes.

CHAPTER FORTY-ONE

'So, that's the state of things,' Gina said as she added Samuel Avery to the board under Francesca Carter's photo. Everyone in the room now knew of her daughter's involvement with this man. Wyre had almost offered her deepest condolences. She grabbed a pain au chocolat from the packet that Jacob had brought in and she took a bite. Briggs brushed past O'Connor and PCs Smith and Kapoor, before catching Gina's gaze for a second.

He sat at the head of the table. 'Bernard, can you kick off? I know you have something to say.'

Bernard flicked through the many pages of his report. 'All findings so far have been emailed to you all. As you all know, we are still working through evidence gathered at Cleevesford Manor and the clearing. We are trying to compare as much as possible to evidence collected at Francesca Carter's house and we now have a link. The size nine shoe impression that was discovered just outside Francesca Carter's back fence is a direct match to a partial print we found in the clearing in the woodland at the back of Cleevesford Manor. The Cleevesford Manor print was the hardest to distinguish. As it was only a partial print, we had to scrutinise it closer but a person's gait is quite unique, there is a slight wearing at one side of the shoe. The print at the Carter household was deep and a cast was taken, giving us all dimensions.' He reached into his folder and pulled out a photo of the cast with measurements and dimensions overlaid. 'See that wear on the sole? It is an exact match of one of the partial prints found at the clearing. Same make, same size.

'There's something else. We recovered a couple of visible prints on the slabs by the gate of the Carter's garden. It looks like the perpetrator had stepped on the grass, leaving prints leading from the garden. The visible prints show us a splayed softer version of this person's footprint with the impression just coming through lightly. When magnified there is pattern to the print, such as that of the material used on boot covers. The covers are again a common brand, the same as those used by estate agents and tradespeople when they work in our homes.'

'So our perpetrator went well prepared?'

'Definitely.'

'Anything else for the time being other than what we've received in your initial findings report?'

He shook his head. 'We'll keep ploughing on and I'll keep feeding you any new information. I know budgets are tight but we've been working around the clock. One of my colleagues messaged me with this news in the early hours. I'm back onto it as soon as I've finished here.'

'Thank you. Smith, any news on Samuel Avery, Phillip Brighton or Edward Powell? All three were not where they should have been at the time of Francesca's murder.'

'Uniform have reported that Edward Powell arrived home in the early hours.'

'I want to speak to our groom. We'll head back to the Powell household after we've finished here. Wyre, O'Connor, can you keep trying to find out the whereabouts of Samuel Avery and Phillip Brighton? As we know, Avery turned up at the Cleevesford Cleaver to see my daughter, Hannah, at ten in the evening last night. I want to know what he was doing before that.'

'Yes, guv,' Wyre replied.

O'Connor took his second pain au chocolat and bit into it.

'Do we know when Francesca Carter's post-mortem is scheduled?'

Bernard glanced at his notes. 'Sixteen hundred hours, today.'

'Thank you. Wyre, O'Connor, can you two attend and feed straight back to me when it's over. I want to know if they find something in her throat.'

Placing his pain au chocolat down, O'Connor clapped his hands to dislodge the greasy crumbs. 'I think I'll save this for later, much later.'

Gina glanced at the receipt from Piccolo's. 'This receipt from around a month ago which Charlie Carter found in his wife's bag shows her to have ordered a couple of sharing platters. The vegetable and the meat. Then we have the couple of bottles of wine. We need to find out who she was with. It is odd that she'd go there when this was her and Mr Carter's special place. She never mentioned it to him at all. Who was she with? Why had she hidden it from him?'

She put the receipt down on the table.

'Jacob, you said you have something to share.'

He nodded as he scraped his chair bringing himself closer to the central table. 'This is where it gets interesting. One of the other people at the party has a juvenile record for sexually assaulting one of his classmates at Cleevesford High School ten years ago. Robin Dawkins, also known as Elvis. He was serving that night.'

'We need to put him at the top of our list.'

'Do we know anything about the case?'

'It was at an end of year school disco. The girl called Jill Snaith said she'd fallen asleep by the lockers after being given a few shots of vodka that some of the other kids had brought with them. They were both fifteen at the time. She'd gone to her own locker to retrieve a bag of crisps she'd left there at lunchtime and had felt a little tipsy, so she sat on the floor in the dark. She awoke to him trying to pull her underwear off. He had his trousers pulled

Carla Kovach

down and lay on top of her. Eventually, she managed to push
him off. There had been another witness at this point who veri-
fied that it looked like Jill had been asleep. Anyway, he pleaded
guilty to sexual assault and did a year before coming back out.
No record since.'

'That certainly puts him in the spotlight. Bring him in. I think
we have reasonable grounds there.' Gina closed her notepad.
'There's also our other bridesmaid, Lilly Hill. Given what happened to Holly and Francesca, we need to look out for her. Right,
I'll be out for a while. First stop, Edward Powell.'

CHAPTER FORTY-TWO

Gina tapped on the door and listened out for footsteps. Edward Powell's black SUV was parked up on the drive. It hadn't been there when they'd spoken to Kerry the night before.

'Aha, I can see him coming down the stairs,' Jacob said as the young man opened the door.

With a towel in one hand, Edward began to dry his dark hair. He glanced at his reflection in the door glass. His baby blue shirt hung over his trousers and he'd left his green striped tie looped around his neck. 'Are you here to talk to Kerry? She isn't in at the moment.'

'We're here to talk to you actually. DI Harte and DS Driscoll. May we come in?'

'I'm just getting ready to go to work. I'm already late.'

'This won't take long.'

He glanced at the clock over his shoulder. 'I really have to get going. I don't know anything about what happened to Holly, she was Kerry's friend.'

'Have you spoken to Kerry since last night?'

He finished towel drying his hair and ran his fingers through the tangles. 'We haven't spoken since last night. When I got home, I found a message on the answering machine saying that her mother had collected her. She'd taken her to the family home and she wanted me to call when I got back. It was a bit late so I haven't managed to phone yet. Wait.' He frowned. 'Is everything okay? Nothing's happened to Kerry, has it?'

Gina shook her head. 'It would be best if we came in.' She wanted to go into the house, see if there was anything lying around that would give her more of a clue as to what Edward had been up to the previous evening.

'I'll just message the office and let them know that I'll be late. Come through.' As he typed out a text, he led them to a formal dining room through a door on the left. The table was surrounded by ten hardwood chairs, and a large candelabra adorned the centre of the runner. The huge brick fireplace gave the house an older style even though it looked to be fairly modern from the outside. A framed silhouette photo of the happy couple staring out to sea as the sun set, took pride of place on the hearth. 'Have a seat.'

Gina and Jacob sat by the fireplace while Edward sat at the head of the table in the carver chair.

'Last night, Francesca Carter was murdered in her own home. Could you tell me how well you knew her?'

The bulge of his biceps showed through his shirt as the sleeve stuck to a damp patch on his arm. 'I had no idea. Poor Frannie.' He paused. 'I should've called Kerry last night but I didn't want to disturb her. If I'd heard what happened to Fran, I'd have called straight away.'

'How well did you know Francesca?'

As he leaned back, the chair creaked a little. Deep in thought, he rubbed the index finger and thumb of his left hand together. 'She was just Kerry's friend, going back to her schooldays. Fran, Holly and Lilly would come over and they'd all drink wine and chat away in the kitchen for hours. Most of the time, I left them to it. Conversation was far too deep for me.' He let out a slight laugh. 'They'd talk about how we're ruining the planet with flying, meat and plastic. They all went vegan at one point; Holly lasted the longest at three weeks. That's the sort of thing they would talk about. Me, I'm simpler. I don't worry about anything. What will be, will be.'

'Apart from Francesca coming over to visit your wife, are you saying you didn't really know her?'

He slowly nodded. 'That's right. I don't know anything about her family, her job, or anything. I just know she's Frannie, Kerry's friend.'

'How about Holly? How well did you know her?' Now he was rubbing both of his fingers and thumbs together. He looked almost like he was meditating except for the annoying movement of his digits. Gina looked away, not allowing herself to focus on his habit.

'I didn't really know Holly. Again, she was just Kerry's friend. She visited the house, they went out together. It's really getting on. I should be at work.'

'I thought you sent work a message.' Gina glanced over at Jacob's notes. He too had spotted that Edward Powell seemed a little nervous.

'I did, but I have to meet an external client in about an hour and a half and her office is in Warwick.'

'We'll try not to keep you too long.'

'I heard that Holly was pregnant too. Kerry spoke to her mother.'

Gina nodded. 'That's true.'

'Such a shame for her and her baby.'

'It is. It's a terrible thing that happened. Her mother is devastated. Do you know who Holly was seeing?'

He shook his head and wiped a finger across the bottom of his nose. 'I heard Kerry talking to Lilly on the phone about this. They didn't know who she was seeing either.'

Gina cleared her dry throat. Most people offered them a drink. Today she'd have jumped at the chance to say yes, but the offer hadn't been there. 'What is it you do?'

'I handle acquisitions for Reed Corporation. Normally Kerry and I work on them together but with all that's been happening, she's taking a short bereavement break.' He reached over to the corner of the room, grabbed a pair of shoes and began lacing them up.

'What are those?'

'These?' He held up the scrunched material. 'Shoe covers. When I go into some of the premises just after the new carpets have been laid, I pop these on my feet.'

'Where were you yesterday evening?'

'Why do you want to know?' He sat rigidly in the chair and linked both hands together firmly on the table. His fidgeting had finally stopped.

'We're asking everyone who knew Francesca. It's just a routine question.'

His stare moved from Gina to Jacob and then back again. 'I was at the park, if you must know.'

'Which park?'

'Cleevesford Park. The one with the lake and kids play area. I walked around and then sat on a bench. We've been bickering, Kerry and I. Just over stupid things. She wants me to be here with her all the time but I need some space, just a bit of time on my own so I escaped to the park. I mean, we work together too.'

'You've only been married a couple of weeks.' Gina wondered why he wanted to get away from his wife so badly but she also understood how it felt to be stifled within a relationship. Her years with Terry had shown her exactly what it was like to feel controlled and in front of her sat a man who relied on his wife for everything, including his job. She wondered if she had him right. Was Kerry the one in control or was he? Their stories didn't match up.

'I know and I know it sounds weird. Since what happened to Holly, Kerry has been drinking a lot. When she gets drunk she accuses me of using her for the house, the job, her family's wealth. I mean, it's obvious this house isn't all our doing. But, I'm not like that and she can't get it into her head that I love her. The house and the money – it's just a bonus. I'd choose to be with Kerry if she lived in a bedsit and had nothing. Anyway, last night, I'd had enough. She was lounging around, wallowing and started taking a few snipes at me. I needed to get away for a while so I went to the park.'

Gina tried to stop herself from yawning. It had worked this time, but she might not be as lucky if she needed to yawn again. She hadn't slept all night while wrapped in Briggs's arms, even though he'd slept soundly. 'Did you see anyone while you were there?'

'There were people out with kids on scooters and bikes, dog walkers, joggers. I didn't speak to any of them, if that's what you're asking, but there's a good chance someone saw me. Wait – as it was getting later, a man threw a stick for his dog, it was a Red Setter. The stick landed by my feet so I picked it up and threw it onto the grass. I then stroked the dog and I might have mumbled some pleasantry. Maybe he'd remember me. Then it got dark so I just sat back and smoked while I watched the rippling water under the moon's light. Like I said, I'm simple like that. I enjoy the simpler things in life. I like smoking. Kerry hates me smoking so I enjoyed being there while I puffed away.'

'Is there anything else you can tell us?'

He shook his head. 'I left the park late that evening, probably around midnight and then I came home. Kerry wasn't here so I went to bed and that's it. Look, I really do have to go to work.'

'Just one more question. On the night after your wedding ceremony in Crete, did you notice anyone talking to Holly? Lilly reported hearing Holly talking to someone either in person or on the phone in the early hours of the following morning, telling this person that *she can't keep this to herself.*'

He shrugged his shoulders and gazed into the fireplace for a few seconds before looking back up. 'I have no idea what that was about. I don't remember anything being odd or out of place. I was a bit drunk though. It was my wedding night and the wine had been flowing freely all day long.' Gina watched as his Adam's apple bobbed as he swallowed.

'Thank you.'

'Is that it?'

'Unless you have anything else to tell us.' Gina knew that, since a murder had occurred in the council park in recent years, they had installed a CCTV camera to the car park. If he was where he said he was, his car would show up. 'Here's my card. If you remember anything that might help or you think of anything else, please call me straight away.'

He went to speak but closed his mouth again. 'Did you want to tell me something?'

'No.' He shook his head and smiled as he placed her card in his pocket before doing his tie up. 'I just need to get to work.'

'Thank you. We'll be in touch,' Gina said as they left.

'What did you make of him?' Gina opened the car door and got in.

Jacob pulled a sweet from his pocket and popped it into his mouth. 'I think he's concealing something. He seemed a little nervous. I mean, who spends all evening sitting in a park on their own? How old is he?'

'Late twenties. If we gave him the benefit of the doubt, what did he have to think about that made all those hours pass so easily on a park bench? One other thing, the park is about a thirty-minute walk to Francesca Carter's house. If his car does show up on CCTV, there is still a chance he could have got to her house, murdered her and walked all the way back. When we get the CCTV, we need to use the car registrations to find out who else was at the park while he was there. If these joggers and dog walkers didn't see him, we have to consider him a person of interest, that's for definite. We could do with finding the owner of the Red Setter. Give the council a quick call. Tell them we need yesterday's CCTV, then we'll head over to Lilly Hill's house.'

CHAPTER FORTY-THREE

As he gripped her around the neck, she emitted a choking noise not like any of the others she'd made before, but he couldn't stop. He imagined her to be *the other one* as his clutches tightened. It's no longer about self-preservation. It's more for pure enjoyment. The police were going around in circles and it had been hilarious to watch.

About the other one – he'd been watching her and the more he thought about what he'd do to her, the more turned on he got. He liked a bit of variation and she was different. As he yelled out with pleasure, she pushed him away, giving him the look he hated to see. He'd overstepped the mark this time. She wasn't happy with him, he knew that much. 'I'm sorry,' he whispered as he rolled off her. She ignored him and grabbed her dressing gown. 'Look, I said I'm sorry.' She wasn't going to ignore him – how dare she? That's not how all this worked.

'Keep your voice down or you're going to be even more sorry.' She kneeled on the bed and placed her index finger across his lips before swiping the back of her hand across his face. 'Don't you ever grip me like that again.'

A tingle flushed through his body. Now was the wrong time to say that he'd actually enjoyed her slap. He loved it when she got angry. It was a side of her that their friends never saw and he felt privileged that she'd put on this show, just for him. She tied up her robe, covering her nakedness. For now, she would get on with things and he'd go about his day. Work beckoned and he didn't have long to get onto his scheduled plans – he was now officially in a rush. He'd smooth things over with her later. He always did.

She stared at her reflection in the wall to ceiling mirrored wardrobe as she rubbed her neck. Maybe he'd gripped her a bit too hard. She pulled out a silk scarf and wrapped it expertly around her neck and posed, taking in the look from all angles. Holly was so far in the past now. A distant memory. Francesca would also be nothing more than a memory soon. He hated the way such beautiful memories faded within no time.

He glanced at the bedside clock. He was going to be late for his meeting. But first, his target may be on the move and he didn't want to miss her. He could fit her in before he started his day. He grabbed his phone and sent his apologies. The meeting would have to be rescheduled.

CHAPTER FORTY-FOUR

Gina placed the memory stick containing the CCTV into her bag as she and Jacob prepared themselves to have an unsettling conversation with Lilly Hill, the last bridesmaid.

Jacob eyed the street as they approached the end of terrace house. 'So, this is it. 12 The Fallows. I have it down that Lilly and Brendan Hill live here.'

The Fallows sat in the middle of the old Cleevesford Estate, a mixture of council and privately-owned houses. A block of flats welcomed visitors at the entrance to the street and a corner shop was located at the other end. Several teenagers leaned against a large bin outside the shop, shouting and laughing as one of their friends did a wheelie on his pushbike.

'Shouldn't they be at school?'

'They look older than school age.'

'I'm seriously getting old then. I thought they were about twelve.' He knocked on the red door and waited.

'O'Connor called Mrs Hill to make sure she was in so hopefully she hasn't gone out.' They waited a few more seconds and she opened the door. The twenty-five-year-old had one hand on the door catch and the other on the end of a blonde plait that hung like a rope over her shoulder.

A loud crash followed by crying filled the house. 'You best come in. Ben, what have you done?' She picked up the crawling child and gave his teary eye a kiss. 'He's just learning to walk. You fell over. Didn't you, poppet?'

She gestured for Gina and Jacob to sit on the settee as she sat on the chair. The little boy's intermittent screams were met by cuddles and baby talk. 'Sorry about all the toys.'

Gina placed the activity mat and the stuffed animals to one side. 'That's okay. Hello, little man.' Gina smiled at the toddler. 'How old is he?'

'He's one next month, aren't you, Ben?' The red-cheeked boy slid off his mother's lap and began playing with his toys once again, his tears a distant memory.

He grabbed a large blue cube and passed it to Gina. She swallowed as she thought of Gracie. Her own granddaughter was a few years older but she remembered all of her developmental stages so well. 'Thank you.' She smiled and took the brick. He fell onto the floor and half walked and crawled over to his toys. 'I know you've heard about what happened to Francesca last night. My colleague, DC O'Connor called you.'

She nodded and fanned a hand in front of her eyes as she forced back her tears. 'I haven't stopped thinking about what happened all night. The police knocked a couple of times, telling us that they'd drive-by our house now and again. Am I in any danger?'

'We hope not but just to make sure, I'd like the drive-bys to continue.'

The young woman stretched her long jumper over her knees as she leaned forward in the huge chair. 'I don't know if I'm being paranoid but I keep thinking someone is watching me. I'm the only other living bridesmaid from Kerry's wedding and I keep thinking I'm going to be next and the worst of it is, I keep mulling over everything. It has to be someone we all know and for the life of me, I can't work out who would want to kill Holly and Fran. They were both such lovely people and I'm going to miss them terribly.' She wiped her eyes on her sleeve. 'Brendan had to go to work today but I wanted him to stay here with me.

We're not like Kerry and Fran. We can't afford for him to miss a day and his manager hasn't been so sympathetic.'

'Where does he work?'

'He's an estate agent working for a company in Evesham. My maternity leave will be up soon and I'll be back at work too.'

'What is it you do?' Gina tried to put the woman at ease with some simple questions, while Jacob scribbled a few notes down.

'I'm a nurse. I'll miss him when I'm back at work, won't I, poppet?'

The boy looked up, giving his mother a big smile before falling into her arms.

'We already have your statement with what happened to Holly and we thank you for being so thorough. I need to ask you a few questions about Francesca. Would that be okay?'

'Of course. I just want this person caught. I want to feel safe again. I want my friends to be laid to rest so that we can all mourn properly.'

'Had you heard from Francesca since the wedding reception?' Gina moved a small toy from under her bottom and shuffled back a little into the soft settee. She almost placed her hand on a patch of dried up milk on the arm of the settee.

'We'd spoken on the phone. She'd been fed up that she had to go back to work after what had happened and I suppose she just called to vent about that. We spoke about Holly and how much we'd miss her. We didn't meet up in person after the reception, but then again, we didn't meet up too often anyway. Occasionally, we would all meet up for a wine and nibbles night at Kerry's house or somewhere local, but that was it.'

'We found a receipt for Piccolo's restaurant dated Saturday the eleventh of April amongst Francesca's belongings and her husband Charlie Carter didn't go there with her. Was Francesca seeing anyone that you know of?'

Lilly smiled and let out a nervous laugh. 'No, definitely not. Let me check my diary. Bear with me.' She leaned over and pulled out her phone and scrolled. 'That's one of the things having a child is good for, you always know where you were and when. Kerry, Holly, Fran and I were at Piccolo's. We go out every couple of months for a few snacks and drinks, normally on a Saturday lunchtime. We shared a couple of platters, if I remember rightly.' She paused and opened her mouth as she thought. 'Oh, I know Charlie wouldn't have known that time.'

Gina placed her elbow on the arm of the settee waiting for her to continue. The little boy slipped off his mother's lap and toddled over to Jacob, the legs of his dungarees dragging behind him where the poppers had come apart. Jacob awkwardly smiled.

'He'd tried to cut her spending down and she didn't want him to know. We all take it in turns to pay and it had been Fran's turn. They weren't short of money, he was just a bit tight so I guess she felt she needed to hide the spend from him. She was in no way having any kind of affair though. She loved Charlie – went on about him all the time.'

That cleared up one mystery. Gina crossed that note from her list.

'Can you tell me a little about Francesca and Charlie's relationship?'

'As I said, they were close. She'd never lie about the big things. It was just lunch. He was a saver, she was a spender. That's all. I never worried about her or him, not like I do Kerry.'

Gina arched her brows. 'In what way do you worry about Kerry?'

'I don't want her to know I've been talking about her. I shouldn't have said anything.'

'It may help with the case.'

'It's nothing to do with the case.'

'It may not help us directly but it'll give us a better picture of everyone.'

Her shoulders dropped. 'It's not a biggie. We were all just worried as to how much of a player Ed comes across as. Brendan gets angry when he sees him. Kerry never notices, but he has this way about him that has women flocking towards him. He's charming and over complimentary. He flirts a lot and he's good-looking, I get that. But in my view, it's not on. He says how much he loves Kerry and that's she's his everything. I just don't feel he comes across as genuine, but that's more my opinion. I don't want Kerry to know that came from me. She wouldn't be too happy. She moans about him sometimes, but if anyone were to say a bad word against him she'd give them what for. She'd give me what for.'

'Thank you. Moving onto you and your safety. Has a community officer come by to talk about home security?'

'Not yet. I'm not sure if we need that. The garden gate has a lock on it and all our doors are double lockable.'

'When you open the door to anyone, can you keep your chain on? Any worries at all, call us straight away, even if you think you're just being silly or that it might be nothing. We need to put your safety first given what's happened to your friends. Best still, do you have any relatives you can stay with for a short while?'

She shook her head. 'No. We do but Brendan said we're not being scared out of our own home even after—'

'After what?'

'It's stupid. I feel stupid. It was nothing.'

Gina leaned forward as Jacob played pass the brick back and forth with a dribble-mouthed Ben.

'Last night, I thought I heard something at the back gate. Brendan went out to look but there was no one there. I thought I saw movement in the shrubbery that lines the bus route. It looked like someone was out there, standing still. It was probably someone waiting for their dog to do its business or something like that. When he went out, they'd gone; that's if there was anyone there in the first place. I haven't had much sleep lately. I saw a flash of white in the darkness. It could have been a carrier bag trapped in branches for all I know. It could have been anything. I was just jittery, that's all.'

'Well, if ever you're worried again, just call us.'

Lilly hurried over to Jacob, rescuing him from the many coloured bricks that were piling up in his lap. The child screamed as she scooped him up.

'He's okay,' Jacob said with a smile. 'You best have your bricks back.' He passed Ben a brick and the boy stopped crying for a moment.

As they tied up the conversation, Gina and Jacob said their goodbyes and headed out, back into the May sunshine. The weather was starting to change for the better. Daffodils grew in clumps on the communal patches of grass and birds tweeted from the trees. Lilly and Ben waved to them as she closed the door.

'Do you think someone was hanging around, watching them, guv?' Jacob stood beside the car.

'I don't know. What I do know is that we have two dead bridesmaids and I don't want anything to happen to her. I'm going to up the patrols on this house. We'll add in a patrol of the street too. If officers are checking around the back regularly, that may act as a deterrent. My biggest fear is that our perpetrator is known to her. She may let our killer straight in through the front door. This person could be trusted by all, seen as harmless. How do we guard against that?' She grabbed her phone and dialled the incident room. 'Wyre, it's Harte. I want a panic alarm fitted at Lilly Hill's house as soon as possible. Can you ask PC Kapoor to head over as soon as she can?' She paused as Wyre spoke. 'What? We're on our way back now.' She ended the call.

'What was that about?' Jacob tapped his nails on the roof of her car.

'Phillip Brighton checked in as a part of his bail conditions, albeit late. He's there now. Wyre and O'Connor are preparing for Francesca's post-mortem so let's hurry back.'

'Was that all?'

'No. The plot thickens. I'll tell you in the car. We have a witness coming in to make a statement against Samuel Avery. It's all happening at the moment.'

CHAPTER FORTY-FIVE

Midday had passed and Cass had already received two calls from work. They really didn't trust her when she'd told them that she was sick in bed with a tummy upset. Now, it was more of a bind and she'd have to face a back to work interview the next day, a company procedure she'd come to fear. Two sick days in a year, that's all she'd had. She couldn't face work and the idea of calling in with a sickie had appealed at eight in the morning. She did feel ill but it was all self-inflicted. The fried food hadn't sat well at all but she knew it wouldn't when she was scoffing it down.

She tied the silky scarf in a different way. That was better. It looked far nicer in a loose bow. That's how Kerry would wear it. Cass wore the same black trousers or leggings every day but she knew Kerry would have racks of amazing designer clothes and that wearing them would command respect as soon as she entered a room. She had to conjure up her inner Kerry and she had to do it on a budget. She did a half turn and flinched as the lights and radio went off. Heart beating like a hammer drill, she let out a laugh. The emergency button needed pressing on the meter; that was all.

Hurrying out of the front door, she opened the cupboard and pressed. Everything came back to life. Heavy footsteps clunked up the stairs. She gazed down, trying to spot who was coming up another flight. 'What are you doing back?'

Elvis's shoulders dropped. 'You're meant to be at work.' He pushed past her and hurried into the bathroom, locking the door behind him. Moments later, she heard the shower running.

She turned the radio off and waited for him to come out and interrogate her.

Kerry still hadn't replied to her message. Last night, Cass had watched from the bushes as her drunken friend's mother had helped her stagger into the car before driving her away. Then the detective had heard her, the one who'd been at the reception on the night of Holly's murder. When she approached, Cass had held her breath until she'd got into her car and drove off with her partner. She had no reason for being in Kerry's bushes and had no idea what to say if she'd have been caught.

She fiddled with the white scarf and smelled it. The free sample of expensive perfume still lingered. A flowery fragrance of quality. Kerry would approve.

Her stomach turned as she waited for Elvis to make an appearance.

As the shower stopped spraying, a loud hammering knock at the door startled her.

'Who the hell is that?' Elvis unlocked the bathroom door and trod wet footsteps over the carpet.

She shrugged her shoulders. 'Shall I answer it?'

'Durr, yes! What the hell have you done to your face?'

He obviously didn't approve of her make-up. She hurried to the door. 'Hello, who is it?'

'Police.'

'It's the police,' she mouthed.

The knocking continued.

She gently opened the door with the chain across it. 'Hello.'

The bald man in a suit and the woman with straight shoulder-length black hair held up their identification. 'Detective Constables Wyre and O'Connor,' the woman said. 'We're looking for Robin Dawkins.'

She glanced across at the lounge as his jaw dropped and he rubbed his chin.

'May we come in?' DC Wyre asked.

She removed the chain and opened the door.

'Cassandra Wilson?'

'Yes, that's me.'

As the two detectives entered the lounge, Cass took a step back and nervously clasped both hands in front of her, gripping them tightly.

'What do you want?' Elvis grabbed an old hoodie from the back of the chair and slipped it over his head.

'We're going to need you to come to the station to make a statement under caution. Francesca Carter was found murdered in her home last night and we need to ask you a few questions.'

'What? No way. Am I under arrest?'

'No, not yet.'

'Then I'm not going anywhere.' He sat on the chair and placed an unlit cigarette between his lips.

'Okay, we can arrest you on suspicion of murder and keep you in for questioning for twenty-four hours or you can come with us voluntarily and this could be over within a couple of hours.'

Cass felt a quiver at her knees. Had Fran been the woman who was messaging her boyfriend? Had he committed the unthinkable? She hated herself for doubting him but he had given her every reason. 'What's happening, Elvis?'

He huffed and stood, grabbed his jeans and began pulling them up under the towel around his waist. As he zipped them up, the towel dropped to the floor. 'Just get this over with quick and, for the record, I haven't hurt anyone. I'm not the person I was back then. I've changed. I know why you're here. I've done my time and you're harassing me. I was just a kid.'

'What have you done?' That's the first Cass had heard about her boyfriend doing time.

'Nothing. It's in the past and I just want to forget it but this lot won't let me, ever.'

She stared at him as he finished getting ready. She didn't know him at all. Was he dangerous? She'd been living with him all this time and she had no idea he'd been in prison. The news of Elvis getting arrested would soon sweep around the community. Would the press start to hassle them? Maybe Kerry would find out. If Elvis had committed the unthinkable against Kerry's two best friends, would there be room for Cass in her life? Everything was falling apart. Had it been Elvis, the very man she lived with, who had been lurking outside Lilly's house the night before when she'd arrived? Had he scared the life out of her as he followed her back to the flat? She opened her mouth to speak to the police but Elvis glared right at her. There was no way she'd say a thing. The look in his eyes told her that she'd regret uttering anything.

As they led him out, she closed the door and rushed to the window, watching as they bundled him into the car and drove off.

Leaning against the kitchen wall, she kicked back and wiped the tear that slid down her face. 'Please message me, Kerry. I need a friend too,' she murmured.

CHAPTER FORTY-SIX

'Phillip Brighton, please answer yes or no for the tape. Did you know Holly Long?' Gina waited for him to lie again. Jacob kept his gaze on Phillip too.

'I swear I don't. Why have you got me in here for questioning again? I checked in as per my bail conditions. I've done everything I had to do.' He plunged both hands into the pockets of his denim jacket.

'For the tape, you checked in late. We have a witness who claims that you knew Holly. We also have CCTV evidence showing you pressing the buzzer to Holly's apartment on Wednesday the twenty-fifth of March.' She removed a camera still from the folder and slid it across the table. The resolution wasn't perfect but the man had Phillip Brighton's hair and was wearing the same jacket. 'Can you confirm that this is you?' The video wasn't clear enough to tell which buzzer he'd pressed but Gina wasn't about to mention that yet.

He reached for the photo and stared at it. 'Okay, it's me in the picture.'

'Why did you say you didn't know Holly when clearly you do?'

'Look, I didn't even know her name was Holly.'

'But you recognised her?'

'I thought I'd be in trouble. I was in the toilet at the time of her murder and I told you that already. I don't have an alibi and you lot hate me. That's why I didn't say anything.'

'What size shoes do you wear?'

'Nine. Why?'

Gina exhaled. 'Where were you last night? That's Monday the eleventh of May, between six and eight in the evening?'

'At home?' His gaze darted from Gina to Jacob, then back to Gina.

'We visited you last night and you weren't at home. I will repeat the question, where were you last night?'

'I want my solicitor.' He made a zip motion across his lips with his grubby fingers and his left eye twitched a little.

'Interview terminated at thirteen twenty-two hours.' Gina slammed her folder shut and stood to leave the room. 'I suggest we get Mr Ullah here straight away. We are going to get to the bottom of this. It's not looking good for you, Mr Brighton.'

CHAPTER FORTY-SEVEN

The strip light above flickered as Gina and Jacob headed away from the interview rooms.

'Phillip Brighton was definitely up to no good last night, but did he kill Francesca and if he did, why? He has no history of violence whatsoever. Why won't he just tell us where he was and get this over with? But he's not making it that easy. His solicitor, Mr Ullah, will take ages to get here. He'll then tell him to keep his mouth shut and we'll be none the wiser.'

Gina rolled up the sleeves of her oversized shirt and undid her top button. It was stuffy at the station or maybe she was having a flush. One or the other. She continued leading the way along the corridor. 'If he has no history and he did murder Holly and Francesca, what triggered it? I don't feel as though he has the intelligence to have committed the crimes. Francesca's murder was well thought out. The assailant wore boot covers, possibly gloves too as no unexplained prints were found. So far, there has been no DNA evidence turn up.'

Jacob followed her and loosened his tie.

Gina stopped outside the closed incident room door as she continued to ponder. 'I just don't get it. He wears size nines, that's a start but not much else fits. He had opportunity but no motive. Maybe Holly was buying drugs from Phillip Brighton and she threatened to shop him at the reception. Would he care that much? None of this is making sense. We need to find the father of Holly's baby. I checked the system. The foetus's DNA has been catalogued but there was no match on the system.'

'One thing we can confirm, although it's not much, is that the baby's father was neither Phillip Brighton nor Robin Dawkins. They both have a past. We have them well and truly logged.'

'Elimination is a start. One thing to consider though is the murderer may not have been the baby's father either.' She twisted the strands of hair that framed her face and pulled a frustrated expression. 'We're close you know.' She pressed her lips together. 'Maybe Francesca's post-mortem might throw us a lead. Also, do we have access to Holly's bank statements yet?'

'Yes. They arrived this morning.'

'Great. I want to delve into her lifestyle. I can't see how she could have afforded everything she had on her salary.'

Jacob nodded. 'Yes, that's a mystery.'

'And, Trevor Reed, our witness who saw what Samuel Avery was up to on the night of the reception, do we know when he's due in?'

'Not as yet.' He pushed the door open.

Wyre removed her coat as O'Connor slumped into the swivel chair next to his computer.

'Alright, guv? We've just brought Robin Dawkins, AKA Elvis, into custody. He's in interview room one at the moment. PC Kapoor is with Lilly Hill, setting up the panic alarm and we have concrete confirmation that Holly's manager at the microbrewery, Rick Elder, was skyping his sister in Australia at the time of Holly's murder. The sister's girlfriend took a piece of time-stamped video footage of them doing stupid impressions and joking around. The communications provider has also backed this up.' O'Connor smiled as he clicked his email icon.

'I suppose we can finally eliminate him for now. Good work. What time is Trevor Reed due in to make his statement?' Gina grinned. Finally, she'd be able to convince her daughter once and for all that Samuel Avery was bad news.

'He's just arrived,' Wyre interjected.

'Robin Dawkins can stew for a while. I'll grab a drink and then take his statement. This, I'm looking forward to.' She pulled her sleeves back down and tucked her loose strands of hair behind her ears.

'We're just leaving for the morgue, guv,' O'Connor said. 'We'll catch up later.'

'Great. Anything to do with flowers anywhere in the body, let me know immediately. Any sign yet of Samuel Avery?'

Wyre shook her head. 'None at all. His staff opened the pub. They said he'd headed to his sister's in London last night, just for a visit apparently. They also said he'd be back later today.'

'Mystery solved. That's if he ever even went to his sister's.' As far as Gina was concerned, until that information and his timings had been confirmed, he was still a suspect in Francesca's murder. She inhaled, taking a moment. Time to nail Avery on other charges for now. With two witnesses he had a lot more explaining to do. Since the last time she interviewed him, things were looking even worse now that Francesca, the one witness, had been murdered. In the absence of any carnations placed at the scene, she had to consider that someone else was involved and that maybe it was Avery.

CHAPTER FORTY-EIGHT

Gina entered the room to find Trevor Reed already seated and sipping a machine coffee. The man looked to be in his early fifties and was equally as well preened as Alison Reed had been when Gina saw her the night before. He smoothed his full head of hair down with one hand and rested his other on the leather wallet and phone that lay on the table that divided them. Jacob shuffled behind him in the snug room and sat next to Gina.

'Thank you for coming in so promptly,' she said.

'Once I heard what had happened to Fran, I had no choice. I can tell you, our family are deeply saddened by what has happened. Holly and Fran have been a part of our lives for years, on and off. They were Kerry's best friends. I remember the slumber parties, the cinema nights. I picked them up when they all went to their first night club.' He paused. 'My wife and I treated them all like our own and I saw how that man was treating Fran at our daughter's reception. To think I paid good money for him to provide the guest ale bar, then I see him upsetting one of her bridesmaids.' The man closed his eyes and swallowed. 'I'm sorry. I'm still taking all this in.'

'That's okay. Take your time.'

He took a long deep breath and opened his eyes. 'I heard shouting when I left the function room to use the men's room. Fran was telling him to get away from her, in fact she was shouting it. I couldn't hear every word over the music but I caught some of it.'

'Would you confirm who you are referring to?'

'That prick, Samuel Avery. I hired him to pull pints not bridesmaids. I digress. He wasn't pulling her, he was gripping her by the wrist and she was telling him that it hurt and that what he'd done to her was unforgivable. She said a few things like "stay away from me".'

'What time was this?'

He shook his head and pursed his lips. 'I can't be sure. I know the gatecrashers had arrived as a bit of a ruckus had begun. I was heading to the toilet before I took care of matters.' Gina flicked back to the previous report that Francesca Carter had given. She claimed to have been sexually assaulted before the gatecrashers arrived. Maybe this was a separate incident.

'She yelled at him to get his hands off her and that she'd already told him to leave her alone.'

'Did you intervene?'

'No, I didn't think it was my place. It also ended as quickly as it started. I didn't want her to know I'd overheard what had happened so I ducked into the toilets and when I came out, they were gone. Francesca was back in the function room having a drink.' He scrunched his brow.

'How did she seem?'

'A little deep in thought. She was sitting alone for a minute or two. I thought of asking if she was okay but Kerry grabbed her and pulled her onto the dance floor. Within what seemed like seconds, I spotted another gatecrasher. That took me away from my concerns about Fran. They were already drunk and loud, they took a bit of manhandling out of the room. I forgot all about what had happened between Fran and Sam until last night, when I found out about her murder. I didn't know if what I'd seen was even relevant. I just knew that if it was and he had something to do with her murder, I'd never forgive myself for keeping quiet.' He exhaled and rubbed his tired eyes. 'Sorry, my daughter has been upset most of the night, upset and severely drunk. It's taken it out of my wife and me.'

'Going back to the reception, you say Samuel Avery grabbed her wrist. Can you tell me any more?' Gina felt her pulse quickening. He was helping with the case against Avery more than he realised.

'He was gripping it. She was trying to pull away but he wouldn't let go. He said something on the lines of "you wanted it too. I could tell you were turned on". To begin with, I thought they'd had some sort of tryst but there was something defensive in her tone, a quiver to her voice, almost like fear or anger. That's when I heard her say that he was hurting her. I definitely heard her shout, "stay away from me" but he treated it like a joke and replied with something like she'd been flirting with him. That really is it. I didn't hear any more.'

Gina thought about Holly; maybe Trevor Reed would remember something he hadn't previously thought of. 'Do you remember seeing Holly around this time?'

'I can't say that I do. I said that in my statement. I had gatecrashers to deal with. I wasn't really switched on to who was around me.'

Gina knew that Holly left the room around this time. Other witness statements had confirmed that. The gatecrashing incident had acted like one big distraction. Had Phillip Brighton come in and sneaked past everyone, following Holly to her room? Had Samuel Avery given up on Fran and taken his frustrations out on Holly? Everyone said that Cassandra Wilson was working alone through a lot of the evening while Samuel Avery and Robin Dawkins enjoyed the party. Had Robin succumbed to the same dark urges buried in his past and followed Holly up to her room? Maybe the party had triggered his behaviour. She now had what she felt were three firm suspects who had opportunity and motive and all three of them had failed to provide an alibi for the night of Francesca's murder. 'Thank you for coming forward.'

'It was my moral obligation to do so. I have a daughter and when it comes down to it, I know I should have intervened but, as I say, it was over so quickly. I suppose I failed Fran. If I'd have said something, she may still be here. The focus was all on Holly after what had happened. None of us were thinking straight that night.' He fiddled with the cufflinks on his sleeve. 'That's something I'll have to live with.'

Gina let out a small cough. She knew exactly how it felt to live with guilt, although her guilt was darker in nature. She placed her hand around the side of her neck and swallowed. Terry had felt no guilt at all for what he'd done to her. She wondered if he'd have felt any remorse if he'd have killed her when he had his hands gripped around her neck. All this talk of weddings was starting to play on her mind.

'Thank you so much for coming and telling us what you remember.' She fished a card from the folder. 'If you remember anything else, call me. Do you remember seeing the other bar-person around, Robin Dawkins?'

'Oh him. Useless, he was. Fancies himself as an Elvis impersonator. He was chatting up all the women in the room with his little Elvis sound bites but I think most of them found him annoying. I don't remember seeing him when the gatecrashers came but I may have just missed him. As I keep saying, my mind was on other things. He could have been there all along. His girlfriend looked upset though.'

'Cassandra Wilson?'

'That's the one. Short, ample and curly-haired. It was sad to see her being ignored while he flirted away. I felt a bit sorry for her but these things happen. You hope that young women with toads for boyfriends finally see sense.' He glanced at his watch.

Gina thought of Robin Dawkins waiting in another interview room. He was next on her list.

'Did you see this man at all?' She passed him a mugshot of Phillip Brighton.

He pulled a pair of glasses from his pocket and slid them up his nose. 'Ah yes. That's Phil. I don't know him well but I have seen him in the Angel Arms once or twice, he always looks stoned. My daughter does goofy impressions of him, the way he slouches and twitches. I know that doesn't sound kind but it's done in good humour. He was there on the night of the reception. I saw him later on in the evening but when you arrived, he'd gone. I can't say that I took much notice of him. He wasn't the rowdiest of the gatecrashers. He came across as a little weasel but that's as far as it goes. As I said before, I had a lot of other things to take care of and once we found out what happened to Holly, my family were distraught. It was like time stood still and I lost all focus on what was happening. The whole night after that was a blur. I'm sorry I can't be of more help.'

Gina smiled. 'You've been a great help, Mr Reed. I won't take up any more of your time. Is there anything else you'd like to tell me before we finish?'

Jacob caught up with the notes on the witness statement as Gina waited for him to answer.

'Not that I can think of. If I do remember anything, I'll let you know straight away.' He placed her card in his shirt pocket and patted it. 'For now, I have some work to do, then I'm heading home to be with my family.'

Jacob scribbled out the blank end of the form and turned it around. 'Could you please sign and date each page.' The man obliged before standing to put his jacket on. 'I'll see you out.'

As they left, Gina grabbed her phone and checked to see if Hannah had messaged but there was nothing. She hoped that Samuel Avery had gone to his sister's in London because that would mean that Hannah was nowhere near him. She now had the witness statement of a dead woman and Trevor Reed. This had to be enough to make a charge stick.

She'd left Robin Dawkins long enough to sweat it out. It was his turn next.

Briggs hurried along the corridor. 'Update with regards to Robin Dawkins and you're going to like this.' That was just what she needed, some ammunition to enter the next interview with.

CHAPTER FORTY-NINE

Cass's finger hovered over the message she'd prepared for Kerry.

Kerry, is everything alright? I thought I'd have heard from you this morning. Hope you're okay. Please message me when you read this.

The icon flashed, telling her that Kerry had read her message. She paced around her tiny lounge, stomach churning as she thought about Elvis and everything he was hiding. Had the neighbours seen him getting into the back of a police car? She pulled the curtain aside and scanned the streets and road below. No one was looking up at the house. No reporters had arrived to get a photo and dredge up Elvis's past. As her mind ran away with that thought, she imagined trying to get out of the communal door below and being mobbed by people with microphones. Holly's murder had already been on the news daily; they were hungry for a lead. Maybe they'd ask questions she didn't have an answer to. Was Elvis having a relationship with Holly? What had he done time for? Maybe she'd been living with a rapist or a murderer. She'd read stories in her magazines, stories about women who'd lived with people and later found out that they'd done something terrible. Would she be another story?

She stared at her phone. Why wasn't Kerry answering? Cass had skived off work and she wasn't going back soon. Not only because she couldn't face her judgmental colleagues if the news broke out about Elvis but also because she wanted to be there for Kerry. Today would test whether Kerry could be there for her too and now Kerry was ignoring her. Be patient, she kept telling herself. Besides, she couldn't tell Kerry what had happened. Her mouth watered as she imagined Kerry finding out that Elvis had killed Fran. Is that what she thought?

Yes, he had been acting weirdly.

He'd been out at the time of her murder.

Maybe he'd been at Lilly's house after the murder, at the same time Cass had been checking the last bridesmaid out, trying to decipher what Lilly had that she didn't.

She felt her stomach roll as she imagined the headlines when it all came out. Elvis the Bridesmaid Killer. It had to have been him, especially with this past she had no idea about. The police had come for him and he had no option but to go, that confirmed his guilt.

She thought back to all the messages he was getting at all hours, the passwords on his phone and laptop, his evasiveness and his increasing irritation towards her; the fact that he was pushing her away when she wanted affection. All the signs were there. She had to find out what he'd been up to but he'd been one step ahead. She was sick of passwords. She hit send on another message.

Kerry, please answer me. I'm worried about you.

Maybe Kerry had been hurt. She had been fine when they'd been drinking together. Elvis had been out. Maybe when he went back out he'd hurt Kerry. *Stop it, Cass. You're letting your imagination run away with you.*

Just tell me you're okay then I'll stop messaging. I need to know you're safe. Please message me. Cass.

Phew, Kerry had now read all of her messages. Cass held her breath. Kerry was typing, then she stopped. She swallowed and swiftly went back to Kerry's Facebook page, her trembling fingers almost accidentally closing the app. The last thing Kerry had posted was how sad she was over what had happened to Fran. She flicked over to Instagram. Kerry always posted at least a couple of selfies a day, but nothing. Not a selfie in sight. Twitter – nothing. Kerry started typing again. Cass bit her bottom lip as she waited.

Cass, please stop messagin me ov and over again. I've got nough to deal with and I cant handle all these messages. I've just lost my 2 best friends.

Kerry was still drunk. That was it. That had to be it, otherwise she'd want Cass to go over to be with her. The spelling in the message told her all she needed to know. She almost tripped over her rug as she started to pace again. Then again, didn't drunken people always tell the truth? Maybe she was being officially friend dumped again. After all she'd done to change, all for Kerry.

I'm sorry. I just wanted to help you. I didn't mean to upset you. Cass.

She couldn't help sending another message. She had to smooth things over. She waited and waited. This time Kerry hadn't read the message and her photo greyed out. She'd been blocked. She flung the phone onto the coffee table and slumped into the threadbare armchair. At this moment, she had no one. How dare Kerry dump her again? How dare she?

Cass gripped her over-spilling muffin top under her jumper and punched it with the other hand.

She wasn't good enough. She hadn't tried hard enough.

She stood and ran to the bathroom, taking a moment to stare at her reflection. The crooked eyeliner and deep pink lipstick made her look like a clown. Elvis was right. She looked ridiculous. She pulled a few sheets of dry loo roll and rubbed her face like she was scrubbing tidemarks from the bath. That's all she was to everyone, a dirty, ugly, tidemark. She rubbed and rubbed at the make-up until it had smudged and her face had reddened. She looked even more revolting when she sobbed, knowing that she'd never be a Lilly, a Holly or a Frannie. Never would she be good enough for Kerry. She wouldn't look good in a wedding photo.

She had to make Kerry see that they could become the best of friends still. She was upset, that was all. She hadn't meant to block Cass from messaging her. Cass had to speak to her before rumour got out about Elvis going down to the station. This would not defeat her. She had some investigating of her own to get on with and it started with her boyfriend.

Hurrying to the bedroom, she emptied Elvis's drawers, feeling along the backs of them for a clue, anything. She checked under his side of the bed and amongst his shoes. As she tipped his old Doc Martens boot upside down, several packages dropped out onto the floor. Tiny cellophane wrapped white powder and lumps of black, which she knew was cannabis resin. Wiping the tears from her face, she stood and put her coat on. She couldn't sit around any longer. Kerry had made a mistake in blocking her and she was going to fix it.

CHAPTER FIFTY

Gina and Briggs sat as they waited for Robin Dawkins to say something. A twinge ran through her hand – she wanted to slam it onto the table and demand that he talk. Also, Phillip Brighton's solicitor had turned up. Jacob and PC Smith were interviewing him at that very moment. Gina felt a warmth coming from Briggs as she pulled her chair in closer.

'Mr Dawkins, please answer the question. Where were you last night between six and eight in the evening?' It was the third time she'd asked him and her patience was wearing thin. Given his past assault on a girl at school he had now shot up to the top of her list of suspects. She pictured her hand slamming onto the table and him recoiling as he spilled out all the answers. She gripped her hands together in her lap.

Briggs maintained eye contact and the man looked away, his hair bouncing as he did. He looked different without his quiff, if not a little scruffy with a few kinks around his ear.

'I was out.'

'As you know, Francesca Carter's body was found last night. She'd been murdered in her home. Can you imagine how her family felt? I need to know where you were!' Gina glanced at the wall clock and all they could hear was the hand ticking away.

'I didn't do anything to her. I was nowhere near her house. This is all because of my past, isn't it? I've paid for what I did. I got rehabilitated and took some hospitality qualifications. I did everything I was supposed to do. They said I could start afresh and have a normal life and now this happens. You have nothing on me because I wasn't there.' He scratched his arm under his jacket. Welts began to surface on his pasty flesh and his cheeks flushed.

'All you need to do to clear this up is tell us where you were.'

He shook his head several times and closed his eyes.

'Mr Dawkins, a woman was murdered and, yes, you have a past conviction that involves sexually assaulting a girl. That puts you in the picture. Where were you?'

Eyes still closed, Robin snorted and rolled his shoulders. 'I can't.'

'You have no choice, Mr Dawkins.'

Briggs maintained his stare but it was no good, the man refused to even open his eyes. He began grinding his teeth and his tiny sideburns moved up and down with every clench.

'What size shoes do you wear?'

He opened his eyes and scrunched his nose. 'What?'

'Shoe size?' Gina eased off slightly.

'Nine. What's that got to do with anything?'

'Thank you.' She made a note on the file and paused for a moment, just long enough to make him feel comfortable once again. 'Where were you last night?'

His hands shook as he gripped the plastic cup of water and took a sip. 'Work.'

'We know you weren't at work.' Briggs had filled her in with their most recent update before stepping into the interview room. On checking out his workplace, the truth had come to light. Elvis had not been at work during the time of the murder.

'Maybe I wasn't. I work all shifts. I can't remember what time I finished.'

'How about Monday night? You were fired. You were the one who tipped off the gatecrashers, weren't you, and Mr Avery found out and fired you? One of your colleagues confirmed that today. Why are you lying to us?'

He exhaled slowly and scratched his nose. 'I haven't told Cass that I was fired. I was out walking the streets so that she'd think I was at work.'

'Which streets?'

'Really?' He scraped the chair across the floor and crossed his ankles as he slouched back.

'Yes. A woman was murdered while you were out walking the streets. Which streets?'

'I. Can't. Remember.'

'Did you know Holly Long?'

He shrugged his shoulders.

'For the tape, Mr Dawkins shrugged his shoulders. Does that mean you don't know if you knew her?'

'Okay, I knew her. I saw her drinking on a couple of occasions in the Angel Arms but I don't really know her. I barely recognised her at the reception but when the news reports came out, I recognised her from the pub.'

Gina glanced down at her notes and flicked to the next page. 'No one can place you behind the bar at the time of her murder. The statements we have state that your girlfriend, Cassandra Wilson, was manning the bar all night and was mostly on her own.'

'I was there. I may have popped out for a cigarette but that was it. I knew some of the people at the party and she was managing okay.'

'You say you knew some of the party attendees, did that include Francesca Carter?'

Jaw clenched, he half smiled. 'No. I didn't know Francesca Carter.'

'Where were you last night?'

He grinned and leaned back. The little bit of cooperation they were receiving had come to an end. Briggs nodded her way.

'Robin Dawkins. I'm arresting you on suspicion of the murder of Francesca Carter on the evening of Monday, the eleventh of

May. You do not have to say anything, but it may harm your defence if you do not mention when questioned something which you later rely on in court. Anything you do say may be given in evidence.' She only hoped that twenty-four hours would be long enough to gather the evidence needed but with another bridesmaid in potential danger, she couldn't let him back out on the streets without doing all she could. He had size nine feet and he had no alibi during Francesca or Holly's murders. He also had opportunity in both cases.

'I'm not saying another word until I speak to a solicitor.' He kicked the table leg and turned to the side, refusing to look at her.

'Interview terminated at seventeen twelve. Let's book you in.'

Her thoughts drifted to Phillip Brighton and his interview. She hoped that her colleagues had managed to get more out of him. She was missing something that was right in front of her. Phillip Brighton and Robin Dawkins, both of them refusing to speak, both of them not having alibis. Maybe there was a connection between them. She had to keep the possibility of there being more than one person involved at the front of her mind. Two similar murders but different murder methods.

Briggs hurried to her side as she left Robin with the desk sergeant and a PC.

'Maybe a few hours in a cell will make him remember where he was and hopefully his solicitor will drum some sense into him.' Gina paused. 'I can't stop thinking about the girl he assaulted all those years ago. Can a person really change that much and not have the same urges, or maybe he needed to go further to satiate his urges? And, if Robin Dawkins gave into such urges, what would have triggered him to have done so? The party maybe?' The questions were coming thick and fast and she had no answers.

'We have twenty-four hours to work that one out. Wyre and O'Connor should be back soon. Maybe the post-mortem will tell us something.' Briggs smiled.

As they entered the incident room, it seemed a little quiet. The Phillip Brighton interview was still going on and most of the others were chasing up leads. PC Kapoor walked in.

'Any updates?'

'No, guv,' PC Kapoor replied before turning to Briggs. 'Only the press. They keep calling. Annie told us that she's preparing a press release for you.'

Briggs nodded. 'Great. I best head over to corporate communications and get onto that. I'll catch you later.'

Gina hoped he wouldn't. She needed a rest from everything and she needed to find out why her daughter hadn't called back. She hurried to her office and logged onto the system. Samuel Avery still hadn't been located. At the very least, she had Trevor Reed's statement about his behaviour towards Francesca at the wedding reception. There was a knock and her door was pushed open.

'Alright, guv. We have news.' Jacob sidled into her office and sat.

'Hit me with it.' She needed news. 'I have a list of suspects with no concrete evidence and I'm now on the twenty-four hour timer with Robin Dawkins. Is it to do with Phillip Brighton?'

'Yes, we've just finished his interview. He was on a bus at the time of Francesca's murder. With stops, that takes care of forty minutes. We're just checking out the pubs in Redditch he said he was drinking at. I suspect he went there to deal but we're not likely to get a confession out of him.'

That wasn't what she wanted to hear. She wanted something that could tie him to Francesca Carter's murder.

'We've had to let him go for now.'

'Okay, thank you.'

'We'll catch this person.'

She smiled. There didn't seem to be enough to go on. 'Organise a search of Robin Dawkins's flat for first thing but in the meantime, keep digging. We can speak to his girlfriend too. A six o'clock wake-up call will ensure she's in and catch her off guard. Does Cassandra Wilson have a record?'

'No, not a jot.'

'Have we managed to crack Robin Dawkins's phone?'

'Not yet, but that should come back soon. It takes a lot to keep our tech team out.'

'At least he has a phone. We still haven't come across the phone or tablet that Holly Long had been using.'

'Oh, Wyre and O'Connor are back.'

'It's all happening at once. I'll come through in a second. Maybe Francesca Carter's post-mortem will tell us something.' She quickly scanned the system. Holly Long's bank statements had been fully uploaded. She needed to delve further into Holly's life and take a closer look at the flags against certain transactions.

Her mind flashed back to Francesca's body lying in the bathtub, her hair splayed out and her bleeding toes, then she shivered. There was no putting it off.

She tried Hannah one more time but her phone was switched off. Hannah had to be with Samuel Avery, regardless of her daughter's reservations when she spoke to her the other night. Her stomach fluttered as she pushed the image of the two of them out of her mind. What was Avery playing at?

CHAPTER FIFTY-ONE

He hurried through the door and scurried down to the cellar to see his victim. He'd been gone a while but his absence had been unavoidable.

The light flickered on. There she was, waiting for him. Exactly where he'd left her with her hands bound behind her back only a couple of hours earlier. She'd drifted off to sleep, her head leaning against a dusty shelf.

He hadn't meant to be gone so long. Her low-cut top exposed his fingermarks on her neck and he grinned. The damsel-in-distress look suited her so well, better than he'd ever have thought. He only wished she was enough for him but she had merely been the catalyst for what he'd done wrong – not that he regretted it. His fingers twitched, but not for her. His body craved a release, and she couldn't help. His mind craved a new memory, one that could be replayed for an eternity, but it wasn't craving memories of her.

'Let me go,' she whimpered.

She looked so insincere he almost wanted to burst into laughter. 'You're awake.' He pulled a bottle of water from his bag and held it to her berry-coloured lips. She guzzled down half the contents before spluttering a mouthful into her lap. He bent down to stare into her eyes but she turned away. 'You hungry?'

She shook her head.

He kissed her gently on the forehead taking in the damp smell that had seeped through her clothes and hair. 'You're cold.' He grabbed a fleecy blanket and pulled it over her shoulders. She still wouldn't look at him even though he was doing everything possible to make her comfortable. This was a game he hadn't played before. He didn't know what his next move would be. All he could do was improvise.

He dragged a chair from under the stairs and slumped into it. It had been a long tense day, which was evident by the smell seeping from his pits. 'Look at me.' She looked down. He grabbed her hair and turned her face to his before locking his lips over hers. 'There, that's better.' Was it better? It didn't feel right at all. He didn't know why he was bothering. It wasn't working. This was all too weird.

She wasn't enough – this woman in front of him. There was another on the horizon and he knew just where to find her. He pulled the phone from his pocket and reread the stored messages.

'Okay, if you won't be nice, I guess I'll have to leave you here a bit longer.' As he stood to leave, he slipped his hand behind a bottle of wine and checked to see if Holly's tablet and phone were still there. They were. She glanced across at the pink tablet then looked away again. The woman in front of him had read everything on that phone and tablet already.

Once again, she leaned her head on the shelving and closed her eyes. He hurried back up the creaky steps and locked the door behind him. He had some business to attend to, some paperwork to straighten, then he'd be leaving for good. All the plans had been made and starting again would be fun, a whole new world of opportunities was about to open up. However, one opportunity lay on his doorstep and the urge to take it made him feel like an addict chasing a fix. He knew exactly who was next in line.

CHAPTER FIFTY-TWO

Wyre stood in front of the boards while she added to the notes under the photos of Francesca, and O'Connor leaned back in his seat at the other end of the room. He reached into his pocket and pulled out a squashed pasty. Gina felt the saliva building up in her mouth. She'd barely eaten over the course of the day and he was making her hungry.

'Are you okay going through the post-mortem with us?'

'Yes, guv,' Wyre replied. 'Thankfully everything went without a hitch. O'Connor didn't heave once – result. It was pretty much as described at the scene. We can confirm that Francesca Carter definitely drowned in her own bathwater. A huge clump of her hair was missing from her head and that too was found at the scene. There was evidence of several knocks to the back of her head, consistent with being dunked repeatedly. I'm afraid there wasn't much more to report. No evidence of previous abuse. No evidence of strangulation like we found on Holly Long's neck. She was slightly underweight for a twenty-five-year-old.' Wyre did the zip up on her black jacket and shivered a little.

'Anything flag up in the post-mortems to link Francesca Carter to Holly Long? They were both asphyxiated, one in water and one with a pillow, but was there anything else?'

Wyre flicked through her notes and scanned a few pages. 'No.'

'Okay, what are we missing? Holly was pregnant.'

'Francesca definitely wasn't,' Wyre interrupted.

'Any sign of a flower or petals on her body?'

'No, guv.'

Gina's mind whirred. 'I have a theory. Francesca wasn't pregnant. Carnations are Mother's day flowers. The petals had been sprinkled across Holly's stomach, the murderer trying to tell us that Holly was a mother. The flower head in Holly's throat, was that to gag her, to stop her from talking about her pregnancy? And now I'm bouncing back to there being two suspects.' Gina stared at the wall as she let the cases flood her mind. 'How about the scene? Anything else to report?'

Wyre shook her head. 'They are still processing evidence. As we know, the main exhibit is the footprint.'

'Problem is, the two we've had in today are both a size nine and as it's a popular size, I'm guessing we'll get more size nine suspects. We still have Edward Powell to consider. Have we located the owner of the Red Setter yet?'

O'Connor swallowed a lump of pasty and swigged his drink. 'It's not for the want of trying. We've watched that footage several times and not one person gets out of a car with a Red Setter. They're big dogs too. I wouldn't have missed it.'

Gina flinched as the voice came from behind.

'I've included an appeal for this particular dog walker or anyone who may have seen them in the press release that has just gone out. Expect to be bombarded with calls, it's already hit the locals and social media.' Briggs leaned against the doorframe as he placed his hands in his trouser pockets.

'Thank you.' She took a few steps and looked out into the potholed car park lined with police cars and her phone rang. 'Bernard.' She listened and smiled as he reeled off his information.

'What is it, Harte?' Briggs asked.

Everyone in the room waited in silence for her to break the news. 'The foetus, Holly's baby, we have a DNA lead, on the father's side. Officers in Cardiff have arrested a woman for driving under the influence and she is a twenty-five per cent match, which means she could be a grandparent or aunt of the baby's father. Problem is, we don't know her name as yet. She's apparently so drunk they're letting her sleep it off for a while. She was also caught in a stolen car. The owner pulled up to post a letter and she drove off in the car. They're going to keep disturbing her to see if she can talk. As soon as they have anything, they're going to message back. Her mugshot is on its way. Let's hope she bears some resemblance to one of our suspects.'

A slight cheer filtered through the room. It was the biggest breakthrough they'd had. All they had to do was check out her family tree to work out who they needed to bring in.

Gina kept hitting refresh on the computer screen next to the boards but the photo still hadn't arrived. She glanced up at Holly and Francesca's photos. Her fingers tingled with excitement. The email pinged up from Cardiff Police.

Everyone crowded around and waited for the photo to load. Seconds later, they had a mugshot of their drunk driver. A short, round-faced woman with greasy hair. She had one eye open and the other half shut and her nose was a sore shade of pink with a couple of scabs around the edge.

'She doesn't look like anyone we know.' Jacob slumped back over to his chair and fell into it.

'I guess we'll just have to wait until she's sobered up a bit.' Gina grabbed her notebook and popped it into her laptop bag. 'Anything else?'

A low hum of noes filled the room.

'I'm going to be working from home. If anything comes in from the press releases, call me any time, whatever the hour. I'll go through everything we have on the system again and again until I find something.'

She took one last glance at the woman in the photo and tilted her head. She couldn't see a resemblance to anyone she knew. She tilted her head the other way. The shape of the woman's chin seemed familiar. She looked away. It was just a chin. Any familiarity she thought she may have seen had now long gone. She stared for a further second and zipped her bag up.

CHAPTER FIFTY-THREE

Gina threw her keys onto the kitchen table. Ebony jumped through the cat flap and began rubbing her head against Gina's black trousers, depositing hair all over them. She bent down and lifted the cat up, stroking her before kissing her on the head. She put the cat on the table and pushed a sachet of food into the cat bowl, before heading to the living room and booting her laptop up. She had come home to work in comfort, not to take the rest of the night off.

She tried Hannah again but the phone kept going to voicemail. It was no good, she was going to have to call Nanny Hetty, her ex-husband's mother. Her daughter had been there when they last spoke. She pressed the number and waited.

'Hello,' came the gruff voice on the other end, a voice that sent a shiver through her.

'Hetty, it's Gina.' She swallowed and wiped a bead of sweat from her brow.

'I know who you are. What the hell do you want? How you've got the nerve to call here after all that you've done.' The woman coughed as one would expect when she smoked about eighty a day.

'I need to know if Hannah's there.'

The sounds of Gracie playing made Gina smile. At least Gracie was okay. Hetty had many faults but she knew that her grand-daughter would be safe with the woman. It was Gina she hated. 'I'm surprised you had the nerve to call after what your lovely colleague did to my Stephen last year. You tried to set him up.

Told him to shut up or the planted evidence would come out. I may be a thick-looking old boot but I know more than I make out. You're nothing but a devious bitch.'

Hetty was right. The secret that Gina was now keeping for Briggs had consequences and Hetty's hatred of her was one of them. Stephen's withdrawal from making her life a misery was another, which she was thankful of. There was no way she'd ever admit a thing. Briggs's secret was as safe with her as hers was with him. That's the way it would be, for life.

'Hetty, this is ridiculous. I'm worried about Hannah. Is she there?'

'Have it your way, but we know what you're like. We know.' She paused. 'Hannah isn't here. She left after you woke us all up with your call and said she was going back to the B&B as the settee was hurting her back. I want to spend time with Gracie, not like you, so I said she should go out and enjoy herself for the remains of her stay.'

A tear filled Gina's eye. That had stung. She loved spending time with Gracie but she had a job, a demanding job that she loved. Hetty was retired.

'You were always selfish, even when our Terry were alive. You didn't even care when he died. I saw you drinking at his funeral, that emotionless face. I tell you something and it plays on my mind. I saw my boy come back on many an occasion after a skinful and not once did he fall down – not over a step or down any stairs. Anyway, snowflake, you get back to your duties. Go back to work while I look after this beautiful little girl.' Hetty slammed the phone down.

Gina's heart hummed as the pace picked up. Soon it was booming, threatening to burst through her ribs. Pain seared across her chest and she gasped for breath. She tried to scream but a burst of sobs escaped as she slipped to the floor, pulling the door handle off a cupboard as she dropped. Her wedding night flashed through her mind as her vision peppered. The light of the kitchen being replaced by that of her mind's eye. Terry's hands gripping her neck as he forced himself on her. The pleasure in his eyes as he gripped harder. The main light of their bedroom was still on and so was her dress, the cheap thing she'd bought from the high street. From that moment, he owned her.

She opened her eyes to Ebony's meows. She breathed in and out until she'd regained control. The tremor in her fingers reached all the way to her elbows as she breathed in the air around her. The pains subsided but her stomach churned. Ebony forced her head under her arm so she stroked her gently until the shaking went. She threw the door handle across the kitchen floor, scaring Ebony out of the cat flap. 'I'm sorry,' she called out. She hadn't meant to scare her furry companion away. *Pull yourself together, Harte.*

She staggered to a stand, a wash of weakness set in her muscles and bones. Yawning, she'd love nothing more than to go to bed and ruminate over her conversation with Hetty. The woman had been right. She knew both of her sons better than Gina would ever know Hannah and she understood deep down that something more than a stumble on the stairs had happened to Terry. Gina would never tell her how she held back on calling for that ambulance as he took his dying breath. She'd never tell Hetty about all the times she thought she'd die at his hands while he was alive. That was her bit of control. She knew the truth about everything, Hetty knew nothing. That was her ultimate win. It was her only win.

Leading with her weary legs, she flopped onto the settee and grabbed her laptop. She scrolled through the case files methodically.

She'd stared at the photo of the drunk driver who shared DNA with their murdered woman's baby. She couldn't pinpoint the familiarity even though she'd been through all the suspect photos. She checked her watch – it was almost eleven and she had to be back at the station for five to prepare for the search of Robin Dawkins's flat. It was going to be another long day. She opened the files containing Holly Long's bank statements and reread all the notes that had been made beside them.

Her phone rang and she grabbed it. 'Any news?'

Briggs paused for a second before speaking. 'Only that the press release went out. I also saw a report out tonight that questioned our competency. The link has been made that both victims were at the same wedding reception. They're dubbing it "The Bridesmaid Murders". It's a nightmare. What are you up to?'

'I'm just scrutinising Holly Long's bank statements. Her spending exceeded her income by several hundred pounds per month. She had no credit at all. Had she not been receiving a regular payment of fifteen hundred pounds per month on top of her meagre salary, she'd be in major debt by now.' Gina glanced at the dates as she bit her nails. 'She'd been receiving this supplementary income since moving into her flat over a year ago from…' She looked at the reference. It was a series of numbers, the length of an account number. 'I mean, could she have had another job that we don't know about? She received the same amount on the same date, every month. This suggests a permanent contract.'

'That is odd. Or blackmail? Something to consider.' Briggs paused.

'Definitely. I'm not ruling anything out right now. We need to go full throttle on this. We need to find out whom this account number belongs to and where the account is registered.'

Gina reached across and grabbed the black coffee from the table and took a swig.

'It was lovely spending the night at yours, I'm just sorry I went out like a light on the couch. Are you okay?'

'I'm fine.' A slight smile emerged from her lips. 'Anyway, I have about five hours sleep and then I need to be up to raid Dawkins's flat. I'll see you tomorrow when I get back to the station.' There was no way she was going to tell him about her panic attack or how niggled she felt about the photo of the drink driver who seemed key to progressing with the case. She only hoped that the woman spoke some coherent words soon.

'I'll catch you tomorrow. Goodnight, Gina.' He paused for a few seconds then ended the call.

She swapped the screens over and glanced back at the photo. She leaned in, studying the contours of the woman's face, the shape of her nose, the distance of her eyes. She stopped at the chin, slightly wide, then her eyes were pulled to the nose again. It was more of an all over resemblance to someone who was familiar but it wasn't obvious. A subtle bit here and a slight likeness there. Nothing definite was pointing her to the person this woman reminded her of. She slammed the lid down and closed her eyes with that face etched into her mind.

CHAPTER FIFTY-FOUR

Wednesday, 13 May 2020

Lilly stood in the garden under the moon's light enjoying every puff on her vape. She'd given up smoking when she'd found out she was pregnant with Ben. She and Brendan ceremoniously tore up their cigarettes and threw them in the bin. She hadn't told Brendan that all through her pregnancy she'd obsessed over giving birth so that she could have a smoke. Instead, as soon as her stitches had healed enough for her to get to a shop, she'd taken up vaping and still hid the habit like the secret that it was.

She inhaled the vanilla vapour, enjoying the slight rush through her body as she puffed into the air. It floated straight past their bedroom window. If Brendan woke up, he'd not only wonder where she was, he might wonder why a thick cloud of smoke was visible through the slight gap in the curtains. She took a few steps down the garden towards the back gate and inhaled again. The security light clicked off. If he woke to that, she could always say she couldn't sleep or she felt a bit yuck. Whatever – she'd find an excuse. As long as he didn't see vapour, she was in the clear.

She loved the silence. It was rare. Since Ben had come along, their house had been filled with the sound of cartoons, Ben's crying and more often, his laughter. She loved it all but still, the lure of her night-time secret puffs on the vape while enjoying the night's silence was strong. This moment was hers and no one else's. As she took another puff, she held the vapour in her mouth as she listened to a shuffle at the other side of the gate. Silently exhaling, she crept backwards, triggering the security light again. That was twice. She was sure she'd wake Brendan up now. For once, she really hoped she had. She'd have to tell him that she'd heard a noise and came for a look, but he'd be angry. He'd tell her she should have woken him and he'd be right. No, the shuffling had been nothing more than a figment of her imagination. The other night when they saw someone loitering, that could have been nothing more than a person passing by. Having the panic alarm fitted was overkill.

Another shuffle came from behind the gate. She checked her pocket and all she could hear was her booming heart. The panic alarm was on the kitchen worktop. She'd changed her mind. It wasn't overkill. The gate rattled and she spotted something that sent her head in a whirl – they'd forgot to lock the gate after all that talking about security. She took another step away from it. The bar on the catch lifted. He was coming for her, the third and final bridesmaid. She didn't want to believe it but she knew he would find her and he had.

She turned to run and stumbled on the mossy slab. Glancing back, she caught sight of the hooded figure entering her garden. Run – she had to run. She darted straight over the rest of the slabs in her slippers, treading as carefully as she could as her assailant sped up. She felt the air of his chase on her back as she reached for the door handle. It was no good. He wrenched her back by the hood of her dressing gown. As she tried to scream a hand covered her mouth. She thought of Ben and his cute little chuckles as she willed Brendan to wake up. He was normally a light sleeper but not tonight. Then she thought of the panic button on the side. How could she have been so stupid?

CHAPTER FIFTY-FIVE

Knees knocking, Gina entered the red room to catch the back of a man. The hulk-like figure brought the cleaver down onto the butcher's block. Blood splattered and Gina let out a yelp. She shouldn't have said a word. Now he knew she was there and she was going to be next. He turned. Through the welder's mask, she could see his beady eyes but what startled her more was the cage that his bulky frame had been masking; the cage containing Hannah as she held a single carnation. She wanted to run but she couldn't leave her own flesh and blood. As he removed the welder's mask, she recognised the face instantly but the face wasn't the owner of the eyes she'd seen only a few seconds earlier. Hannah's sobs had turned into laughter as Nanny Hetty came at her with the meat cleaver. 'Whose eyes were they?' she yelled as she ran from the red room, into the vacuous dark space. The figure had gone but she was alone with no answers. Whose eyes had she been staring into?

Gina tipped the glass of water into her lap as the phone's ringing brought her out of her nightmare. She grabbed the lit-up phone. 'Jacob. What have you got?' She placed her hand on her chest hoping that her heart would calm down. Glancing around the dark room, the moon shone a beam against the main wall through her open curtains. There was no cleaver-wielding Hetty chasing her. She was safe, alone and in her living room. Ebony jumped onto the settee and changed her mind about nestling into Gina's lap when she realised it was soaking wet. 'Damn!'

'You okay, guv?'

'Yes. I fell asleep holding a glass of water and now I've poured it all over myself. What an idiot.' She grabbed the snuggle blanket that had slipped off her knees and mopped up what she could as she balanced the phone between her ear and shoulder. 'What you got?'

'The panic button has just been pressed over at Lilly and Brendan Hill's residence. Uniform are on their way over. They let us know as soon as the call came in. Did you want to head over? I can meet you there?'

She threw the blanket to the floor. 'I'm on my way.' She ran up the stairs for a quick wash and change, yawning as she ran her fingers through her hair. She glanced at the shower, almost gutted at not having time to soak under a flow of warm water to properly wake herself up.

Grappling with the closest pair of trousers and a light V-neck jumper, she checked her appearance once before running out of the door. An image flashed through her mind. The eyes in her dream before the mask had been lifted wouldn't leave her alone. The slight crinkle to the corners as the assailant smiled behind the mask, and the way he – it was a he – the way his brows raised as he spoke. It couldn't be. She knew exactly who that drunk driver in Wales reminded her of and he had a lot of explaining to do.

CHAPTER FIFTY-SIX

Shaking his arm several times, he managed to ease his battered muscles. He hadn't banked on her grabbing him the way she had. She was definitely stronger than Frannie. Unrolling the scarf from around his mouth and nose, he dropped it to the floor. Not the best disguise but with his oversized hood, a lot was concealed. Mummy bridesmaid would keep. That was his nickname for Lilly.

He removed the hoodie and grabbed the phone off the side. It wasn't his phone. He'd never be seen dead with a purple diamanté case and a screensaver of a dog wearing a crown. The messages on the phone had been interesting; they'd definitely brought a smile to his face. That poor desperate girl certainly was a needy one but he'd seen that in her already. As he followed her the other night from Lilly's house, he sensed her tension, but she had interrupted his plans. The odd bang of a fence panel here, the throwing of a stone there. That's why she'd started to run although he had to chuckle, she wasn't good at running. He'd go as far as to say, he thought she was flat-footed and her moves reminded him of a duck trying to balance on a frozen pond.

Her pitiful life was worthless. She wasn't his type, not like Holly or Frannie but they all looked the same when they went purple while being gripped around the jugular.

The chair below screeched across the tiled floor. The woman in the cellar had woken up.

He pressed send on the message.

I'm so sorry about earlier. Everything has been getting to me. I shouldn't have cut you off like that. Forgive me. I'll message you tomorrow. I promise. K. Xxx

And he would. He wouldn't leave her wondering if a message would come but he had to get this right. This wasn't for him; tomorrow he would share this pleasure with another. Someone who deserved the gift he was about to give them.

He smiled as he read her message.

I totally understand and I just want to help you, as friends do. Message me tomorrow and we'll talk or we can talk now if you want. I'm always here for you. Shall I call? C. Xxx

His new friend had responded in exactly the same way as he had messaged. Three kisses and an initial. She trusted him. He smiled as a fuzzy feeling washed through his body. Trust – given far too easily once again. She trusted a message on a phone sent by someone she couldn't hear or see.

I'm a bit tired at the moment but I'd love to talk tomorrow. Can't wait. Take care and sleep well. K. Xxx.

He turned the phone off and placed it into his pocket. Again, there was a scraping noise coming from the cellar. There was something far more important that he needed to attend to and she was waiting exactly where he'd left her. He kicked the hoodie out of the way and opened the door to the cellar.

Tomorrow, he will have his answer. Who was he coming for? Only one of them would be the lucky winner. Time was ticking and he had a new life waiting for him.

CHAPTER FIFTY-SEVEN

Gina pulled up behind the police car on the road beside Lilly and Brendan Hill's house. A couple of lights were on despite the hour and a woman cradling a baby let go of her curtain when Gina glanced her way. She hurried to the door and knocked. Lilly answered, her hair scooped messily into a topknot. 'Come in. The police are just talking to Brendan in the lounge.'

'Thank you.' Gina stepped into the hallway and followed Lilly into the lounge. Jacob smiled as she sat in the same seat as she'd sat on last time she'd spoken to Lilly Hill. She glanced around the room. PC Kapoor had just finished making notes and was ending her talk with Brendan. The man stood and pulled the back of his T-shirt out of his checked lounge pants. Lilly tied the belt of her dressing gown that covered her blue pyjamas. Gina smiled at PC Kapoor. 'Can I just have a quick word?'

The young officer nodded and followed her into the kitchen as Jacob continued speaking to the Hills.

'I thought I'd ask you what happened before speaking to Mrs Hill.'

In a squeaky half whisper, Kapoor began to relay what she'd been told with added hand movements for emphasis. 'When I got here, guv, Mrs Hill was a bit shaken. She has a grazed wrist. As she went to open the back door, she fell into the wall and scraped her arm. She said the intruder grabbed her from behind by the hood of her dressing gown and placed his hand over her mouth. She managed to wriggle free and scream. She thinks she scared him off as he ran away at that point.'

'What time was this?'

Kapoor glanced at her notes and her black eyebrows arched. 'About one thirty. She said she was in the garden, alone, and she heard a noise coming from behind the gate. She then saw the gate open so she ran. The intruder chased her into her garden.'

'Do we have a description?'

She scrunched her nose and shook her head. 'Not really. The intruder was wearing a black hoodie and gloves. That's all she saw. She said it happened too quickly.'

'Would you call forensics while I sit with Mrs Hill? Has anyone been in the garden since the attack?'

'PC Smith is still out there looking but we saw no one when we checked. Just us. Lilly and Brendan Hill haven't been outside since the incident.'

Gina hoped they hadn't trampled any evidence but she knew that they'd have to go out and check to see if the intruder was still around. The security light flashed on in the garden seconds before Smith entered through the back door. 'Alright, guv. Definitely no one out there now. I've walked through two streets and there's not a soul around.'

Gina glanced through the window into the garden. 'After forensics have been called, could you please start a door to door, find out if any of the neighbours saw anything. Start with the houses that have lights on.'

'On it, guv.' Smith nodded and left with Kapoor in tow.

She continued glancing out of the window. The gate had to have been about fifteen meters from the door. The slabs were a little mossy. She scrunched her eyes so that she could see a little better. A skid mark across the slimy garden slab caught her attention. Maybe this time the attacker had left them a little more to go on. That's if the intruder had anything to do with Holly and Francesca's murders. With the gate closed, the garden scene was secured for now. It wasn't a particularly breezy night and there had been no rain. For a change, the weather was on their side.

'Lilly, may I speak with you?' Gina asked as she entered the living room.

The young woman nodded and followed her to the kitchen, leaving Jacob with Brendan Hill.

'PC Kapoor has briefly gone through your statement with me. I'd like to ask a few more questions. First of all though, would you like to be checked over by a paramedic? That scrape to your hand looks sore and you look a bit pale.'

Lilly shook her head and took a seat at the kitchen table. A tear slid down her cheek. 'My heart has just stopped thumping but no, I don't need a paramedic. It's nothing a little antiseptic won't sort.'

'Okay, this happened about one thirty, is that correct?'

'Yes, I pressed the button a couple of minutes after that so it must have been about then.'

Gina opened her notebook and titled up the page as she continued to speak. 'Were you still up or had you gone to bed and woken up? How did you come to be in the garden?'

Lilly shrugged and sat back a little. 'I don't want Brendan to know.' She stood and closed the kitchen door and continued speaking in a hushed tone. 'I couldn't sleep. With what happened to Fran and Holly, I kept having weird dreams and waking up. At one point I was shaking and I just had to get out of bed. Brendan doesn't know, but I vape. I didn't want the smell to fill the house. Sometimes I do it in the garden when he's asleep. That's what I was doing. While I was out there, I heard a shuffle outside the gate. I guess this was about one twenty-five. It all happened so fast really.' She pulled the sleeve of her dressing gown over her hand and wiped her cheek and sniffed. 'I saw the latch on the gate move. The bar, it lifted. I knew someone was coming in so I ran back to the house. I was so scared, especially when I slid on the slab. I thought that was it. I thought he'd get me but I kept going and reached the door.' The woman traced the wood grain on the table with her finger.

Lilly had slipped, not the intruder. Gina made a note so that she could pass that information onto forensics. 'Can you tell me anything else? You say the intruder was wearing a hoodie and gloves.'

She bit her bottom lip. 'I can't think.' She closed her eyes. 'I think he was wearing boots, dark boots. Yes, I'm sure I saw boots and laces. I can't remember anything else. The hood hung over his eyes, oh, and he seemed to have a scarf wrapped around his mouth – a black or dark coloured scarf. The figure looked masculine. He was white. I caught a glimpse of his cheeks.'

'Did you by any chance see or hear in which direction your attacker ran away?'

Lilly clasped her lips together. 'No. I was so upset and I slammed the door as quick as I could and locked it. I don't know which way he went.'

'Thank you. If something else comes to mind after we've spoken, call me at any time. Sometimes after the initial shock has worn off, further details may come to mind.' Gina knew that most of what she'd get from Lilly was right here and now, but she still hoped that something else would come to light. 'Forensics will be here soon. They will want to have a look at your back garden and they'll look for evidence outside your gate and along the path. They'll also need your dressing gown. PCs Smith and Kapoor have already started door-to-door enquiries. It's possible that one of your neighbours may have seen something.'

Another tear slid down Lilly's cheek. 'Why is this happening to us? Holly and Fran were both harmless. I don't think they had an enemy between them and now someone's after me. I was so scared when he grabbed me. I really thought my time was up and now I feel guilty. I shook him off but the others were killed. I keep thinking, if I hadn't have fought back and screamed, I'd be dead, like them. My baby boy wouldn't have a mummy and Brendan would be on his own and I can't bear those thoughts.' She grabbed a green stuffed rabbit from the chair beside her and hugged it.

A loud cry pierced the air. 'Mummy.'

'I best go to him.'

As Lilly left there was a knock at the door. Jacob almost bumped into Gina in the hallway as they both went to open the door at the same time. Gina stepped aside and thanked Keith, the crime scene manager, for coming as they led him into the kitchen.

'What a week it's been.' Keith struggled past with a bag and his sample box.

'Do you want a hand?'

Gina took the bag from him and he gave out a slight yelp as he placed the box on the kitchen table. 'My back is getting worse.' He ran his hand through his grey comb-over and exhaled. 'Right, the intruder was in the back garden. Is that right?'

'Yes. He chased Lilly Hill over the slabs to her back door. He grabbed her from behind but she managed to fight him off while screaming. He ran away after that. In which direction, we don't know. That streak of mossy slime on the slab was caused by Lilly. She said she slipped. She did say that the attacker was wearing boots. Boot covers weren't mentioned. If you can find another imprint in the garden or outside, that might just prove that our assailant was the same person who was at Cleevesford Manor and Francesca Carter's house.'

'I'll get my creaky old back out there now. One of the assistants should be here in a moment but I'll make a start for now. As soon as I have anything, I'll call you. It's a big enough garden and then there's the path outside. Could be a while.'

'Thanks, Keith.'

He unlocked the door leaving Gina and Jacob alone in the kitchen.

'Can we speak outside?'

Jacob followed her through the front door and over towards her car. 'What is it?' He suddenly looked more awake than he had a few moments ago as he waited for her to speak.

'That drunk driver that they arrested in Cardiff, I see a resemblance to someone we've interviewed recently and I wanted to run it by you to see if you could see it too.'

'Who?' He leaned against her car.

As she went to speak, her phone rang. 'It's a Cardiff number. Before I answer this call: I see Edward Powell in her.' As she listened to the officer with the Welsh accent reel off the name of the woman, she smiled before relaying the information for Jacob's benefit. 'So just to confirm, the woman's name is Sally Powell. Thank you so much. That's really helped us. If you could send all information you have on her, that would be fantastic.' She ended the call. 'There are a couple more checks we can do just to confirm my suspicions but DNA doesn't lie and the surname matches too. I want Edward Powell brought in as soon as possible. He is without a doubt the person who got Holly pregnant and he's yet to provide an alibi as to where he was on the night of Fran's murder. As far as I'm aware, no owner of a Red Setter dog has come forward since the appeals have been put out. He's well in the frame.' She paused. 'Maybe Holly was blackmailing him or maybe he was helping her out with money. She had regular payments going into her account. We need to concentrate our efforts into nailing who owns that account number and sort code. Where exactly is the money coming from? It's possible Holly was about to tell Kerry of their relationship. Did that push him to murder her? Why would he kill Francesca? Did she know about Holly and Edward? He has a cushy life with Kerry. A gorgeous home, plenty of money and a job that came with the package. He'd lose it all if everything came out in the open. Bring him in.'

'Where does all this leave Robin Dawkins?' Jacob rubbed his eyes and yawned.

Gina stared at the pavement for a moment as she processed all that had happened. They had until five in the afternoon to prove he had something to do with Holly and Francesca's murders. 'He was in custody when Lilly was attacked but until we know more, he is still a suspect. I can't eliminate the possibility that there might be more than one person involved and he won't tell us where he was at the time of Francesca's murder. Let's hope the search of his apartment sheds some light on the case. I also want to speak to his girlfriend. Let the search commence.'

CHAPTER FIFTY-EIGHT

Bang! Cass flinched and threw the quilt back. She turned her lamp on and squinted as she focused on the time. Six in the morning. Maybe the police had released Elvis. She knew he hadn't taken his door key with him. She threw her legs over the side of the bed and wedged her toes into her slippers before padding across the threadbare carpet. A loud bang filled the silence again. 'Police, open up.'

Cass swallowed. Something had happened, she knew it. After tossing and turning all night, she'd only been asleep for a couple of hours, kept awake by this sense of foreboding. She'd been happy when Kerry had messaged. Her happiness was always short-lived. She knew something bad had to follow. 'I'm coming,' she called as she removed the chain from the door and opened up.

'DI Harte, Cleevesford Police. We have a warrant to search the property. May we come in?'

The detective stood still, awaiting Cass's response. Her brown hair was falling out of a tangled rubber band reminding Cass of her own unkempt self. While Cass had been watching Kerry's house, the police detective in front of her had come out with Kerry and her mother. Her heart rate picked up. It was down to luck that she hadn't been found in the bushes.

Cass also knew that she didn't have an option but to let the police in. She knew what a warrant meant, she'd seen police programmes on the television. The fact that DI Harte was asking was more about being polite and not trying to alarm her. She opened the door, letting them into the small hall that led to all rooms. 'Of course. What's happened?'

'Do you have the keys to Robin Dawkins's car and can you tell us where he keeps it?'

'He doesn't use it. The MOT ran out ages ago. It's in the garage rotting away – number three in the block opposite the flats.' She passed the DI the car keys that had been dangling off the key hook for months. The DI handed them to the suited male officer, then he left.

'Shall we sit down?' DI Harte led her to the kitchen and they sat at the kitchen table while the other officers carried on with their duties. She watched through the gap in the kitchen door as gloves were snapped on and hair was covered. The DI loosened her stab vest and wriggled a little until she got comfortable. 'That's better. These things are a little tight. I know this looks scary and I know you're probably wondering what's happening. We have your partner Robin Dawkins in custody at the moment, as you know. As it stands, we can't place where he was at the time of Francesca Carter's murder. I was hoping we could have a little chat.'

Cass knew that police didn't just chat. This was an interview and everything she said would be duly noted. Her mind flitted back to Elvis and how secretive he'd become. She swallowed again as she thought about the drugs she'd poured out of his boot earlier. They'd long gone. If the police found more drugs, would she be arrested? 'I know Elvis has done time, he said something when the officers came to take him. What did he do?'

'You'll be able to speak to him yourself soon. For now, would you mind if I ask a couple of questions?'

She shook her head. She did mind really. She didn't want to be associated with anything as vile as the murder of Kerry's friends and now her boyfriend was in the frame. She thought of the messages that Kerry had sent. Her friend wouldn't want to know her if all this came out.

The DI gave her a reassuring smile. 'I know this is worrying for you but I will try to make it as easy as possible. Would you like some water?'

'No. Am I in trouble?'

'We just need to ask you a few questions, that's all. Can you tell me if you saw Mr Dawkins on Monday the eleventh of May between six and eight in the evening, that's this Monday just gone?'

'Let me think.' That was the night she'd visited Kerry after work. 'I tried calling him a few times to tell him that I wouldn't be home when he finished work but his phone kept going to voicemail so I left a message.'

'Where did you go?'

Cass straightened her back and spat out the stray hair that had made its way into her mouth. She stared at the DI, slightly open-mouthed as she realised that she was probably a suspect. Could they think that she helped Elvis to kill Fran? 'I haven't hurt anyone.' Why did she feel so guilty even though she was telling the truth? Cass knew she had one of those faces that screamed guilt even though she'd done nothing wrong. Maybe Elvis had said something and was trying to push the blame onto her for something he'd done.

'I'm not saying you have but we just need to establish where you were so that we can eliminate you. This is nothing more than routine questioning. We've been asking everyone the same questions.' The DI smiled lightly as she placed her pen on her notebook.

'Okay. I visited Kerry, that's Kerry Powell. We're old school friends and after what happened at her wedding, I wanted her to know that I was there for her. I thought she might need to talk.'

'I'm sure she appreciated you going around. What time did you arrive?'

Cass pulled the loose end of her thumbnail away and dropped it onto the kitchen floor. 'She told me to get there for eight so

I got there for eight.' The DI made a few notes. 'I don't know where Elvis was between five and seven. I know where I was. I finished work at six, went to the Co-op on Cleevesford High Street and I bought a bottle of wine; this was about half six. I then waited at the bus stop for an hour so that I wouldn't get to Kerry's house too early. There were lots of people there and the man who runs the chippy waved at me. I didn't want to go home, didn't see the point so I just waited and played games on my phone. At about seven thirty, I got on the bus, went six stops to the edge of Cleevesford, then got off the bus and I walked along the roadside until I reached Kerry's house.' She paused for a moment and gasped for breath, realising that she'd reeled off her whereabouts without breathing. 'I was a little early but that didn't seem to matter. She let me in anyway. We had a glass of wine and she spoke about Holly and how upset she was, but she was quite drunk. I had a Sambuca with her. Then, about forty minutes later, I left and went home.'

Her mind whirred. She'd been waffling and she looked too nervous. She pulled the top of another nail away and dropped it into her lap. The detective glanced up at her, waiting for more. Should she speak? She placed her finger in her mouth and began chewing the ragged nail. She couldn't give Elvis an alibi. He didn't text her back or answer her calls during the time that Fran was being murdered. The more she thought about it, the more she knew that Elvis wouldn't stand a chance with a woman like Fran. He was a scally, poor and uneducated, not the type a sophisticated young woman would go for. But Cass had seen women when they'd had a few, playing up to him when he performed as Elvis and they'd downed too much Prosecco. He could put on a show, albeit a very average show.

'What time did you hear from Mr Dawkins after you visited Kerry's house?'

'I remember Elvis messaging me when I was on the bus home but he didn't say when he was coming back.' She pulled her phone out and scrolled through her messages. 'Look, he said he'd be home soon, it was nearly nine when he sent this message.' The DI glanced over and made a note.

'When did he get home?'

Cass remembered the foul mood he'd been in, especially as she hadn't bought him anything from the chip shop. 'I guess he got home about half ten. I got back to Cleevesford High Street about quarter past nine, I went to the chippy and walked home.'

'How did he seem?'

Should she tell the DI that he was angry? She crossed her ankles under the table and continued picking at the same nail. She pulled and almost yelped as the sting of pulling nail from skin hit her. 'Short-tempered.' Her eyes watered up as she rubbed her sore finger.

'In what way?'

'He told me he was with friends when I asked him where he'd been. He basically told me to mind my own business and he was angry that I didn't get him any chips.' Their relationship problems went beyond chips but she couldn't explain why he was the way he was. 'I think he was cheating on me. He would never tell me where he was going or who he was with. He had all his gadgets password protected.' She spotted a forensics-suited officer through a gap in the door. He was bagging and tagging Elvis's laptop. 'He didn't want to touch me. I could just tell. He was very secretive.'

The detective scribbled everything down. 'Can I ask about the night of Kerry Powell's wedding reception? You were working at the party, not there as a guest?'

Cass stared at the detective. What was she getting at? She was saying that Cass wasn't a good enough friend to get an invite. They'd just been distanced over the years, that was all and now they were going to be best friends again. The DI wouldn't understand that. 'I wanted the best for her and I knew if I helped out with the guest ale bar, it would all go well. She was happy with me doing that. I was behind the bar all night. I didn't even get a chance to pee.'

'Were Robin Dawkins and Samuel Avery working behind the bar with you?'

She shrugged her shoulders and began chewing on another nail. 'They seemed to be enjoying the party. I was run off my feet, I didn't see what they were doing all night. I've already given a statement.' She did remember something that was said, something by Samuel Avery and it had upset her that Elvis thought it was funny. It wasn't funny at all. She couldn't tell the detective, not before speaking to Elvis first. Or could she? He'd been treating her horribly. Maybe she should tell. What they were saying definitely wasn't funny.

'Cassandra, are you okay?'

She snapped out of her thoughts and pasted a fake smile across her face. 'Yes. That's all I have. I didn't look up that night. Sorry, I was just run off my feet.'

Boots shuffled in the hallway and Jacob entered. 'Guv, we've found something in the car.'

'Excuse me.' DI Harte stood and followed the other detective out of the room. Cass stood and listened by the door, just out of sight.

'There are twenty wraps of cocaine and a huge collection of multi-coloured pills – looks like ecstasy. He had to be dealing.'

The voices hushed a little. Cass flinched as the DI was coming back. She'd disposed of the drugs she'd found in his Doc Martens in the bin outside the shops. Her heart rate ramped up. If Elvis had stashed any more drugs in their flat, her home, she'd do what? He already walked all over her. Fingers trembling, she only hoped he wouldn't drag her down with him. The DI entered. 'We've unfortunately found a large quantity of drugs in the boot of Mr Dawkins's car. Can you tell us anything about these?'

She shook her head. 'I'm not allowed to go anywhere near his garage or his car.' In her mind, she now knew exactly why he was getting calls all the time and she'd thought he was having an affair.

'Did you know that Mr Dawkins was fired from his job on Monday night?'

A tear welled up in the corner of her eye. She knew nothing about the man she'd been living with. A dangerous secretive past, a drug dealing present and on top of everything, she knew full well that he was a suspect in Holly and Fran's murders. 'I had no idea. I'm so stupid.' She snivelled a little as she tried to hold back her tears.

'No you're not. We will need you to come to the station and make a formal statement. Can you do that?'

She nodded. The DI may have been asking her a question but she knew there wasn't an option to say no. Not now they'd found drugs in the garage.

'Is the garage tenancy in your name too?'

'No. It was Elvis's garage. I've never actually been in it, had no reason to.' She paused and bit the skin on the side of her mouth. The DI had kind eyes. Maybe she should tell her what Elvis and Sam had been talking about at the reception. She wouldn't let Elvis bring her down any more. As she went to speak the male detective came back in to move them out of the kitchen, ready for more searching. Now wasn't the time. She held her phone to her heart knowing Kerry would message again soon. Kerry would be able to help her get through all this. They'd help each other.

CHAPTER FIFTY-NINE

'Tick-tock. Tick-tock. Time is passing. Who's next?' He stared into the eyes of cellar woman. That wasn't her name but names weren't needed between them, fleeting references would do the job.

He ran his fingers through her silky hair and gazed into her eyes – he was getting into it now. A slight look of panic flashed across her face. He removed the scarf that he'd tied around her mouth and she screamed. He'd expected that. Hell, he'd banked on it, it was all part of the fun. He grinned as he kneeled down in front of her. The screaming ended and he ran his fingertips gently over her slender neck, pressing on the pulsing vein. He stopped as she coughed then placed the scarf back across her mouth, retying it tighter behind her head.

'Don't worry. I won't trap your hair in the scarf, not like last time.' He kissed her on the cheek. 'Won't be long now.' He turned off the light and hurried up the stairs, slamming the door behind him. He didn't stop at one flight, he headed straight to the master bedroom in the eaves of the house and moved the large picture in front of the safe. In it, the passports and tickets were exactly as he'd left them.

He kissed the tickets and placed them in the holdall.

Would the last one be enough? Who would live and who would die? Maybe he should toss a coin. Choosing was hard.

CHAPTER SIXTY

Gina swallowed the rest of the coffee down, enjoying the slight kick it was giving her. Nothing would ease the sense of fatigue that was building up in her body after barely having any sleep for days. She glanced at Edward Powell across the table and then back at Wyre whose black hair shone on the top under the stark strip light, almost making a patch of it look white.

'There's no point in you continuing to deny it,' Gina said as Edward Powell sighed. 'DNA doesn't lie and concealing the truth from us isn't doing you any good.'

He swallowed. 'I didn't kill her. I wouldn't!' He scraped the chair across the floor and leaned his elbows on his knees as he bent over and ran his fingers through his gelled hair. His tie dangled on his thigh. 'I don't want to hurt Kerry.'

'Her two best friends are dead. She's already been hurt. Kerry needs to know the truth.'

'Okay.' He paused and sat back up, staring at Gina before fixing his gaze on Wyre. 'Have you never made a mistake?'

Gina had heard this one before and it irked her that he was arrogantly trying to turn this back on them. 'This isn't about me, Mr Powell. This is about you being the father of the baby that Holly was carrying when she was murdered.'

His cheeks twitched as he clenched his jaw. Edward Powell was used to being believed. He was used to charming his way out of situations, Gina could see that now. 'Tell me about your relationship with Holly.'

'There was no relationship. We slept together once and my being the father was purely bad luck. Why me?'

'Go on.'

He slowly shook his head from side to side. A bead of sweat formed at his hairline and began to trickle down his cheek. He wiped it away with the handkerchief from his suit pocket before removing the jacket. 'It was at the end of January, this year. The weather was as frosty as Kerry had been that day. We'd had a bit of a tiff. It's ironic that she was going on about having a baby. She kept bleating on and on about how cute Lilly's kid was and that she was ready. I wasn't. We had planned our wedding and I wanted to enjoy us being free for a couple of years. Anyway, in her words, she said I was a selfish bastard. Instead of shouting my mouth off, I walked out. That's what I do and I know it upsets Kerry. She'd rather battle it out. I went to the newsagents, bought some cigarettes and kept walking until I arrived at the park. It was full of parents with screaming brats and my stomach was churning with anxiety at the thought of fatherhood becoming my life. I hate myself for thinking all this. When we got together—'

'Is that with Kerry or Holly?'

'Kerry, of course.' He paused and tilted his head slightly to the side. 'I know I'd promised her everything, kids, the lot. I suppose with the wedding coming up, I was beginning to feel trapped and that argument had sent me over the edge. I arrived at the park and I sat on the bench, the same bench I was sitting on the other night. It was where I bumped into Holly, then one thing led to another and that's it. I didn't hurt her. It was just the once.' He threw his head back and took a deep breath.

'What happened next?'

'Do we have to? Isn't it obvious?'

The mechanics were very obvious but Gina needed more than that, she needed to know how he felt and if there was something in his story that would lead her to believe he killed Holly and or Fran. 'Please go on.'

'She was jogging, going for it good and proper, really pushing herself. I spotted her and waved. I remember her bending over while she got her breath back and at that moment I saw an escape from all my problems. Her red hair was in a long plait down her back and she had such a warm smile. She could see I was upset so we spoke for a while, she reassured me that one day I'd be a good father and it was normal to be nervous with the wedding coming up. I felt like a shedload had been lifted off my shoulders. I then listened to her and she spilled that she was in some sort of relationship that she thought was going nowhere. She got a little upset and I don't know what happened. Her hand brushed against mine. We were both in a bad place and we both felt something. We went straight back to hers and had the most passionate sexual encounter I've ever had in my life. There, is that all? Do you want the details? Positions, maybe?'

Gina cleared her throat. 'What happened after?'

'I awkwardly dressed and I don't know why, I kept apologising. I have cheated on Kerry before but it seemed weird with Holly and I could tell she felt the same. She was one of Kerry's best friends. As I was about to leave, I heard her crying so I stayed a while. We both agreed that we were going through confused times in our lives and we said we'd never mention what happened again. She was happy with that and I was. I went to get a drink from her kitchen and there was a man's shirt hanging over the back of the chair so I know there was someone else in her life.'

'Did you ask her who this other person was?'

He paused for a moment. 'No. I didn't want to know but during her teary moments, she admitted he was married but she couldn't let him go. By this time, I just wanted to get out of there so I made my excuses and left. I didn't even know she was pregnant until it came out after she was murdered.'

'Thank you for being so open. As it stands, we don't have any witnesses who can confirm that you were at the park on the night of Francesca Carter's murder. Did Holly tell Francesca that you were her baby's father, putting her at risk?'

'No. Way! I did not kill Fran. I did not kill Holly. If I'd have got caught out, I'd have handled it. It wouldn't have been the first time Kerry had found out I'd cheated. I wouldn't kill to keep that to myself.'

Gina flicked through the case notes. Through the chaos of his wedding reception, no one could vouch for him being in the function room or garden at all times. Like many of the others, he had opportunity when it came to killing Holly. 'Did you murder Holly Long on the night of your wedding reception?'

'I can't believe you lot. I didn't murder Holly and I didn't murder Fran.'

'Was Holly threatening to tell your new wife about the baby?'

'No. Holly hadn't spoken to me since we slept together that one time. I told you.'

Gina could see his hands tensing up.

'Was Francesca Carter threatening to say something to Kerry about what happened between you and Holly? No one can vouch for you being at the park. All those appeals on the news and not one person has come forward to say they saw you. We've reviewed hours of footage and no one passed the camera in the car park with a Red Setter dog.'

'They probably walked. There is more than one entrance to the park!'

Opening a poly pocket, Gina slid out a bank statement with most of the transactions blacked out. 'Do you recognise this account number and sort code.'

He stared at the numbers for a few minutes and grimaced. He glanced up at Gina then at Wyre before looking down once more. Rubbing his thumb and index finger together, he turned away. 'Never seen them.'

Gina slammed her notes together in front of her and maintained eye contact with Edward Powell. When his eyes were on the numbers she could see a flicker of recognition. He continued to rub his fingers together. 'Where were you last night between one and two in the morning?'

He laughed a little then leaned back, his hair now sodden with sweat. 'At home in bed. Kerry was there. Has something else happened? Something you can't pin on me.'

'We've already spoken to Kerry. She confirmed that you slept in separate bedrooms last night.' That was her trump card.

'I want my solicitor. I didn't kill or hurt anyone and I'm not saying another word.'

Gina and Wyre sat in silence for a few moments as the tape continued to run. Edward Powell literally looked like he'd been through a ringer. He had no alibi for all three incidents, then there was the question of him having shoe covers at his disposal. The more she researched his work, the more she realised he'd own a pair of proper safety boots too, probably similar to the imprint of the popular brand they'd found at both murder scenes, and he had motive. Edward Powell had only told them about his encounter with Holly because he'd had no choice. She realised he was going to be tough to crack. She nearly had him, but why was there a niggling doubt at the back of her mind? 'What size shoe do you take?'

He shrugged. Sticking to his silence. 'Can I go?'

'If you leave, I'll have no option but to place you under arrest. We'll wait for your solicitor to arrive before continuing with questioning.'

All she had was circumstantial evidence. She couldn't get this wrong. He would wait. She could see it in his demeanour. He wasn't going anywhere.

CHAPTER SIXTY-ONE

Cass hurried away as quickly as possible. She never wanted to go into a police station again. The two men that were being booked in for fighting had scared her a little but the officers who interviewed her were happy with her statement. Still, she had no news on Elvis. They wouldn't tell her anything, only that he was safe and in their custody.

Her phone beeped and a rush of adrenaline dashed through her veins.

Cass, I really need a friend and I trust you. Can you come over? I need to talk to someone or I'll go insane. You're a true friend, I should have seen that all those years ago, I regret that now. My true, best friend. I'm not at home. I'll message you the address in a moment. K.

At last, Kerry could see that they were meant to be the best of friends, just like they had been at junior school. Another message beeped through – the address. She smiled. She'd been to this house on many occasions. It was odd that Kerry wasn't at home but maybe she'd had an argument with her new husband. None of that mattered to Cass, she was sure that Kerry would explain all once they got to speak in person. Last night, she'd felt hopeless, but now, she saw the start of a new future opening up.

She had time to freshen up. Elvis had been wrong about her make-up and her scarf. He'd been jealous that she was making new friends. He loved it when she was down and when she overate. She now knew that this made him secure in that she'd never find anyone else, that she'd always be at his beck and call. Not now. She had Kerry and with what he was putting her through, he'd soon be history.

Maybe she and Kerry would become newly single together. They could go on holidays, nights out, spa days, do all those things that really good friends do together, all those things that the trio of bitches had deprived her of. Holly and Fran were no more and Lilly, who's Lilly? Kerry wasn't asking Lilly to go over and be with her. She wanted her oldest, most trusted friend by her side. Besides, when Cass had watched Lilly, she could see that Lilly wouldn't have time for Kerry any more. Not since she'd had her child. Friendships moved on, just like Lilly's and Kerry's had.

She hurried past the Co-op and along the back, straight to her flat. Glancing behind her, she could see that no one was following her, not like the other night. It had to have been a coincidence. That person who was outside Lilly's house had just been going the same way.

Time for a quick freshen up then her new life would begin. Given all the bad things that had happened, Cass couldn't help but beam a smile. She almost skipped up the stairs to her flat. Everything always works out for the best in the end.

CHAPTER SIXTY-TWO

Gina stuffed the last of the cheese sandwich into her mouth and pressed play on the CCTV footage again. No one as yet could verify that they'd seen Edward Powell at the park. Cars came and went. She slowed it down, searching every inch of the screen, frame by frame.

As the timeframe of the murder got nearer she watched as the family of four stepped out of the four-wheel drive before opening the boot for three bouncy terriers. Each child held a dog on a lead and the man held the third dog. They left. She scanned the side of the car for anything, a glimmer of something that may help – nothing stood out.

Screwing up the sandwich wrapper, she lined it up with the bin in the corner of her office and threw it. Straight in.

She moved onto the next frame. A woman got out of a small red car and bent down to tie her laces. Again, nothing out of the ordinary was happening.

Someone knocked on her door. 'Come in.'

Jacob sat opposite her and went to speak.

'Bear with me. Sorry,' she said as she flicked back a frame. A glint had caught her eye. She played the frame again and slammed her fist on the table. 'How on earth could we miss this?' She knew she should have poured over the footage herself.

'What is it?'

She turned the screen around on the desk and they both watched as she played the clip again.

'Did I miss something there? A woman got out of a red car.' He scratched his head.

She flicked to a screenshot of the frame she wanted him to properly look at and magnified it, as she did the image became more pixelated. 'It's not the clearest of photos but see in the rear-view mirror of the jogger's car.'

'Could be the tail of a Red Setter in the boot of a car?'

'Yes, and in the reflection, we have a partial plate of a silver Volvo.' She flicked to another screen and fast-forwarded. A surge of adrenaline passed through her body. 'Here. Check out the road footage. There's the whole plate of the same silver Volvo and in the back, what do you see.'

'It's a reddish-coloured spaniel.'

'I think Edward Powell has got his dogs mixed up. We need to speak to the man with the red spaniel. Can you get onto it?'

'That would confirm he was where he said he was. We may have just proven his innocence when it comes to Francesca Carter's murder.'

Gina slumped back in her chair. 'How could we have missed this?'

'In all fairness, I don't know how you spotted it, guv.' He squinted as she flicked back to the previous screen. 'And, let's not forget, he did say he saw a Red Setter. That dog is clearly a spaniel.'

She shook her head. They were back to square one if the footage proved that Edward Powell was at the park. 'Sorry, what did you need me for?'

'Robin Dawkins. He's ready to talk. He's spoken to his solicitor and he's waiting in interview room one. Before we speak to him, you need to see the CCTV footage that just came in from a pub in Redditch.'

She grabbed her jacket and stood. 'I'll be there in a few minutes. Will you join me in the interview?' She made a note on a piece of paper and passed it across her desk. 'In the meantime, pass that registration to O'Connor, tell him to speak to the owner of the Volvo then meet me in the interview room in ten minutes.' That was just enough time to finish her drink before she got to the bottom of what Dawkins had to reveal. Jacob smiled and left.

She pursed her lips together, grabbed her phone and checked for messages. Still nothing from Hannah. She flicked over to Facebook. Hannah had posted a selfie an hour ago, one of her eating an ice cream. Her hand trembled with anger. With all that was going on, her own daughter couldn't manage a quick message to tell her she was okay. It certainly was a day where the reflections in the pictures gave her the bigger story. In the window behind Hannah, she could see Samuel Avery laughing. Her daughter was out having a good time with a man who'd twice been accused of harassing one of their victim's. She threw the phone on her desk, buttoned up her suit jacket and left.

Robin Dawkins had been in custody all night. One thing she knew for sure was that he had been nowhere near Lilly Hill's house last night. He couldn't be her attacker. They were about to lose Edward Powell and Robin Dawkins as suspects. If they were gone, who else could it have been? She was at a loss. One thing she was sure of, Robin Dawkins wasn't an innocent man. With the drugs connection to Holly's apartment, she wanted to know everything Robin had to say. It may not have been him but he could still be hiding something that might lead them to the killer and she wanted to know what.

CHAPTER SIXTY-THREE

Cass smiled all the way up the winding path as she passed the shrubbery. The greenhouse in the distance reminded her of summers gone by when she and Kerry picked the tomatoes for lunch. The scenery across the Warwickshire countryside was breathtaking, sectioned off patchwork fields led the eye into the distance. She re-tied her scarf and checked out her reflection in the tall door with the glass side panel. Her make-up was just right and the lipstick did suit her; she'd keep it. She ran her fingers through her freshly washed curls to break them up a little.

Her phone beeped and a text popped up.

Come around the back.

She breathed in and slowly walked in her low-heeled boots on the cobbled path around the house. As she passed the large front window, a memory of a Christmas past flashed though her mind. That's where the Christmas tree used to be, right next to the white grand piano that Kerry would play badly. A warmth filled her heart and she smiled as she remembered them trying to play 'Chopsticks' over and over again until they were eventually told to stop. Mustn't keep Kerry waiting, not now Cass was needed. As she turned the last corner the large garden brought back the fuzziest of memories. The tyre swing and treehouse were still at the bottom of the garden. The long summer days, making dens and swinging back and forth, while eating lumps of cheese that they'd pilfered from the fridge.

Another text arrived as she reached the back door.

Come in. I'm in the wine cellar checking out the drinks. Today calls for a celebration. K. Xxx.

She pressed the handle and as expected, the door wasn't locked. As she entered the boot room she bent over and unzipped her boots before slipping them off. Kerry wouldn't appreciate the white carpets getting stained and she knew the house rules – shoes off. Taking a deep breath, she pushed the door open and entered the kitchen, her tights making her slip a little on the porcelain tiles. She held her arms out for balance and gripped the kitchen island, allowing her handbag to dangle around her neck. 'Kerry?' she called. There was no answer. Cass swallowed and felt a shiver running through her body. 'Kerry.'

As she stood in silence, she heard the back door closing and locking.

CHAPTER SIXTY-FOUR

Gina glanced at Robin, then at his solicitor. Several minutes of silence was too much considering her other leads were screaming for attention. She placed her hands under the table and tapped her foot. The suited woman whispered in his ear and Robin whispered back. Jacob leaned back and yawned as they waited.

'My client wishes to make a brief statement.' The solicitor pulled up the sleeves of her shirt, picked up her refill pad and began to read. 'On the night of Monday, the eleventh of May, between eighteen hundred hours and twenty hundred hours, my client was in Redditch and can prove his whereabouts. He entered several pubs in Redditch and he is certain there will be CCTV footage to prove that he had no involvement in the murder of Francesca Carter. He will give you a list of the establishments that he went to.'

Gina slid one of the CCTV stills across the table. 'We already know. Unfortunately, a certain piece of CCTV footage shows us something of great concern. What were you doing here, Mr Dawkins?' The photo clearly showed the man in front of her passing a small packet of something white to another man in the foyer of a pub. There was no chance of it being anyone else, the sideburns and quiff were a huge giveaway and it wasn't a look many other young locals followed.

The solicitor scrunched her brow and gave her client a glance.

'He, the man, dropped something on the floor. I was just passing it back to him. That's the truth.' He cast a pleading look in his solicitor's direction.

'You don't have to say anything.' The solicitor moved her ash blonde hair to the side before whispering in his ear again.

His shoulders slumped as he finished whispering back. After taking a few seconds to brush his sideburns with his fingers, he pulled his chair closer to the table.

'In the footage before this frame, we see you pulling several of these packets from your pocket and passing this man one of them. A few seconds later, he passed you some cash which you put in your pocket. You then go outside where we have a second camera pointing in your direction as you count a wad of cash with Phillip Brighton. A search of your garage also came up with a large quantity of cocaine that had been stored in the boot of your car. The cocaine is portioned out into neat little wraps, all perfectly weighed out and they look the same as the wraps in this footage. Please explain yourself?'

Gina knew Robin Dawkins and Phillip Brighton had nothing to do with Francesca's murder. They were both together, drug dealing in Redditch at the time. She had all the evidence she needed. Phillip Brighton had breached his bail conditions and would be hauled back in and this session would end with Robin Dawkins being charged.

'Okay.' He held both hands up and leaned back before linking them behind his head. Closing his eyes, he took a deep breath. 'I was stupid. I lost my job and I did a stupid thing. I've never done anything like this before. I knew I'd let Cass down and we needed the money.'

'Cassandra Wilson.'

He stared at the wall behind them. 'She knew something was up and she's going to be angry with me, especially when Kerry finds out what I've done. She was so fixated on what Kerry thought of her.'

'What do you mean?'

'She wanted the reception to go off well. Kept asking me to go and speak to Kerry to see if Kerry remembered her from school. Kerry did know who she was, I saw her looking over several times. I don't know why Cass wanted to know her. Kerry was a bitch. I could see her laughing and glancing over with Fran.'

Gina leaned in. 'I thought Cassandra and Kerry were friends. She visited Kerry the other night.'

'Well if they are, she never told me.' He parted his lips before continuing. 'Kerry picked on Cass at school. When we got to the party, I told her to rise above everything that happened in the past and get on with the job. I said it was all in the past but Cass was hell-bent on getting back in touch with the girl who made her school life a misery. I didn't understand it and we had a bicker about it before we got there. I just couldn't understand why she was punishing herself, trying to be something she isn't.'

Gina knew from her notes that Kerry and Cassandra had been in touch but Cass had spoken about Kerry in nice ways. Her upset had been directed at the man sitting in front of Gina. A slight churn in her stomach told her something wasn't right. Cass had come to the station, made a statement stating that she knew nothing of the drugs in the garage and left. She hadn't said much about Kerry. Gina made a note on the next page of her pad. Cassandra's name with a question mark next to it.

'How do you know Phil?'

'From the pub. Everyone knows Phil the Pill.'

'Where were you during Holly Long's murder? Several people say you were out of the room when her murder could have taken place.'

His solicitor sighed.

'Yeah, and so were many of the others. It's a big place, we were all over it.' He paused. 'Okay, I'll fess up. I'm not being nailed for this. I have a past yes, but I also have someone who will vouch for me. At the time I was in the toilets with Phil, scoring something to relax me when I got home. That was the only time I headed towards the stairs.'

Gina knew they were both up to no good but now they both had an alibi. As long as Phillip Brighton said the same thing, she had to brush them aside in the murder investigations. She felt her hands tensing up. She wanted to screw them into a ball and slam them into the table. All that time wasted on Phillip Brighton and Robin Dawkins and there was still a murderer out there. Her mind wandered back to Edward Powell. She still couldn't confirm if he was in the park alone and the answer would be revealed just as soon as O'Connor had contacted the owner of the Volvo. Powell had recognised the account number on Holly's statement and he was Holly's baby's father.

'If you're not going to charge my client, you need to let him go. It's seventeen hundred hours. He's never been convicted of a drug-related offence before and he is being cooperative.'

No, Robin, Elvis, Mr Dawkins – whatever he wanted to be called – he was not getting off with a slap on the wrists. She wouldn't allow it. He'd hindered a murder investigation with his lies. 'Robin Dawkins, we will be charging you with the supply of Class A drugs. You do not have to say anything. But it may harm your defence if you do not mention now when questioned something which you later rely on in court. Anything you do say may be given in evidence.' Gina slid the paperwork to Jacob. 'Can you follow up on the charges with the CPS?' Jacob nodded as Gina stood to leave.

Hurrying along the corridors of the station, she almost bumped into O'Connor as he came from the incident room. 'I was just coming to see you, guv. Take a look at these bank statements.

Wyre dug a little deeper and found the company that this account number was registered to, a TAR Holdings Ltd.' She stared at the company name. She'd never heard of a TAR Holdings, it certainly wasn't a local company – then it clicked.

Her heart began to pound but what she was thinking didn't make sense. She'd have never suspected that this person could be involved but the more she went over his interview her hands shook. He'd taken full control of everything, misdirecting the investigation, casting suspicion on another. The *another* he'd brought up might not be innocent of everything but this person had been clever. Not any more. She wanted answers and she was going to get them. If her mind had drawn the right conclusions, she had to rethink everything. Had Holly told him that the baby was his?

'What is it, guv?'

'Is this company based abroad?'

'Grand Cayman, guv.' She knew it. What she'd seen of him, business-wise, was only the tip of the iceberg. It was easy to look at the Phillip Brighton's and Robin Dawkins's of the world and see guilt; they were guilty of things and trouble for them was easy to get into. But looking at the man whose image filled her mind, all she could see was respectability. He was clever but he wasn't going to outwit Gina.

'You and Wyre are a pair of geniuses! Did you get me the owner of the Volvo?'

'Yes, guv.' A smile spread across Gina's face. 'I just spoke to him myself. He can confirm that he remembers someone matching Edward Powell's description sitting on the bench. His family walked around the lake a couple of times with their dog and he said that Powell was there the whole time. Apparently, he looked worried so the man with the dog made some light conversation with him when the dog's stick had landed by his feet.'

'Is he prepared to put that in a statement?'

O'Connor nodded. 'Yes, his wife can confirm the same too.'

'I need to check something but I think we have him.'

'Who?'

She smiled. 'Give me five and be ready to leave. I'm on my way. I just need to grab Jacob from the interview room. Someone else can finish up with Dawkins.'

In her mind she saw Holly struggling under the pillow until she'd breathed her last. She saw his strong fingers clenching her around the throat, digging his nails into the back of her neck. The hairs on the back of her own neck prickled, the same as they had on her wedding night when Terry held her down on the bed and strangled her until she almost turned blue. As she escaped his clutches, falling off the bed, he lay back and laughed as she coughed.

She gasped for breath and leaned against the wall. Now wasn't the time for dwelling on her past. A surge of adrenaline had kicked in, giving her just what she needed to finish the job. She had to stop this very same thing from happening to anyone else. He was not going to get away with his crimes.

CHAPTER SIXTY-FIVE

Cass half opened her swollen eye and flinched as an ice-pick headache struck. She tried to shout but the taste of her own scarf in her mouth mingling with metallic blood was making her gag. One of them turned her way; she clenched her eyelids closed. If they knew she'd seen what had just happened, she'd die, she was sure of that. *Don't let them see I'm awake.*

Her stomach clenched as she thought of Holly and Fran. Why had he killed them? She knew from the way he was standing that he was the man who'd followed her home from Lilly's house. What she couldn't understand was why he'd tied his wife up in their cellar.

'Get a move on. Let's go,' the man shouted as the wine rattled on the shelves. 'Move it, we don't have much time.'

Cass half opened an eye and spotted the man placing a pink tablet into a holdall.

'I am moving it. We've got an hour and ten before check in closes. We'll be fine.'

'Shut up!'

As they glanced over Cass closed her eyes again. A moment passed. She could feel her pulse hammering through her head. She slightly opened one eye and the man stared right at her, the same man who'd once been like a second father. A trickle of blood hindered her vision. As she went to speak, her muffled words were lost behind the material, then he laughed before pressing his firm fingers around her throat. How could she have been so stupid as to think that Kerry wanted to be her friend? Was this Kerry's doing? Kerry had messaged her, she'd lured her here with the promise of friendship and Cass had fallen prey to the trap. Once again, she'd been humiliated, just like back then in the school playground as she lay there crying over her bloodied knee, now she was weeping over the fact her friend had deceived her. Nothing had changed over the years except instead of being on the ground with a bleeding knee she was tied to a chair with a banging, bloodied head.

The cellar looked like it had tilted and shifted as more blood seeped into her eye. As she gasped, he gripped harder. In the distance she heard a laugh. Who was laughing? The jewel like bottles of red and white were beginning to fade as her peppering vision took her sight. Her head flopped and the chair overturned, banging her ear against the stone floor. As the laughing faded she knew her end had come. No one would save her, she couldn't be saved. Maybe she didn't want to be saved. There was no point in fighting an end she half wanted. Everyone had to die, at least she had nothing to live for. She had no family, her colleagues hated her, Kerry was never going to like her and her boyfriend wasn't who she thought he was. Lying in a pool of her own blood in a dark cellar was her end. She shivered as her short sharp breaths became less frequent. It was time to say goodbye to the world.

CHAPTER SIXTY-SIX

Gina knocked at the door of Kerry Powell's house and the woman eventually answered. She leaned against the doorframe, barely able to stand. 'What the hell is it now?' A scab had formed in the corner of Kerry's mouth and her cheeks burned a deep crimson colour. She wasn't the beautiful bride Gina remembered seeing only a few days ago, the young woman standing in front of her looked as though her world had been ripped apart.

'We need to speak to you. May we come in?'

Jacob waited beside her and the whole station was on standby. At the moment, Gina wanted to do as little as possible to unnerve Kerry Powell.

'Don't you think I've been through enough?' A fresh tear rolled down, refreshing the old tear tracks on her face, mingling with what looked like sleep in her eyes and yesterday's make-up. 'My friends are dead. My husband just happens to be the father of my dead friend's baby. What the hell? My dad is livid.' She kicked the door open and held onto the staircase as she headed towards the kitchen.

In Gina's book that was an invite. Jacob closed the hefty door behind them. Several suitcases lined the hallway. Shirts stuck out the gaps, jamming the zips, and coats had been flung over the top. A carrier bag of shoes had toppled over.

'He's a gonna,' she said as she swigged wine straight from the bottle.

'Is your husband in?'

She shook her head and stared out of the bi-fold doors. 'I told him to go. He's meant to be back in a couple of hours for his bags. I never want to see him again.' She leaned back on the stool and slammed the wine onto the kitchen island. The stool creaked and Gina wondered for one moment if Kerry and the stool would tip backwards but her slight frame was secure, for now.

'Kerry, I need to ask you about TAR Holdings Ltd.'

She grabbed the kitchen roll and blew her nose. 'What has that got to do with anything?'

'The company is registered in your name.'

'No it's not.'

Gina placed the paperwork on the island and Kerry squinted as she read. 'My head hurts. I don't get it.'

'What don't you get?'

'I don't know.' She placed her folded arms on the worktop and lay her head on them.

Gina gave her a slight shake. 'Kerry, stay with us.' The woman was as drunk as she could be and Gina thought for a moment she'd started to snore. 'We tried to call you, to say we were coming.'

With one eye closed, Kerry sat back up. 'Have you found my phone?'

Gina shook her head. 'No, sorry. Have you lost it?'

'I haven't had it since yesterday. I must have left it at my parents.'

Gina glanced at Jacob.

'Have you spoken to your parents today?'

'No. Should I have? Do I look like I want to speak to anyone? I just want the world to go away and I'm sick of my mother fussing. I wish people would stop hassling me.'

'Hassling you.'

'I'm glad I haven't got my phone. Between Ed and Cass, I can't deal with it all.'

'Cass?'

'She kept messaging me but I just need to be alone. I know she means well but I can't face things yet, not after what Ed has done to me. It's not her fault. I should have messaged her back, but what can I say? I couldn't find my phone.'

Sitting on the stool next to Kerry, Gina placed an elbow on the worktop and faced her. 'Kerry, we have a company registered in your name that you say you know nothing about. Does the TAR stand for Trevor Alison Reed?'

A laugh escaped Kerry's lips as she grabbed the wine bottle once more and took a huge swig of the liquid. Gina gently took the bottle and placed it on the worktop.

'Kerry, we need to know what's going on here. Payments were made monthly to Holly Long's bank account and these large amounts came from an account that has been traced back to TAR Holdings Limited. Why would TAR Holdings Limited, registered in Grand Cayman, be paying Holly a regular income? We need to know.'

Kerry's laughter turned hysterical. 'I want the answer to that question too. Ed came home yesterday and before making his sleazy confession, he asked me the very same thing. Just what the bloody hell is going on here?'

'We have also found something else out. It's not only the company you own, you own every asset too. You own this house, your parents' house and a whole smattering of rental properties, businesses and restaurants, including Reed Corporation. You own every car, every office – the whole lot, it's yours. It has been for years.'

'The lot?' In an instant, it was as if Kerry had sobered up slightly. 'Does Ed know this?'

Gina shrugged. 'Did you or anyone tell him?'

'I've only just found out. How could I have told him? I might get away with just giving him half of this house.' Kerry grabbed the wine bottle and hurled it at the oven, glass shattering everywhere.

'My father told me to get a prenup but I just laughed. We fell out over it. Am I going to have to share everything with that cheating prick? Everything my parents worked so hard to build up? I suppose I'll have to speak to Dad when—' The woman's face paled as she stood. 'Excuse me.' She half ran and staggered out of the room and Gina heard her retching as she ran along the hallway.

The distribution of her family's wealth was the least of her problems but Kerry couldn't see that yet. Gina had confirmed everything they needed to know. She gave Jacob the nod to get everyone on standby and in position. Jacob showed her the message from Wyre that had been emailed to both of their phones.

The warrant has come through. Give me a call when you get a moment. I have something, it may or may not help.

She called Wyre. 'What have you got?'

'We bailed Robin Dawkins and he called us when he arrived home. He said he can't get hold of Cassandra Wilson, his partner. She's not answering her phone and that's not like her. He called her work and they told him that she hasn't been in today. He's concerned. I don't know if this is anything to worry about or if it has anything to do with the case but given that she's cropped up a few times, I thought I best mention it.'

'You were right to. Alert everyone. Leave now and we'll meet you at the house.'

Gina slid off the stool and hurried to the door. As they left, she spotted PC Kapoor pulling up on the drive. 'Stay with her. She's in the bathroom at the moment and I don't want her left alone.' Kapoor nodded and Jacob followed. 'We have to go – now!'

CHAPTER SIXTY-SEVEN

Gina crept around Trevor and Alison Reed's large house, hitching her black trousers up her waist. Her shirt had rolled up under her stab vest. Passing the kitchen window, she peered in. 'I can't see anything unusual. I can't see the Reeds either.'

Jacob followed her closely. PC Smith nodded as he received news that Wyre and O'Connor were covering the front door.

Silently, Gina stepped around the planters and stopped at the back door before trying the handle. 'It's open.'

She nodded back to PC Smith. 'Call Kapoor, tell her to keep Kerry there.'

As Gina leaned against the door it creaked open.

'I recognise those boots. Cassandra Wilson was wearing them when she made her statement.' She held up a hand to silence the chafing of coats against stab vests. Nothing, not a sound came from the house. She crept through the boot room and pushed the kitchen door open. 'Mr Reed, Mrs Reed. It's DI Harte and DS Driscoll from Cleevesford Station. We have a warrant to search the property.' She pulled the paperwork from her pocket along with her identification and held it in front of her as she headed through the kitchen. Silence followed. 'Cassandra Wilson?'

Jacob and a further two officers followed her in, all of them listening intently. She thought Kerry's kitchen had been large but it paled into insignificance compared to this vast open plan kitchen diner. Two couches and a coffee table adorned the one end, complete with coffee table books on wildlife and business.

Everything gleamed and the dark shaker kitchen looked newly installed. As Gina passed a large dresser full of best china, she spotted a scuff mark on a white door. Maybe it was the pantry or it could lead to the hall. She edged closer and pressed the handle. 'Mr Reed. Mrs Reed. Cassandra?' Again, there was no answer. She pushed the door open and gestured for the two officers to continue to the lounge while she and Jacob headed down the cellar steps.

Jacob reached for the cord and the light flickered on. 'DI Harte and DS Driscoll. Hello.' Three steps down, Gina spotted the wine racks.

'Anything, guv?' Jacob whispered.

The light flickered again and all she could hear was the intermittent buzzing noise they made. Gina felt a surge of adrenaline run through her body as she spotted the red pool. 'Get a paramedic,' she said as she hurried down and kneeled beside Cassandra. She began to untie the woman's hands to release her from the chair. Removing the gag, she leaned in and hoped more than anything she would feel the young woman's warm breath on her cheek, but there was nothing. Blood seeped from her head where she'd hit the floor. An angry cut from her temple to her ear led Gina's gaze to the red marks on her neck. She reached for her wrist and felt for a pulse. 'Where are the paramedics?'

'They're coming, guv.'

'Hurry, I can feel a pulse.'

Cassandra coughed and began to choke. Gina kept her on her side and reached into her mouth with her index finger. She coughed again and a piece of tooth escaped from the side of her mouth as she tried to murmur. 'You're safe. I'm DI Harte and help is on its way.' She snatched the scarf that had been in Cassandra's mouth and placed it hard against the wound on her head to try to stem the bleeding from her face.

'Mr Reed…' A blood bubble escaped the side of her mouth.

'Shh, try to remain still.'

'Airport.' As the word escaped her mouth, she let out a pained scream and her head flopped back.

Gina listened as the paramedics thundered down the steps and pushed her aside.

'You're going to be alright. You're safe now,' Gina called over the commotion in the hope that Cassandra had heard her. She stepped back and pulled out her phone, getting immediately connected to Briggs. 'It's the Reeds, Trevor and Alison Reed. We've just found Cassandra Wilson in their basement left for dead. She managed to say airport. They're leaving the country. Get word to all the airports and, for good measure, the ports and the Eurotunnel too.'

'Good work, Harte.' He ended the call.

She wiped her bloodied hands on her jacket. The younger paramedic spoke softly in Cassandra's ear and she responded with a pained smile.

'Guv,' O'Connor called. 'I've just found an almost blank piece of paper in the study. It has today's date and Birmingham Airport printed on the top right on an almost blank page. It's page three of three. The other two have gone.'

She grabbed her phone again and got straight through to Briggs. 'I'm heading to Birmingham Airport.' She ran up the stairs and into the lounge. On the grand piano sat a large silver framed photo of Mr and Mrs Reed. She snapped it with her phone. 'I'm sending you a photo of the Reeds. Send it to the force control room to get a log set up and to radio airport police and tell the duty inspector to meet me there. Tell them to look at the log urgently. If needs be, text them the photo. Just hurry. The Reeds can't be allowed to leave the country.'

'Okay. Doing it now.'

She hung up and pressed send.

'Jacob. We've got to go.'

He ran across the kitchen. 'The airport it is.'

'We better not have missed them.'

CHAPTER SIXTY-EIGHT

He couldn't have timed it any better. They hurried through check in and he knew that a cold glass of champagne had his name on it. He'd earned it. The house he'd purchased under the new company name in Dubai awaited their arrival. The staff had made up the rooms and were prepped to pick them up at the airport when they landed. He thought of the desperate girl, lying dead in the cellar. No one would find her for ages and he knew they would both treasure that last memory forever – this time it was a shared memory.

He admired the beautiful woman walking next to him as they entered the executive lounge. He'd never loved anyone so much and Holly had threatened everything. That woman hadn't been a patch on his wife. They had an understanding, a shared darkness. Other people would never understand. They reached highs that only being on the brink of death produced.

'Let's make a toast.' He topped up her glass.

She took the bubbly and followed him to the vacant seats by the window. 'I don't want to make a toast.'

'Just drink it, will you?' He gently gripped her neck and felt her warm breath on his cheek.

'I killed someone and the baby wasn't even yours! I can't get over this, I can't—'

He couldn't allow her to lose it. They were so close to their new life, besides, there was no going back. 'Come on. Why did you play along then if you were so fed up with me?'

She shrugged. 'I wasn't prepared to lose everything. I've turned into something I hate. I've turned into you.'

'I wasn't a killer until you started that ball rolling, you can't blame me for that one.'

'What have I done? When I thought the baby was yours—' Her eyes watered a little. 'I wanted her dead and when I told you what I'd done, I thought you'd be horrified but you weren't. Why weren't you disgusted? Why didn't you tell the police? It should have ended that night.'

'I'm sorry.'

'I knew then we'd started something and...' She paused and stared into his eyes. 'I wanted it. I looked into her eyes as she gagged for breath and I understood you. I enjoyed it and I wanted it and I wanted to share it with you.'

He let that sink in. His loving wife had done what came naturally to them, asphyxiation had been a part of their life for so long. He also loved that she played his victim in the cellar and he was happy to play hers sometime soon. He stroked his neck under his shirt – she certainly liked role-play. Trevor leaned over and kissed her. Was she enough? She had to be. For now, she was all he needed. Her gaze met his and he knew he could never upset her again, he could never be sure if she would end him. She could never be sure if he would end her either. Trust was so easily given and so easily lost.

'Tell me again, what was it like, you know, when you—'

'When I gripped her skinny neck in my hands?'

He nodded.

'I felt it, her pulse, running through my fingertips and all through it, I thought of you, of us and I couldn't stop. You felt it too, with Fran, didn't you?'

'Yes.' A warm feeling rushed through his body as he thought of Cass, their shared kill. 'We get to start again.' They both had blood on their hands. He didn't know if he could stop or if he'd want to. The final call was announced over the tannoy. Their flight was boarding. 'We best go. No going back.'

'I've been thinking about Kerry.' Trevor knew their daughter would know everything before the day was out and that bothered him. Maybe he wasn't as cold as he thought he was.

'Don't.' She placed her finger against his lips. 'We have to start again. We're no longer Trevor and Alison. We've left her enough. If she blows it all, she's on her own.'

'We were never that close as a family were we?' He held her tight and stroked her long fine hair, inhaling her flowery shampoo.

She shook her head. 'Let's go.'

As they waited in the passport queue, he smiled at the man checking their passports. Peter and Eleanor Hemming were about to board a plane. The new names would take some getting used to but he liked Peter and he thought Eleanor suited his wife. She could go with Ellie, Elle or simply Eleanor. 'Goodbye, Trevor,' he whispered as he passed and joined another queue of people. Their new life in Dubai was only a few hours away. 'Come on, Eleanor.' He kissed her on the cheek and grabbed her trembling hand.

CHAPTER SIXTY-NINE

Gina ran through the airport, flashing her identification at every checkpoint. A police officer wearing a cap and uniform hurried over and guided them through the barriers.

'Duty Inspector Buckley? I'm DI Harte, this is DS Driscoll,' Gina said as she tried to get her breath back.

'Hurry, one of the constables has just this second radioed. He's spotted a couple that might be them getting ready to board a plane to Dubai. I've asked him to hold back until backup arrives. Follow me. We'll head through the staff gate.' He pushed through a crowd that had huddled with trolleys and bags. Jacob and Gina remained close.

'Tell me the plane doesn't have permission to take off.' She wanted to make the arrest on British soil, right now.

As they hurried along a corridor, the whiff of several different Duty Free perfumes caused Gina to sneeze. The police officer wasn't slowing for anyone or anything, in fact, he'd sped up. They continued in a sprint, nearly crashing into a pair of airline staff. She kept his cap in sight, fighting through the stitch in her side that was aching like mad.

'Straight down. Just keep going,' the young male police officer called as they exited into departures and followed them.

'Has the plane,' she gasped for breath and continued as she reached the officer's side, 'been grounded?'

'That's them. They're just heading onto the plane now.' The young officer pointed. Gina spotted Mrs Reed as she disappeared through the door.

'No.' Inspector Buckley stood in front of the desk and the young man in a waistcoat stepped from behind it as he went to close it off. 'This is DI Harte and—' His face was a deep berry colour as he caught his breath.

'DS Driscoll.' Jacob caught up and stood beside Gina.

'Who were the last people to join the queue?' Gina tried to peer down the corridor but could no longer see anyone.

The waistcoated man held the list of names up.

'Let's get them.' Gina smiled. This was for Holly, Francesca and now Cassandra. From the scene she encountered at the Reeds' house, she wondered how much involvement Mrs Reed had. Cassandra had named Mr Reed before she'd passed out. How could Alison Reed have missed it all? She was arresting them both. At the very least, Alison Reed was trying to leave the county using a fake identification.

Gina hurried behind Inspector Buckley straight onto the plane. Jacob and several more airport police had joined them. The air steward let them board and stood aside. The man on row twelve turned to check what was going on and Gina recognised him immediately. 'Mr and Mrs Reed, you are required to come with me immediately.'

They stood. Alison Reed tried to grab her case and the bag next to it from hand luggage. Shaking so much, she dropped her case on the head of the passenger in row eleven.

'I'll get that.' Gina took the cabin case and the bag next to it and passed one to Inspector Buckley and the other to Jacob before leading the two of them off the plane. 'Stand.' Mrs Reed stood. 'Turn around.' Gina gestured for Inspector Buckley to cuff her. Gina moved her along and then took another pair of cuffs from the young constable. He was hers. The cuffs clinked into place.

Passengers glanced over, babies cried and children fidgeted. She saw the line of sweat running down Trevor's face. She could see something in him, something Holly would have been attracted to. Not only was he in good shape, he looked younger than his years and exuded wealth from the way his hair had been trimmed to the smell of his aftershave. As soon as they reached the main building Jacob took Alison Reed to one side and Gina took Trevor Reed to another.

He went to speak but stopped and stared at Gina. 'I want my solicitor.'

'And that is your right. Trevor Reed, I'm arresting you on suspicion of the murders of Holly Long and Francesca Carter, and of the attempted murder of Cassandra Wilson. You do not have to say anything. But it may harm your defence if you do not mention when questioned something which you later rely on in court. Anything you do say may be given in evidence.'

All he could offer her was a forced grin. Trevor Reed was clearly used to getting his own way in life but nothing was going to get him out of trouble now. As Gina cuffed him all she could hear was Mrs Reed's loud sobbing. She stumbled on her pink wedge shoes as they were led away, brushing her hair from her sodden face. They had a lot of explaining to do and Gina was looking forward to hearing all about it once they had been transported back to the station. Her phone beeped and two messages flashed up. One from Hannah and another from Briggs. She had a stop to make on the way and it couldn't wait.

CHAPTER SEVENTY

'Her injuries aren't as bad as they look but she is suffering with concussion, so go gently,' the nurse said as Gina followed her through to a corner booth. The curtain was drawn. 'Cassandra, the detectives are here. How do you feel about talking to them?'

The young woman's face had reddened more with the bruising. Blood had congealed in her hair but the wound to her face and her one ear had been dressed. Gina walked around and sat beside her, smiling warmly. 'You look better than when I found you. How are you feeling?'

Cassandra forced a smile but the tears that were forming in the corners of her eyes gave her sadness away. 'Sore,' she croaked.

'We've arrested Mr and Mrs Reed at the airport, thanks to you.'

Cassandra scrunched up her nose and let out a small cry. She brought her shaky hand towards her face and traced her bloodstained fingers down the dressing. 'You caught them.' Her grimace turned into a smile.

'What happened in the cellar, Cassandra? Are you able to tell us?'

She gave a slight nod. 'I... I got a message on my phone.' She closed her eyes and swallowed. 'I thought Kerry wanted me to go over. When I got there, I got a message from Kerry telling me she was in the cellar. Then I heard the kitchen door close behind me and I panicked and ran to the cellar. That's when I saw Mrs Reed bound to a chair and he hit me.' She flinched.

'Mrs Reed was bound to a chair?'

'Mr Reed had her tied up in the cellar. It's all a sick game. They were getting off on it.' Her bottom lip began to quiver and she buried the side of her face in the pillow.

'It's okay, Cassandra, you're safe now.'

She wiped her eyes on the crisp white sheet, bloodying it with the streaks of tear-mingled blood from her cheek. 'When I came around, they were both there, all turned on, hands all over each other. I had to pretend not to be looking. I thought they were going to kill me. That's when I heard them talking about the airport.' Her voice had almost gone.

Gina poured her a glass of water and held it under the woman's cracked lip and tilted it. Cassandra brought her trembling hand from under the sheet and sipped the water, almost spilling it down her chin.

'He strangled me and I remained still, hoping that he'd think I was dead. The chair tipped and my face hurt. I can't remember much after that. I remember you being there, only for a few seconds and then I remember being in the ambulance.'

Gina pulled the chair a little closer as Jacob remained standing by the curtain. 'You've been really helpful. Is there anyone I can call to be with you?'

The woman shook her head, her curls sticking to her face, her stare fixed on the glass of water she'd placed on the metal table.

'Hello.' Robin Dawkins peered around the curtain. 'Cass, oh my God!' He hurried over to her side and took her hand. Gina stepped back, allowing him to sit. She felt a pang of sadness. Cassandra had no one apart from Robin and he had let her down. He had a record he'd failed to mention to her and he'd been bailed that day for dealing drugs.

He went to place his hand over hers. She pulled away and looked down. 'You lied to me.'

He ran his fingers through his hair and hunched over. 'Cass, I understand if you never want to see me again. I did something stupid when I was at school and I know it was wrong and I hurt someone. I've changed and not a day goes by when I don't think about the hurt I caused. I've been so, so, stupid.' He placed his head in his hands.

'I don't know if I can ever forgive you. You made me feel horrible about myself and look at me. Look at the wreck I've become. You hurt me. You always make me feel like I'm not good enough.'

Gina stepped outside the curtain and listened as Robin Dawkins continued to plead how sorry he was.

'Just post your key through my letterbox when you've packed your things.'

He stormed out of the bay without glancing back at Gina and Jacob. Gina hurried back as Cass began to sob.

'I don't want all this any more. I can do this on my own and I don't need him. It's funny, for the first time in my life, I feel free.' A smile spread across her face.

'I'll come back to speak to you later when you've had a bit more time to recover. Are you sure there's no one I can call?'

She shook her head and paused. 'I have something to tell you, something I should have said when I came to the station.' Gina sat back in the plastic chair.

CHAPTER SEVENTY-ONE

Gina sat opposite Alison Reed. Several minutes had passed and she'd refused to speak, just like her husband had. The cracks were beginning to show. It was as if the longer they all sat there, the more she was itching to say something. Her solicitor whispered a few words to her. She pushed him away. 'I know what I'm doing.' The solicitor rolled his eyes and leaned back on the creaky chair, throwing his pad and pen to the table.

'Mr Reed had a lot to tell us.' That was a bluff but one she was willing to go with. Despite all the messages on Holly's tablet and phone that they found in his hand luggage, he still wouldn't say a word. They didn't need him to talk. The search of his house had produced the size nine work shoes. The pink tablet and the phone that Holly had used, both of which had been paid for by one of their companies, had been found in his hand luggage along with all the messages between Trevor and Holly. Gina had read them all through and the passionate messages had turned dismissive at the mention of a baby. Trevor hadn't wanted a child. Gina almost wanted to let out a small disbelieving laugh. After all that, the baby's father was Trevor's very own cheating son-in-law.

With faded make-up Alison Reed's complexion took on a grey tone. Her honey-streaked hair stuck to the side of her face and her lipstick had been smudged away with only the faintest of lines remaining around the Cupid's bow.

'I'll ask you again, did you go anywhere near Holly Long's room on the night of her murder?' Gina could feel the weight of her own stare bearing down on Alison Reed. Her knees were shaking a little. *Come on, Alison, you know you want to tell.*

'I didn't want to hurt her. I just wanted to tell her to keep the hell away from my husband. I read the messages on his phone. She was pregnant and I couldn't have it, he didn't want a baby either. I couldn't let her ruin what we had. I had to help him.'

'So you killed her?'

She nodded and a tear streamed down her face. 'It was just like the games we play. I wanted to feel the power he had.' She undid the top button of her shirt and revealed her bruised neck. 'I wanted her to pay for everything. The rage, everything, I couldn't control it.'

'We know about your games. Cassandra Wilson is going to make a full recovery. She told us what happened in the cellar. We also saw the messages you sent from your daughter's phone, telling Cassandra to come over. You both planned for her to come and find you in the cellar when you found Kerry's phone, the one she accidentally left at your house. It was a part of your little game, then the tables turned. You thought she'd die and you'd be living in Dubai before any of this came out.'

She shrugged her shoulders and looked away.

'And Francesca Carter. What about her?'

Alison Reed frowned. 'He hasn't said anything, has he?'

'We have enough evidence already. The families of these young women deserve to know what happened. Neither you nor Mr Reed will be walking amongst the general populous for a long time. I'd be surprised if you ever will. All you have left is the truth.'

Her shoulders dropped. 'I didn't want him to leave me. I got drawn into his games. One minute I disgusted myself, the next, it almost thrilled me.' She paused. 'I don't know where it all went wrong. I started it. I shouldn't have gone up to Holly's room. I can't explain what came over me, I can't.' She paused and wiped her face. 'It just felt like another game. I didn't go anywhere near Francesca though.'

'What are you saying?'

'Will it help my case if I tell you everything? I can't stay in prison forever, I just can't.'

Gina couldn't make any promises but she'd always note that the perpetrator had been helpful if they had. 'It always helps to tell the truth. The courts will look more favourably on you.'

'Trevor killed Francesca. When I told him what I'd done to Holly, he became really turned on and wanted to know every detail. I've never seen that side of him. It's like I unleashed something within him, some transfixed beast. He had to try it for himself.'

Gina sat a little closer, keeping the woman engaged. The two killings had enough differences to be inflicted by two different people. She continued to listen, feeling numb to everything Alison Reed was saying. She'd experienced too much horror in a few short years and she hated that she almost felt immune to that horror. She wanted to feel something, anything. Hatred, upset, sadness – anything. All she could do was sit and listen as Alison bleated on about how distraught she was that her daughter would now know everything.

'And the worst of it, knowing now that the baby wasn't Trevor's,' she said. 'Had I have known that, I would have stayed away from Holly but she lied to Trevor. She wanted his money to bring her baby up. She wanted to take him away from me. She wanted security and she was trying to steal everything I had. I wasn't going to sit by and let that happen… I had to keep him. I turned into a monster.'

Gina had to agree. Alison and Trevor Reed had killed and hurt people for pleasure, for their own perversions. 'Kerry had known Holly and Francesca since school? Those young women had trusted the Reeds.'

Alison burst into tears of self-pity. 'They used to come and stay with us for sleepovers. Cass did too for a while.'

'They probably looked up to you like you were a second mother to them. They trusted you and you breached that trust when you took Holly's life and almost killed Cassandra.'

Alison's tears began to dry up and she folded her arms. 'I did.' Still, Alison Reed was playing a game, a part. She had no empathy for her victims, she was just saying what she thought she should say.

All signs of emotion left the woman's face. 'I think I've said all I want to say. I did it. I killed Holly and I left Cass in the cellar, tied to a chair.' She shrugged. 'Make a note. I didn't kill Francesca. Tell that to the judge.'

'One more thing, why the carnations?'

She let out a small laugh. 'I stared at her dead body and I saw the carnation in her room. Kerry buys me those and Trevor and I buy them for our mother's. The Mother's day flower. That was the closest Holly would ever get to a Mother's day gift.'

Gina had seen enough. She had all she needed for the Crown Prosecution Service and she was ready to make that call.

CHAPTER SEVENTY-TWO

Gina stepped out of her car and stood outside the Angel Arms, smiling at what Cassandra had told her. Wyre followed her closely. Several men roared with glee as one of their teammates scored a one eighty on the dartboard.

Hannah took a sip of her gin and tonic as she rolled her eyes at Gina. 'Mum, I said I'd pop over in a bit. There was no need to come here and get me, for heaven's sake.'

'I'm not here for you, Hannah.'

Cass told her what she needed to arrest Samuel Avery on charges of sexual assault against Francesca Carter on the night of Kerry's wedding. The woman had heard everything that Robin Dawkins and Samuel Avery had said after the gatecrashers had gone.

'What's going on?' Hannah slipped off the bar stool, landing clumsily on her heels as she watched the scene unfold.

Even in her most painful moments, Cassandra had made sure Francesca had got justice too, even though she was helping a woman who'd made her life a misery as a schoolchild.

'I heard them boasting and laughing. Sam had forced his hand up Fran's skirt and she'd tried to push him away but he carried on, touching her. He went on, laughing like he thought he was some sort of stud. He kept saying women like it and they'll do anything when they're hot for you, that they just need convincing,' Cass had said.

She had heard everything and with the statements that Francesca and Cassandra had given, she finally had enough to make him pay for his crime. She doubted Trevor Reed's statement would help given that he turned out to be Francesca Carter's murderer.

'Samuel Avery, I'm arresting you on suspicion of the sexual assault of Francesca Carter on the evening of Saturday the ninth of May. You do not have to say anything. But it may harm your defence if you do not mention when questioned something which you later rely on in court. Anything you do say may be given in evidence.' With Cassandra as a new and willing witness, she was finally able to progress with this case too.

'Not this again, this is police harassment.' He let out a sneer and a laugh at the same time. 'You've already tried that one, Inspector. Whatever. The girl is dead anyway.' He came from behind the bar and stood next to Hannah, placing an arm around her waist and his head next to hers as he squeezed her.

He knew exactly who he was and his grin was no more than a façade. She felt her shoulders tense and her hands begin to roll into a ball. For a split second, she imagined grabbing his scarecrow hair and slamming his face into the bar until he bled. She shook her head, hating her thoughts – but he'd messed with her daughter. *Keep calm, Harte.* 'Another witness has come forward. You will need to come with us to the station.' He was worth losing a hot bath over. She was going to spend the evening interviewing and charging him herself. He was hers and she'd waited a long time.

Hannah batted his hand away from her. 'I didn't say you could touch me.'

'Like mother, like daughter.' He cast Hannah a sleazy look.

Hannah grabbed the full gin balloon and tossed the contents of the drink into his face. Gina only hoped that she'd seen everything of Samuel Avery that she'd need to see and that any friendship with him would be over. The darts players had stopped and the pub was silent.

'Come on. Time to go.'

Gina recognised the girl behind the bar. Leslie Benton. She'd spoken to her earlier in the week when she came to interview Avery. Her mouth was ajar and her braces were in full view. She threw a beer towel at the bar. 'He touched me too. I want to make a statement.'

Gina knew this time he wasn't going to slip away. His time had come too. It was the perfect end to the day. Hannah's gaze flitted between Avery, Gina and Leslie before she stormed out of the pub.

CHAPTER SEVENTY-THREE

Cass lay on the ward, eyes closed as she kept recounting what had happened in the basement. Why her? All she wanted was a friend and Kerry had come back into her life. At first, she'd wanted to know why they were all so cruel to her and why Kerry had allowed it to happen when they had been so close. Now she'd never know.

Kerry had money and she couldn't imagine her sticking around to be with a husband who didn't care in a town where her parents were about to be exposed as murderers. She recalled the look on Elvis's face as she'd told him she wanted him to go. He was bad for her. Deep down, she thought people could change as she hoped Kerry had, but Elvis had kept such a dark secret from her and she knew she'd never be able to forgive him. The call he made on his way to the hospital, telling her the whole truth about what he'd done had shocked her to the core. She hadn't stopped thinking about that poor schoolgirl since.

She reached for her neck and swallowed. The pain was getting worse. No one was coming for her, no one wanted to be with her; she was definitely one of life's loners. Maybe that's how it would stay.

'Cass?' She felt the breeze of someone pulling the curtain back a little.

'Kerry?'

'I'm so sorry. I can't believe what they did to you.' Kerry hurried to her side and placed a hand on her arm. She pulled the sleeves of her sweater up and a tear trickled down her cheek.

'Thank you for coming.'

'I had to come.' She paused. 'I don't know what to do, what to say.'

Cass yelped a little as Kerry leaned in to embrace her and then she flinched. It hurt, everything hurt. Her heart hurt and her mind was all over the place. All she knew was that people deserved second chances. She'd lived through her ordeal and she felt like a warrior. She'd survived and she'd lived to tell the tale. There were moments that she thought she didn't want to live but after being so close to death and accepting that her time was over, she'd never felt so alive. 'Everyone deserves a second chance.'

'I don't know how you can still want to be anywhere near me after all that has happened. I won't let you down, Cass.'

Cass smiled, clapped her hands twice and clapped Kerry's and then her own again in a little clapping sequence they learnt in junior school. Kerry laughed through her tears. They'd both lost a lot and they could both start again.

'Hurry up and get better. We have so much catching up to do.'

'We do.' Cass lay back down with a smile on her sore face. She had her flat, she had a job and she had a friend – that was a start. Those women at work were going to see a new side to her once she was well enough to go back. Through all that pain came a strength she never believed she could ever possess.

EPILOGUE

Two days later

'Mum,' Hannah called as she let herself into Gina's house.

Gina remained seated at her kitchen table, staring out at the squirrel feeder nailed to the fence as she dwelled on the conversations she'd had with Marianne Long and Charlie Carter. At least the families could now start planning funerals and lay their loved ones to rest. A squirrel perched on the nut feeder. Gracie ran through the house and straight into Gina's arms.

'Hello, chicken. It's so lovely to see you.' She kissed the giggling child's forehead.

'I've been to Cadbury World, Nanny.'

'Gracie, come with Mummy a moment.' Hannah put some cartoons on the television. 'Here, you can have the chocolate buttons. Mummy just needs to speak to Nanny for a minute.' She came back into the kitchen and pulled out a chair. 'I guess he's been charged. Sam?'

Gina nodded. 'I told you he was a bad one but you wouldn't listen.'

'I'm sorry, okay.' Hannah's face was beginning to redden, just like it always did when she was stressed.

'Where were you when I was trying to get hold of you?'

Hannah swallowed and nervously scratched her forehead. 'Sam had gone to his sister's in London and he called to see if I wanted to join him. He promised to show me the sights.'

'So you just went?'

She nodded.

'Were you sleeping with him?'

'No way. When you came to the Cleaver and he was there, he'd helped me home from the pub. I'd had too many and I really thought he was simply being a nice person. I guess I just enjoyed feeling wanted for a while. Now I see through him, he was just trying to rile you. He wasn't my friend at all.'

Gina could see that there was more to Hannah's story. 'What's going on, love? You can't fool me. There's more to this than you just getting drunk in the Angel.'

'It's stupid.'

Gina placed her hand over her daughter's. 'It's not.'

She shrugged her shoulders and stared at the table. 'Greg has been working away a lot and we'd been arguing so I went out a few weeks ago. I just wanted to feel like I was free, just for a while and I met a man. I cheated on Greg.'

That wasn't what Gina had expected. For some reason she imagined the blame would lie with Greg, an assumption she wasn't proud of making. 'I gather he found out.'

'I told him. I couldn't base our relationship on lies and secrets.'

Gina almost felt the pain of her statement. Her relationship with her daughter was littered with secrets and she knew the tension they caused. 'And?'

'We muddled along for a while but then he said he needed time to think which is why I came here. He was so upset, Mum. He cried. I broke him.' She smiled. 'The good thing is, he called. We're giving it all another go. He's going to cut down on working away and I am going to do everything in my power to make him trust me again.' Hannah paused. 'When I came here, I wanted to tell you but as always you were called away, and I'm sorry I acted the way I did. I was just so confused and I was angry that you'd gone again.'

Gina gripped Hannah and hugged her. 'I may be called away for work but I am always here for you. You can always talk to me, tell me anything and I'll listen without judgement.'

Hannah hugged her mum back. 'Thanks, Mum. I have to get going now. Greg is waiting for us. I need to get home and try to fix my little family.'

'I'll miss you.'

Hannah wiped her damp eyes and stood. 'Come on, Gracie. Come and say bye to Nanny before we go.'

The little girl ran in and held out her chocolate-coated fingers and gripped Gina in a clumsy embrace. 'Love you, chicken. You be a good girl for Mummy and Daddy and I'll see you soon.'

'Bye, Nanny.'

'Catch you soon, Mum.'

As quickly as she'd arrived, Hannah had left. A tear trickled down Gina's cheek. Those few moments between her and her daughter had meant everything. Whatever the future held, Hannah would always have her and now Hannah knew that. Gina glanced at the returning squirrel as it continued to crunch on nuts. She shivered in the silence of her cold house that lacked love and happiness. Ebony meowed. She bent over and stroked the cat.

Her phone beeped. It was a message from Briggs.

Gina, please come over tonight. Let me cook for you. We don't need to talk. In fact, number one rule, no talking. That's a promise. Just us, having dinner – and it won't be egg and chips. I promise. We could take Jessie for a walk too. X

Gina smiled. She'd love to go over and walk his dog, then be treated to a lovely dinner without the pressure of talking about her horrible past. Her smile faded as she replied. But was it a good idea? She pressed reply and typed away. Maybe it was time to live a little.

A LETTER FROM CARLA KOVACH

Dear Reader,

I'd like to say a huge thank you. At a time when millions of books are available at the press of one click, you chose to read *Her Last Mistake*. For that, I remain truly grateful.

If you'd like to be kept up to date with my news and new releases, sign up to the following link. Your email address will never be shared and you can unsubscribe at any time.

www.bookouture.com/carla-kovach

Without you, my journey as a writer wouldn't be complete. Every writer wants their stories to be enjoyed and their words to be read. It still makes me smile that people are enjoying Gina Harte's world and the cases that she solves.

This particular book made me think a little deeper about Hannah and Gina's relationship. At the end of the day, sometimes families don't get on at all but, more often than not, they are there to help and support when needed.

If you enjoyed *Her Last Mistake*, I'd be truly appreciative if you'd leave me a review on Amazon, iBookstore, Google or Kobo. This also helps other readers when they come to choose a book.

As some of you might know, I do love a chat on social media and can be found most days hanging out on my Facebook page and on Instagram, so please pop along for a chat.

Once again, thank you so much for choosing *Her Last Mistake*.

Carla Kovach

CKovachAuthor

CarlaKovachAuthor

carla_kovach

ACKNOWLEDGMENTS

It takes more than just me to produce a book, so this is where I get to express my gratitude to all those who helped me along the way with *Her Last Mistake*.

Firstly, my editor Helen Jenner is the best. Her edits are invaluable and I don't know how I'd manage without her. I like to think that I know it all but I don't – hehe. Helen helps me to shape my manuscript and she definitely makes it sparkle. On top of that, I love working with her. Thank you, Helen. May we continue to create more books together.

I'm always in awe of the Bookouture publicity team. Noelle Holten and Kim Nash – you're the best. Thank you so much for making my publication day special and spreading the word far and wide, and thank you for shouting about promotions and news as it arises. I couldn't do this without you both.

Bloggers – you are amazing. You give your precious time to read and review our books and I can't thank you enough. I'm grateful to everyone on the blog tour and for making my publication week so exciting. I'm also thankful to the NetGalley reviewers for their time too.

Bookouture authors, you are a fantastic and encouraging team so thank you millions. The Bookouture family is a truly unique group of people. The encouragement that is given and received almost makes me want to shed a tear of happiness. Long may our lovely relationship continue.

Carla Kovach

Thank you to my brother-in-law, Clive Buckley, who helped me with the airport policing procedures. Also, I'm hugely appreciative of DS Bruce Irving for patiently answering all my police procedural questions. I love our chats and may they long continue. Any errors are my own and I'm grateful for their input and expertise.

I'd like to thank a very special group of people, my beta readers. Brooke Venables, Vanessa Morgan, Su Biela, Anna Wallace and Derek Coleman. Your feedback really helps and I'm grateful to have such good friends. You're also an incredibly talented bunch and I'm honoured to know you all.

Another quick thank you to cover designer, Toby Clarke, and Helen Jenner! I love this cover. It is absolutely stunning.

And there's more! I have so many people to thank. Thank you Peta Nightingale for keeping me up to date with everything. It's always a pleasure to hear from you.

Lastly, I'd like to thank my husband, Nigel Buckley. This particular book was difficult to write as my father has been in and out of hospital. I appreciate all the encouragement you gave me when it came to knuckling down with work during hard and emotional times. Mega big fat thank you!

Manufactured by Amazon.ca
Bolton, ON